Dedicated to my Dear Uncles,

James Pettit and Charles Winn

God's answers to prayer.

You took an interest in my writing from early on. You encouraged me, pushed me in a good way, and helped make this book a reality.

Thank you.

Special thanks as well to my husband Chris, best friend M.H., my godly mom, and everyone who has supported my publishing endeavors, both in the past and present.

Thanks also to John Stone, my epic editor (and my dad!), M. Hanlon, my superb cover artist, John Lutheran, my awesome formatter, and to my talented friend Bryan, who supplied the first page artwork inside this book.

- STARGANAUTS -

<1>

The Prophetess

"Judgment!"

Samantha Harris' words echoed in the marketplace square of the coastal town of Vogul Bay. Shoppers shook their heads and muttered under their breath as they passed by the "crazed woman." Samantha Harris' reputation for being mentally ill preceded her, and today was no different. Society had learned to ignore her weekly rantings.

"The world will END!" Samantha cried, lifting her arms skyward. "Doom will fall before the sun sets, but there is hope! Believe in the Lord Jesus! Believe in Christ the Son, and look on Him for salvation, and He will show you the way to life!"

"Hogwash!" a man shouted, and a boy threw a tomato at Samantha. The vegetable hit her clothes but didn't leave a visible stain on her red sundress. She stood on a dais in the middle of the market square, crowded with many tourists and residents and surrounded by Vogul Bay's poshest shops. Two policemen moved toward the dais after her last statement. At the same time, a man in coveralls rushed forward, speaking quickly to the men. The officers halted and waited while Matthew Sanchez approached his cousin.

"Samantha, I think you need to go home now," he said gently. Samantha came out of her fervor and raised an eyebrow at him.

"I will not be silenced," she said in a low tone, "not even by you, though you doubt. The Lord has given me this task to save as many as can be saved. You agreed to help me salvage the old shuttle, but when it comes to my message, you suddenly change your mind? Today is the day, Matt. The hour is come! It will descend from the sky!"

"The police are finally coming to take you away." Matthew Sanchez gestured imploringly. "People have put up with you for a while, but their patience is running out. Is that what you want? You've been doing this for seven months! What makes you think people will listen?"

"I just need to pray." Samantha glanced at the officers for the first time. "Please let them know. I won't run, but I must discern whether the Lord is done using me here. I have things I must do, before the Gathering."

"Yes, *Prima*, of course!" Matt said, using the Spanish word for cousin. He felt relieved to finally get through to her. He knew Samantha wasn't crazy in the mental sense. She was simply too avid a Bible reader, and too obsessed with End Times prophecy.

Samantha dropped her arms and cast her face downward, her springy curls falling forward. She closed her brown eyes and, after a long while, Matt saw her lips part in a smile. She leaped down from the dais and linked her arm through his.

"My work here is done for the present," she announced cheerfully. "Take me home, Matt. We've got another load of rations to deliver and then I've got a wedding to attend."

"You're still going through with this?"

"*Primo*, if I don't go to that wedding, Sharko and Kaity's marriage will end today. Many events in a distant galaxy won't be set into motion, and we won't be living our destiny."

"Sure...whatever." Matt's tone dripped skepticism as they neared the parking lot. Matt took the opportunity to shake his head before sitting in the driver's seat and closing the door. Samantha climbed into his idling car, and they were soon speeding along the palm-lined road to her house. Why had he ever agreed to go along with her insane plans? Although Matt couldn't fathom his cousin's obsessions, every moment spent with her caused him to question his own sanity.

THE COOL SAND SQUISHED beneath Kaity Cox's feet as she walked, barefoot, along the beach of Vogul Bay. The ocean's pleasant roar filled her ears, the violent tides of night settling into calm eddies of morning. Buildings peeked at Kaity over the tropical flora, overshadowed by high mountains which backed the small town. The red rays of the rising sun tinged the heavens a goldenrod color, bathing Vogul Bay's resort hotels in a soft, crimson light. Cars began to dot the highway and streets, increasing in number until the sparse lanes flooded with their daily deluge of traffic. Despite the hurried atmosphere, a pleasant calmness pervaded the monotony. For most, it was a typical coastal day, but for Kaity, "ordinary" was the last way she'd describe it.

I can't believe I'm getting married today! Kaity thought to herself, nervous but unable to keep from smiling. *On this very beach, I'll be joining my life with Sharko Anderson's. Wow.*

Derek "Sharko" Anderson was a truck driver by trade. He had spent long hours hauling cold goods to save up for their wedding. Kaity had met Sharko in college four years earlier. Her fiancé had only made it to his junior year before financial difficulties forced him to abandon education for survival. Truck driving had offered decent pay but horrible hours. Sharko started attending Kaity's church when he could, and it was there the two grew closer, their friendship blossoming into romance.

Now, after saving up and renting their first apartment, Sharko would welcome Kaity under the same roof as his wife. It blew her mind, but she recalled more pressing matters. Hair, makeup, and dressing needed to be done, bridesmaid's photos taken...Kaity's brain raced with the amount of things to be accomplished before the clock struck four.

It didn't matter. Her best friend, Nancy Cooper, would oversee the details. Her aunt had also volunteered as their wedding coordinator. Kaity felt a thrill of happiness as she imagined walking down the aisle with her father. A pang of regret tempered it. Sharko's parents wouldn't be present to witness the occasion. They had died in a plane crash when her fiancé was seventeen. Even now, eight years later, it still brought sadness to his face. Kaity knew how hard it was hitting him, particularly on this day. Their wedding day. Once, she'd tried to comfort Sharko by pointing out that her parents were present. The Cox's were long-time friends of Sharko's and almost like surrogate parents. Yet this did nothing to alleviate his disappointment.

Kaity paused to enjoy the salty air that whipped her hair in every direction. Then she turned and trudged inland, refreshed and relaxed. Going on a walk before the fuss of wedding preparations had been Nancy's idea, and Kaity felt thankful for it. The rest of her morning passed in chaos. She had never felt so much fuss being made over her, but she secretly enjoyed it. Finally, after much curling, styling, painting, layering, and blending by various beauticians, Kaity emerged looking more radiant than before.

"My goodness, you're more beautiful than you were at Prom!" Nancy exclaimed, surveying her friend with a broad smile.

"I can't wait until Sharko sees me!" Kaity exclaimed, bouncing in her seat. "You're a gorgeous maid of honor, yourself."

A blush spread over Nancy's cheeks, but it was true. Nancy's straight, coal-black hair was plaited in an ornate bun, her sapphire eyes framed by subtle shadow and her plump lips tinted a cherry red.

"I'm a plain Jane compared to you," she shot back, and Kaity turned and admired herself in the mirror. Pinkish eyeshadow that matched her lipstick brought out Kaity's light blue pupils, while caramel-brown hair crowned her head in curls. Nancy handed her friend a gorgeous bouquet, which Kaity nearly dropped as she tried to tilt it forward properly.

"Don't worry about the bouquet." Nancy's words were kind, but she couldn't hide a grin. "They say when you're in love, your brain goes out the window!"

"Pray yours will fly out the window someday, too!" Kaity remarked cheekily, and her best friend laughed. "Think of it, Nance! I'm spending my last moments as a Cox. In a few hours, I'll have a new identity. I'll be Kaity Anderson! Our wedding will take place, and the rest of our lives will begin!"

SAMANTHA HARRIS' HOUSE was a cramped, two-room bungalow. Really, in Matt's opinion, it qualified as a shack by the sea. The uncertain dwelling sat upon an outcropping of cliff, the waves crashing against the natural jetty before bursting into a thousand drops of spray. Inside, the cramped space was its usual mess. Newspaper clippings and verses littered one wall, while the other boasted neatly-arranged pictures and wall décor. How aptly it suited his cousin! Part of her personality revealed the engineer she'd once been—rational and logical. The other part displayed chaos and confusion. Yet one thing he knew to be true: she had good intentions beneath her Bible-thumping.

At least she's living by the Bible, Matt thought, *instead of arguing with me at the mere mention of Jesus' name.* He remembered the day his cousin had approached him with news of her salvation. A feather could have blown him over. While he'd been delighted at first, her extreme behavior soon worried him.

The back wall of Samantha's dwelling culminated in a single, huge window that overlooked the restless ocean. Matt thumbed through a pile of unopened bills on her kitchen counter, noting that the newer ones were marked "urgent."

"Sam, you do realize you haven't paid these?" he raised his eyebrows at her. "Are you spending all your money on food, water, and canned goods? I don't understand it. You quit your job. Your job as an *engineer*! You haven't even paid rent! What's wrong with you?"

"The world is coming to an end," Samantha said factually. "Today is the last time we'll walk upon this terrestrial soil. What bother are bills, when Earth is to be decimated?"

"Doesn't Revelation say that no one will know the time—?"

"It does," Samantha cut in, grabbing a handful of canned vegetables and stuffing them in a bag. "That's speaking of the End of Time, when God will bring all things under judgment and create all things anew—Heaven, Earth, the planets."

"That again?" Matt asked tiredly. "I'd believe you if you weren't so...so *E.T.* about this."

"The Universe is *so* much bigger than we can comprehend!" Samantha's voice quavered in wonder. "If you'd only seen what I did, Matt! The Lord showed me stars! Not just our stars, but planets with different constellations, in other solar systems, in another galaxy! One day Earth will be repopulated, and the events in Revelation shall take place. But for now, judgement. Humanity will be severed from Earth for a time, much as Noah was severed from land."

"Why?" Matt asked. "I thought God was supposed to be loving. Would he really kill all these people? The entire world?"

"Do you think when I say judgment I refer to His? Matthew Sanchez, God is allowing evil to triumph only for a time. When I say judgment, I refer to the judgment of someone upon this Earth. Not even I know who, but I'm aware that any who wish to survive must come with us to the Tower."

"I hope you're right." Matt's irritation came out in his voice. "I wasted a lot of weekends fixing up that old shuttle for you."

"On the contrary, you'd do well to wish I was wrong." Samantha's words caught Matt by surprise. She handed him a case of bottled water and shouldered the bag of food. "'*El Señor es paciente con nosotros, no quiere que nadie perezca.*' God doesn't desire that anyone should perish, so neither do I."

Her badly-pronounced Spanish broke some of the tension between them. Being only half Latina, Samantha hadn't grown up speaking Spanish, as Matt did.

"God has a purpose even in this," she continued. "These next months will be harder than anything we've faced, but He will get us through them. Remember that!"

A MAN IN BLACK-AND-yellow board shorts dashed along the beach. His chest heaved beneath a black rash-guard which matched his hair, and his skin was covered in droplets. The early morning waves lapped gently onto the shore, but urgency radiated from the young man's face.

Sharko Anderson and two groomsmen stood farther down the beach, waiting to get their pictures taken. Sharko had a kind, rectangular face and wiry build. He was slightly taller than the muscular newcomer. As the man approached the small gathering on the beach, Sharko's face lit up.

"Dudeman!" The truck driver smiled and gave his friend a manly embrace that ended in a noogie. "Or should I call you James today?"

"Sorry I'm late, dude," James Erskin said, shifting his feet self-consciously.

"Hey, it's okay," Sharko countered. "You made it in time for photos. 'Late' would've been right before the wedding!"

The two chuckled, and Dudeman slapped Sharko on the back. As childhood friends, Derek and James had conjured nicknames for themselves. Derek's was Sharko, after his favorite sea animal, while James chose Dudeman because he loved surfing.

"I caught some sick waves this morning," Dudeman said, removing his sunglasses. "I scored a 20. Got second place. I just wish the competition hadn't been before the wedding."

"Don't worry," Sharko said wryly, "we'll catch you if you start floating away!"

Dudeman entered a changing stall adjacent to the beach's restrooms. Sharko and his groomsmen waited until James emerged in a tuxedo, then all four men posed for the photographer.

Meanwhile, Nancy Cooper put the final makeup on one of Kaity's bridesmaids. One of her hobbies was doing makeup, and she had slender, nimble fingers that allowed for skill in both her hobby and vocation. Nancy worked as a secretary at the local police station, typing up reports with legendary speed. However, her original choice of vocation had been nursing. Nancy had wanted to be in medicine from a young age, but failure to pass the nurse's exam stifled those hopes. Thus, her secretarial position.

Kaity still remembered the day they'd met, even though they'd both been in kindergarten. As an only child, she'd considered Nancy to be like a sister, and picking her to be Maid of Honor was a given. Sharko had siblings, and one of his younger brothers served as their groomsman—the other being off in the military. Yet Kaity's only immediate family members were her parents. Her mother currently stood with her, making final adjustments and speaking words of encouragement between exclamations of how beautiful her daughter looked.

Kaity felt nervous, joyful, and lightheaded all at once. The hour finally came and she took her place at the chapel door. Outside, guests sat in white chairs arranged before a brick pathway through a grassy lawn. The path culminated at a beautiful gazebo twined with purple flowers, which sat on a dais in front of the sandy beach. The pastor waited beside Sharko. The bridal procession began. The guests alone noticed a stiff wind and graying skies as the bridal procession threaded its way down the walk.

Kaity peeked through the window of the chapel door and watched as her mother and the bridal party walked down the aisle. She hesitated slightly, biting her lip to keep back a wellspring of emotion. Her father laid a comforting hand on her shoulder. She took his arm, reminded herself to hold the bouquet per Nancy's instructions, and marched out into the sunlight.

Her father's arm guided her down the paved pathway of happy destiny. She did not notice the guests stand. She paid no heed to the girls who gaped at her flowing gown, or the women who squeezed their husbands' arm in remembrance of their own special day. Her eyes transfixed on one place alone: Sharko's face. Her soon-to-be husband was beaming with emotions too wonderful to describe. Disbelief, joy, and amazement washed over him like the pounding surf on the shoreline. Her heart pulsated with delight. Everything seemed so wonderful and perfect that she almost doubted her wedding could be happening.

Sharko slid his broad hand over hers, and they faced each other. Before the Lord and happy spectators, she pledged her life, heart, and future to the man smiling down at her. Her days as a Cox drew to a close, and her future as Kaity Anderson began.

———✝╫╲╲╚╠———

MATT SANCHEZ DROVE as fast as he dared along Shoreside Road. Samantha urged him to go faster, but he reminded her that a speeding ticket wasn't something he needed. Shoreside ran parallel to the ocean, rising in elevation until they were zipping along the coastal cliffs. Mountains towered above them and clouds started gathering. Matt slowed through a particularly bad turn, knuckles white around the wheel.

At last, they arrived at their destination. A barbed wire fence surrounded the flat, grassy surface of a promontory containing a single building. The Tower, as locals called it, was perched on the edge of a sheer-sided peninsula like a nesting hawk. Waves dashed against the cliff face of the promontory, and the Tower's seaward side had rusted from the relentless spray of the ocean. The landward side displayed the bright colors of the space administration, with its faded logo near the top. The cousins approached the fence. Matt unlocked the gate with his key, then helped his cousin carry in their latest haul of supplies.

The Tower's interior was dark and ribbed with metal and piping. Its conical roof appeared retractable, but in the middle rested the most amazing feature of the building. In a deep pit, surrounded by a gantry, rested a space shuttle. Most of its booster engines sat down in the pit, yet they were so tall that they rose above it some twenty feet. The body of the shuttle rose much higher. Samantha treated the sight as if it was ordinary, but Matt marveled every time he entered the Tower.

The 100-foot shuttle had come from a deep-space expeditionary program. This model possessed more compact boosters, a shorter tank, and a thicker hull than other craft. It was also designed differently, having a conical body, the exterior of which connected to six rocket boosters. Between these jutted six wings, each inset into an engine. A metal ladder spanned the shuttle's exterior, leading to a door in its middle deck. The brainchild of a local scientist, the project had been abandoned a year before due to the defunding of the space program.

Matt, being in the scrap and salvage business, had taken the worthless shuttle as something to tinker with in his spare time. The space program had removed all of the shuttle's important gadgetry, leaving Matt with an empty shell that he would have dismantled but for Samantha. His cousin had pleaded with him to repair the shuttle. Since Matt enjoyed working with his hands, he was easily persuaded. However, his "weekend project" brought new and often unwelcome surprises every month.

Somehow, Samantha procured rocket fuel for the craft. Outdated electronic equipment, first aid kits, and solar sails followed, until Matt realized she was trying to make it space-worthy. Her story about the end of the world had convinced him at first, but months of hard labor were causing him to question.

Now, as he strained to carry a heavy pack of water cartons up the metal ladder, he chastised himself for consenting to his cousin's whims. He was certain what they were doing must be illegal. Yet his mechanical side felt that restoring a condemned spacecraft was rather awesome. He deposited the cartons in the shuttle's storage bay and shook his head. There were enough rations, toiletries, and supplies for an army. He suspected his cousin's unpaid bills were the result of funding this, but she didn't seem to mind. Her apathy both intrigued and annoyed him.

"Well, that's taken care of," Samantha said cheerily, glancing around. "Let's hurry back to the bay! We've a wedding to attend!"

"Whoa, ¡esperas un momento!" Matt placed a restraining hand on her arm. "Earth is about to go boom or something, and you're headed to a wedding?"

"Kaity is someone the Lord told me about. She and her husband are integral to His plans." Samantha followed up her comment with a determined look, which Matt had often seen since their childhoods. He shrugged and turned toward the door. *That* facial expression rendered all arguing pointless.

Matt drove his cousin back to Vogul Bay. She directed him to park in the plaza lot once more. The quickest route to the beach was through the marketplace and, as Matt followed, he noticed something wrong with the weather. The day had started sunny and warm. Now, a brisk wind whipped his cousin's hair back from her face. The bottom of her sundress was flaring out, and ominous storm clouds began forming directly overhead. Shoppers paused in the plaza, gazing at the sky and pointing at the looming tumult. For once, Samantha wasn't drawing their attention.

A storm at this time of summer wasn't uncommon, but something about this one seemed—wrong. It was spreading across the entire horizon. A middle-aged woman made a remark that the major cities were experiencing a similar phenomenon, with storm clouds even in the deserts.

Matt stopped walking without even realizing it. The heavens felt menacing and paralyzed him with a fear he couldn't explain. Only his cousin's arm brought him back to reality. Yanking him toward the street that led to the ocean, she walked hurriedly across the square.

KAITY ANDERSON STOOD in front of the bathroom mirror in a bit of a stupor. The ceremony had passed in a rush. She had paused for her bridesmaids to adjust her skirts, and to simply look at herself in disbelief. She was a married woman! Kaity had so much to look forward to—and to be! The best part of it all? Spending her future with such a wonderful husband like Sharko.

Nancy finished sorting out her skirt layers, which had been whipped into chaos by the wind. Bride and bridesmaids then entered the grand wedding reception room. Kaity and Sharko had rented this place at a discounted rate from a friend. The floor of radiant marble glistened beneath lights that added cheer to the space, while white table linens, fine silverware, and glass rails made everything feel elegant. The tall roof contained a series of skylights, normally affording a view of the picturesque blue sky. Today, they served as portals to the storm overhead, affording the guests an occasional flash of lightning and the steady drumming of rain on glass. It was abysmal how the unexpected storm picked up during their wedding. The gray clouds, heavy with the threat of rain, had caused them to rush the ceremony. Now, all of the guests sat safely indoors, no longer prey to the elements. The busy reception commenced.

Kaity and Nancy approached a long banquet table, elevated from the rest of the floor and situated by an open space for dancing. A waiter pulled a chair out for the bride, and Kaity sat down and tucked the voluminous skirt in around her.

The man she had just married ceased conversing with his best man and turned to greet her. Sharko looked exceedingly handsome in his tuxedo, with his brown hair combed back and his hazel eyes sparkling. She felt his hand taking hers, and she gazed into his eyes and could not help but beam with joy.

Most of their friends had been confused when the wedding invitations were sent out for Kaity Cox and "Derek" Anderson, largely because Derek went by Sharko. The trucker felt that his given name was too bookish for his occupation. As a big-rig driver, some people looked down on him. Kaity didn't care. He was a gentleman and the finest man of character she knew, and it hadn't been hard to fall in love with him. She smiled as she thought of recent events. Sharko gazed at her with a puzzled expression.

"What?" he asked.

"I was just thinking," Kaity remarked. "You were on time for our wedding, but you're usually late for everything else. You know that's going to drive me crazy when we're older?"

"It may, but I bet it doesn't now!"

Sharko grinned, tickling her side playfully. Kaity fought him off in mock protest. Soon she was leaning her head on his shoulder. Their food arrived, and she scarfed it down. There wasn't much time to eat, after all. She and Sharko gave a toast of thanks to everyone involved, and then they rose to cut the cake. They'd barely returned to their seats when Dudeman leaned toward Sharko, a worried expression on his face.

"I hate to mention it," he said, "but do you hear that?"

"What?"

"The thunder," Dudeman said. "It's getting louder, and...it's steady."

Sharko stiffened and Kaity listened intently. For the first time, she noticed the noise. It was like a constant droning, and Sharko started to speak when a cry of alarm escaped from one of the guests. The woman's eyes seemed glued to the ceiling. Everyone looked up at the skylights, and Kaity craned her neck to behold a sight that took her breath away. A massive object blocked out the light. Black, tubular, and lower than the clouds, it was filling up the stormy sky...and hanging directly *above* them.

<2>

Apocalypse

Kaity couldn't tell what direction the gigantic object was moving until she saw a sliver of gray sky. Whatever the thing was, it appeared to be tilting vertically.

"Is this some sort of joke?" Sharko asked Dudeman, in response to his comment. The surfer was known to pull pranks.

"N-no, I swear, man, it isn't!" Dudeman exclaimed. He seemed genuinely frightened. "What in the name of—?"

The guests in the reception room started to panic. Many quaked with fear, while others gazed in silent curiosity. The storm's rage and violence increased in intensity. Kaity couldn't begin to imagine what was happening, but everything seemed so unreal that she felt riveted to the spot. Her parents, only a table away, likewise froze in place.

A commotion erupted in the hallway of the main building. The double doors of the restaurant burst open and a soaking-wet woman in a red dress rushed in. Panting, she dashed up to the bride and groom's table. A reluctant-looking workman in coveralls trailed after.

"Kaity! Sharko! Come quickly!" Samantha leaped up the steps and grabbed the bride by her arm. Kaity yanked it away.

"Excuse me, do I know you?" she demanded. The storm and the unknown object in the sky had frightened her, and she had little thought for cordiality.

"You will soon, if you listen to me!" the stranger cried. "I'm the woman who's going to save your lives, and if you don't follow me out of here immediately, you'll perish along with the rest of them!"

"Rest of 'them?'" Kaity was utterly perplexed. "Now hang on a minute!"

"There is no time!" the woman insisted. "You *must* come with me! You've got a vital part to play in the destiny of the galaxy, though Earth ceases to exist!"

Kaity's eyebrows rose. Under normal circumstances, she would've written the stranger off as insane and asked the waiters to remove her. But something in the woman's tone held her captive. Urgency rose in her heart, and the object in the sky felt like confirmation. Could it be? Was Armageddon really happening? Cloaked in a mysterious, cylindrical form...and on her wedding day? The woman in the red dress backed up, whirling to face the guests seated around the dance floor.

"Come, all who desire to live!" she proclaimed. "God has given me this message so that you might be saved! Earth will be destroyed in less than an hour, but there is a way out, for those who come!"

The pleading in her tone could not have been more sincere. Sharko appeared stunned. Dudeman merely rose and beckoned to the waiters.

"Who is this raging lunatic?" he demanded. "God? The end of the world? Why the devil would I get up and go with you?"

"Because the God of your father has chosen you," Samantha exclaimed, her eyes flashing as the storm outside intensified. "Your foster father, the church deacon! You may have rejected him, but God has a place for him in His kingdom. God knows how much it hurt you when your parents revealed you were adopted! He was there, witnessing your shame, as you viewed images you wish you could forget!"

JAMES ERSKIN FROZE. A look of rage passed over his countenance. Yet utter amazement replaced it, and he motioned the waiters away. He vaulted over the wedding table, landing on the dance floor and practically grabbing Samantha by the arm.

"*Who* are you?" he demanded, his voice barely a whisper. Kaity and Sharko rose together, heading down to the floor. Nancy reluctantly joined her friend, and Kaity's parents and a few others gathered around Samantha. The woman gave a bittersweet smile, and started leading the group out of the restaurant and into the parking lot.

"I wished for more," she said, "but I am so happy you have come! We must leave immediately!"

"Hold on, where are we going?" Kaity's father questioned. "My wife and I have some bank accounts we'd like to cash out, and some things that would come in useful for the journey."

"You cannot linger, not for earthly possessions or anything," Samantha commanded. "We make for the Tower!"

"We can't just leave them!" Kaity's mother protested. "We'll gather what we can and meet you there!"

Kaity, walking next to her new husband, was shocked. The thought of gathering her possessions had also entered her mind, but the woman's voice...the urgency...

As if in a daze, Kaity watched her parents approach her. Each gave her a heartfelt hug. Somehow, she knew this was the end, and she couldn't believe their materialism. They were Christians, too. They believed the woman in the red dress, didn't they? Why were they risking death for some money and a few items of stuff?

"We'll see you there," they promised. "We love you!"

Kaity could barely tell them she loved them, too, before they were gone. She watched, dazed, as they climbed into their car. They tore out of the lot, heading quickly for their beachfront house. Kaity could only mouth a "no," but it was voiceless, formless—unable to fully escape her throat. What happened next unfolded like a bad dream. Samantha grabbed her by the wrist. Others who'd joined them headed for their cars, to go and gather their earthly possessions. Samantha warned them that there was no time.

"Following me, *now*, is the one chance you have to be saved!" she exclaimed.

The people ignored her. The manager of the restaurant was storming toward them, upset and demanding an explanation. A young couple who had just parked their car ran over, greeting Samantha. Kaity could not afterward remember what transpired, but as they emerged into the wet, windy parking lot, there were only eight. Sharko, James, the woman, the man in coveralls, the young couple, Nancy, and she. Kaity was struck by the tragedy and numbness of a loss even before it happened, yet checked herself.

Was she overreacting to this woman's story? Was she crazy to be following a stranger? Kaity couldn't know whether hysteria was getting the best of her, but that unknown *thing* in the sky could not be ignored.

Samantha helped her into a car, speaking words of reassurance. Kaity didn't hear them. The world rushed by in a haze of spattering rain. She gazed out of the car window, out at the blurry world which she couldn't believe would soon end. The sun-filled bay, the sparkling waves, the golden beaches, the verdant mountains. All would cease, this day, today—upon her wedding day.

Kaity's body shook with sobs. Sharko bowed his head beside her, and she saw a few tears running down her groom's stalwart cheeks. Putting his arm around her, Sharko Anderson drew in his new bride with a grip that could have warded off death. Though not a word was spoken, he seemed to say; "I am here, I will always be here, and I will never, ever let you go."

THE CAR RACED ALONG the cliff-side highway, Matt driving as fast as he dared in the pounding rain. Samantha clung grimly to the sides of the passenger's seat, glancing back frequently to make sure Kaity, Sharko, and James were all right. Behind them, Nancy's red mustang skidded as she rounded a curve, causing Samantha to caution her cousin.

"Slow down a little," she ordered. "We have time enough. And here I was urging speed earlier!"

"Are you so certain?" Matt questioned, an edge of fear to his voice. In the sky above, the black object hung near-vertically. A pinkish light emanated from its base, revealing a hollow interior ribbed with metal.

"What is that *thing*?" Matt asked. "You've talked about aliens and distant galaxies and E.T.! Is this object...alien?"

"Very much so," Samantha remarked, half in wonder, half in sorrow. "It is an alien gunship, manned by an alien crew but for one man—one person from Earth who was forsaken but has now returned to destroy his home."

"Wait a moment!" Dudeman protested, crossing his arms. He alone appeared unaffected by Samantha's words. "We're running like scared cats just because of some UFO? And some storm? How do I know you aren't pulling one over on us, Miss—?"

"Samantha Harris, prophetess of God," the woman replied, reaching back a hand to shake his. James coughed.

"Pardon? Wait, you really just called yourself a prophetess? Oh this is rich!"

James burst into a fit of chuckling which was ended by a sharp jab from Sharko. His laughter only intensified Kaity's grief.

"How can you laugh at a time like this, and at God's servant?" Kaity snapped. A bolt of lightning suddenly struck a tree dangerously close to their car, and James gulped nervously.

"Okay, maybe I jumped to conclusions," he said hastily. The rest of their drive, he stayed wide-eyed and silent.

They reached the Tower after the rain abated. No longer were droplets falling from the sky, but the entire atmosphere was starting to ionize. The storm clouds remained, lightning cutting through the clouds and striking the side of the monstrous, barrel-shaped object in the sky with no effect. Samantha hurried to the side of the building, to a door badly in need of paint. Nancy's mustang squealed to a halt behind them, so they were all present. Sharko ushered Kaity into the Tower ahead of him, and the others followed. Nancy and Matt began unloading the back of her mustang, for it held Sharko and Kaity's honeymoon luggage. The plan had been for Nancy to chauffeur them to the airport, but fate had other ideas.

Kaity would have been shocked to see a spacecraft inside of a dilapidated tower, under normal circumstances. After recent events, she hardly noticed. She was still in a daze. As she climbed up the ladder to the hatch-like door, her fingers missed a rung and her foot slipped on her wedding dress. Sharko, just starting his climb, reached up a hand and caught her. With his support, she made it the rest of the way, collapsing inside of the space shuttle. Her head spinning, her heart pounding, Kaity felt sick with grief.

"It's going to be okay," Sharko soothed. He kneeled, pulling her up into his comforting arms. "I promised to be with you in sickness and health, for richer or poorer, in times of good and times of sadness. This is the latter, but I won't abandon you, do you hear me? We'll make it, through God who sustains us."

Kaity nodded weakly and nestled her head against his chest. Painful as it was, she knew his words were true. Hadn't God used His prophetess to fetch them, to save them? Surely He had a purpose in this, but she thought of her parents, and grief stabbed her heart afresh. Lucid thought gave way to a wall of emotion, and she collapsed into Sharko's arms.

The young couple introduced themselves to Sharko as Mike and Chrysta Taylor. Mike, a college student, had blond hair and clear, blue eyes. Chrysta was a green-eyed, fiery redhead and a seamstress. At present, she appeared as much an emotional mess as Kaity.

Nancy and Mike had enough emotional stamina to ask if they could assist. Mike helped James carry luggage from Nancy's car up the ladder, then closed the docking hatch with a solid clunk. Nancy gently assisted Chrysta and Kaity into chairs. The section of the shuttle they were in contained ten seats, all set against the wall and featuring belts. Two porthole windows faced each other from opposite sides of the round room. Kaity ended up next to one of these windows, through which she saw the interior of the Tower. Sharko took his place in the chair nearest her.

In the background, Samantha and Matt climbed up the metal ladder to the spartan cockpit of the spacecraft. Stripped of much of its advanced gadgetry, Matt had inserted or modified what he could so that the cockpit had just enough control panels to get them off the ground. The cousins flipped switches, pressed buttons, and readied the shuttle for takeoff.

"Would you do the honors, *Primo*?" Samantha questioned. Matt glanced at her in surprise. He still wasn't convinced that the world was coming to an end. Nonetheless, it might be fun going on a trip into space with his mad cousin and the few who chose to believe her. Though he'd never admit it, Matthew Sanchez had secretly dreamed of being an astronaut. Now, he would get an opportunity to enter the stars.

Palms sweating, Matt initiated the launch sequence. The Tower's ceiling hatch retracted and, with a roar, the engines propelled them skyward. The entire space shuttle vibrated, the porthole windows filled with smoke, and then they were soaring upward.

Out of the gantry the shuttle zoomed, rocketing into the storm clouds with such incredible speed that the force pushed Kaity against her seat. Her vision blackened. She reached for Sharko's comforting hand, fingers clamping on with frightened desperation as they roared upward. Their craft climbed out of the smoke at an intense velocity.

From the porthole and some distance away, Kaity beheld the dreaded, black object. Completely vertical to the ground, it hovered against the fading horizon, ominous and dark. The pinkish glow was brighter now and, as she watched, a solid beam of energy shot out from the barrel of the object. It struck earth, pummeling the ground like an impacting comet. The energy seemed to coalesce right beneath the object, and shockwaves of pinkish plasma spread in every direction. Not an inch was spared as the substance rippled outward. It enveloped everything around Shoreside Road, growing and moving faster, racing across sea and land, over mountains and under bridges, with equal voracity.

Kaity watched in fascinated horror as the walls of plasma swept through the landscape. Their unquenchable fury wiped out every shred of vegetation, animal life, and civilization in its path. She gazed, unable to look away despite her heart desperately wishing to. The wall of death smashed into Vogul Bay, leaving nothing in its wake but bare, stripped earth. The shuttle was still climbing away from it. As Kaity's field of vision increased, she could see more of the world she once called home. The wave of energy continued spreading. Details faded from her vision, but as they neared the thermosphere, she saw every inch of Earth shrouded in the murderous substance.

She had no time to process the utter destruction happening before her eyes. Kaity was too numb to consider the depth of what was being lost, or the tragedy of losing all she'd ever known. She slouched in the chair, her clenched fingers loosening limply from Sharko's. The walls, windows, seats, and people—even Sharko—faded from view. The world felt empty and static. Only the shuttle's sudden lurch as it entered the thermosphere interrupted her reverie.

Kaity blinked, trying in vain to stop the tears flowing down her face. In that single blink, the exterior of the shuttle burst into flames. Earth faded from view. Her last image of home was through fire, enveloped in pink, the black object of destruction lingering above the planet like an insatiable vulture.

She had lost her parents. She had lost her home. It was too much for Kaity to handle. The apathy of shock held her captive as fire outside the porthole gave way to shadow. The space shuttle shot out from the thermosphere—the end of the world complete. Their journey into space had begun, and they were leaving the naked rock which had once been Earth far, far behind.

THE BLACKNESS OF SPACE swept by as Kaity stared out the porthole window. Earth—everything—was no more. Nothing but a bare, rocky planet was left of a thriving world of billions. No buildings, traffic, or plant life remained. All lay empty, silent, dead. Kaity turned her face from the window and buried her head in her hands, heart bursting with pain. Though still strapped into her launch chair, she felt Sharko's comforting arm encircle her shoulders.

Sharko's pained face conveyed both anger and sadness. He couldn't speak. Mike and Nancy looked shocked, and Chrysta Taylor melted into an outburst. Unstrapping herself, she raced to a porthole window and banged her fists against the solid glass.

"Take me back!" she cried. "Mother! Father! Sisters! Brother! They can't all be gone! I can't accept this!"

She collapsed against the wall, and only Mike could raise his pitiful wife and help her back to a seat. The others watched him calm Chrysta down. She was the most emotional of them all, expressing externally what they were feeling inside. Then again, Kaity couldn't blame her. Who was she to judge someone else's expression of grief, on the day of Earth's apocalypse? Matt Sanchez reacted to the destruction with a curious mixture of realization and outrage. As soon as he descended the ladder from the cockpit with his cousin, Kaity heard him voice a confession to Samantha.

"All those times I argued with you as if you were crazy..." Matt trailed off. "I'm gonna shut up now, because you were majorly right!"

Samantha alone possessed enough calmness and clarity to chuckle at his comment. Then again, that calmness came from having known about the grim future of Earth.

"Only I knew this would happen." Her words hung heavily in the recycled air. "I grieved ahead of time, but for you, it's painfully fresh. Many of your family and friends are now in heaven. That doesn't ease the pain. Anger, sadness, disbelief—it's going to be an emotional journey. But we must keep moving."

"Why?" Mike asked, clenching his teeth. "What else is there in this God-forsaken Universe than Earth?"

"We have an enemy."

Samantha spoke quietly, but her words chilled them.

"This did not happen, man!" Dudeman pointed an accusing finger at Samantha. "It's all a hoax to make us believe your crazed lies!"

"Are you blind, James?" Kaity was compelled to shout, through tears. "It's all destroyed. Earth just got obliterated. She didn't lie—she *saved* us!"

"I refuse to believe it!" Dudeman snapped. "Chrysta's the one with real sense! Take us back! Let me out! This is fake! Somewhere behind the screens and special effects is Earth, just as alive as ever! You can't make me believe anything!"

"An accurate self-assessment, Mr. Erskin," Samantha stated coolly. "Earth's demise, however, does not require faith. I wish, oh how I wish, it wasn't true! But here we are, we eight, bound for a destiny beyond our stars and for a purpose greater than we may recognize in our lifetimes."

"How can you be sure of that?" Sharko at last found his voice. "Forgive me, but I barely just met you."

"God has shown me things," Samantha stated with authority. "This may seem a tragic end, but it's really just a beginning. I can't pretend that any words I say will dull your pain. These next months and years are appropriate for grieving. I simply want to encourage you by saying that God has a plan for each and every one of you—a wonderful plan—and He will make beauty out of these ashes." She gestured meaningfully to the barren orb of Earth.

Her last words were like a salve to a burn. Kaity and several others felt their heartache lessen at the thought of a hopeful future. Dudeman simply crossed his arms before storming towards the ladder, to the two bedroom decks above. Sharko tried to head him off, but James Erskin wanted to be alone.

"Buzz off!" he exclaimed, and that was the end of the matter.

"You should all get some sleep." Samantha broke the awkwardness. "Matt and I will keep the shuttle going. We've had a long day—especially you two."

She nodded to Sharko and Kaity, whom she escorted up the ladder to the fourth floor of the shuttle—the top bedroom deck. Here, she stopped by an alcove sealed off by a sliding door. With a kind smile, Samantha drew the door aside to show them a room she'd prepared for them. It was a decent-sized space carved out of the shuttle, but to Kaity, who'd anticipated a Hawaiian bungalow, it looked pathetic. The alcove was very narrow by the doorway. It widened as it deepened, providing the couple with just enough space to lie next to each other near the back.

The rumbling of the engines reverberated through the ship's cold walls. Kaity hung her head, but Sharko understood the value of the privacy Samantha had granted them. He thanked her sincerely, and she left the two to their wedding night. Neither Sharko nor Kaity had the heart for anything but huddling beneath a thick blanket and whispering about the day. After crying for nearly an hour, Kaity found her voice again.

"We wanted an unforgettable honeymoon," she said bitterly. "This fits the bill, in so many negative ways!"

"I'm so sorry," Sharko murmured, his voice breaking. "I wanted to give you a better wedding night than this—a better honeymoon—a better life."

"Hey, it's okay." Kaity stroked his hair tenderly, concern for him overriding her personal disappointment. "You couldn't exactly help it, Dear, and—remember our vows? To love one another and be faithful no matter what?"

"We've hit 'no matter what.'"

"We have, so what do we do about it? Crumble and fall, or face it together?"

"I still feel bad..." Sharko began. Kaity put a hushing finger to his lips.

"Don't! God is with us, and we can still have a good marriage. Of all the thoughts flashing through my mind this past hour, one thing makes me grateful—both of us have survived."

Sharko said nothing for several moments. Kaity was uncertain whether her words had encouraged him or rendered the opposite effect...until he squeezed her hand.

"Regardless of where the future takes us," Sharko pledged, "I will strive to love and protect you. You're right. Though we live in a time when Earth is lifeless, at least we'll face it together."

"Together always," Kaity agreed. She snuggled her head against his chest and, for a few brief moments, let herself forget the unhappiness of the universe.

A WEEK OF SPACE VOYAGE passed Kaity without registering. Devoid of the comforting sun or the cycle of day and night, the eight survivors of Earth experienced insomnia, disorientation, and cabin fever. None of them were used to space travel. Kaity knew they were fortunate that *The Deliverer*, as Samantha dubbed their craft, was an experimental shuttle designed for deep space voyages. The Australian Space Agency had constructed and launched something like it several years earlier, sending the youngest astronaut into space aboard it. Kaity still recalled the story of how they'd eventually lost contact with their astronauts. It had made global headlines.

The body of *The Deliverer* was tubular and divided into five levels. Kaity's muscles grew sore as she adapted to everyday climbing, and the artificial gravity meant traversing each deck with care. The bottom floor of *The Deliverer* contained a storage hold. It sat beneath the Commons, the room ringed by ten seats which Kaity and the others had occupied during takeoff. Above the Commons, the third deck housed four bedrooms, a galley kitchen, and a crammed pantry the size of a closet. On the floor above were six bedrooms, all the size of closets and boasting only single beds. Kaity knew Samantha had given them their special, curtained-off alcove because of this, and expressed her gratitude.

At the top of *The Deliverer* sat the cockpit, filled with gadgetry Kaity couldn't name. She seldom made the climb up the long ship's ladder to see it. Instead, like everyone else, she spent most of her time in the Commons. Smooth-topped tables rose from the sterile white floor, with foldable chairs that could be retrieved from the wall. All was compartmentalized, clean and modern. Every level had windows except the storage area, for the engines and fuel tanks attached to its exterior.

The storage hold was full to bursting. Samantha had literally invested all of her money in *The Deliverer* and its rations. Water sat everywhere—in tanks, gallon jugs, and bottles. Crates of clothing, blankets, kitchenware, and other dry goods abounded. Plastic-wrapped food, canned vegetables, dried fruit, a freezer stuffed with frozen meals—Samantha had anticipated all of their needs. There was even ammunition for Matt's revolver. Once, as Kaity and Mike were down there with Samantha, the young man ventured a question.

"Is there any...pizza...and a microwave to cook it?" he asked.

"Even pizza, *and* a microwave," Samantha said, with a grin. "I brought some frozen hamburgers along, too. They don't taste as good as the real thing, but hamburgers are my weakness." She pointed comically to her broad hips.

"I'm a college student," Mike answered, seizing a packaged pizza with gusto. "Frozen food is my friend!"

He winked so mischievously that Kaity nearly laughed. Yet it came out as a weak chuckle, for their spirits were greatly dampened.

It was no small thing, losing all. Everything they'd known had burned with Earth, and it was truly life-changing. Kaity counted her blessings that Sharko was present. As newlyweds, they were the happiest of the group. Experiencing the joys of loving and living together gave them energy—and hope—the others lacked. They had little time completely to themselves in the cramped ship. What moments they did have were sweet, and Kaity found much comfort in Sharko's soothing arms. Learning to be a wife and a lover was a joy, yet her heart still throbbed with pain. Her parents' faces on that final day haunted her. *They would still be alive*, she thought chokingly, *if they hadn't insisted on gathering stuff. Plain, worthless, miserable *stuff*!*

Whenever Kaity thought of it, she turned to Sharko for comfort. As someone who'd lost his parents in a plane crash, Sharko understood her pain. Kaity remembered the day he'd lost his own parents. She and Sharko had waved goodbye to them as they boarded their plane to visit relatives in Vermont. Work and military training had kept Sharko and his two brothers from going—an ironic mercy. On the return flight, his parents' plane had suffered engine failure and crashed into the Rockies. All of the crew and passengers had been instantly killed.

It had happened so suddenly, so unexpectedly. Sharko hadn't flown since news of their deaths. He'd avoided planes like the plague, only agreeing to fly to Hawaii for their honeymoon because of the occasion. Now, he was trapped in a space vessel. He bore their circumstances bravely, but Kaity sensed the added layer of grief it brought. She suggested he speak to Dudeman about it, yet that proved nearly impossible.

James stayed cold and aloof during the entire week. Kaity wondered if it tied in with an absence of family. Although he wept for Earth lost, James Erskin had no true relatives to grieve. A foster child, there existed only scant information about his parents. His mother had been a waitress and his father a professor. Somewhere in his heritage was a bit of Pacific Islander mixed with Jamaican, though he didn't know from which side. He liked to think that his love of surfing extended back to these ancestors.

"Dudeman" had given his foster parents, the Erskins, more than a few gray hairs. Always the rebel, James had nearly spiraled down into the world of partying and drinking before Sharko's influence pulled him out. Dudeman could be downright stubborn, but Sharko spoke to him in a way no other human could. Thus Kaity's husband tried to communicate with his childhood friend, but James kept withdrawing. He merely moped about, pausing occasionally to argue with Samantha.

Why he hated the calming prophetess eluded Kaity. She viewed Samantha as their one bastion in a galaxy of madness. Kaity couldn't fathom how she did it, but Samantha set a course as confidently as if she'd been plotting a route home. She alone knew where they were heading, and believed in a future worth voyaging towards. In an existence as shattered as theirs, it was a surety to be thankful for.

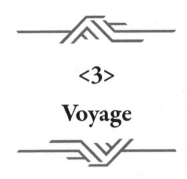

<3>

Voyage

The Deliverer continued onward under Matt's simple piloting. Another week slipped by, then two. They glided easily through open space using solar sails, only steering around a handful of obstacles. The flat, panel-like sails used solar winds from the sun as propulsion, much like sailing ships on Earth had used trade winds.

As they continued travelling, Kaity grew sick and tired of space. The monotony of shuttle life didn't help. She spent her days grieving, praying, talking to Nancy, and growing closer to her husband. She also conversed with Chrysta, learning that the seamstress and Mike had joined Samantha at the last minute because of the prophetess' preaching. Both churchgoers, they had listened to her message of doom in the marketplace. After praying about it, they had felt led by the Spirit to the restaurant parking lot. Kaity took a liking to Chrysta, but Mike seldom opened up.

Thirty days after their departure, Samantha made an announcement over their ship's intercom. It was a system Matt had repaired as part of his tinkering, and she sent a message from the cockpit to the Commons. *The Deliverer* was nearing a planet. Kaity dashed to the nearest porthole window, gazing out in wonder at the red world they were floating by.

Mars! A mottled palette of crimson orange, a giant marble suspended in the heavens that had captured the imagination of many astronauts. Kaity beheld the Martian planet and wished it was habitable. What secrets lurked upon its barren surface? From the porthole window, she beheld the towering mass of Olympus Mons and the deep labyrinths of the Valles Marineris. Three smaller but equally impressive volcanoes ran in a chain between them. Kaity knew that nightly temperatures plunged too far for any hope of ter-

raforming, but Mars tugged at her heartstrings and brought on a terrible realization.

Out of eight planets, only Earth was suitable for life. Suppose there were
no more? What if the extraterrestrial planets portrayed in films were merely
that—the stuff of fantasy? Samantha spoke of distant galaxies where they be-
longed, but what of distant peoples? If there were aliens, what did they look
like? Why would God isolate them from humanity? Did God love them, too,
and were some of them Christians?

It blew her mind. Yet Kaity felt, as they passed Mars by, that any chances
of habitation passed with it. The great Red Planet slowly faded into the con-
suming blackness. They were adrift again—one tiny shuttle in a massive void.

Feeling saddened, Kaity decided to pay a visit to her chief confidante.
She climbed *The Deliverer*'s ladder and found her friend in her tiny room,
studying a photograph which the tutor recognized too well. Crease marks
ran through an image of two smiling parents and three beaming children.
The figures stood in front of a house in a field, a detached garage and tractor
in the background. The secretary seemed to finally notice her friend's presence. She folded the photo, tucking it into a leather wallet that boasted debit
and credit cards, now useless.

"I look at it every day," Nancy said, after a moment of silence. Her body
language conveyed embarrassment and wistfulness all at once. Kaity knew
the practical secretary didn't like to be thought of as sentimental.

"Who could blame you?" Kaity forced a reassuring smile. "I wish I had a
picture of my family. My last memory of them..."

"I'm so sorry," Nancy said, after a few silent moments. "I know it must've
been hard. We both knew they weren't going to make it to the Tower."

"They died for possessions! For THINGS!" Tears formed in Kaity's eyes.
"What a worthless way to go! They were wonderful parents, Nancy! They
were *Christians*. Why didn't they come? I keep playing that day over and over
in my head. I keep wondering if there was anything I could've done differently, so that more could've been saved. So that my parents would have come!"

Nancy reached out and squeezed Kaity's hand in a sympathetic gesture.

"I know," she said simply. "Why did I have to move to Vogul Bay while
my family stayed in Montana? Why did I, the oldest, outlive all my younger
siblings? I had neither the time to warn my family nor the opportunity to say

goodbye. We were rushing out, driving, and boarding the shuttle before calling them even entered my mind!" Nancy's lower lip started trembling as she added, "I know the feeling, friend. Even though hindsight is 20/20, you keep asking yourself over and over: Could I have done more? Could I have done something to save them?"

"There was nothing."

An authoritative voice spoke from behind them. Kaity and Nancy whirled around to see Samantha.

"Day after day, I preached doom on the street corners," Samantha stated. "Night after night, I prophesied of that very day! Only you seven listened. Perhaps it was the will of God. Maybe it was men's stubborn hearts. I cannot say."

"Yes, but if you had spoken the truth more persuasively—?" Nancy ventured.

"The hearts of humankind are naturally wicked." Samantha's words sounded unusually harsh. "Their ears are deaf and their eyes, unseeing. Jesus performed miracles before the Pharisees, but did that turn them? We can't know why people make the choices they do, yet humankind has the capacity to look truth squarely in the face and reject it. I'm sorry about your parents," she finished, giving both of them a sympathetic look.

"What of your own parents and family?" Kaity asked. "In all our time together, seated around the tables at mealtime, I've never heard you mention relatives. Even James said something about his foster parents, and Heaven knows he gave them a fair share of headaches!"

Samantha's face darkened.

"You were aware in advance of the doomsday," Nancy chimed in. "Did your own parents reject the truth?"

"My parents..."

Samantha, for once, looked pained. She couldn't finish, and it was a strange reaction for the normally-staunch prophetess. Out of compassion, Kaity quickly changed the subject, yet the look on Samantha's face lingered in her memory. Samantha Harris usually appeared strong and stoic, only breaking into awestruck emotion when speaking of God. She was their leader, their rock. To see her shaken by a simple question made Kaity wonder just how much of Samantha's story remained to be unearthed. At the end of the day, how much did they really know about the prophetess?

SAMANTHA HARRIS DREW her hands together in prayer. In the quietude of her cramped shuttle room, she reflected on her interchange with Kaity mere minutes before. Few things riled her, but her parents...oh, how she mourned her parents! No amount of preparedness for the apocalypse could assuage the ache within her soul. A sorrow that her calling didn't give her time to process. This group of survivors needed her, every second of every day. She alone knew who pursued them—the individual who sought their annihilation, despite sating himself on the population of Earth. Yet if she couldn't take the time to deal with her own grief, perhaps she could help others through theirs.

Samantha gathered everyone in the Commons for their fortieth dinner since Doomsday. Every night had been a solemn affair, but this particular evening, Samantha was determined to address her crewmates' grief. The prophetess had brought along a calendar, and Nancy took it upon herself to mark each day that passed with an X. As it was Sunday, Samantha led them in a church service. Dudeman usually skipped out, but tonight, after their singing and prayer time, he joined them. Samantha brought out a sturdy, space-grade box with a hole in the top, as well as some papers and pens.

"I want you to write the names of all the people you miss," she said, "and drop it into this box. We're going to set it afloat in space, and pray that centuries from now, it will fall into the atmosphere of a revitalized Earth."

"Hear, hear!" Matt cried, and Samantha's heart warmed as they set about the task eagerly. Some of them finished quickly, recalling names fondly. Others, like Chrysta, could not see the paper for tears. Samantha surprised herself by only writing down a dozen or so names. Her list was as short as James'. Kaity and Sharko, in contrast, seemed to be running out of space on their papers. Both had been friends to a lot of people, with a fair sum of relatives between them. Kaity dropped her paper in last, and Samantha sealed the box tightly.

"To our friends and family, we say goodbye!" she declared, her voice catching. "Some we will not see until the Judgement. Others, we will walk with again in Heaven. We miss them all, but let us remember that this life is not the end. Death is merely a portal to eternity. One day, our present cares and sorrows will be washed away, and the Son of God will wipe away our tears."

A single, mocking clap sounded in the space. Dudeman half-sat, leaning against the back of a chair, an expression of disbelief written across his face.

"I hope He will," Dudeman jeered, "because I'm telling you, man, He's the one who put those tears there in the first place!"

"Lay off it!" Sharko countered. "We all know you aren't a Christian, James, but for Heaven's sake, this isn't a theological debate! This is a time of honoring everyone we knew who died."

"Where was God when Earth burned up?" Dudeman spat. "How could your God send those who died, innocent, straight to Hell? I just don't get it! God didn't give me nothin'! I was born on the wrong side of the bed and I've lived on the wrong side of everything, and now I'm the 'lucky' survivor of the end of Earth! Whoopee! Somehow that victory tastes about as good as ashes!"

"All of us feel a measure of survivor's guilt," Nancy defended, "and just because God allowed this doesn't make Him bad!"

Dudeman continued his string of accusations, and Samantha could tell this was heading nowhere good. *Spirit, help me with this stubborn surfer*! She prayed, closing her eyes. Suddenly, a vision flashed across her mind. Images played out before her, and she smiled confidently and opened her eyes.

"He was there, that rainy morning, in your bedroom," she said. James' eyes bugged slightly.

"Excuse me?"

"Did you think it was mere coincidence that your mother arrived home an hour early from her church meeting?

"I don't know what you're talkin' about!"

"Sure you do." Samantha was undaunted. "It was a rainy November morning. You were so depressed. You'd woken up in an alleyway with no memory of getting there, shaky and surrounded by vomit. You faintly remembered drinking, a woman—your mind blanked. That scared you, so much that you returned home and grabbed the second knife down in the butcher block. You almost did it, James. You almost slit your own throat, you were so depressed, so angry—so tired of it all. It seemed you'd always been searching and coming up empty, so why continue? Then your mother came home with the news that Sharko's parents had died, and you suddenly forgot the desire to kill yourself and be rid of this world."

Dudeman had been listening like a cornered animal. As soon as Samantha finished, he shook his fist in rage.

"GO TO HELL!" he shouted, his anger shocking everyone. The young surfer practically flew up the ladder to the 3rd level, and the spell of the evening was broken. Samantha leaped up to follow him, yet halted in exasperation as Sharko darted in front of her.

"Are you sure that's wise?" he asked. Samantha gave him a withering look. She recognized the signs of someone actively avoiding God. Didn't he care about his friend's salvation? Sharko was about to step aside from the power of her gaze when Mike's voice drew their attention to a window.

"Um, you guys might want to look at this," he said slowly. The seven humans approached the porthole beside him, looking down towards the shuttle's stern. They couldn't believe their eyes.

A GREAT, CYLINDRICAL object voyaged in space behind them. It was the gunship, and it was gaining on their position! Kaity blinked, believing herself to be in a nightmare, but *The Deliverer*'s walls and the porthole window were as real as ever. Memories of the object in the sky assaulted her. Panic gripped her heart, and she couldn't move. How could this be? Why would the alien object that had incinerated Earth *follow* them?

"We have company!" Matt exclaimed, and everyone turned to Samantha. She was their natural leader—the only person who had a clue what she was doing.

The prophetess simply closed her eyes. This past year had been the strangest of her existence. First a voice had spoken to her as she gazed across a crowded street, telling her that life would soon change for her and everyone she knew. Quiet but commanding, she'd assumed it must be God's. Then visions, dreams, an overwhelming desire to build this Ark, compelled her to work overtime and exhaust her savings. This one ship to house humanity's survivors had been her focus, her bent...but another dream had come as well. She recalled falling slowly through space. The stars blazed all around, and a nebula's wispy gasses seemed to embrace her. She felt warm, not cold. The voice came to her again—*His* Voice—which had comforted her after giving her the prophecy of Earth's destruction.

"But how can you let everyone die, God?" She had whispered, feeling saddened and afraid.

"My Child," the Speaker replied, "if you could fathom the galaxies and stars, if you could understand the cosmos as I do, you would know the simple answer. My purposes extend beyond the stars. My Will overshadows all human understanding. I have a greater purpose than you could ever comprehend. It is not My hand that sweeps down upon the earth. I am allowing evil to triumph for a time. Yet grief will not last long, and Earth will be restored. But as for you, Child, I have something which no human of Earth could possibly imagine!"

The Voice rose in intensity and power as it spoke. With a final, loud exclamation, the world had burst into light and color. Samantha felt herself being propelled, as if from a slingshot, through the heavens. Her body felt no force, no rushing wind, and yet her consciousness crossed galaxies and distant solar systems. She saw dark planets gleaming with lights, bright planets glistening in splendor, thousands of stars and constellations she couldn't name, and then...this very day. She could not explain it, though Matt inquired a hundred times where they were going and how she knew. Samantha simply *felt* the course corrections that were necessary. Gazing at the space around them, she was certain they were here. The time had come. This was the moment of destiny.

"Matt, take the pilot's chair!" Samantha commanded. "Retract the solar sails and prepare for some interesting maneuvers!"

Her cousin gripped the ladder and hauled himself up with ease borne of frequent use. Samantha stood by the intercom console, waiting to issue Matt orders as the situation unfolded. She could tell Kaity and Chrysta felt sheer terror. Who could blame them? The object which had blasted Earth was coming for them!

The gunship drew closer. Samantha noticed that its barrel was hollow and far more massive than it had appeared from Earth. She saw Kaity begin to quake, though Sharko slipped a comforting arm around her waist to calm her. Mike was likewise holding his cowering wife in the crook of his shoulder. The couples' care for each other warmed her heart slightly, even in the midst of the tension.

"I said we had an enemy." Samantha surveyed each one of them. "He hunts us with an obsession honed by madness and the Great Liar; the first Enemy of us all."

"Who hunts us?" Mike demanded shakily.

"One of the most evil men in history."

"There's something you haven't been telling us, isn't there?" Nancy ventured. She had observed an almost furtive look on the prophetess' face. "You know who it is!"

"You're very astute, Miss Cooper," Samantha complimented. "I won't avoid the question, but now's not the time to discuss identities. If we get out of this scrape, I'll make everything plain."

"What do you mean, *if*?" Chrysta squeaked.

"We're going to be swallowed by his ship, of course." Samantha's tone dripped practicality. At that moment, the darker maw of the gunship blocked out the blackness of space. Kaity cried in dismay. The enormous vessel had overtaken them! Like a fish being consumed by a shark, their vessel disappeared into a massive, metallic throat devoid of light. Their enemy had caught up with them.

KAITY FELT LIKE HER very essence had been consumed. Terror enveloped her, and only Sharko's steadying presence kept her from fainting. Brilliant lights suddenly snapped on. The entire inside of the enveloping space burst into stark detail, and Kaity and Sharko squinted simultaneously. Rows of hundreds of lights encircled their shuttle, revealing the utilitarian maw of the alien vessel. She beheld a cold, metallic barrel fashioned out of plates resembling cast iron, with ribbing composed of lighter, steel-like girders.

Fear waned in the face of Kaity's curiosity. This ship had been construct-ed, but where? The sheer enormity and power of the creation surpassed any of Earth's known capabilities. Samantha must be right. She was looking at the insides of an *alien* gunship! Before Earth's doom, Kaity would have scoffed at the thought. Now, this felt like yet another anomaly in their strange, new reality.

Catwalks traced the trajectories of the steel ribbing, figures moving along them. Silhouettes advanced—human in shape, but taller and thinner. There were a hundred of them, clad in spacesuits that hid their faces. They were heading for the shuttle when *The Deliverer* gave an unexpected lurch. Kaity looked upward through the porthole window to see metal arms extending from the girders. They had latched on to two of their fuel tanks. *The Deliverer* was caught by the great, black beast that had ravaged Earth.

"Samantha," Matt's voice crackled over the intercom, "what should we do? They've sunk their hooks into us!"

"We're trapped!" Chrysta sobbed, slamming her hand against the win-dow. "Oh why, oh why, did I ever come along on this suicide mission?"

Mike merely stood, visibly unsure what to do. Nancy Cooper rushed in to salvage the situation. Taking Chrysta away from her fumbling husband, she put a soothing arm around the younger woman.

"Please get a hold of yourself," she said, firmly but not unkindly. "Saman-tha and Matt know what they're doing, and God is with us."

"Wait for it...!" Samantha told her cousin. Kaity wanted to back away from the window, yet her limbs were lead weights. The alien beings halted, a new figure emerging from their midst. Its manner and gait were unnervingly familiar. The aliens in spacesuits stood at attention to let him by. The obvi-ously-male figure strode like an emperor of ancient Rome, his poise speaking of power. A helmet covered his head, yet the visor was clear. He outpaced the ranks of what must be his underlings, coming so near that Kaity could tell the suit didn't fit him properly. It was alien in make, but his face—a sneering face—it was...it couldn't be...!

"By all that's sacred, he's a human!" Sharko exclaimed, breathless. The fig-ure must have seen their faces in the porthole windows, because he raised an arm and pointed at them. Kaity felt her blood freeze. The expression on his

face resembled madness twisted by rage. *This* must be the man who had destroyed Earth. He seemed more monstrous than human.

"Boosters, NOW!!!!"

Samantha shouted the order over the intercom. There was a rumble, the
shuttle shook, and the metal arms outside of their craft groaned. *The Deliverer* lurched, buckled, and lurched again. With a horrid snap of metal, their
space shuttle broke free of the arms. Kaity looked back to see two of their engines still held in the clutches of the restraining pincers. *The Deliverer* blasted
out of the gunship on a wobbly course. Fuel trailed from the spaces where
two engines had been, and from Matt's tone, it was a fight to keep their craft
steady.

"Sam, I need you here IMMEDIATELY!" The panic in his tone surprised Kaity. "We just left the frying pan for the fire!"

"Be there in a sec!" Samantha exclaimed. Leaping onto the ladder and
climbing like a madwoman, she met Dudeman halfway up. James Erskin had
heard and felt everything happening, and his rage was quite forgotten. The
two passed each other awkwardly on the steep rungs, Dudeman dropping the
rest of the way.

"What's up?" he asked, bewildered. "We hit some solar wake or something?"

He'd barely uttered the inquiry when Samantha's voice issued authoritatively over the intercom.

"Everyone, strap yourselves in! We're about to face one heck of a roller
coaster!"

"Roller coaster?" Dudeman's confusion deepened an instant before the
shuttle abruptly veered away from the gunship's barrel. Kaity glanced out of
the window on her way to a chair, expecting to see open space. Instead, a
swirling vortex of purple whirled in front of them. The gunship appeared to
be shooting a beam into it. Kaity couldn't believe her eyes, but Sharko forced
his new wife into a seat. Strapping her in securely, he tightened and double-
checked all of her fastenings. Crouching beside her, Sharko gazed lovingly into the eyes of his new bride. The fear and uncertainty of galaxies faded away
before her husband's strong countenance.

"Wherever we're headed," he said sincerely, "I love you. If we survive, I
cherish the thought of spending my life with you. Should we perish, I want

you to know that you're the most precious thing to me in the universe. These last few weeks have been the worst of our lives, but because of you, they've also been the best. Whatever comes, I shall not regret it, so long as I face it with you."

KAITY'S HEART WARMED at Sharko's words. Husband and wife leaned toward each other for a kiss. At the same time, *The Deliverer* careened wildly. With the artificial gravity on, Sharko was thrown by the force. He skittered to the middle of the room, catching his fingers on the seam of the tabletop which was folded into the floor. Dudeman slid across the slick flooring as well, bumping against the wall and catching on to an empty chair.

The jolt of unseen impacts sent shudders throughout the ship. *The Deliverer* veered in the opposite direction, bumped against something again, and started spinning. All control was lost as it screamed crazily through whatever anomaly blotted out open space. Kaity could only see the purple mass, rushing by so quickly it became a blur.

In the cockpit of the shuttle, Matt fought madly to avoid the invisible boundaries of whatever had sucked them in. Samantha, strapped next to him, clung to her seat and prayed fervently. From the cockpit, they could see a purplish tunnel stretching onward for what seemed eternity. The walls were streaks of mottled white and purple, and their shuttle was accelerating. Neither Samantha nor Matt said a word. The prophetess knew that whatever surrounded them—wormhole, warp tunnel, vortex—they had lost control.

The Deliverer continued to spin. Sharko and Dudeman clung grimly to the objects in their fingers. Kaity felt like nothing was right-side up. Faster and faster they went, spinning, whirling, screaming along through an unknown phenomenon of space that saved them only to prolong their suffering. Dudeman lost his grip, slid across the room, and smashed into Mike. The young man held the surfer fast—James wincing with pain. Sharko's strength was failing, and Kaity feared he would be flung about until the ship battered him to death. She felt her own straps straining, straining as if they would snap as she moved upside down, sideways, and right-side up again.

As if by magic, they shot out of the purple tunnel. They were in space again, still spinning, but directly ahead of them loomed an orb of tan. Their acceleration could not be slowed. *The Deliverer* hit some sort of atmospheric turbulence. The exterior of the ship lit up like a firecracker, fire bursting into the ruptures where the two engines had been. A fuel tank exploded as the shuttle went whirling ever downward, ever spiraling, until it broke free of the thermosphere at last. They plummeted toward a sea of sand. Matt managed to lift the shuttle's nose, but she was still falling.

"The chute, Sam! Deploy the chute!" he cried. Samantha had been so busy praying and panicking that she was oblivious to more practical concerns. She slammed a button on the console. Out of the back of the craft rocketed a large parachute made of Kevlar. The shuttle started to slow...in vain! Massive sand dunes, multilayered bluffs, and plains of cracked earth flashed into view. The shuttle hit the top of a sand dune, jumped, and skittered across a bluff. Kaity slammed back violently into her seat. Mike's straps snapped from the impact, and he and James went flying. Sharko too lost his grip, and Kaity closed her eyes and couldn't watch.

A horrendous tearing sound and a jolt caused Kaity to open them. Sharko had caught hold of a loose strap, but Mike and Dudeman were still sliding across the floor. Chrysta let out a scream, and Nancy screwed her eyes shut. A sand dune hurtled past in the window. The shuttle plowed violently into something, and all fell into darkness. With a dizzying jolt, their craft stopped, and Kaity knew no more.

<4>

The Alien World

An immovable sun cast rosy hues over rocky, purple terrain. Great mountains rose sharply above plains with wavy grass and shadowy lakes. A spacecraft of alien make skimmed above the grass, soaring high into the air to crest the mountains before plummeting with the steep decline of their slopes. Over their lofty peaks, the sun could not reach.

In shadow lay a kingdom ancient and exhausted. Its power waning, its grip loosening, its war-weary leader returned. His craft came over the mountains, followed by two others. The trio of identical ships landed together to confuse a would-be assassin. Out of the leftmost craft, a figure emerged unlike anything from terrestrial soil. Lithe and blue-skinned, the figure had gracefully-shaped limbs, a heart-shaped head, and stumpy feet clad in metal boots. He pressed a button on a silver belt and immediately hovered a foot into the air. The male shot off across a walkway that twisted between trees glowing with orange, iridescent light. Four bodyguards followed closely.

The male zipped past purple-leafed trees, luminescent flowers, and teal palms with upside-down fronds. He zoomed by the cozy façades of white houses framed in purplewood, until he reached a building set upon a smooth, stone foundation. The entire exterior was made of white, semi-translucent, glowing trees, intertwined to form almost solid walls. Multicolored glass filled any gaps where the trees didn't meet. A synthetic, thatched roof presided over a dark, polished floor that reflected the glow of bluish wall lights.

At one end of the tree-palace was a round entranceway and, at the other, a gleaming throne room. Dozens of aliens that looked like the hovering male crowded the doorway, but the alien passed through them without heed. His bodyguards took up positions by the door. Crossing the grand hall alone, he flicked off his boots and landed with a clank in front of the throne. Sitting, he held up a blue, four-fingered hand as a male a few decades younger than him approached. He was the male's nephew, a youth named Jixa, who served as his royal advisor.

Murmuring could be heard at the doorway of the throne hall. Jixa gazed at his uncle before turning around and proclaiming, in a booming voice, "Tormac Durag has returned from Qorqar!"

"I do not wish to see anyone!" Durag snarled, his tone low and ill-tempered. He crossed his arms over his chest, which was protected by a small breastplate made of two axe blades.

"The Tormac does not wish to see anyone at this moment!" Jixa exclaimed. Disappointed cries could be heard from the entry, but every Trylithian slowly turned and abandoned the line outside the throne hall. The hall and its occupants were left in peace, with only guards standing to attention by the throne room's entrance.

Durag sighed. He was tormac, or "king" of Lidexid, in the land of Duskrealm. His was not the only colmit, or country, in the realm. For years, his colmit had waged war with their neighbors, leaving Durag as exhausted as he appeared. Most of the other nations of Trylithia, the world of the blue-skins, hated Lidexid. Durag knew that leaving the planet was their only escape, as he couldn't bring himself to surrender. Like most Trylithians, a defiant streak ran through his blood.

Jixa turned to Durag with a disapproving glare. His eyes were the most expressive part of him, because he covered the lower portion of his face with a decorated cloth. All modest Trylithians did.

"What in the Gorvan was that?" Jixa demanded. "My Tormac, you cannot continually dismiss your subjects and servants!"

"I am tired of them!" Durag snapped. "Tired of this entire business! I can see but one way out, and that is leaving Trylithia. There is not enough room in Duskrealm for all our colmits. Get me Vogul! I must have his report on the effectiveness of the *Draxalis*!"

"Of course," Jixa pledged, grabbing a flat device from a pocket of his kilt-ed loincloth. A few buttons later, a holographic screen projected from the floor. Tormac Durag leaned forward eagerly as Jixa cleaned up the deep space transmission. A Trylithian captain answered and replied that Vogul would be fetched. Several minutes later, the pinched visage of a middle-aged human from Earth came onto the screen.

Willum Vogul. His gaunt cheeks, fiery eyes, and downturned mouth spoke of good breeding as much as insanity. Vogul had been born into privilege. Even now, with a crew of Trylithians outnumbering him, he still maintained an aristocratic bearing.

"The test was an absolute success," Vogul said proudly. "Earth is wiped clean of all life, and even its skyscrapers are now skeletons. An entire planet of 8 billion was snuffed out. Your weapon will strike terror into the hearts of the Gorvan races, and Lidexid will find ample worlds willing to accommodate them in the face of annihilation!"

Vogul gave a ranting laugh. *As humans are inclined to do*, Durag supposed. He smiled beneath his mouth cloth.

"I am pleased," he praised. "You did not disappoint me! How long will the plasma take to recharge?"

"A month, at most," Vogul answered.

"How did the *Draxalis* fare?" Durag's anxiety came out in his words. "It is a powerful gun, and we took it from spacedock prematurely."

"Structural integrity held," Vogul reported. "Some minor systems blew out, such as our planetary sensors and temperature regulation. We will strive to make repairs on our own."

"Good! Take the wormhole back to our galaxy and hide in Stattar Nebula. I will inform you of your next target world there. It will be a place with few habitants, but enough to catch the attention of the System."

Vogul's glee faded, and his mouth stretched taut with anger.

"My Tormac," he said, "I cannot directly follow that order. It has come to my attention that there were...*survivors*...from Earth. I trapped them inside the barrel, and meant to bring them to you as specimens. But the cursed Earthlings broke free and used the wormhole ahead of me! Two of their engines ripped off as they fled, and one intersected with our stabilization beam. There was an explosion and our beam is offline. It will take a month to replenish enough plasma to stabilize the wormhole again."

"Then you will be stuck in this...Clouded Way Galaxy?" Durag asked. "Are your supplies sufficient?"

"Milky Way," Vogul corrected, "and yes. When we do return to the Gorvan, I would like your permission to follow the survivors and obliterate their craft."

"Why do you desire this, Vogul?" the tormac questioned. "I'm well aware that you hate your kind, and they have trapped you in your home galaxy. But how many survivors were there?"

"Eight!" Vogul nearly foamed with rage.

"Eight? Eight measly survivors?" Durag threw back his head and laughed. "I'm not going to waste one plasma ion against eight individuals! This gunship was designed to kill billions."

"You don't understand," Vogul said quietly, coldly. "Eight humans might not mean much to a Trylithian. I wouldn't even give them the time of day but for one fact! One infuriating truth: I know something about them you don't. They're a stench in my nostrils, and one day, your precious Trylithia will suffer because of them. The fate of our galaxy will forever change when the last humans from Earth find what was prophesied. Mark my words."

"Murmurings. Delusions!" Durag waved a dismissive hand. "You cannot know the future, pitiful Earthling! Go back to the work with which I entrusted you. Or would you rather be commanding a jail cell than a gunship?"

"No need to get nasty, Tormac." Vogul flinched. "I will always do as you say. We will be returning to the Gorvan System once we can."

The human smiled, and bowed so nobly to Durag that the tormac was convinced of his loyalty. The transmission ended, the screen flicked off, and Durag leaned back against his throne in a satisfied manner.

"You may now send in my visitors," he remarked. "That human is so unpredictable!"

Jixa was not as dismissive. The younger Trylithian, always more observant than his uncle, had sensed something in Vogul's outward calmness that unnerved him. Where Durag saw an amusing man with a changeable mind, Jixa saw a calculating genius whose smile came laced with poison.

"I know Vogul is unpredictable," he said, as the first visitor entered his uncle's throne room. "That's what concerns me."

LIGHT BROKE INTO KAITY Anderson's dark world. An undefined mass of tan met her blurry eyes, and Kaity blinked to clear them. A granular surface of sand came into focus, along with the metallic walls of their shuttle. Sitting up uncertainly, Kaity took in her altered surroundings, wincing as her temples pounded with pain. Their craft appeared to be lying on its side, with sand partly burying it to form a sort of floor. Sunbeams slanted through a hole in the shuttle's side, which now served as its roof. In front of her stood the crumpled metal floor of the room, now vertical like a wall—its doorway still intact.

The unconscious forms of Nancy, Dudeman, Mike, and Chrysta surrounded her. Kaity wanted desperately to help her companions. Some were still strapped to their chairs, while others showed signs of injury. However, she didn't know anything about First Aid. Only her husband and Nancy possessed any degree of healing knowledge, but Nancy hung out of reach, unconscious and fastened to a chair high above her. Sharko was...! A lump of fear formed in Kaity's throat as she realized he wasn't there.

She vaguely remembered the straps of her chair snapping and her body being thrown. A bump on her forehead and resultant headache confirmed this, along with many scrapes and bruises. Dazed, she rose from the ground. She *must* find Sharko, and why not begin with the storage bay? Walking toward the doorway with a throbbing head, she found nothing but a gaping hole. Her heart sank. All of their supplies, their conveniences...gone? The hull had ripped and bent during the crash, the lower section torn off by sheer force. Beyond the twisted cavity lay many sand dunes.

Kaity stepped out into the light, quickly covering her eyes from the blinding fierceness of the sun. Amazement overcame her fear. She was on an alien world! A lone cactus stood, starkly silhouetted against the horizon, bearing a shape familiar but twisted. Bluffs loomed in the far distance beyond an undulating ocean of dunes, and not a drop of water could be seen. It was as if this land had always existed parched and forgotten by rain. Only the desert stretched on, endless.

We truly are alone here, aren't we? Kaity realized, with a pang. They were eight small humans, trapped in a universe so overwhelmingly bigger than them. It nearly blew her mind, but she remembered Sharko's absence. The icy hand of fear gripped her heart again. Suppose...the storage room...? The hold had separated from the rest of *The Deliverer* during the crash. What if Sharko had lost his grip and fallen out of the doorway at high altitude?

Kaity's heart felt close to bursting. Losing Sharko was her greatest fear. Forgetting her headache, Kaity raced out of the protective cover of the shuttle and across the sand. She stumbled many times as her legs sank in past her ankles. Yet determination compelled her to retrace the large furrow which marked their crash course. She had progressed from the shuttle perhaps thirty feet when a human voice stopped her.

"I'm not sure where you're going," it shouted, "but you might want to check with your husband first!"

Kaity skidded to a halt. She whirled around to see Sharko a ways behind her, leaning against the outer hull of *The Deliverer*! Embarrassment colored her features. She'd let her heart get the best of her, dashing recklessly into the dunes instead of checking inside or around the shuttle. What would logical Nancy say about that?

Relieved beyond expression to see him, she trudged toward him with renewed energy. From her new vantage, Kaity saw the barrier responsible for stopping their ship—a sand dune! *The Deliverer* had plowed straight into its slip-face, and over half of it lay buried in the tan embankment. The sand inside the Commons had poured in through a broken porthole window.

"You're hurt," Kaity said, before Sharko pulled her into a tender kiss. He kissed her so long that Kaity almost ran out of breath, but he eventually let her go, save for a hand. This he grasped onto fervently, and would not release.

"I'm so glad you're all right," he told her emotionally. "My arms are really sore, but these little bleeding scrapes are nothing." He gestured to some scratches on his dusty face.

"Where did you end up? I was thrown from my seat right before we stopped."

"Under the sand, would you believe it?" Sharko spat some of the particulates out. "Got a mouthful, ptheh! I'm out like a light. Next thing, I'm waking from a knock-out, watching my own knock-out walk out."

"Oh heavens, are you going to be this cheesy always?" Kaity rolled her eyes, but Sharko grinned so winsomely that she couldn't suppress a laugh, which hurt her head. "Ouch!"

"Sorry, Dear," Sharko teased, then grew serious. "We'd better go in and see if the others need help."

"Dudeman has a broken arm," Kaity affirmed, as they walked. "Mike looks pretty awful, and I think Nancy's unconscious. I've got no idea how we'll get her down, and I recall Chrysta fainting before the impact."

"What of Matt and Samantha?" Sharko asked.

"No clue. That part of the vessel is either intact, buried, or..." she trailed off, and Sharko didn't need his wife to voice her fear that they might be crushed inside a crumpled fuselage.

Inside the shuttle, husband and wife found Nancy conscious and panicked. Nancy Cooper, strapped into a chair now oriented sideways, hung about twenty feet off the sand. Despite being brave about many things, Nancy was averse to heights, and being unable to move scared her. Kaity sympathized with her friend's fear.

"Thank the Lord you two are here!" Nancy exclaimed. "Please get me down! I have to help them—" she nodded toward the two injured men "—and I hate being trapped!"

"There's got to be a ladder somewhere," Sharko supplied. His eyes roved the space, and he snapped his fingers. The ladder running through all the levels of their ship! They'd needed it to traverse all of the decks but now, with the ship sideways, what purpose did it serve? Sharko rushed to the ladder, yet bolts anchored it in place. A storage locker inset into the shuttle wall was within reach. He opened it but could find no wrench. Nancy, growing desperate, called to him.

"I hesitate to ask, but can you catch me?"

Sharko looked to Kaity. The tutor could tell he wanted her approval, for he felt awkward putting his arms around another woman, even to rescue her.

"It's all right," Kaity affirmed, and Sharko braced himself directly below Nancy's chair. The secretary unfastened first one strap, then the other. She slid out of the slanting seat and Sharko caught her awkwardly. Nancy gained her balance and stood, visibly glad to be vertical.

"Time to use my nurse's training," she commented wryly. Kaity observed her examination of Dudeman, Chrysta, and Mike from a distance. Chrysta's predicament mirrored Nancy's—strapped sideways in a chair. However, the arm of her seat rested mere inches above the sand. Nancy determined that she, of the entire group, bore the fewest physical injuries. Mike proved a different matter. The poor man lay in the sand, on his stomach. Nancy rolled him over, instantly noticing a sharp piece of metal sticking out of his chest. A moderate amount of blood flowed from the wound, and Nancy propped him upright. Mike moaned slightly.

"I can't remove this!" Nancy exclaimed, her palms growing sweaty from nervousness. "I need equipment and bandages, and we've got to have something to stop that bleeding!"

"There should be a first aid cabinet on the upper deck," Kaity recalled.

"I'll go," Sharko volunteered, and Kaity stayed to help her best friend.

SHARKO ENTERED THE slanted bedroom level of the shuttle carefully. Everything was sideways, and a rock had punctured through part of the hull, jutting right through Dudeman's current bedroom. Sharko poked around in the dark space. Traversing the walls now as walkways, he made his way along the sandy surface which had come in through the rupture. He tried pressing a light switch, but nothing came on. Only the glow of emergency lights offered a dim view of the area.

Unable to locate a first aid kit, Sharko hiked to a higher deck. A metal box fronted by a painted, red cross sat on the floor, barely visible. The medical cabinet that had contained it was open, its doors flung back in the tumult. Sharko bent to retrieve it, yet a thought occurred to him. Samantha and Matt had been in the cockpit. Had anyone checked on them since the crash?

Sharko made his way to the doorway, through which stretched their now-useless ladder. The floor creaked slightly as he entered the ten foot-long corridor which led to the cockpit. Crouching, he worked his way along in the dim light, afraid of what he might find. Sand covered the "floor" of the tunnel. Sharko emerged into the cockpit beyond and gasped. Samantha and Matt were seated at their posts, buried from the chest down in sand! Matt appeared to be unconscious, but Samantha was very much awake—and struggling.

The cockpit hull was intact, yet the windshield had blown out. Sand and glass had blasted in, filling half of the room. Sharko noticed that Samantha and Matt's chair straps still held them securely to their chairs. There were many lacerations on the cousins' skin from the glass shards.

"Thank the Almighty!" Samantha declared. "With all this sand, my legs are stuck beneath the console and I can't find the belt release for this darn chair!"

Sharko gingerly brushed away the glass bits and, with Samantha's help, he unearthed the dusty prophetess. She roused her cousin, who looked groggily around the cabin.

"Glad we made it," Matt said dazedly. His head fell forward onto the sandy console. "It's a dessert!"

"Desert, Matt, desert!" Samantha corrected. "Wake up!"

"Leave me alone!" He snorted, batting her hand away in such a drunken manner that Sharko almost smiled.

"Are you injured? Is your head okay?" Samantha scrutinized him for bleeding and bumps. Matt abruptly leaned back and laughed.

"My head's been screwy ever since I agreed to your schemes!" he laughed. "For months I didn't believe you, and now 'I told you so' just doesn't do it justice! I was napping, if you must know. I woke up, saw we were buried in a bunch of sand, saw you trying vainly to dig out, and thought heck, why not fetch a siesta?"

"Oh, you are insufferable!" Samantha scolded, flicking sand at him.

"I hate to interrupt this very mature moment," Sharko said sarcastically, "but I came for a first aid kit."

"The others...?" Samantha suddenly remembered they weren't alone.

"Mike's condition is uncertain and Dudeman has a broken arm."

At Sharko's words, Samantha finished digging herself out, rose, and marched down the tunnel to the bedroom deck below. Without waiting for anyone, she fetched up the medical kit and strode to the Commons. Sharko trailed after, slightly annoyed yet relieved to find the prophetess and the mechanic in one piece. As long as Samantha lived, hope on this desert planet lived as well.

NANCY REMOVED THE CHUNK of shrapnel from Mike's chest with the utmost care. The college student gritted his teeth, and Kaity couldn't watch as she drew it out. She turned around again after Nancy had cleaned the wound, wrapping bandages around his midsection. The nurse flitted from Mike to Dudeman. James still lay, unconscious, on the sandy floor. Samantha stood by, holding the first aid kit, while Nancy conducted her examination. Kaity wondered if they should awaken the surfer, and voiced her thoughts.

"It's best not to wake him," Nancy warned. "He'd only be in agony. He's got a broken ulna and radius, from the looks of it—very common in forearm fractures. Egad, I hope I can remember all that stuff from my medical book! It's because I couldn't that I failed!"

Nancy trembled slightly. The movement surprised Kaity, for it was so unlike her calm, collected friend. She put a comforting arm around Nancy's shoulders.

"You can do it," she said staunchly. "Many qualified people fail the nursing program for reasons other than skill."

"Yes, but do you really want a failed nurse tending to your medical needs?" Nancy questioned. "I didn't even get that far."

"You appeared confident with Mike," Samantha interjected. "Why this hesitancy with Dudeman?"

"Setting a broken bone is different from removing shrapnel!" Nancy pursed her lips. "If I don't set his bones correctly, he'll be impaired for life. What life would he have here, in this isolation? I don't even know where we landed, but it's far from home, and there are no hospitals. There never will be any hospitals, because we're it. We're alone...trapped...isolated—!"

Kaity could sense Nancy nearing hysteria. She drew her uncertain friend into a gentle hug.

"Nancy, I couldn't ask for a better physician," she said genuinely. "The fact that you care so much, and you aren't overconfident, means you'll be the best person in the world for this job. I'm certain God knew that."

"God chose each one of us for a reason," Samantha added. "It's no accident that we eight are here."

Nancy smiled wanly, somewhat reassured. It was painful, watching and hearing her set the broken arm. Yet Dudeman's forearm soon rested, bandaged, in a makeshift splint. Nancy moved on to treating his head wound, which had caused his unconsciousness, before giving him a drug for the pain. By the time Dudeman awoke, his condition was stabilized. He grimaced with pain, yet thanked Nancy for tending him. Mike soon came out of his semi-conscious state, and Chrysta recovered from her swoon. All of them stood together on the sand inside *The Deliverer* and pondered what should be done. They were eight humans, crash-landed on a barren alien world which seemed as inhospitable as the mysterious gunship.

Grief had held them captive for so long, but a question now loomed to be answered. What would they do now? They'd arrived in the last place Kaity expected, and the future seemed a blank canvas of obscurity.

"*Prima*, who was that man?"

Matt's inquiry broke a long silence. The company of eight had been assessing their situation, and Samantha's news about their food and water had dampened the proceedings. Their supplies were running low—in large part due to the loss of their storage bay. The prophetess did not answer her cousin's question for several more moments. When she did, she mouthed the name bitterly.

"He is Willum Vogul."

"You mean one of *the* Vogul family?" Sharko's eyebrows rose. "The aristocratic family who founded our town?"

"Few know his full history," Samantha said cryptically. "Once a promising young astronaut, he left in a space shuttle to survey Saturn. The idea was preposterous back then, as the trip took years. Willum and the crew disappeared into the stars and were not heard from. Everyone assumed they'd died in space. Two years later, the shuttle reappeared with only Vogul aboard. He seemed none the worse for the trip, and never explained what happened to his crewmates."

"He spoke of a distant world with blue-skinned aliens, whose language he'd learned. He claimed they welcomed him as a king. Of course, no one believed it. His reputation ruined, Willum became the laughingstock of

the Bay. I still remember seeing him, before he left for his second—and final—time."

Samantha paused, a faraway look in her sympathetic brown eyes.

"You were there?" Sharko questioned.

"I was only a girl..."

Samantha trailed off as a memory flashed before her. Rain poured from a
gray sky, pattering on an umbrella overhead. She was ten and hiding behind
her father's raincoat. Sirens screamed as police and emergency vehicles raced
toward a towering rocket gantry to prevent an unauthorized launch. The
steady drumming of February rain was interrupted by a *boom* that shook
the earth. Smoke erupted from the rocket's engines, and Samantha's eyes followed it skyward. She didn't fully understand the situation, but she knew this
moment would have consequences. Vogul's words, spoken in his final broad-
cast before departure, chilled her as she recalled them.

"What is it?"

Samantha came back to herself, realizing she'd shuddered involuntarily
in the present. Everyone stared at her in anticipation.

"I stood on the runway of the nearby airport, hiding behind my father
and watching Vogul's shuttle rocket into the sky. It was a rainy morning I'll
never forget. My father thought it a shame Willum should lose his mind. He
used to be the brightest and best. However, the mockery of men drove him
to madness. Oh how the mighty fall!"

"On his last TV interview, Willum vowed to return to Earth with evidence and 'make our skeptical planet pay.' These words never made it into
the history books. They were merely printed in the back pages of a couple
of newspapers, and yet...they would reflect the dark end of humanity! His
words, and the man, passed into obscurity. Willum Vogul faded from memory, and most forgot him—*I* forgot him—until the dream."

"Dream?" Chrysta's red eyebrows perked up with curiosity.

"I dreamt a dark shadow was spreading across Earth." Samantha shivered
as she recalled it. "I saw the stars blocked out by a massive, barrel-shaped object. My eyes focused in on the ship, until I found myself gazing into the window of an alien bridge. Vogul's face flashed before me, vile and pinched into
a sneer, and I recalled that rainy day. I woke in a cold sweat, but God spoke

to me. He said 'Daughter, do not fear. What man intends for evil, I will use for good.'"

"Some good!" Dudeman snorted. All eyes turned to him. "So far, we've had nothing but pain, misery, and misfortune. We crashed on a desert planet. Our storage bay is gone. Poof went a lot of water and supplies! Seems like your God made you save a bunch of food and water for nothing!"

Kaity's heart sickened at his remark. Although the past weeks had been filled with grief and heartache, her faith in God remained unshaken. James had no faith to begin with, and that was becoming more apparent with each day they spent together. Kaity had always considered Dudeman to be a nice, relaxed sort of man, but their present predicament brought out his true colors.

"How can you question God at a time like this?" Nancy spoke up. Samantha, however, understood James in a way none of the others could.

"No, he has a valid point," she countered, surprising the group. "Let me posit this: why did we survive the crash? How did we happen to get sucked into another galaxy and delivered from death? You see only misery and trials. I see God's hand at work. He will not suffer us to perish. Mark my words, and learn from them, Skeptic!"

Dudeman snorted, crossing his arms. Chrysta seemed to agree with him, Matt looked uncomfortable, but the majority of the eight were believers. In the end, Nancy won out.

"Say what you will," she remarked, "but is it any coincidence we crashed with an engineer, a nurse, a seamstress, and a mechanic? How about a former Eagle Scout, biology major, truck driver, and tutor? I can't think of a more perfect blend of people to start a new society, can you?"

Nancy's comment effectively silenced Dudeman, to his great consternation. Samantha appreciated it. With James' arguments shut down for now, the group of eight survivors could turn their attention to a much more pressing matter—*survival*.

———————✝———————

THE WORLD THE EIGHT had crashed upon was a barren wasteland. Nothing but sand stretched for miles, with one plateau of rock alone, stand-

ing out against the far horizon. A quick trip to the top of the dune burying
their shuttle revealed no water or signs of animal life. The only promise of
vegetation lay in a single cactus, visible to Samantha in the hazy distance. She
appropriately dubbed the desert world Sahara, and the name stuck.

Their first priority was making the wrecked vessel habitable. Buried in
the sand and sideways, *The Deliverer* had lost power. Only the emergency
lights, fed by batteries, offered illumination. Samantha tasked Matt with
digging the shuttle's backup generator out of the sand. The main generator
proved to be ruined beyond repair, but the salvager knew he could fix the
backup. Samantha assigned taking stock of their food to Kaity and Chrysta.
The two women crawled around the cramped, tilted supply room above the
Commons for hours, pencils and notepads in hand while recording every
scrap of food and every container of water. At the end of the day, Kaity had
never been more exhausted. She couldn't stop feeling an ache for home, or
for quiet evenings by the sea with her parents.

The prophetess herself spent hours surveying the damage to their crashed
ship. She let her engineering side take over as she marked notes on a pad
of paper, grateful for writing supplies from the upper decks. She brought
Sharko along to help her dig sections out and render a second opinion. In the
end, both concluded that restoring *The Deliverer* to its space-worthy shape
would be impossible.

"Even *if* we had someplace to go," Sharko wryly pointed out.

Samantha wondered if there might be worlds other than Sahara, inhabit-
ed by aliens, but she couldn't know if they'd be friendly. Vogul's blue-skinned
crew proved that at least some were hostile. Therefore, prophetess and truck
driver made plans to shore up *The Deliverer*. It was the best shelter they could
manage, and being inside of a dune provided cover from hostile eyes.

Staying in one place benefited Mike as well. In addition to his chest injury, the college student experienced pain and swelling in his left knee. Nancy had identified the cause as a bone bruise, and the injury rendered Mike
unable to walk. Samantha noted his frustration, as the injury prevented him
from helping. But ideas to keep him busy in a disabled state eluded her.

Evening descended over their second day of work. Matt rerouted emergency power to their kitchen and lighting, and Samantha strictly rationed
the low reserves. The survivors ate microwaved dinners by candlelight. James

passed out the meager meals, cussing as he burned his fingers on the hot, plastic trays. He dug into a chicken dish with a plastic fork, and Sharko asked to try some of it. The truck driver sputtered and sneezed the moment he tasted it. His eyes streamed tears and his cheeks turned red. Dudeman let out a loud guffaw. Samantha chuckled, while Kaity patted her poor husband on the back.

"Are you okay?" she asked, as Sharko coughed and wheezed.

"What's *on* that thing?" he demanded. Dudeman smiled mischievously.

"Just a mild jalapeño rub. I wouldn't be much of a Jamaican if I couldn't handle spice!"

"Wait, you're Jamaican?" Mike's eyes widened in surprise. "I thought you were Samoan."

"I'm a mix of a lot of things." Dudeman crossed his legs and settled into his sandy seat. "A mix of influences, but belonging nowhere. Kinda describes my life."

"You're in buena compañía," Samantha said. "I'm half Hispanic and half European. That's why I sometimes speak Spanglish."

"And badly pronounced Spanish," Matt added humorously.

"I'm all white meat!" Kaity joked, sending chuckles around the group. "If you can classify Swedish, Dutch, English, and Irish as such. It's not fair, because Sharko has Native American and Jewish. He tans in the sun, but I cook like a lobster!"

"We both do!" Nancy chimed in. "I'm half Korean. My mother's maiden name was Kim."

"Strictly Irish and Scots for me," Chrysta spoke up. "Can you tell by the red hair and freckles?"

"I think Sanchez speaks for itself." Matt's eyes sparkled playfully. "My mother was a first-generation immigrant from Ecuador."

"Only poor Arabia is left out," Kaity commented. At this, Mike slowly raised his hand. Everyone but Chrysta eyed him in amazement.

"It's been lost in my family's appearance," he explained, "but somewhere in the family line, a Persian trader fell in love with an Italian noblewoman. If my grandma's stories can be believed."

Silence fell over the group, and Samantha pondered their words. She hadn't considered it before, but their diversity wasn't limited to occupation.

Her fellow Earthlings represented every major ethnic group on planet Earth. Her heart warmed to think of how God had preserved them as a remnant, not only of humanity, but of the nations.

The task of survival hung over Samantha like a load of Matt's scrap metal, despite the evening's pleasantries. The desert posed a threat to them all—especially with low water stores—and Vogul would certainly come to hunt them. Why he hadn't pursued them through the warp tunnel remained a mystery, but she knew he wouldn't give up so easily. No person burning with that much hatred ever did.

<5>

Discovery

Days passed in a blur of work. Sharko and Matt fully excavated the bedroom decks and cockpit. Chrysta and Kaity picked up fallen or broken items, gluing what could be fixed, tossing what couldn't, and generally making every room functional. Samantha oversaw everything, while Dudeman did what odd jobs he could in spite of his arm. Mike simply rested, Nancy keeping a constant eye on him when she wasn't levelling the uneven sand floors with a broom. James helped Samantha and Sharko shore up the wrecked space craft. The shuttle was sideways and at a slight angle, but it was their only shelter in the vast, barren desert.

"A bit of a tilt is the least of our worries," Samantha remarked, as the two men helped her shore up part of the passageway leading to the cockpit. The entire tunnel was unstable due to crash damage. Matt set up the two, white-topped Commons tables on the sandy floor of the sideways space, and the eight survivors met around them routinely to discuss their plight. A week after the crash, Matt shared some good news.

"I packed solar panels in the storage room days before we left Earth," he said. "Although I gave them up for lost, I just remembered a way I might be able to salvage them. Either that, or use materials from them to rig something with the solar sails. Those are still intact and retracted inside our shuttle's walls. Bottom line? We'll definitely be getting the power back on!"

"No more dim emergency lights!" Sharko exclaimed.

Everyone cheered, and Kaity marveled at Matt's resourcefulness. She realized it was God's grace that he'd come along. Then again, didn't they owe their very presence on this planet, *alive*, to His grace?

She heard Samantha rise from her folding chair, and watched the prophetess circle the table. Samantha had seemed distracted during much of their meeting...even through Matt's news. She halted, turning towards them, a frown gracing her mouth.

"I'm glad we'll have power, but our greatest need is water."

The realization caused a flood of anxiety to rise up within Kaity. Sharko squeezed her arm, as if sensing the tension. He looked as grim as he felt while Samantha laid everything out in plain terms. Their water supply would only last about three weeks. Food stores wouldn't give out for several months, but water conservation was paramount. It would be brief showers and hand sanitizer for all. Samantha advised them to quickly close any freezer or refrigerator doors, shut off all lights, and only wash dishes that had touched raw meat.

"In other words, we're camping!" Matt's snarky comment fell on solemn ears. The reality that they were running out of time, even so soon after crashing, could not permit humor. Kaity already missed the conveniences of home, along with its people. This news simply made it worse.

"I think we can all manage conservation," Sharko put in. How Kaity loved the sound of his calming voice! "Samantha, what did you have in mind about our water crisis?"

"I was thinking my cousin and someone else could hunt for signs of it."

"Count me in!" Sharko volunteered, but Dudeman raised his hand.

"As much as I'd love to sit in the shade," he said, "I was an Eagle Scout. Pardon me, but Sharko can't find the broad side of a barn."

Kaity and Nancy suppressed giggles. Sharko shot Dudeman a withering look.

"And how, pray tell, was I able to navigate as a trucker?"

"There's no GPS in the desert," James shot back. "You're all fine and dandy with the proper tech, but remember that time we got lost hiking? *For three hours*? Whose bright idea was it that the creek led home?"

Sharko blinked, his cheeks reddening, and said nothing. Even Mike and Matt had started chuckling. Kaity gave Sharko's shoulder a sympathetic squeeze. She knew he felt embarrassed but was trying to be a good sport about it.

"I suppose that settles matters." Samantha's tone hadn't changed a bit, nor did she crack a smile. "*Primo*, you and James will go looking for water. You're our best, and I suggest you take your revolver."

Matt nodded. Nobody present needed to guess that taking the pistol along brightened his mood. Matt had served for a year in the Army before starting his salvage business. An expert shot, the revolver had been his gift from a commanding officer. Samantha turned towards Kaity, and she felt the effect of the prophetess' intense, brown eyes. The woman still intimidated her a bit.

"I'll need you and Chrysta to venture into the wasteland as well, for a different reason. Think you can handle it?"

Samantha launched into an explanation of what she and Chrysta would be doing. They would backtrack the furrow made by the shuttle's crash-landing, to find and salvage as many of their supplies as possible.

"Thanks for giving us a choice," Chrysta muttered sarcastically. On that note, Samantha adjourned the meeting. Everyone disbanded, but Kaity paused by the ceiling of the Commons, which now served as a wall. On it hung their calendar, and her eyes teared up. Samantha had brought this along to preserve a sense of normalcy, and Nancy was faithfully marking their current day off with a red X.

"Can't believe it's already been a month and a half?" Nancy inquired. "Tell me about it! Sometimes, it feels so unreal. My grief is still pretty raw...a wound no medkit can heal."

Kaity said nothing. How could she adequately express the feelings that tore her heart to shreds and scattered it across star systems? The numbers on the calendar reminded her of time's passage, yes, but it was the picture that brought such agony. That single image of swaying palms against an ocean backdrop evoked such sensations of homesickness that Kaity could hardly speak. Perhaps her body and mind dwelt here, but her heart, oh her heart, resided still on Earth! She only felt at home when she closed her eyes and remembered that sweet, tropic place now impossibly distant. Whatever home they could eke out on Sahara would never compare...could never satisfy.

Nancy noticed tears forming in her friend's eyes, and opened her mouth to comment. Sharko suddenly swept up to them. Grinning playfully, he took Kaity's slender fingers in his.

"I must borrow my wife for a moment!" he informed her impishly. Turning to Kaity, he added, "Come with me and watch the sunset!"

The golden light of evening slanted diagonally into the open storage bay, illuminating the dark, cave-like space. Kaity had to hold her hands in front of her to ward off the glare, but Sharko drew her out of the confines of the bay walls at a jog. Helping her up the flank of a neighboring dune, he stopped at its brink, placing both arms around his wife and standing behind her. Kaity leaned her head against his cheek, and husband and wife watched the alien sunset together in silence.

The fierce orb of red dipped lower toward the far dunes. Its light cast fascinating shadows across the undulating, serpentine waves of sand. The shadows deepened, and the sun seemed to kiss the top of the desert plain. A brisk wind assailed their backs as they stood, watching the burning disc drop from sight in its fading splendor. Despite the sadness of their plight, Kaity felt a sense of peace and security in Sharko's arms. Even desolation could be beautiful, in the right lighting.

"I saw your tears, my dear," Sharko whispered softly, as the wind tossed her brown tresses back against his cheek.

"I miss home and family so much." Kaity let the tears flow, knowing she was safe. "It hurts most of the time. I can function, but an inner pain cuts into me like a barb. The others seem like they've moved on already, but for me..."

"Kaity, don't disparage yourself," Sharko said gently. "Chrysta certainly isn't recovering faster than you, and when did this become a comparison game? We men look calmer, but I can assure you, we're all roiling inside too."

"I guess...I feel...I should be happier than I am." Kaity's mouth was downturned. "We're newlyweds, after all."

"Who dictates that you should be? We never got to have a honeymoon, Dear. Our wedding day turned into a time of tragedy instead of joy. While we're happy as husband and wife, the trials of the present far outweigh the blisses of matrimony."

"You're right," Kaity said thoughtfully, and squeezed his hand.

"I miss my brothers, grandparents—all my friends and relatives," Sharko whispered, a catch to his voice. "It's a daily ache, and every one of us has it. We're in uncharted territory. No group of humans has been in our situation before, so it's okay. I understand."

His words, so comforting, felt like a warm blanket around her heart. Her tears ceased, and Kaity turned around and slipped her arms beneath his, hugging him tightly.

"What would I do without you?" she questioned, as Sharko kissed her forehead.

"You'd still have God," he replied simply. "But I'm thankful to Him, a thousand times over, that I still have you."

THE MORNING SUN BEAT down on Kaity and Chrysta as they traced the crash-path of their shuttle. They crested one dune after another, the straw beach hats they wore barely alleviating the sun's oppressive rays. Large tote bags with beach prints dangled from the women's shoulders, and their skin glistened with sunscreen. Kaity prayed the SPF was high enough to protect them. Practically all of their gear, and the sunscreen, had come from her honeymoon luggage.

The women had departed earlier that morning, at the same time Dudeman and Matt left to look for water. Kaity did not envy the men their task, and she appreciated her sturdy sandals as she trekked the dusty dunes. As they went, they came across a crate here, a food item there—many unusable. Evidence of animals came in the form of half-chewed food, and both women wondered if creatures from another world would prove hostile. They found a butcher knife from storage along the way, so Kaity kept it in her tote just in case. She couldn't handle the thing, since the temperature made the metal too hot for her fingers.

Neither woman was accustomed to the desert heat. Living in a coastal town that peaked around 80 Fahrenheit, the harsh sun felt merciless. Kaity began to curse her sandals as the sand heated, burning the sides of her feet with every step. Chrysta sweated buckets, and they stopped to rest several times, facing away from the sun. Once, Chrysta flipped their last canteen upside-down in frustration. Not a drop left the mouth of the container.

"We're out," she lamented.

"Great!" Kaity commented sarcastically. Both women felt miserable, by this point. Their bags sagged with salvaged goods, and a warm desert wind began whipping up. There was no shade anywhere, yet they hadn't reached their objective. The solar panels, if they remained intact, must still be farther behind them. Kaity glanced toward the sun and, although no expert, realized they'd walked too far. It was well after noon. Without a clock, they'd passed the point of returning before dark. She berated herself for not bringing Samantha's watch, but what could be done? She was about to suggest they turn around when Chrysta squeezed her arm.

"Look! Our solar panels!"

The flat devices lay, broken, along the escarpment of their crash-path. Chrysta and Kaity debated for a moment. They were exhausted, hot, out of water, and with full bags. The panels must surely weigh more than they could bear, so they decided to head back to *The Deliverer* with news of the panels' location. They munched on their food as they walked, yet Kaity felt her grim spirits lift. Trekking across the desert dunes had not only sapped her physically, but emotionally.

Her entire life felt like this day: meaningless suffering without a certain destination. Yet Kaity knew this wasn't true. Just as they had found the solar panels, they would find their purpose. Samantha had said, after all, that God was not done with them. She just needed to keep pressing on...right?

Sharko greeted Kaity with a kiss when the women returned, and a tired Dudeman and Matt sauntered into the base an hour later. News of the solar panels perked the ex-soldier up, however, and he decided to venture out the next day despite the men's long and fruitless search for water. The end result was that the survivors gained a power source within two days. Kaity and Chrysta went out into the dunes again, picking up more salvage from the crash—along with more sunburns. Sharko and Dudeman took a turn looking for water, and life seemed a daily monotony.

On their fourth foray for salvage, Kaity began to thoroughly hate desert travel. Nothing provided relief from the relentless sun, and the women decided to walk parallel to the shuttle's furrow in hopes of finding more debris. They went up and down the undulating dunes, until the sun reached its zenith.

"One more dune crest, and I say we eat lunch and head back," Kaity suggested. Chrysta, panting and sweating heavily, nodded a willing assent.

The last dune seemed like Mount Everest. Kaity's legs burned as she fought against the sand that constantly slid beneath her. For Chrysta, it was all she could bear. At last, they reached the summit.

"Whoa!"

Chrysta pointed northwest of their position. Kaity shielded her eyes from the afternoon sun and squinted, disbelieving. There were glinting things littering the sand! They seemed a half hour's walk away, yet the sheer volume of metal...it blew her mind! Was this debris field their storage bay? That made no sense. Kaity recalled passing enough rubble to account for most of the bay, while this metal comprised a sizeable field. Curiosity overtook exhaustion. She turned to Chrysta.

"We've got to have a look," she cried, "if only for the shade that must be under those large pieces!"

Chrysta couldn't argue with that. The dunes between them and the strange rubble field were small, and both women slipped and slid down to them. Crossing the dunes took less time than anticipated, and as they drew nearer to the shining debris, Kaity gasped in astonishment.

"UH, CHRYSTA, THIS IS *definitely* NOT from our craft!" she exclaimed. Her sentence came too late. Chrysta Taylor's eyes had already reached the size of saucers. The metal rubble didn't look as random, up close. It seemed to form shapes, reminding Kaity of airplane hulls and yet with strange curves and a few thick plates. She recognized the half-buried silhouettes of wings, and her pulse quickened. Could it be...?

"Alien ships!" Chrysta cried aloud, flabbergasted. Before Chrysta could restrain her, Kaity broke into a run toward the nearest one. Much of this ship remained intact, its hull opened to the elements by the gaping hole which had caused its demise. A cursory glance told her everything.

An oddly-curving hull. A dusty, sand-covered control panel. Broken windows formed of purple glass. Strange steering gear. The remains of a pilot's chair. Kaity couldn't speak. That one race of aliens existed in the Universe was enough. Realizing that more than one alien people populated this galaxy made her forget even the heat. She simply sank to her knees in the wreckage of the ship, completely overpowered by the sheer possibilities. Were the aliens all hostile? Were some actually friendly? Did any of this technology work and could they utilize it? Kaity was no history expert, but she could tell these vessels were very old. They'd been here, decomposing beneath the sun, for perhaps centuries.

"Uh, K-Kaity...um...!" Chrysta had braced herself against the side of the hole, and was pointing to the ground near Kaity's left side. The tutor turned to look at the cause of her stuttering, and jumped to her feet in horrified surprise. Both women darted out of the ruin with a burst of energy fueled by revulsion. Once a safe distance away, Kaity found a rock and they sat beneath its shade. Chrysta looked like a frightened rabbit.

"I can't believe you were crouching right next to an alien corpse!" she burst out, shaking hysterically.

"How do you think *I* feel?" Kaity retorted, crossing her arms. "I'm the one who was a foot away from that—that *thing*!"

"I don't like skeletons anyway, but that one wasn't normal! We're definitely not alone, and I don't like our company!"

"At least these neighbors are quiet," Kaity nervously joked. Her attempt at humor fell flat. Chrysta wrung her hands anxiously and stole a nervous glance at the field of ruined alien ships.

"Can we get going?"

"What about lunch?"

Chrysta's stomach growled, as if to emphasize Kaity's point. The seamstress grudgingly agreed to eat, and both women rummaged through their totes and pulled out warm burritos. Kaity still felt grossed-out by the fact she'd nearly touched an alien corpse. The skeleton, mostly buried, hadn't registered in her mind due to its unusual appearance and coating of sand. Not until Chrysta's outburst, at least.

Miserable, Kaity scratched her skin and felt pain. Her shoulders, arms, and legs were already sunburned, and she wished for once she had Samantha's olive skin tone. She heard Chrysta eating between chattering teeth. Whatever could be said, the surprise in the ship graveyard had affected her greatly. Moved to compassion, Kaity set aside her own discomfort and said a few encouraging words to Chrysta. The woman relaxed, her eyes darting less to the debris field than before. Neither spoke for several minutes, until Chrysta stopped eating her burrito.

"How do you do it?" she asked suddenly

"Do what?" Kaity replied.

"We've lost everything!" Chrysta declared. "Life is wretched, but you seem to stay positive."

"What's the alternative? I miss what we've lost, too, but I also know this life isn't all there is."

Chrysta did not respond. She stared away into the distance, and when Kaity leaned forward to look at her face, she saw tears making muddy furrows down her cheeks. A piece of Chrysta's red hair stuck to her face. She brushed it back and sniffed.

"Hey, what's wrong?" Kaity inquired sympathetically. More lay behind the seamstress' distress than simply seeing a skeleton.

"All of it!" Chrysta exclaimed with surprising bitterness, throwing up her hands. "First my greatest dream is crushed, and now *this*!"

"You and your husband are churchgoers, aren't you?" Kaity questioned. "How well do you know the Bible?"

"Well enough," Chrysta sputtered, "to be aware that there are passages saying the righteous sometimes suffer along with the wicked. But why *our* planet? If God is so sovereign, he should have made Vogul incinerate this place! Or, better yet, struck him down with lightning!"

"Life isn't fair. That doesn't mean God isn't good."

"Oh, why do you guys have to go around all preachy?" Chrysta spat. "Maybe James is the only one who has true sense among us."

"Chrysta, let me explain—"

"I'm not hungry." The redhead rose and shouldered her bag. "I lost my appetite, and I'm heading back. I really don't want to talk about this anyway."

"You can't blame God for Vogul's evil," Kaity offered. "It's...it's immature."

Chrysta stiffened at her remark, and Kaity realized she'd said exactly the wrong thing. The rest of their journey continued in silence. Only the wind, rising in intensity, made the experience even worse by blowing sand directly into their faces. By the time they got back to their base, it was nearly gale force. Sharko manually closed the storage bay door behind them, and Chrysta and Kaity dusted themselves off after setting their bursting bags on the floor.

"Honey, is it good to be back!" Kaity exclaimed, kissing Sharko. Her husband smiled to see her, but it quickly faded.

"Where are Dudeman and Matt?" Chrysta asked, sensing that all was not well.

"That's just it," Nancy spoke up. "They haven't returned today, and Sharko says we're in for a sandstorm."

Kaity's blood ran cold. A sandstorm? She had been in a cabin during a blizzard, once, and she imagined a sandstorm must be the desert equivalent. All thoughts of the discovery she'd made slipped from her mind, to be overtaken by worry. Kaity didn't need to know much about survival craft to comprehend that being stuck in a sandstorm, in the open dunes, could spell their demise. Would the men make it? Kaity could do nothing but hug her husband tightly and wait.

SAMANTHA HARRIS SAT in a chair by the wall of the overturned Commons, clutching her arms about her. She traced sand patterns on the floor with her eyes, cognizant that each passing minute decreased Matt and Dudeman's chances for survival. She feared for the surfer nearly as much as her cousin. An immature Christian, Matt had nonetheless given his heart to Christ. In fact, he'd been instrumental in pointing her to Jesus despite her Atheism. Yet Dudeman—James Erskin—was a skeptic through-and-through. Without shelter, the men could suffocate to death. One would go to Heaven, but the other...Samantha prayed fervently both would make it.

What an insane few months she had experienced! Preparing fervently for the day of Earth's doom, stocking up and watching her bank account drain down to zero. Then boarding the shuttle with those few willing to believe her, and just escaping Vogul's destruction! The space journey had been heartbreakingly difficult for the others. Samantha grieved in her own way, yet she'd needed to remain strong. She was their pillar, after all. A year's foreknowledge sort of took the edge off the pain, even if the loss involved the entire world. *And I alone cared enough to get us away from *him**, Samantha thought, shuddering.

She rose, exchanged a few words with a concerned Kaity, and walked down the ship's hallway into the deck housing Matt's room. She staggered as she tripped over a bulkhead. The sideways shuttle still surprised her at times. Entering his space, the scent of his deodorant struck her. He'd probably run out in a few weeks, but Matt was a stickler for hygiene. Even here, in the deserts of an alien world.

A photo of her, Matt, and their respective families graced a frame on his metal bedside shelf. The holiday pic overflowed with people—sixty in all. Their *abuelita*'s 70th birthday gathering. Family had always been important to them both. Memories of Earth ran through her mind, sorrow and nostalgia woven together. Her first day on the job as a structural engineer. Her huge argument about science and Creationism with Matt. The truck which had almost hit her as she drove home in a rage, eager to jump on her computer and prove him wrong. The angelic figure revealed in a flash of lightning, causing her to swerve and miss the corner of a semi trailer. Matt's overjoyed reaction to the news of her conversion. The day God called her to be His prophetess.

Yet worry rose, unbidden, as she recalled these memories connected with Matt. Suppose Sahara proved his grave? God hadn't promised they would survive in their new home...just that a remnant would follow her from Earth. She blushed in embarrassment as she remembered arguing with God. When He'd revealed the coming apocalypse to her, it had been too much to bear. The thought of Him letting so many people perish from one man's sin felt overwhelming. The Lord had spoken to her, audibly, in her mind. His voice, soothing but strong, had gently contradicted her stubborn insistence that she was better off serving Him on an intact Earth.

"But Daughter, that isn't what I have for you," the Speaker said, His voice soothing but strong. "My plan has always been to draw you across the stars. Do you think my love is confined by geography? By borders, boundaries, or the limits of visible space? Behold! Before I set the planets in motion, I numbered every one of your days. I ordained that you should travel to a distant galaxy, to a people not your own, to spread the gospel and save multitudes.

You will do incredible things in My Name, Daughter, but you must give me control."

"It's so hard, Jesus!" Samantha had said.

"I know," the Voice dropped to a gentle whisper. "I never promised your walk with me would be easy. But I do offer to carry your burdens, if you'll only cast them on Me. You must trust me and obey My will."

Samantha still felt ashamed that it had taken her several weeks to surrender to God's will. Yet surrender she had. It had cost her *everything*.

The recollection of Her Savior's words faded into darkness, and a tear slid down Samantha's quavering cheek. *Who am I, to question the Sovereign Creator?* She thought, humbled. *I need to trust God, and we all need to pray. The same Lord who saved us from destruction watches over us, and He can deliver them from any storm. Have faith, Samantha!*

Realizing she still held Matt's photo in her hand, the prophetess replaced the framed picture and slipped out of his tiny room. The outcome of her present trials didn't matter as much as her response to them, and she would make the same decision as she had before. Samantha chose simply to trust.

JAMES ERSKIN HELD HIS compass level, waiting for the spinning arrow to point northward. *At least, if there *is* a northward here*, he thought. Matt stood behind the former Eagle Scout, panting with exertion. Both men glistened with the sweat of several hours' travel. They'd trekked far across the ocean of dunes, using Samantha's compass to head in what seemed an easterly direction. James kept them to the valleys between the dunes until they reached a flat, level plain of earth.

Both men scanned for signs of water—an action that had become automatic, after two weeks. They looked for patterns on the ground, dampness, animal tracks. Not until their sixth hour did Dudeman spot two parallel lines of indentations. They seemed like a small animal's paw prints, and the men scared away several alien lizards and a scorpion as they followed them. A new track joined with the animal's...the slithering contours of a snake. Dudeman paused, shading his eyes from the glaring sunlight to gaze into the far horizon. The tracks continued in the direction of a plateau, just visible from their crash site. Surfer and mechanic trekked toward this lone tableland in the midst of a cracked, barren plain.

As they drew closer, the enormity of the plateau struck Dudeman. It was massive and varied, its face steeply terraced, like a waterfall of sedimentary rock that had frozen while cascading down. Folds and ridges in the stone face were punctuated by holes hollowed by sand and animals. After circling the plateau, both men concluded that no suitable path to the top existed. They paused to rest by its windward side, letting the warm wind cool their soaked clothes. Dudeman drank from his canteen and pointed to the plateau top.

"Water might've hollowed out a basin up there," he said. "In this heat, I'm sure it's dried up."

"Very likely," Matt concluded. "Hey, is it just me, or is the wind picking up? I'm getting sand grains in my mouth!"

Dudeman suddenly realized that the sun had passed its zenith. They needed to return to the shuttle, and something about the wind and eastern horizon lodged a barb of warning in his heart.

"Let's head back," he said aloud, and Matt seconded his decision. The two men trekked in the direction of *The Deliverer*. They were halfway across the dusty plain when James looked back. His jaw dropped. A new plateau had risen in the east, but it wasn't a bluff carved of rock. Matt also saw the looming threat, and both men glanced at each other without needing to voice their fears.

A sandstorm! The wall of dusty fury blew towards the plateau, and already they felt sand grains pelting their faces. James knew they wouldn't reach *The Deliverer* before the storm overtook them. Out in the bare dunes, they risked being buried alive or suffocating. There was no shelter, and the handful of scattered, measly alien cacti offered no reprieve.

"The plateau!" Dudeman exclaimed, breaking into a jog across the ground they'd just covered. "It's our only shelter against the storm's rage."

"We find an alcove or ridge on the leeward side," Matt caught on. "Makes sense!"

"I hope it works, too!" James confessed, leading the way. The two fell into a trot, then an all-out run. It seemed insanity, racing toward the blowing wall of sand. The howling obscurity felt menacing, and a frightening realization gripped James as his legs pumped beneath him. They wouldn't make it!

Twenty yards separated them from the plateau, but the tableland was already engulfed!

Seconds later, the sandstorm struck. The air filled with a howling noise. Particles whipped against James' face, choking his airways. His sunglasses became the only thing separating his eyes from the painful granules. He slogged forward, his visibility reduced by the dust and scratches on his lenses. All he could think of was reaching the plateau's shelter and how intensely he missed the oceans of home! Not even his worst wipeouts, falling face-first onto a sandy beach, compared to the feeling of scratchy, miniscule particles pelting his entire body.

He glanced back to see if Matt still trailed him. He could barely discern the man's bulky frame. Nothing else remained visible in the blizzard of dust. When he turned around, a horrible feeling seized him. *Which* way lay forward? The storm obliterated his bearings, and Matt skidded to a halt beside him. The ex-soldier's eyes were screwed shut, and he'd wrapped his shirt around his face. The wind whipped his thick, brown locks. *We're going to die out here*, Dudeman's brain screamed at him. The buildup in his airways brought on a fit of coughing that didn't help. *We're going to suffocate, and we may be mere feet from the plateau*!

He considered trying to form a bunker of sand to protect them, yet shot his own idea down. It was absurd! Building one would not only consume time, but also fail to solve their problem of breathable air. He imagined he heard Matt trying to speak, but the din carried the man's voice away. It had grown even more difficult to breathe, and James tasted dust in his mouth. Suddenly, he remembered. His compass!

Slowing, he squinted into the nothingness and spat out a wad of sand. Holding the compass in front of him, Dudeman waited for the arrow to indicate north. A great wave of relief washed over him, tempering the panic of suffocation and pending doom. They were facing east...the direction of the plateau! Pain flooded his eyes, causing him to screw them shut. He felt stinging grit beneath his lids. Apparently, his sunglasses weren't stopping every sand grain. Gesturing to Matt, James squinted and raced forward. A dark silhouette materialized from the dust. He nearly smacked into the side of the plateau, but caught himself. They'd made it! The west-facing cliffs sheltered them from the brunt of the storm, and now they simply needed to find an alcove or ridge.

Sand blew in torrents over the top of the sizeable outcropping. The sun was entirely blocked out—a suffocating relief. Sand, sand, everywhere! Dudeman began to feel as though he'd never breathed clean air all his life. He felt along the plateau wall, searching for a fold or alcove in which they could wait out the storm. Matt stayed close to avoid losing contact in the swirling desolation. Dudeman was about to despair of finding anything when his hand felt open space. An odd sensation crept over him, and he realized that he was looking into the opening of a cave!

Too desperate for shelter to hesitate, he and Matt stumbled inside the pitch-black cavern. There was no way of lighting the interior, so they felt their way forward, eyes burning. James took a step forward, only to have his foot encounter air! He tripped, caught himself, then stumbled again. He couldn't be certain, but it felt like he'd encountered a series of steps. Hearing his grunt, Matt dashed toward what he believed to be Dudeman's location. He bumped into something solid and cold, and halted.

"I'm all right, Man," James declared, dusting himself off. "It was a shallow staircase, so I caught myself. Good thing we found—!"

He never finished his thought. Matt froze on the spot. The two men's eyes had adjusted enough to the darkness that they were able to discern silhouettes, yet they soon regretted it. To Dudeman's horror and utter surprise, the shape of a giant scorpion stood directly in front of him. Its stinger raised high, he realized there was no way for him and Matt to avoid its poisonous strike!

THE DRIVING SANDS OF the dust storm settled down. For the group waiting at home base, the howling lasted an eternity. Kaity watched Samantha pace, sit down a few minutes, then pace again. For a woman of faith and certainty, it jarred her to see the prophetess so anxious. The evening had passed uneventfully, with a mutual prayer time, playing the one board game they possessed, and eating food that tasted like the dust in their mouths. Most of them couldn't sleep. Still, Matt and Dudeman did not return.

It was amazing how the loss of only two people could affect them all. Kaity didn't know Matt very well. Dudeman had been a longtime acquaintance, but hardly a friend. Yet she, too, feared for them. Losing two able-bodied men to the desert was no small thing. Kaity's grief came back in full force at the possibility. Life seemed nothing but a string of tragedies. She'd lost parents, home, world...and how likely would their survival be now? Without Dudeman and Matt, their chances fell sharply. They were the last of humanity, so that left only herself, Sharko, and the Taylors to have children. After their children intermarried, who would be left to marry their grandchildren?

This thought crossed both Kaity and Nancy's minds. Nancy, particularly, felt a pang of despair. Their deaths meant she had no one. Her dreams of a husband would never come to pass. Worse, they'd lose their survivalist and their mechanic.

Sharko felt a pit of worry deep within his stomach. He'd been calm initially, but now, his fear showed its full strength. Dudeman was his best friend. A memory of the surfer on his wedding day, in board shorts and running late for photos, flashed across his mind. How many nights had they stayed up talking about God, sports—girls?

Chrysta was the first to notice the desert quiet down. She and Mike alone slept through that long night. Upon waking, Chrysta remarked that the wind had ceased blowing sand down their skylight. Kaity, Sharko, and Samantha clambered to the doorway in a sleepless stupor. *The Deliverer's* open storage bay faced away from the wind, so they exited without encountering a mountain of sand. The same could not be said outside the shelter of the bay.

Sand had blown over from the dune's crest, depositing numerous heaps at the break point that measured several feet high. The entire dune over the craft had shifted from the storm. Kaity noticed this as Sharko led the way up the gritty embankment, to the top of the dune under which their shuttle lay buried. Here, with a better vantage, the three searched desperately for human shapes against the tan obscurity. Only a few, residual dust devils met their eyes, spiraling in the wind.

"Should we set out and look for them?" Samantha wondered aloud.

"It wouldn't do much good," Sharko remarked pragmatically. "I'm as sad to lose them as you, but their tracks are erased. I don't think they made it."

"Ahoy, ugly!" a voice called from a distance. Samantha and the Andersons looked high and low, but could see nobody.

"Yeah, you, truck driver!" it called again. "You barbaric son of a gun! Look this way!"

Filled with amazement, the three humans walked forward. In the valley ahead of them, between the sand dunes, were Dudeman and Matt!

A THICK LAYER OF DUST coated the two men. Sharko ran down the slope, heedless of the sand he sent skittering downward. He slapped James so hard on the back that Kaity couldn't tell if gladness or consternation drove the gesture. The two men hugged, and were soon grinding sand into each other's hair. Kaity rolled her eyes.

"Men!" she muttered good-naturedly, joining Samantha in descending the slope. The prophetess slipped halfway down it, grabbing hold of her cousin tightly.

"You crazy scrapper!" she exclaimed. "Thank the Almighty you're okay! What happened?"

"Oh, y'know, James and I found a cave and bumped into a scorpion." Matt's face remained placid.

"A scorpion?" Samantha nearly looked scolding. "Really now, and how did you survive that?"

"I rode it and kept the stinger away while Matt shot it!" Dudeman cut in. His lie was so obvious that all five burst into laughter.

"Actually, it was a statue," he explained. "You wouldn't believe the place we found, Dude! We couldn't see all of it, but there were other statues and some writings on a wall."

"More than that, there's water!" Matt exclaimed. "A pool lies in one corner of the cave. We could carry some back here and purify it with the shuttle's filters!"

"We really did see a scorpion, though," Dudeman added. "It was normal-sized, though, and skittered across the floor in front of Matt."

"Yeah, I nearly stepped on it!" Matt pulled a face. "Well, we're both starving, as you can imagine. Any food left?"

"I'll cook you a meal myself!" Samantha vowed, placing a hand on both men's shoulders. She was so happy to have them back that she was beaming. Matt's face immediately fell.

"You? *Cook*?" he exclaimed. "No offense, *Prima*, but I'll take my chances with the scorpion!"

"Oh go put your head in the sand!" Samantha scolded, shooing him away.

"Already did!" Matt returned impishly, and he dashed off toward the storage bay. Samantha walked swiftly after him. Dudeman sauntered back with Kaity and Sharko, who eagerly listened to his account of the cave.

The two men tore into an overdue meal, cooked by Samantha and Kaity. Everyone gathered around as Matt and Dudeman took turns babbling about their discovery between bites. Even Mike sat down to listen, despite the pain of his injuries. Samantha smiled to see her taciturn cousin so loquacious. After the men finished both meal and tale, all but the Taylors were eager to raid the strange cave for water. However, Matt cautioned that the distance was too great to traverse before nightfall.

"Let's set out tomorrow morning," Samantha proposed. "I think it'd be wise to keep some of us here, while the rest of us journey to this cave."

"I appreciate that," Chrysta put in. "I'll stay here with my husband."

"I'd better remain, too," Nancy said. The regret and grimness in her tone worried Kaity.

"Count me in!" Matt said, but Samantha shook her head. He raised a quizzical eyebrow at her, but the prophetess gestured to him. Kaity didn't fully understand the exchange, yet figured Samantha would speak to him privately.

"Sharko, Kaity, James," Samantha said, in her authoritative voice, "I'd like you to comprise the team. You two," she pointed at the men, "to carry water. Kaity, because I like your company."

The tutor warmed at the compliment. She was thrilled to be chosen as one of the company.

A day of rest and relief passed, James and Matt lounging after their ordeal. Kaity read a book, helped Chrysta heat canned food for dinner, and did some dishes. As she climbed the ladder to her alcove-room that night, her brain buzzed with tomorrow's trip and all its possibilities. After finding a ship graveyard on her last outing, what alien artifacts might they find next?

Recalling the field of wrecked starships suddenly reminded Kaity that she'd forgotten to tell Samantha about it! She smacked a hand against her forehead. The sandstorm and their missing friends had completely wiped it from her mind. There might be things they could salvage from it, secrets they could learn. Excitement filled her. She cuddled with Sharko as usual that night, but neither could fall asleep for over an hour. Husband and wife were happily talking about what tomorrow could bring. As Kaity finally drifted off to sleep, a thought came to her mind which both saddened and encouraged her. For the first time in almost two months, she was excited about what tomorrow might bring.

On the bedroom deck above, Samantha Harris conversed quietly with her cousin. Matt stood in his blue pajamas, almost asleep on his feet. Nonetheless, he stayed to listen to his cousin.

"I'm leaving you here because of Vogul," Samantha whispered. "I'm sorry if you wanted to go tomorrow."

"It's all good," Matt reassured, yawning. "My feet aren't loving me right now, so it'll give me a chance to rest them. Do you really think Vogul will come after us? The chances are a million to one. What possible motive does he have?"

Samantha raised her eyebrow at him, and Matt held up his hands.

"Alright, I get it. It's a prophetess vibe. Learned my lesson about doubting you when Earth was incinerated."

"Matt, this base is vital to our survival," Samantha said seriously. "Vogul *will* come. I don't fully understand his motivations, but the Spirit has given me this sense. The desert isn't our only danger."

Matt nodded and said goodnight. Samantha stayed in the circular space between rooms for a while, pondering. How glad she was to have him back, and how little he understood! She appreciated the group of people who had fled with her from Earth, but a certain sense of loneliness lingered—a leftover from her prophesying days. In a sense, she'd always be that lone voice in the wilderness. The woman focused on the bigger picture, while others bent their backs to the task of survival. If this was to be her fate and destiny,

Samantha embraced it. And she prayed for the courage to face Vogul, when he inevitably descended...

<6>

The Cave

The form of a gigantic gunship hung against the backdrop of a vast nebula. Frozen gasses of orange, blue, and teal enshrouded the vessel, providing elements the *Draxalis* needed to replenish its plasma storage tanks. These sat at the stern of the ship, in a section comprising its living quarters. Most of the gunship was barrel, with only the rear third housing a barracks, storage, and engine room. At the point where barrel met living quarters, a large ship's bridge rose on an arch-shaped support, windows ringing its front half. Framed in one of them, a human figure gazed out at the unsearchable celestial splendor.

It was Vogul. The madman from Earth, clad in a white-and-gray spacesuit, had his helmet off to reveal neatly-combed blond hair. A plasma pistol hung from his utility belt, and he tapped his foot against the metal flooring in impatience. A Trylithian attendant approached, and Vogul whirled. His piercing, blue eyes flamed with eagerness.

"Tormac Durag has been hailed," the alien reported. Vogul walked to the center of the room, where a large screen hung down. The familiar interior of the glowing throne hall came into view, along with the tormac's blue-skinned form. Durag wore an axe-blade headdress which matched his chest protector.

"Greetings, Most Exalted Tormac!" Vogul exclaimed, bowing winsomely. "We've replenished our plasma and are eager for your instruction. How are things in Lidexid?"

"Terrible," Durag muttered irritably, "which is why you will enter the wormhole and make for Stattar Nebula. Your next target will be Dalar 2. The Teradite colonists there are of little consequence, but their annihilation will herald our strength to the galaxy! The Gorvan System will know that Lidexid has the power to destroy any planet it seeks. If it does not bow, Vexador will be our next target!"

"Of course, my Tormac," Vogul affirmed. "So in the meantime, you wish for me to hide in another nebula?"

"Stealth is essential to our plan. We do not want the galaxy aware of us until we reveal what the *Draxalis* can do. You will need to recharge your banks after stabilizing the wormhole, and what better place than Stattar? Send me a report of the ship's status each week."

"Whatever you command," Vogul said, smiling between his teeth. "All shall be according to plan."

The monitor flicked off. Vogul didn't waste a moment, but added in a murmur, "My plan."

"Trylithians, listen to me!" he exclaimed, snatching a com device. "We make for the wormhole in five *desrec*! I know Durag hid a tracking device on this vessel, and I've got an idea of how to use it against him. My fellow beings, we set a course to mark history! To Dalar 3!"

"I thought it was Dalar 2," the attendant piped up, confused. "What about the plasma? The Tormac's orders?"

"To Hades with Durag!" Vogul sneered. "I have what I need to rid the Universe of this pestilence which crawled out of Earth's muck!"

"Why was I not informed?" the attendant questioned, still baffled.

"Because..." Vogul suddenly whipped out his plasma pistol and pointed it at the Trylithian's chest. "...I needed to test your loyalty, first. Do you serve me, or Durag?"

The surprised male jumped involuntarily, sweat breaking out across his paling blue skin. A click sounded behind him, and the male glanced back to find two other pistols aimed at him. Even his fellow Trylithians supported Vogul! They served the madman fanatically, unlike those who served out of fear. Unlike himself.

"I serve y-you and you alone, T-tormac Vogul!" the attendant stuttered. Vogul smiled coyly, sidling up to the male. The Trylithian screwed his catlike eyes shut as the madman raised his pistol, holding it inches from the alien's face. He stroked the side of the male's face with the barrel, the Trylithian shivering beneath the icy metal.

"Good." Vogul withdrew the firearm, holstering it and motioning for his loyalists to back off. The quivering attendant breathed a sigh of relief, but Vogul shoved past him, uncaring. The madman faced the room of Trylithian bridge officers.

"We make for Dalar 3!" he bellowed. "We will track down the eight survivors, and if our own efforts fail to pry them from the cracks, I'll use this very gunship against them! Nebula or planet, asteroid or Jovian, I will find and erase them!"

MORNING WINDS KICKED up dust in swirling motes, making the ground appear as if steaming. The company of four Earthlings walked silently across the barren desert plain, dotted by the occasional, short cactus. It was a bleak, sunny day without a cloud in the sky—much as the days preceding. For the inhabitants of Vogul Bay, the climate alone felt alien. Coastal tropic was replaced with harsh wasteland. Though the days burned fiercely, the nights felt frigid.

Dudeman led the way over the cracked earth. Samantha followed, with Kaity and Sharko at the back. Kaity carried several canteens, Dudeman had a backpack of bottles, and Sharko lugged a large, empty water carton which Matt had recently repaired. The carton, previously punctured in the crash, would now serve to store water from the mysterious cave of statues.

"It's a fair morning," Samantha remarked, as she travelled at their head. "I hope this is the worst the heat gets."

"With our luck, it's winter," Dudeman rejoined sarcastically.

Kaity Anderson said nothing. She enjoyed holding Sharko's hand, and the steaming sands looked fascinating, but something felt off. This wasn't home. This wasn't Earth. In some ways, Kaity almost hoped that everything would prove a sham. The sand must be fake. The cacti were probably imported. This was not a real desert, and it never would be. Only Earth, her real home, held any tangibility. Yet their approach to the plateau drew her out of homesickness, and Sharko squeezed her hand. Kaity could sense his excitement, for the thrill of discovery ran through her as well. Surely, this place had never seen humans before!

The thought jogged Kaity's memory, and she recalled her need to share about the ship graveyard with Samantha. She whispered to Sharko, then quickened her steps to catch up to the prophetess.

"There's something I need to tell you," she declared.

"Yes? Make it snappy!"

Samantha's tone came off harsh, stinging Kaity a bit. Yet they were drawing closer to the plateau, and she knew the prophetess felt keen to find Matt and Dudeman's cave. Kaity quickly related her and Chrysta's discovery of the ship graveyard. The prophetess chuckled a little as she mentioned the alien skeleton and bolting with Chrysta. Samantha motioned for her to finish, and she did, wishing the woman wasn't so impatient.

"We'll have to check it out later." The prophetess removed a flashlight from the leather travel bag over her shoulder. "Water's the priority, and exploring for the fun of it is a luxury we can't afford yet. However, it's interesting to know there are more aliens than the kind that serve Vogul. Who knows, but that we might get one of their old wrecks space-worthy?"

Kaity understood, yet she felt disappointed. The existence of aliens stirred questions within her mind. Why would God keep their presence hidden from Earth? What purpose could they serve in His kingdom? Could aliens receive Jesus' gift of salvation, too? *Maybe this is the reason God saved us from incineration*, Kaity thought, as they at last reached the plateau.

It was a bitter recompense. Could losing *so much* ever be worth witnessing to aliens? Why hadn't God bothered to save humanity?

The humans approached the mouth of the cavern with wonder. Tucked back behind an outcropping, Dudeman led them around the projecting stone and did a double-take. It was his first time actually seeing the entrance, as the sandstorm had previously obscured his vision. Kaity soon understood why. Far from a natural cave mouth, the entrance appeared carved by hand. Had the same aliens whose ships lay twisted on the sand fashioned this forsaken place?

She bit her lip, and walked into the cave beyond with her husband. Samantha had flicked on their flashlight, and the four humans descended the shallow steps into the heart of the chamber.

The cavern of statues defied expectation. The walls were a curious mixture of roughhewn and natural. Its floor seemed to be sand and rock, with rough steps carved down to it near the entrance. Devoid of stalactites, the cavern roof stretched to thirty feet at its highest. The back of the cave curved downward into a depression, and Kaity noticed a dark, flat surface which could only be water! Their distant lights sent flickering reflections onto the rocks just above the life-giving pool. Yet something more bizarre arrested Kaity's attention.

Fear, then curiosity, gripped her. Directly ahead of her, four large statues surrounded a clear, circular space in the center of the room. In this rested a strange pedestal. The statues stood about ten feet tall and depicted various animals, all facing outward. The piercing illumination of artificial light revealed their shapes and thickness, and Kaity recognized a scorpion, a lizard, an armadillo, and a snake.

Each statue was crafted with such lifelikeness that she understood why Dudeman and Matt had been frightened. All were carved of stone, but the snake's body twisted, the lizard appeared to be scuttling, the scorpion stood with upraised stinger, and the armadillo crouched solidly. Though alien varieties, she marveled that creatures from Earth should be fashioned and placed in such a location.

"Hey, check this out!" Dudeman exclaimed, pointing at the pincers of the scorpion statue. They had been set close together, with a bridge of stone between them. Inset into this small arch, Kaity beheld a gem—a precious stone that flamed with orange color. Dudeman reached forward and drew it out, holding the jewel in his hand. He revolved the perfectly round orb in his hand. It was slightly larger than a golf ball; smooth of surface and without flaw.

"That seems an odd place to leave a jewel," Sharko commented. Kaity heard Samantha give an exclamation from another area of the cave, and rushed to see what caused it. Rounding the armadillo statue, she found the prophetess playing her flashlight over a long, unusually flat section of the cavern wall. Odd carvings had been etched along its length, spaced out, as if separate paragraphs of a narrative. Kaity stared at the strange marks and furrowed her brows in puzzlement. They seemed a sort of language, but the tutor couldn't guess what they said.

"I-I can read these!" Samantha cried, amazed. "As I stare at these, Kaity, the symbols arrange themselves into words. The words become readable. I...I can't explain it!"

"You can make sense of this?" Kaity arched an eyebrow. Samantha nodded, smiled eagerly, and began reading the nearest script.

"'I Kertcha, being in my twentieth year of rule, came hence at the behest of a dream.' Kaity, it's so exciting! Apparently, this monarch named Kertcha was instructed by God to travel here and bring the 'Pride of Paradeesia'—whatever that is! He describes the journey and states that he left the jewel 'in the eye of the Lizard.'"

"Surely not...that thing?" Kaity noticed a smooth stone, gleaming faintly, from within the lizard statue's right eye. Approaching the statue, she reached over its outstretched front leg and removed the round, golden object from an inset that formed the eye's pupil. Despite looking like translucent gold, the object felt unexpectedly light in her hand.

"How strange," she muttered. "Who in the galaxy would make the trouble of a trip here, and why? What is this Paradeesia and its strange king?"

"There's another one!" Samantha exclaimed, growing excited. "'My name's Crosshair, and my story—well—let's just say I was a mercenary. I don't know why, but God spoke to me, audibly. Little old me! Well he told me to come to Dalar 3 and deposit something valuable. Of course, the cops' eyebrows rose through the roof when I asked to bring the Ruby of Vexador here. You don't exactly let a former crook go chargin' off with a priceless gem, right? So I came here and left it. If you've got any sense, you'll find it quick enough.'"

Kaity chuckled, remarking, "She's kind of funny. I can't imagine it, but Crosshair's got to be an alien. I wonder if she even has hands and feet, like us."

"Well, her name certainly suggests a trigger finger." Samantha's lips twisted in a wry smile. She moved to examine another section of writing when a noise startled Kaity. Samantha turned to listen.

"Hold on, let me get it out of your hand!" Sharko's voice called.

"What's happening to me, Man?" Dudeman exclaimed, panicking. "This is *not cool*!"

Kaity and Samantha dashed towards the men, rounding the armadillo statue to suddenly face a blinding light. The prophetess tripped over one of the statue's legs, but caught herself. Kaity skidded to a halt, shielding her eyes from the intense glare. She could barely see Sharko's form outlined against the light, but the place where Dudeman must be was so radiant she couldn't look at it. The surfer had vanished! Nothing remained but a prolonged flash of brilliance, which abruptly faded.

The cave pitching back into darkness caught their eyes off guard. For a moment, they were blinded again. Then, a shadowy figure in armor appeared where Dudeman had stood! Kaity shrieked.

Flame designs shot up and down its plating. The thing wore a helmet of semi-translucent orange, with a black visor obscuring its face and an armor suit in the colors of orange, yellow, and gray. A tank on its back connected to a weapon of some sort via a hose, and Kaity backed away in fear. The creature must be an alien! Who knew what it had done to Dudeman? *Heaven only knows what it will do to us*! Kaity thought, cowering behind her husband.

Sharko stood his ground. He'd brought along Matt's revolver, and he fumbled for the weapon as the intruder took two uncertain steps toward them. The alien raised its gun, and Samantha cringed. Whether it didn't recognize Sharko's revolver as a gun, or was going specifically for the prophetess, Kaity couldn't tell. But the creature's barrel rose, trained directly on Samantha!

"WHAT HAVE YOU DONE with my friend?" Sharko demanded. "Bring him back this instant, or I'll shoot you!"

The creature replied in a strange, mumbling, unintelligible voice. It waved the weapon around wildly. Sharko aimed the revolver at its chest, hoping alien armor would prove as vulnerable to a gun as human.

"It's no use!" Samantha exclaimed, hardly daring to move. "It wouldn't understand our language, and I can't understand *it*."

By now, the alien's arms flailed wildly. It stepped forward, stumbled, and went flying toward Sharko. The truck driver paused for one hair-raising instant before squeezing the trigger. He'd never before fired at another living being, but the gun discharged point-blank into the chest plates of the alien kidnapper. Sharko's arm jerked painfully and the thing fell on top of him, causing both to fall to the sandy floor. The revolver dropped from his hand.

Sharko rolled out from under the alien. Slowly, horrifyingly, the creature rose to its full height. Chucking the weapon in its hand, the alien reached for its black visor and lifted it with gloved fingers. Sharko moved in front of his wife to shield her. Kaity expected a horrid face to peer out at them. Instead, Dudeman's eyes burned into them, his mouth taut with anger!

"A clone! They've cloned him!" Kaity cried.

"I'm not a clone, you idiot!" Dudeman's shouted. "I'm trapped in this freaking thing and I couldn't talk to you guys!" he glared at Sharko. "Dude, you just totally *shot* me!"

"Sorry!" Sharko gestured apologetically. "You can't blame me, can you? We didn't know what was going on, and I hardly recognized you!"

"What *did* happen?" the explanation failed to calm Dudeman down. "I remember reaching for the orange stone thingy. All of a sudden, I couldn't see. My body filled with warmth, and it seemed I was floatin' a million miles away. It was like surfing a perfect wave with no bumps, no wipeout, just me and the board and a smooth ride. Then I got dumped back here, and you're all staring at me for a while before I realize I'm stuck in this suit tryin' to speak but I can't because this stupid visor—!"

Dudeman broke off into a string of complaints. Samantha grinned at his babbling, but Sharko laid a hand on his friend's shoulder.

"James, you're safe. That's good enough for me. We'll find out how to get the suit off later. You know, I DID just shoot it point-blank with a gun and there's only a dent and powder marks."

"Maybe it's alien technology that activates when you touch these crystals?" Kaity speculated, the golden orb from Paradeesia still in her hand.

"Um, hate to break it to you, but touch can't be the answer." Dudeman cast her a withering look.

"You're holding it," Sharko supplied awkwardly. Kaity blushed.

"Oh."

"No matter what triggers it, perhaps this tech can come in useful," Samantha said, examining the rest of the statues for orbs. "Each person who came to this world left a jewel. There were eight inscriptions on the walls of this cavern, meaning..."

"Eight orbs!" Kaity caught on excitedly, and soon all of them were combing the statues for treasures. Another crystal rested in the second eye socket of the lizard. They found one on the back of the armadillo, and two at each end of the snake. Yet two more remained, and no amount of looking could turn them up until Samantha approached the pedestal.

The octagonal sandstone pedestal stood in the center of the room. Wide and squat, it boasted eight round hollows inset into its stone surface. Samantha felt around the pedestal, and a bit of the stonework gave way. Pushing harder, she slid the brick to one side. The movement revealed a tiny niche, in which rested two orbs: one purple, the other blue. Both glowed with faint light, like the other crystals. It was a curious illumination: a light emanating from the center of each. Sharko could only liken it to a trapped sun, just able to glow forth through thick layers of amber.

They marveled at the mysterious orbs. Why had they been brought here? What purpose did they serve? It was obvious they were jewels of value, but the exact nature of the stones eluded their wildest suppositions. At present, the orbs seemed more of a danger than anything else, so the humans handled them with care.

Samantha used a cloth to hold each gem, and Dudeman's gloved hands aided her. She laid the seven remaining orbs in their insets atop the pedestal. It was easier than placing them back into the statues.

"I find it curious there are eight of them," she said, half to herself. "Eight of them, and eight of us..."

"Can anything be done for me?" James wondered aloud.

"I don't know." Samantha snapped out of her reveries, flushing slightly. She felt bad for forgetting Dudeman's plight. "I'm sorry. You aren't in pain, and it doesn't appear to be altering your DNA in any way. All we can do is pray and brainstorm."

"Don't worry, we'll get you out of this thing." Sharko slapped his friend on the back, flinching as he struck the armor too hard. "You have my promise. Ouch!"

"I guess I won't be doing any surfing for a while!" Dudeman laughed sardonically. "Not that a desert has sick waves, anyway. I bet someone would sink like an anchor wearing this stuff!"

"I kind of hope we find out," Kaity teased. "At least it'd mean we found water!"

Discussion left the topic of Dudeman's fate, and Samantha suggested that they gather water. The pool at the back of the cave looked as rancid as it smelled. Sharko felt sorry for his wife as she gagged, and reminded Kaity they'd be running the water through their shuttle's purifier. The four survivors filled up their canteens and containers to the brim. Sharko figured he'd be sent back with Dudeman and Matt, as enough water remained to be collected for about four or five trips. He didn't look forward to it.

A blast of heat hit the survivors as they emerged from the underground grotto. The plain which appeared so mesmerizing now danced with shimmering waves, the harsh afternoon sun baking their skin. Heat waves also rose from Dudeman's armor, yet the surfer seemed unfazed. Whatever the orb's effects, it enabled him to carry both the backpack and large container of water. Sharko estimated they must weigh eighty pounds altogether. Amazingly, Dudeman seemed to take the weight in stride, unaffected by the heat.

"Whatever happened to him may prove useful in the end," the trucker whispered to Kaity. "If we can find a way to switch this alien tech on and off, who knows what we could accomplish?"

"I only pray he can get out of it," his wife replied dubiously, and Sharko nodded. They crossed the remainder of the desert plain in silence, with only the wind and their thoughts to keep them company.

DUDEMAN RECEIVED MORE than a few stares from the others at their home base. Matt was amazed that the orange orb had entrapped him in an alien spacesuit, while Nancy thought it humorous. James went in specially to show Mike his "impervious" armor suit. He clunked across the horizontal walls of the bedroom deck, ducking into the small space where Mike lay. It was a tiny bedroom with two cots pushed together. The stainless steel walls and white floor glistened dully, and only a pencil sketch of Vogul Bay hanging on the floor—now serving as a wall—offered anything to see.

Mike Taylor stretched out on one cot, a thin, blue coverlet draped over him. Dudeman's visit, and the news of water, cheered him slightly. His knee was still bruised in a bad way, though with Chrysta's support, he could attempt about a dozen paces. Walking proved tricky, in the slanted space, and Dudeman heard the depression in Mike's tone.

"Believe me," Mike said bad-temperedly, "I'd give a thousand bucks just to be moving around, suit or no! So you found water? Is it a spring or river?"

"Sadly, no," Dudeman confessed. "It's just a pool of yuck, man. We still need to find a better source."

"I wish I could've seen it." Mike gazed at the map of Vogul Bay wistfully. "I'm pretty useless to you all right now. Chrysta does more than me, and my chest...well..."

Mike coughed painfully before pulling down the paper-thin coverlet to reveal his injured torso. The wound was anything but pretty. Despite the bandage covering it, a slight trickle of yellow flowed out of the site. The skin surrounding the puncture looked swollen.

"Nancy tries to make light of it, but I'm not doing so hot. I may have needed a doctor, but Nancy and the medkit's all we've got."

"You take care of yourself, Man." James' heart stirred with compassion. He forgot his own predicament, in light of Mike's. Footsteps sounded outside of the room, and Mike quickly pulled the coverlet back up. Chrysta trudged in, looking tired, and Dudeman bade the college student farewell. He felt it best to give husband and wife some time alone. Chrysta nodded to him as he exited. She leaned down by her injured husband, taking his hand between both of her smooth palms.

"Do you know what today is?" she asked, her face lit up by the knowledge of a secret.

"Tuesday? Monday? Do they even have weeks on an alien planet?"

"It's our anniversary, Silly!" Chrysta exclaimed, handing him a rolled-up piece of paper tied with a string. "Samantha wants to ration the paper, but I couldn't help myself!"

Mike opened the present and smiled. Another of Chrysta's drawings! The gift, though modest, meant the world to him. His wife cut two strips of tape from a roll and placed the picture on an unoccupied wall. In an alien wasteland, even simple things like drawings relieved the tension of their situation.

"How do you feel today?" Chrysta asked eagerly, turning around. "Under normal circumstances, I always wanted to recreate our wedding dance. But anything you're up for will do."

Mike looked into his wife's beaming face and couldn't answer her question honestly. How *did* he feel? Depressed, sick, hopeless, useless—utterly unable to express even the simplest thoughts to his wordy, emotive wife! He still hadn't told her why his wound was leaking and discolored. Chrysta would grow so horribly worried and...hadn't they endured enough pain in their two years of marriage?

He was determined to get better, anyway. The infection could be worse, and Nancy came in frequently to change his bandages. An unspoken agreement hung in the silence between them to keep Chrysta in the dark about his precarious health. Nancy reluctantly followed his wishes. Only in occasional moments, if Chrysta slipped out of the room, would Nancy discuss the gravity of his infection.

"I am praying for you," she'd said, "and your wife should be, too."

"If you knew what pain I've caused her." Mike shook his head vehemently. "I won't be the cause of further distress."

"It's not likely, but there's a chance you could die," Nancy would counter. "Do you want her to find that out suddenly, or have time to prepare?"

"Mike?"

The Taylor's mind flashed back to the present. He'd been lost in memories which seemed daydreams. Managing a forced smile, he allowed his wife to help him up. His knee hurt horribly as he accidentally put weight on it, but he deflected the flinch. Putting his arms around Chrysta's slender waist, he rested his weight against her and the two gently began to sway back and forth. Chrysta sank her face into the top of his shoulder, her bright red hair falling forward against his face.

There they danced, one full of joy while the other choked on the guilt of knowledge hidden. Chrysta ignored the smell of her husband's injury. As he pulled his hand up and drew her head farther in, Mike uttered a quick prayer to God. However their days progressed, he prayed for healing and provision in this barren wilderness. And if he could not have those, he prayed that God would imbue his wife with the strength to live after his death.

DUDEMAN REMAINED TRAPPED in the alien armor suit for two weeks. In Kaity's opinion, it did nothing to improve his volatile personality. Only trudging out to the plateau with Sharko and Matt to fetch water kept him from frustrated outbursts, and this proved a mixed mercy. Though Kaity appreciated this break, she saw less of Sharko than she wished. True, each man rotated hauling duty so that they got every third day off. Sharko *was* back every night, but Kaity missed him. Even if he went out for merely a day, his absence revealed how greatly she depended on him. After she finished scrubbing dishes in the kitchen, Kaity descended to the Commons to occupy her wait time.

Today was Matt's day off. The scrap worker generally spoke little and kept to himself, but on this occasion, Kaity observed something about him which struck a chord. He was sitting with his back against the slanting, metal wall of the shuttle, reading. Kaity, being a book-lover, sauntered over. A book with a Grecian-style cover rested in his tanned hand. She inquired if it was the *Iliad,* because she'd read Homer's classic in college.

"Nope, this is *Jason and the Argonauts,*" Matt replied. "Sam told me to pack some reading material, and this is a favorite. I didn't get much time to read in the Army, so I use whatever opportunity I can."

"Are you a fan of the classics?" Kaity asked.

"I don't know." Matt chuckled wryly. "I just like adventure tales. *Jason and the Argonauts* is about a guy who assembles a team and goes off on a quest. We've also been sent off on one, seeking our life-giving golden fleece: water. If you ever want to read it or any other books I brought along, let me know."

Kaity smiled gratefully. "Thanks. I guess that's why we read them. Fantasy can give us hope when the real world seems dismal."

"Right now, it's pretty dismal for *him.*" Matt nodded casually toward Dudeman, pacing frantically at the other side of the Commons.

The surfer, more distraught and oversensitive than usual, was certain he'd never be free again. Sharko and the others tried their best to cheer him up. They pointed out—quite accurately—that his broken arm was healing rapidly in the alien suit. However, James longed to be free of the armor's confines. Sleeping and eating in it felt like a chore. While the suit enhanced his strength and endurance, he began to feel claustrophobic and irate. His descent into a dark mood could be marked daily, until it reached the point where he would even snap at Sharko.

The orange orb was a part of his suit. After his transformation, it appeared in the center of his breastplate, inset into the plating. Dudeman could remove it, yet nothing happened when he did. The suit became like a constant ball and chain. One afternoon, during their customary water search, Dudeman felt particularly unkind. His mood came out in an angry tirade. Sharko finally threw down the water jugs, pivoted, and grabbed his friend around the shoulder pauldrons.

"What is wrong with you?" he demanded. James looked stunned.

"I—I don't really know," he confessed. "As the days go on, I guess it's like I feel urges to be mean, or negative, that I can't control."

"You've never exactly been a choir boy," Sharko pointed out.

"No, I mean, I CAN'T help it!" Dudeman repeated. "Lay off my case, okay? Would you like me to use this gun on you? It's a flamethrower. I tested it on a lizard. Little stinker went up in a poof of smoke, Man!"

"Stop it!" Sharko exclaimed. "You're right. It *has* to be this crystal. Back on Earth, one thing that always bothered you was cruelty to animals. You found a dying seal on the beach once, and it affected you more than you care to admit. The James I know wouldn't hurt an animal."

"Then what can I do?" Dudeman questioned angrily, tugging in vain at the elastic part of the suit. "It's like a second skin—can't get the freaking thing off. I tried."

"How did you become this way in the first place?" Sharko asked.

"I guess I...took the orb and held it up," Dudeman said slowly.

"Did you try holding it up?" Sharko asked. "I hate to be obvious."

"Of course!" Dudeman returned curtly. "It doesn't do anything!" He grabbed the crystal with a roll of his eyes, pulled it out of his armor, and raised it a bit. Nothing. "See? I told you, Man! I'm not an idiot...unlike you!"

"Hey, knock it off!" Sharko exclaimed. "It's one thing to lift it slowly. Didn't you shove it straight into the air the first time?"

James now felt thoroughly insulted.

"Oh, I suppose this thing responds to one's degree of motion?" His tone dripped sarcasm, but he thrust the crystal skyward with a smirk. He was certain he'd prove his antagonizing friend wrong.

Immediately, there was a blinding flash of light. Warmth enveloped James' entire body, and he emerged to find Sharko blinking. The skeptical surfer felt the familiar texture of his black board shorts and rash guard, and his arm hung in its sling once more, though now whole. He was free of the armor! It was gone, as if he'd never been trapped in an alien suit at all. Dudeman's mouth dropped open.

"Dude, I feel like an idiot!" Despite his skin browning from the outdoors, James blushed so deeply that he resembled Sharko's sunburn.

"Hey, we're all idiots on occasion," Sharko responded, with a twinkle in his eye. "Didn't I shoot you with a gun? Friends are God's way of pulling us out of stupidity. Or further into it!" He reached toward his best friend and gave him a brief but hearty hug. "It's good to have you back!"

"Thanks Man!" James exclaimed. "I can't wait until the others see me!"

He shouldered the strap on his heavy water jug and took off at a run across the sand, excited for the first time in days. Sharko nearly had to jog to keep up with him.

THE *Draxalis* emerged from the wormhole within sight of Dalar 3. The uninhabited desert planet hung amidst the stars, the gunship assuming orbit and hovering above it like a bird of prey. Its polished surface dully reflected the sandy planet and surrounding space. From a hangar bay in the vessel, a starship flew out. The *Draxalis* was large enough to carry six, plus a few dropships. The starship opened a warp tunnel, similar to the wormhole yet green and with a chosen destination. It blasted off towards Stattar Nebula, carrying the tracker Durag had hidden on the *Draxalis*. Stattar disrupted sensors and blocked communication, so the pilot hoped to remove the device and slip away once he entered the nebula's expanse.

Inside, Willum paced the hangar bay agitatedly. His plan to misdirect Durag by sending a ship to Stattar seemed poised to succeed, but a roadblock stood in the way of searching Dalar 3. He had stolen the gunship right out of space dock, so several operating systems remained unfinished. Their temperature controls could only cool the craft, not warm it. Their landing gear was incomplete, and their plasma rechargers worked inefficiently. Yet worse than this, the builders of the gunship had installed only a fraction of its sensors. These few sensors had become fried when the gunship discharged over Earth, the blast sending an unexpected power surge through their systems.

In a sense, the *Draxalis* operated blind. Vogul thus kept a ship or two out in space around the gunship, because no amount of repairs could compensate for parts that simply weren't present. Consequently, Vogul would be sending crews of search teams to Dalar 3 via starship. The smaller vessels could scan the planet in a matter of hours, while the hovercrafts would detect living beings within a radius of 50 Earth miles. The search would take far more effort and time than he wanted, but it would be worth it. Destiny could not be thwarted by a simple technological deficiency.

Seven search teams of Trylithians funneled into the hangar, faces obscured by the signature mouth cloth. Vogul gave them an impassioned speech in their language. It was a tough tongue to master, but they dared not laugh at his translation blunders. Vogul's wrath turned fatal, if provoked.

"You have all been instructed!" Willum concluded. "Scour the sands! Any signs of wreckage will be clue enough they are here. Otherwise, we go to the next planet. Now begone! Do my bidding, and do not report until you have results!"

The Trylithians responded with slight bows, holding their hands to their left shoulders and sweeping them outward and upward in a traditional Trylithian salute. Some manned the starships that would sweep the planet's surface. Others boarded a transport, fueled and ready for departure. With a whoosh, the airlocks of the vessels closed behind them. Vogul exited the bay, watching on a monitor as the ships and transport rocketed into space.

The transport was a square-shaped ship, bulky and painted in the Trylithian colors of green-and-yellow between gray plating. As it entered the thermosphere, it practically fell to Dalar 3's surface. Descending rapidly, the transport slowed to a landing when a series of jets activated beneath it. Its sister vessels, the Trylithian fighters, levelled off about 1,000 feet above it. The same colors as the transport, the starships were sleek, long, and shaped like slender tadpoles. Their wings formed a thin half-circle with a hollow in the middle, while their sterns tapered to a flat, round tip. A glass bubble protected each crew of three Trylithians that manned it. Each fighter zoomed in a different direction over the desert landscape, to scan for life-signs and wreckage. Above, the Draxalis maintained a watchful orbit.

Vogul felt grateful to have such capable pilots. Trylithians pilots had a reputation as the best in the Gorvan System, and Vogul's flight crew was no exception. Handpicked by Tormac Durag, they were meant for defense of the gunship if an enemy force attacked. Vogul happily put them to work for other purposes. He waited on the bridge of the *Draxalis*, knowing the air search alone could take half a day.

Early reports flooded back from the starships. It was impossible for them to read heat signatures on the scorching planet, and the ground teams reported the same. The temperature and reflectivity of the soil confounded their heat-based detectors. Twice, the searchers found life signs, only to discover animals. Other false alarms came as the old wrecks of Gorvan ships were discovered. Still, Vogul ordered them to look.

"Fly over every acre of sand, if you must!" he cried. "Just tell me when you find any sign of our quarry!"

Hours, a day, a night, passed. Vogul's advisors counseled searching only at night, as the temperature dropped enough for their sensors to work somewhat. Vogul seemed insensate to their words. He would not cease pacing, or ranting to himself behind a closed door, and could not be coaxed to sleep.

"The day of destiny hangs upon this search!" he would exclaim, striking any Trylithian foolish enough to enter. "You have no concept of the importance of finding and killing my pathetic race!"

Finally, after the ships and ground forces searched for two weeks, news reached the *Draxalis* from Dalar 3. The bottom of the Earthlings' shuttle had been found! A small remnant of the storage bay, ripped from the craft, was discovered a little ways from a bluff. It had been half-buried and missed by an aerial crew hours earlier. Vogul made a note of the names, but he would deal with their failure later. At present, the news felt like sweet vengeance to his parched soul. At last! At long last he'd found evidence that the survivors crashed on *this* planet! They might even be dead from the crash, and so ease his task.

But no! Vogul sensed in his dark heart that they must be alive, out there, struggling in vain to thwart him. Phase two of the search would proceed. A sandstorm had obscured the shuttle's crash course, but at least Vogul knew where to start. A simple group of eight humans from Earth couldn't hope to outlast him. Once he located them, Vogul would personally enjoy their executions. Yet even if they eluded his search parties, he could incinerate their planet. Whether it took a simple hunt, or the obliteration of Dalar 3, Vogul would see to their doom. It was his calling, his purpose—his fated culmination.

<7>

A Vision

News of Dudeman's freedom from the suit cheered the survivors. Even before most of them saw the surfer, all knew of it and celebrated with him. Samantha drew a star on their calendar to mark the event. For once in his life, James Erskin felt like someone other than Sharko actually valued him. He'd never exactly been popular, but with his restoration and help finding water, he became second only to Samantha. The sensation was wonderfully odd.

Dudeman had lived many years as a rebel. His lack of respect for authority and others had made him unpopular. Deprived of feeling special much of his life, he basked in the warm glow of acceptance, and Samantha observed this. Perhaps a way to win this surfer to Christ was by making him feel valued?

Likeability came naturally to Samantha...when she didn't ruffle feathers with prophecies. She led the survivors in prayer each morning, and tried to personally check in on Mike, whose condition didn't appear to be improving. Her fellow Earthlings respected her and sought her counsel in decisions. Though the water in the orb cave ran out, it made a difference when combined with what reserves they already had. Things were looking up, and Samantha had to confess that popularity felt refreshing after being branded a lunatic by most of Earth's journalists.

One evening, the prophetess ascended the slipface of the dune above their shuttle. She settled cross-legged onto the shifting sand, watching the stars burst forth in a tapestry of splendor. A week had passed since Dudeman's restoration, and neither he nor Matt could spot any surface water no matter how far they traveled. Samantha decided to forego panicking. Their reserves from the mysterious cave would see them through at least three more weeks, and she trusted God hadn't led them here to die. The evening air felt pleasant. A relaxing warmth, it contrasted with the cooling sands.

Besides, wasn't she out here to enjoy the stars? The burning celestial orbs took her mind off the responsibility she bore as leader. Knowledge of Earth's destruction had been on her shoulders for a year. Now, she was weighted down with the responsibility of keeping these people motivated and alive. She supposed this constituted the usual routine for a prophetess. Hardship came with the job description.

With Dudeman back to normal, Samantha could simply focus on advising the men and encouraging her fellow women. She had performed this task ever since they left Earth. Kaity and Chrysta especially needed her reassurance, for they grieved the loss of loved ones most deeply. Rarely did Samantha steal a moment to herself, like the one she enjoyed now. Usually, she was busy until she drew the curtain across her bedroom doorway, bowed, and started praying to her Heavenly Father. Most times, she fell asleep in that position.

However, her joy at *being* a leader eclipsed the exhaustion of leading. Samantha enjoyed taking charge. Being in control suited her, and she possessed a natural confidence many had admired in the engineering world. She could be deeply sympathetic one moment and businesslike the next. Maybe that was why everyone—Dudeman excepted—approached her with equal ease. She felt truly comfortable in her role as God's prophetess, only wishing that this mantle could be borne in happier circumstances.

The sorrows of the group were real to her, and she sought not only to counsel but to comfort. Always needed, yet seldom needing—that was how Samantha saw herself. At least, she needed little when it came to earthly matters. As for the spiritual, it amazed Samantha how dynamic her relationship with God was. Whenever she seemed to make great progress and growth, she would relax, sigh, and settle into a rut. Then God would rip the rug of self-deception away, revealing to her just how much change remained for Him to work.

Samantha stretched her legs out, bowed her head, and spread her arms wide in a posture of surrender. Once, she'd been a woman who held everything back from God. She'd wrestled with His call, refused to go to the street corners to speak, and clung grimly to possessions and relationships that did her harm. Only through His painful prying did she learn to loosen her grip, and only then did she experience true peace.

Peace was the last thing in Nancy Cooper's heart as she tended Mike Taylor that night. Every week, she had watched Mike's condition deteriorate. Every day, she tended to his bandages, but the wound worsened. Chrysta always stood by, watching. Nancy could sense the woman slowly realizing that her husband's condition was serious.

"You need to tell your wife!" Nancy exclaimed, as Chrysta popped out for a moment. "Mike, you still may come out of this, but there's an increasing chance you'll die. I can't do anything about it, because I don't have the proper equipment. I—"

Nancy forced back the tears starting to rise to her eyes. Chrysta returned, saw her face, and instantly grew suspicious.

"What's wrong? What's going on?"

"Mike's getting worse," Nancy blurted.

"How dare you!" the college student roared, stiffening. Yet the strain forced him to wince. Chrysta kneeled beside him, her lips quivering.

"Don't try to protect me from a truth I already feel." She frowned. "You're not better, and if things continue, you'll die."

"Sweetheart, I love you," Mike said brokenly. "I don't want to hurt you again by—"

"By what? I'm not a child!" Chrysta turned away from him. "Thank you, Nancy. Please leave us."

The secretary willingly obliged. She left the couple and crawled into bed. Her cot felt horribly uncomfortable. Nothing seemed to induce sleep, and she could hear Mike and Chrysta arguing through the thin walls as she mulled over his condition. She couldn't let him die. She didn't want to! Yet, what more could she do? They were alone here, on a desert world, with nothing but the shuttle and what it contained. If God didn't work a miracle soon, they might lose a member of their group. And for Nancy, losing a patient was the worst failure of all...

KAITY ANDERSON TREKKED with Sharko over the undulating dunes of Sahara. The day dawned oppressively hot, so she wore beachwear, with a straw hat tied under her chin. Sharko walked on sandals, beating the heat in a loose T-shirt and a borrowed pair of Dudeman's board shorts. The two searched the unforgiving wastes for cacti and scrub brush. Samantha had assigned them the task of gathering native plants and sap to analyze, for their supplies in *The Deliverer* would not last forever. She hoped to find a food source, but after a few hours, Kaity felt the task was hopeless. She and Sharko only found a handful of plants in their entire trek. They gathered a cactus branch and some sap, along with a bit of scraggly bush. Sharko could only see a use for their items in the form of clothing and medicine. The gooey cacti sap tasted abysmal.

"It's halfway to cough medicine," Sharko remarked, "so why not utilize it as such?"

He poked Kaity playfully, hoping his words would amuse her. Kaity, however, could not be diverted. The heat and sand assailed her body, while her mind hovered galaxies away. It dwelt back on Earth, remembering all of the good times, the comforts—the warmth of a fireside chat on a drizzly December day. Vogul Bay got colder than it did hot. Though snow only graced the high mountainsides, there could be bitter, foggy mornings. Then the fog would lift, revealing an ocean that looked like a dazzling plain of gray. The ocean's edge blended with the horizon, and Kaity had always felt like she could walk out onto the waves and continue until she ascended to where sky met sea.

There were memories of family gatherings, rounds of lively table games, and lovely strolls with Sharko. She envisioned the office where she'd worked as a tutor: the faces of the little children who came and went and learned beneath her dutiful instruction. To think that all of them were dead was a burden too great to bear. Kaity began choking with tears, and Sharko ceased his monologue about desert types and sand textures. He turned to his wife. He knew Kaity hadn't heard a word of it.

"My Love, what's wrong?"

Kaity merely collapsed against him, her head leaning on his sweaty chest.

"I hate it here!" she cried. "I want everything to go back to the way it was. I'm sick of heat and sand and ugly desert! I'm sick of five-minute showers, energy conservation, no cell service, no restaurants, no social activities and family to gather with, no—!"

"Calm down, my Love." Sharko gently stroked the back of her head. "I know. I'm sick of it, too. But you can't keep dreaming about the past and wishing for something that simply won't be. We have a life. We have each other."

"*This* isn't a life!" Kaity accused. "It's a purgatory! Why did God cast us down into this horrible place to die?"

"The Children of Israel once wondered the same," Sharko replied, keeping a calm voice. "They had been slaves in Egypt, yearning for freedom longer than many could remember. God granted them that kindness. He liberated His people and sustained them through the desert journey, to the place He had especially prepared for them. Yet Israel began to question Him. They stopped having faith in God's provision and sovereign will. Eventually, they came to the Promised Land which so many had yearned for...and it wasn't what they expected. God was showing them an opportunity. All they saw were giants and fortresses."

"What is the point of this story?" Kaity asked wearily. "I've studied this in Exodus. I know how cantankerous they were."

"My point," Sharko continued earnestly, "is that where you see giants, God sees the Promised Land. We are finite on the tapestry of life. We only see the pieces right in front of us, as they are woven. We can't see His grand design. Remember how Samantha told us we had a purpose beyond our solar system? We've traveled beyond the Milky Way, and I do not believe sand, heat, and desert will be our ultimate future."

"I appreciate your positivity, but I'm still grieving! I lost everything, Sharko!" She bit her lip. She'd come off sounding harsher than she felt.

"You didn't lose *me*!" Sharko's voice rose, impassioned. He drew Kaity back and gazed into her eyes. "My Love, I understand your pain. Truly. I lost my parents, and for a long time, I hated my life as well! All this adult responsibility fell on my shoulders. I had to be a leader when I just wanted to rest, grieve, and finish my senior year! There comes a time when you have to let go of how things were, and accept how they are. Can you do that...for us?"

Kaity said nothing for several moments. The couple simply stood, sweating, beneath the burning sun. The hot wind whipped their hair and clothes, sending tickling grains over their sandaled feet.

"I will try," Kaity said at last, and Sharko squeezed her hand.

"That's all I ask. Let's head back to Base now."

The tutor heartily agreed, and they brought back their meager supplies and laid them on the Commons table. Yet Kaity couldn't shake her nostalgia the rest of the day, and she drifted off to sleep with a painful longing in her heart.

WAVES WASHED OVER A sandy shore stretching out of sight in both directions. The soothing surf pounded against sand and rock, leaving foamy skirts of water that receded as quickly as they came. A lighthouse perched upon a jutting cliff in the distance, the ocean nearby appearing to spread out indefinitely until it melted into the grayish horizon. Shadows of palm trees danced on the beach, a gentle breeze ruffling their fronds. In the midst of this natural beauty, Kaity Anderson lay on a white chaise lounge chair. A novel in one hand, she sipped ice-cold water beneath the swaying shade.

She was in college. Her parents had finally moved into the beachfront house they'd always wanted. Kaity had just taken her Final exams for the semester, and she relished a Summer Break yet to unfold. More than this, Sharko Anderson had finally asked her out! Kaity flushed every time she thought of him. Yes, she had it bad! Who could blame her, when Sharko possessed something...something mature, noble, understanding, and strong? His persistence and faith inspired her. Developing a crush on him had been easy.

God was good, life was good, and their little strip of paradise on the beach? A seaside dream come true. Kaity drank from her glass, feeling the cold liquid slide between her lips and savoring the delicious sensation. Ice water! Why did it seem ages since she'd tasted it?

"Kaity! Kaity, wake up!"

Sharko's concerned face roused her from sweet slumber. She awakened feeling homesick and confused.

"Wha—?" Kaity questioned, as Sharko flicked on the battery-powered light. As a rule, they tried to conserve energy, but Sharko appeared desperate. "What time is it?"

"Samantha is missing," he said urgently. "Matt woke me because he went to get something from her room, and she wasn't in bed. It's 4 o' clock, by the way." Sharko gave the time before Kaity's question could fully form on her lips. "We combed *The Deliverer* and the area around, but there's no trace of her."

His last words fully awakened Kaity. How could their leader be gone? The prophetess was more valuable to them than even water, as they owed their very lives to this dauntless woman. What could possibly have drawn her out in the middle of the night? Or, worse...?

Kaity's mind couldn't go there. The thought that they might not be alone on this alien world scared her too much, bringing back ugly memories of the alien corpse in the wreck. She rose, threw on mismatched clothes, and followed her husband into the Commons. The light of their only lantern revealed Matt's haggard face. The scrap worker was usually so chill and even-keeled that his expression took her aback. Wordlessly, he handed Sharko the lantern.

"We *must* find her." The ex-soldier beckoned to the doorway. "I've seen her footprints. She can't have gone far."

"I'll help you," Sharko affirmed. "Kaity, I suggest you stay behind to let the others know we've gone. We don't want a second group of us waking up to find missing persons."

"Agreed!" Kaity eagerly followed his lead, being in no mood to trek out. Her heart pined for family and for Earth. Sharko hugged her tightly, then followed Matt out of their sideways base camp. They set out across the pre-dawn landscape together. The morning sun lay beneath the horizon, the dunes pale and bathed in deep shadow. The men trekked the lightening wasteland, tracing the solitary tracks of the prophetess who had been an ordinary engineer on Earth but was irreplaceable to them.

SAMANTHA HARRIS TOSSED and turned restlessly. The cave of orbs tormented her waking mind. The texts on the wall, the crystals set in stone, the accounts of names and places unseen—they agitated her and kept sleep maddeningly at bay. Somehow, everything resounded with a strange familiarity. A deep sense of déjà vu stirred within her soul, bothering her. She hadn't given it much thought, due to the importance of survival. The orbs seemed as dangerous as they were unknown, and she didn't like things beyond her understanding.

"Samantha."

A voice spoke softly in the darkness. It was barely a whisper. She rolled over, brushing her curly, dark hair out of her face.

"Samantha."

This time, the voice sounded as a loud whisper. The prophetess sat up, annoyed.

"Yes? What do you want?" she questioned, assuming it must be Matt. Finding and hearing no one, Samantha rose.

What did tossing and turning accomplish, anyway? She trudged into the Commons where the silence of the base greeted her. Samantha knew they were fortunate to have crashed into a dune. God had provided them with security, shelter, and insulation from the extreme climate. She slid into a chair by their communal table, purposely diverting her mind to their supplies. Anything but this obsession with the jewel cave!

Samantha calculated how they stood on food and water. Even with the storage bay's absence, they possessed enough food to make it for a few months. Water would be a different story. Samantha figured they'd run out in less than a month, unless they could find another source. The cold, hard fact weighed heavily on her heart, troubling her for different reasons.

Her mind meandered to James "Dudeman" Erskin. As much as he exasperated her, she pitied him. A foster child, Dudeman only knew pain and his own confusion over his parents. His heart chose to reject the Creator despite what God had given him, and Samantha understood his stubborn pride only too well. In a way, Dudeman resembled her at an earlier stage. Perhaps this explained why they butted heads so badly. Regardless, Samantha hoped that one day, the Holy Spirit would open his eyes to his need for Living Water. For the present, finding the real deal was challenge enough.

"Samantha!"

There it came again! Samantha turned every which way, yet beheld no one. Suddenly, a bemused smile spread across her lips.

"I am here, Lord," she answered. "I'm listening."

A wind unexpectedly picked up, blowing into the base from the skylight in a way no ordinary wind could. It stirred her thick tresses and filled her soul with its refreshing coolness. Samantha felt an urge to walk outside that she couldn't explain. Already wearing pajamas, she retrieved her sandals and stepped into the nighttime desert. The stars and dark silhouettes of the dunes greeted her. The first twinkled like brilliant diamonds, forming constellations she did not know. The second were like frozen waves reclining against a dark sky. Wind blew skittering grains of sand over their crests, but all lay otherwise still in the soothing pall of night.

A large crescent moon hung midway above the horizon. Samantha felt the tug to walk toward it. As if in a dream, she wandered up and down the dunes, passing only a cactus and a slithering snake. Yet she feared not the animals of nature, nor the harsh environment around her.

At the brink of one dune, she stopped. It seemed as though she passed into another realm, into another world. The night was banished. Before her lay a glistening city of skyscrapers. People, people, hurried everywhere, and the hustle and bustle of the streets could only be matched by the skies. Starships of all varieties hovered and zoomed above her. She glimpsed sand dunes more massive than any upon this world, and then her gaze left the terrestrial altogether.

Wars burned across her mind. Battles she could not name loomed into her field of vision. She saw falling ships and burning metropolises. She beheld dying warriors and heroes vanquishing cruel foes. Worlds flew by where the cycle of day and night was nonexistent; planets where the sun dimmed and planets where it blinded her. Forms both humanoid and strange met her gaze, but more intense than these visions flashing before her were her emotions. Fear, pain, loss, longing, hope, despair—they seized her heart in sequence, tearing at it, threatening to overwhelm her very psyche. She did not understand. It was too much! How could anyone bear the history of galaxies?

SAMANTHA FELT CLOSE to bursting from it all. Suddenly, she saw herself walking among stars. Upon the surfaces of planets their light had been subdued but here, oh here, they glistened with an intensity that burned into her! But a lightness of soul filled her, rather than pain. She couldn't explain it. Samantha trod amidst stars as if on an invisible lane, unafraid of falling though her eyes saw no path. It was some time before she noticed a figure strolling beside her. A human clad in fine robes, his face looked young yet his eyes seemed aged. They were weighted with the sorrows of solar systems—distant, but not unkind. He gave her a reassuring smile.

"Where am I? What is this?" Samantha asked shakily. "The voice I heard..."

"It was Him, you are correct." The man's voice boomed, majestic. "The Creator calls only His chosen. You are to be honored, Daughter. It is a privilege given to few mortals, but then, you are no ordinary woman."

"I am from Earth, it is true," Samantha affirmed. One look from the being made her realize she'd misunderstood his meaning.

"Daughter, if you knew half of your role in history!" The young, aged man shook his head humorously. "If you could fathom the scope of what has begun..."

"Who are you, if I may ask?" Samantha ventured. The male smiled.

"I am a Servant of the Lord," he said mysteriously. "Anything further is not required."

"Why am I seeing these things?"

"Because the time for being ordinary is over. Your premonition is correct. The crystals haunt you because deep within your heart, you feel they were meant for you. God prepares everything in advance for those who do His good works. Your journey through space, crashing upon Sahara, finding the orbs—it was destined to be. Simply discovering *them* is far more significant than Vogul, or survival, or anything else you could accomplish here."

Samantha frowned.

"Your explanations only merit more questions."

"The most accurate assessment of *my* character ever given!" The young man chuckled. "Your time in the desert will bring many tests. Do not waver in your faith, Samantha Harris. Continue following the Lord's commands, no matter what logic or feelings may dictate."

"Do this, Daughter, and no force of evil shall consume you. Through your planet 2,000 years ago, the worlds were blessed. They are about to be blessed again by the World without Magicians. But there is one trial you must face soon, and you will have a hard time of it. Remember my advice, Daughter: let go."

"World without magicians? *Let go?*" Samantha scrunched her brows together in confusion.

"The Lord is pleased with your oversight of the survivors," the man said carefully, "but there is one among you who is destined to become leader. It is *his* responsibility to step up, and yours, to step down."

At that, Samantha's puzzlement morphed to offense. She was about to question him again, but the stars and the mysterious man faded. She stood on the dune top again, now bathed in the rosy light of dawn. Samantha's chest heaved. She'd been breathing hard, yet her heart warmed strangely at this visitation. What did the man's final statements matter when she had witnessed the future of solar systems? An overwhelming realization of what she just experienced washed over her. Samantha fell to her knees in amazement and stayed that way for a while. When Matt and Sharko finally found her, she kneeled there still, a smile upon her face and her lips whispering praises to God.

"I'VE HAD A VISION!" Samantha exclaimed excitedly, clearing the dusty table of everything but a piece of paper and a pencil. Nancy, Kaity, Sharko, Matt, Dudeman, Chrysta and even Mike gathered around her. They had just finished breakfast, and Samantha surveyed each eagerly. Dudeman looked like he expected another rant, Chrysta appeared disgruntled, Nancy and Kaity seemed intrigued, and Matt merely rolled his eyes. Only Sharko appeared as eager as Samantha. After her apology for worrying them, Matt was back to his old, critical self, raising an eyebrow at his cousin as if her sanity teetered on the edge of a cliff. Sharko understood that, sometimes, faith trumped even a relative's emotions.

The prophetess summarized the experience, sharing about her encounter with the mysterious Servant of the Lord.

"See? I told you God was at work even in tragedy!" Samantha finished. "His plan all along was to bring us here. We were meant to find the crystals."

"For what purpose?" Mike questioned weakly.

"I'm...still working it out," Samantha admitted.

"What can you tell us about their function, then?" Dudeman asked testily. "Any insights on how to prevent all of us from getting trapped in suits?"

"Not much," Samantha admitted again.

"So you're saying that these crystals do something," Matt cut in, "you're not sure what. And we have a purpose finding them, though it's unclear. Great. Not vague at all!"

Samantha sighed in frustration.

"I understand your skepticism. I would feel the same in your shoes, but I am God's prophetess. He has spoken to me through a vision, and we'll have need of these orbs for many trials to come."

"Maybe so," Chrysta put in, "but what if we all end up like James? Or we can't revert back despite what we do?"

"That *thing* caused me to behave out-of-control," Dudeman added.

"Can *I* say something?" Kaity spoke up. Everyone looked her way, causing her to blush. She loathed being the center of attention.

"I saw my husband shoot Dudeman point-blank," she continued, "and I noticed what his bullet did. Nothing! If those crystals can give us protection from bullets, think of the potential! It might be hard to sleep in, but what if we can run faster? Lift more? Heal sooner? In a time of survival, strength and technology may be the advantage we need."

Most of those assembled stared at her in surprise. Sharko beamed with pride to hear his wife sound so practical. Samantha played off of Kaity's words.

"It's a risk, yes," she said, "but when God gives you a gift and tells you to use it, only the faithless walk away."

"In that case, *adios*!" Dudeman said simply. He marched out of the room through the storage doorway.

"I can't believe him!" Nancy muttered, disgusted.

"We cannot force him to share our faith," Samantha reminded. "Who here is willing to embrace the unknown? Who is willing to go with me to gather those crystals?"

Kaity and Sharko raised their hands unflinchingly. Nancy reluctantly shot hers up, and Matt gave an aggravated sigh.

"Oh, why not?" he asked. "I already built you an entire shuttle out of scrap! How much crazier can this be?"

Samantha turned her gaze to Chrysta and Mike. The college student looked rather pale, so she did not expect him to come along, but Chrysta appeared to waver.

"I heard how the suit healed Dudeman's arm," she said, at length. "I guess it wouldn't hurt to see if it can help my husband. I'll come along."

Mike gave a weak smile and squeezed her hand before letting it go. Chrysta smiled lovingly at him and joined the group of five. *She has a lovely smile*, Mike thought, secretly hoping his wife was right. His condition kept worsening. Nobody said a word, but he sensed all of them were aware of his health. *He* knew what only his body and nurse could tell him—the infection threatened his life.

Samantha led the way to the familiar cave. After the bright desert daylight, the darkness of the interior made them squint. Matt and Sharko gathered water in containers while the women picked up the orbs. Samantha had left them on the pedestal their last time in the cave. Retrieving them proved easy enough, and they set out across the flat, sandy plain with both water and orbs in hand.

"What's that approaching us?"

Nancy gestured at some dunes to the north, over which zoomed a black speck which was rapidly growing larger.

"Could it be—?" Samantha broke off. The object in the distance screamed toward them, and in a matter of seconds, it came close enough for them to identify it. A metal craft moving directly toward them, its front displayed the familiar emblem of the enemy aliens. *It has begun*, Samantha thought, her heart rapidly sinking. *Willum Vogul has finally tracked us down*!

THE HOVERCRAFT SLOWED suddenly and stopped about a dozen yards away. Gray and yellow in coloring, the machine seemed more like a platform than a spaceship, with metal railings for sides. The afternoon light revealed its occupants as blue-skinned, with long kilts, metallic hoverboots, cloths covering the lower halves of their faces, and pectorals made of axe blades. Their hair was combed upward and outward, forming a sort of coronal around high foreheads. The aliens' eyes narrowed, and one jumped from the hovercraft, brandishing a weapon. Sharko felt rooted to the spot.

"Run!" he heard Samantha shout. He and Matt dropped their water jugs. Kaity looked so terrified that she couldn't think clearly. She broke into a run with Nancy beside her, and Sharko chased after them before Samantha's voice changed his mind.

"Split up!" she ordered, rushing away after Chrysta. Sharko didn't want to split off from his wife. Everything in him yearned to go with her, yet the prophetess had a point. He joined Matt, and the two men purposely ran parallel to the hovercraft, hoping to draw the aliens' attention. The hovercraft pilot headed after Samantha. One of the hovering blue-skins peeled off to pursue them, while his confederate chased after Nancy and Kaity.

Sharko and Matt carried the revolver between them, but no crystals. The two men rushed directly for the sand dunes, hoping to shoot at the alien while it ascended a slope. They broke into a sweat as heat and exertion took hold. The Trylithian didn't seem much faster than they, but he had the advantage of propulsion. They reached the first dune and raced up the slippery incline. The sand slid beneath their feet, making progress nearly impossible. Matt whirled around. The alien was closing, and the blue-skin took aim just as the ex-soldier did.

A green bolt of energy shot out from the alien's weapon, smacking into the sand only inches from Samantha's cousin. Matt's eyes widened as hot sand fell on his jeans. He pulled the trigger. The report of his revolver rang out, his firearm training proving itself as the alien took the revolver round in the neck. He fell in mid-hover but the boots propelled him forward, plowing his body painfully into the side of the dune and sending dust flying. His entire front was abraded from the crash when they turned him over. Green seeped from the hole in his neck, and it didn't take an expert to realize that he was thoroughly dead.

"Nice shooting," Sharko muttered to Matt, who grunted in acknowledgement. The ex-soldier's eyes swept over the landscape for signs of the others.

"There!" Matt cried, pointing to the hovercraft. The alien pilot had left it beside the plateau, several hundred yards from their current position.

"Are you seriously suggesting we try flying that thing?" Sharko stared at Matt as if the heat had seared away his sanity.

"We could, but I was thinking it marked the direction Samantha and Chrysta took!"

"What about my wife?" Sharko questioned. "Aren't Kaity and Nancy far more defenseless than your cousin?"

Matt paused. A slight grin turned up the corners of his mouth.

"Good point." He patted Sharko on the back. "I'll wager she can handle them, and I wouldn't be surprised if *the alien* needs rescuing before she's through!"

Sharko nodded gratefully and charged down the slope, bent on retracing their steps to the place where they'd scattered. Matt followed him, and they soon spotted the two women's tracks. Legs pumping, Sharko and Matt raced off to rescue the tutor and secretary.

<8>

Transformations

S amantha ran hard. While soldiers in hoverboots pursued the others, she got pursued by the hovercraft! Chrysta somehow kept pace with her, the effort seeming to take everything the seamstress possessed. Samantha felt her own heart racing with adrenaline and effort. The alien hovercraft zoomed ahead of them, the pilot turning it hard to starboard and swinging right in front of them. Samantha grabbed Chrysta and yanked her around it.

Again, the pilot raced forward, cutting his engines and swinging around to cut off their escape. Samantha and Chrysta ducked, dashing beneath the vibrating alien machine. A blast of superheated air hit them momentarily before they were out from under it and running pell-mell. Samantha realized in that moment that the pilot wasn't trying to run her down. He intended to stop them in their tracks, likely to capture them. That meant...Vogul wanted them alive! Yet how in the galaxy could they evade a hovership?

Samantha suddenly switched course. Chrysta followed, and the women dashed for the plateau. They avoided the weaving hovercraft a third time, then a fourth. The plateau was so close! Lungs bursting, chests heaving, the women hit the stonier ground ringing the mesa and flew, skidding, into the cave of orbs.

Their breath sounded painfully loud in the dark, echoing space. The prophetess hoped to ambush their enemy in the shadows, and prayed they could. She would do anything to protect Mike's wife.

They heard an engine turn off, and the dull whine of the male's approaching hoverboots. Samantha shoved Chrysta toward the farthest statue, the armadillo, and rolled under the scorpion herself. A light flicked on in the darkness. The alien moved his searchlight around the space, giving an exclamation when it revealed the menacing figure of the scorpion. The light passed right by Samantha, the prophetess holding her breath.

The alien moved beyond. He hadn't seen her, and Samantha waited until he hovered a yard or so past. The alien kept glancing around, but she carefully and quietly crawled out from under the statue anyway. The statue now between her and the alien, and she reached deftly into the sack of crystals. She had taken four of them—Nancy carrying the rest—and she prayed that raising any crystal quickly enough would transform her into someone invulnerable.

Nothing. No blinding flash of light. No change of adornment. Panicking, she fumbled for another of the orbs. The alien was nearing Chrysta's hiding place. He turned off his boots and began walking, crouching down to peer beneath the statues. She knew he would discover Chrysta any moment.

Frantically, the prophetess picked up another orb with the same, maddening result. The alien now noticed something by the armadillo statue. She heard Chrysta shriek, and running footsteps sounded across the rocky floor, joined by the fast clanking of metallic boots. Throwing caution to the wind, Samantha jumped up with the sack of crystals in hand. She slid out from between the scorpion and snake statues. Chrysta almost bumped into her, the alien hot on her heels. Without thinking, Samantha grasped the throat of the sack firmly, twirled it high over her head, and threw her arm out.

The bag seemed to pass through an energy barrier, hitting the running alien squarely in the forehead. He dropped like Samantha's sack of stones. Chrysta skidded to a halt.

"D-did you k-kill him?" she questioned, breathless.

"Maybe," Samantha declared, "but let's not wait to find out! It's back to Base for us."

"What about the others?"

"We can only trust that God is with them!" Samantha picked up the alien's gun. "With our luck, Vogul has been alerted to our presence. We *must* hide our base. I don't know how long they've been here or how they found us, but he's got an entire ship's crew up there! I think we know why God gave us these crystals!"

KAITY COULDN'T REMEMBER being more out of breath. The sand bogged her legs down, and she and Nancy struggled to stay ahead of their pursuer. Sweat drenched them as they dashed pell-mell across the open flatland with no destination in mind. Their steps involuntarily carried them away from the Base, fear clouding their judgment. Before they could run far, the alien overtook them. He struck Kaity across the back with his gun, causing the tutor to trip and fall into the dust. Nancy skidded to a halt, the bag of crystals still in her hand. The alien faced both of them, hovering in place and brandishing his weapon.

"Zezz tae jejin!" the alien growled, motioning with the gun for them to stand together. "You I cap-shur."

Nancy Cooper was completely blown away. Kaity rose to her feet and stood by her friend, quivering slightly with fear.

"You speak...*English*?" Nancy asked, shocked.

"You speak Vojel speak!" the alien replied harshly. "We Trylithian. You I cap-shur!"

"Look, we don't want to resist you." Nancy chose her words carefully. Kaity glanced at her with eyes the size of saucers.

"Like heck we don't!" she whispered hoarsely.

"Trust me!" Nancy replied in a low tone, adding aloud, "Please allow me to set down my bag of...rocks. They're awfully heavy."

The Trylithian motioned tensely with his weapon, in what Nancy assumed must be an acknowledgement. She deftly reached her hand in while she lowered the bag, withdrawing a crystal and letting the sack drop. The Trylithian narrowed his cat-like eyes.

"Vaaht you do?" he demanded, his buzz-like voice threatening.

"Relax." Nancy smiled disarmingly. "This isn't a weapon, I just felt like stretching a bit."

The Trylithian cocked his head to one side as Nancy raised the crystal toward the sky, gulping loudly. She didn't know if any orb would do, but what alternative did they have? A blinding light shot out from her in every direction. Kaity avoided the brunt of the brilliance because she was beside Nancy, but the Trylithian wasn't so lucky. He seemed blinded, and swiftly moved a hand in front of his milky eyes.

Kaity turned to observe her friend as the light of transformation faded. Nancy's very form had changed. Her dark hair and blue eyes remained, but she looked somewhat different, taller, and wore a black-and-white medic's frock. A white weapon rested in her hand, its barrel capped by a clear section tinted in blue.

The Trylithian looked as if he had been hit. He raised his gun and fired at Nancy, but the shot was instantly absorbed by an energy shield. Nancy aimed at him and squeezed the trigger. To Kaity's utter bafflement, a ray of blue shot forth, hitting the alien and having no effect. The Trylithian appeared too panicked to care. His blue face paled, his hands shook, and he turned tail and fled. Wordlessly, Nancy pursued, and the hunter became the hunted.

"Wait up!" Kaity cried, dashing after. "Why can't we just let him go?"

"I must stop him!" Nancy said, but her voice wasn't quite Nancy's. It sounded deeper, more authoritative. "I simply wish I could figure this gun!"

Her fingers fumbled with a number of buttons on the weapon's body. The tip of the barrel suddenly turned red, and Nancy took aim at a run and fired. Her shot was surprisingly accurate and singed the Trylithian's boots. The alien cursed.

"Are you...all right in that thing, Nance?" Kaity questioned.

"I feel more alive than ever!" The secretary glanced back at her friend. "Why call me Nance? My name is Apotheka."

"Apothi—what?" Kaity asked, panting heavily. She slowed down, her strength to run utterly spent.

With her friend out of the race, Nancy put on an extra burst of speed. Kaity watched in awe as the secretary gained on the hovering Trylithian. The male glanced back in amazement to see a human woman outpacing his technology. Then Nancy leaped, tackling the alien to the ground. They fell together, but the Trylithian's rocket boots sent them twirling across the sand. First Nancy, then the alien, scraped against the ground, screaming along and creating a furrow where their bodies connected with the sand. The alien pressed a button on his metallic belt, turning the boots suddenly off. He plowed face-first into the ground, flipping over and over as Nancy let go.

Nancy herself skidded, but leaped quickly to her feet, unharmed. The shield had protected her the entire time. Kaity reached the scene to find Nancy flicking her gun to its blue setting. She held it over the alien's battered body.

"Are you going to kill him?" Kaity questioned, between gulps of air.

"I'm healing him," Nancy explained quickly. She looked her friend in the eyes. "I-I don't know how. One setting takes life, the other restores it. I feel as if I've always known that, yet it's entirely new information."

Her face shone with sincerity. She looked as baffled as Kaity, but not unsettled. The gun indeed was healing the Trylithian, and Kaity gazed on as the blue flesh began to knit and heal. The green flow of blood stopped, and the Trylithian opened his eyes weakly. They widened in fear once he saw who knelt over him.

"Stay still!" Nancy urged, holding him down easily with a gloved hand. "We won't hurt you! We simply want to know—how did Vogul find us? How many more of you are there?"

The alien did not reply. He merely clicked another button on his belt, and Nancy stood up in horror as his eyes started to cloud over. His body convulsed several moments, and he exhaled painfully and lay still.

"Did he just...kill himself?" Kaity asked disbelievingly, as Nancy scanned him. The sight of his passing disturbed her.

"I'm afraid so," Nancy said, hanging her head, "and you know what this means. If Vogul's minions will go to these lengths at the command of their master, how much farther will Vogul go to pursue us?"

The women dug away at the side of a dune and buried the dead Trylithian unceremoniously. Neither of them said a word as they headed back to the plateau. To their relief, four figures appeared in the distance. Sharko raced toward his wife, almost tackling her in a hug. Chrysta breathed a loud sigh of relief to see Kaity unharmed, and gaped at Nancy's appearance.

The Earthlings headed back to Base. Nancy kept an eye—and weapon—out for more alien foes. None approached, however, and they reached the base unharmed but not unshaken. All of them had survived, but they counted themselves lucky. Vogul's crew was doubtless out there combing the sands, so fortifying their base became everyone's foremost preoccupation. Samantha grabbed pencils and paper, and even Dudeman pitched in with the brainstorming.

They were all so busy making plans that no one noticed Mike Taylor. No one observed the college student limp into the room, feverish and pale. Taking two shaky steps forward, he collapsed on the floor of the Commons in the midst of their flurry of activity.

"MIKE! MY DEAREST! MY darling! Don't leave me!"

Chrysta's voice floated faintly from far away. The world ran together in a feverish blur. Mike Taylor shivered as if cold, yet his temperature registered at 103. His breaths came rapidly, and the only face he knew was Chrysta's. Earth, the crash, Vogul—all fled from his disoriented mind. His wound stank, foul from seepage.

"He may be going into septic shock!" Nancy's voice said, through a haze. "It's now or never!"

Mike saw the fuzzy silhouette of a woman in a white frock. She lowered a gun barrel directly at his infected chest, squeezing the trigger. Her eyes seemed full of compassion, and in that moment, Mike's brain burst into startling clarity. *This is it*, Lord, Mike thought. *They're putting me down. I can understand. Chrysta will be better for not having to watch me die slowly. It's ironic, really. I accomplished so little in life. I wanted to be a baseball player. I never completed it. I started college. I never finished. I wanted to be a father. I...*

Mike stiffened suddenly, gasping in pain. He felt as though a knife was being thrust into his chest cavity. The burning, the agony, ripped through his very being. He wondered if the sheer pain would slay him, until—bliss. The coolest, most refreshing feeling settled over his tormented body. His fever dissipated. The rotting flesh renewed. The gaping injury knit, his heart beats slowed, and in moments, Mike was sleeping as soundly as a newborn baby.

Chrysta stood by, clinging grimly to Samantha's arm during the entire process. While her husband thrashed in fever, she sobbed. When he cried out in agony, she almost fainted. Yet when he settled down, and she saw the pain and decay flowing out of him, a smile of deepest joy took captive her face. She was beaming and crying in one breath, and hugging Apotheka so hard that the secretary hurt.

Kaity Anderson watched the entire scene from a distance—Sharko next to her. Though unable to feel the pain herself, she could imagine what Chrysta was experiencing. *How stupid I am, to cling to the past instead of my husband,* Kaity thought, taking Sharko's hand as he finished praying for Mike. Husband and wife looked over to see the college student falling peacefully asleep. The wound in his chest looked clean and mended, and Samantha left Chrysta's side and walked by them. Kaity reached out and caught her arm.

"One thing I don't understand," she said. "Why did it have to hurt so much before he got better?"

"Sometimes, one can only be made clean through pain," Samantha answered meaningfully. "Sometimes, healing carries a cost. But if we endure, the bliss we experience afterwards far outweighs it."

"It is a taste of Heaven," Apotheka added. "This life is our moment of pain, but the Lord *will* follow it with the bliss of Eternal Life."

"Your 'merciful' God is sure giving us an awfully long 'moment,'" Dudeman put in scathingly.

"Shut your trap!" Matt snapped. "God just saved Mike's life and protected us from Vogul's men!"

"Nancy and Matt are right." Samantha's tone was far gentler than her cousin's, but she cast Dudeman a withering glance. "Better words were never spoken. I knew God would meet our needs, and He has proven His faithfulness! Think! If He hadn't granted me that vision, we wouldn't have retrieved these orbs. Mike would've died...but God had others plans."

Apotheka removed the crystal from her medic's gun. Raising the translucent orb high, she disappeared in a flash of brilliant light, to be re-transformed into the simple, dark-haired secretary from Earth. Chrysta merely sank to her knees and leaned over her husband, her gratitude pouring out silently in exhausted tears.

A MIXTURE OF INTEREST and anger crossed Willum Vogul's face. He listened to the report from his Trylithian captain in charge of search parties, noticing how the man quivered before him with nerves. As well he should. His news of a missing patrol strangely delighted the human, however. Vogul rubbed his hands together with glee and, smacking a flattened hand on the tabletop in his study, he declared; "Finally!"

"Finally *what*, my master?" the Trylithian asked, somewhat fearful.

"We are getting close, as I suspected!"

"Do you think they are prisoners of the humans?" the Trylithian ventured.

"Who can say? But the survivors *must* be involved, which means they are near! You will find out what happened to that patrol, captain! The moment you have news, send me a com from the surface."

"Yes, my master," the Trylithian said, with false enthusiasm. He departed quickly from Vogul's room, leaving the madman from Earth to stroke his chin and mutter happily to himself. Vogul rose from his chair and paced his quarters in the *Draxalis*. His bedroom and study were quite exotic, comprising two rooms housed under the curving front of the gunship's bridge. Two small windows boasted a view down the craft's long barrel, while the thick outer wall curved slightly and a staircase descending from the bridge to the study gave Vogul easy access between spaces.

Dull brown walls and gray flooring clashed with the wild patterns of Trylithia. Vogul regarded it as sterility mixed with vibrancy—a juxtaposition of the utilitarian Myd builders with the colorful Trylithian occupiers. A tapestry of mind-bending patterns hung opposite his study window, while a door to the left provided entrance into his bedroom. Two rugs made of a black-furred, alien beast rested on the cold floor, nearly touching the twisting supports of his study table. This was abutted by two chairs made of a single piece of alien wood, carved on the back with dizzying designs.

Vogul paused in front of his bedroom window and gazed out. He pondered the *Draxalis*—its length, girth, and power. If only the plasma tanks didn't take so blasted long to replenish! Plasma needed matter and heat, and though they possessed matter rechargers, it was a very slow process. Their reload time sat at two months, and only half that time had elapsed. Vogul grinned. With confirmation of their general vicinity, he wouldn't need plasma to destroy the Earthlings now.

They were drawing closer to capturing them! Wild beasts alone couldn't make armed and shielded men disappear, and Dalar 3 was known for being uninhabited. What they'd found of the shuttle wreckage, the disappearance of the search crew—excitement welled up inside of Vogul.

His entire life's work had been bound up in this solitary pursuit. Justice. Vengeance! Vogul remembered becoming lost in the fathomless expanse of space as a young man. He'd been an astronaut several decades after the Space Race, attempting the first manned flight to Mars with a team of six. A wormhole pulled their craft in, ejecting it after much turmoil into a solar system without recognizable constellations. Hurling it here, within sight of this very planet. After determining the desert world held no surface water, Vogul and his colleagues voyaged months before finding a life-giving planet. Yet to their absolute amazement, a party of alien ships greeted them. Amazement gave way to horror as the spacecraft opened fire. All the others were killed, but Willum Vogul survived. Burns from a console fire during the attack disfigured him, and the blue-skinned marauders, despite all hostile intent, must have pitied him.

That was how he discovered Trylithia. Or rather, how Trylithia discovered *him*. His injuries healed by technology beyond comprehension. His mind opened to accept that Earth wasn't alone. Learning the language of the Trylithians and meeting the tormac of the powerful colmit, Lidexid. Vogul recalled each sequence of memory with nostalgic pride. He'd become a celebrated curiosity, a welcomed "alien," a worshipped celebrity! Overwhelmed with so much discovery and popularity, Vogul had departed from Trylithia on a mission: to spread word of this alien planet and turn skeptics into believers. Finding the wormhole by Dalar 3, he had journeyed many thousands of lightyears back to his home galaxy, buoyed by cheerful naivety.

Earth refused to take his good news seriously. Even his proof was regarded as forgery. His own family disowned him, and he could still recall the feelings of galling shame as an interviewer discredited him on live TV.

He should have been hailed as a hero! His name should have been written in every history book alongside that of Neil Armstrong! But no, that hadn't been good enough for the puny-minded people of Earth! Vogul instead was ostracized, hospitalized, and branded as insane. The only way he'd procured a shuttle to leave Earth was through the pity of his father, whose emotional distance even then surpassed any physical separation that space could put between them.

Vogul snarled and kicked the small table over. *These* memories made him angry, and anger moved him to action. Why did he sit like a cowardly tormac and wait aboard ship for news? The net was closing around the survivors! He should be there to finally end the last of his pathetic, small-minded race! Besides, he knew more about them than they could ever know about him.

A face-to-face confrontation was the way to conduct it, and Vogul longed to meet one individual in particular. The prophetess named Samantha intrigued him. He gazed at the shadows on the far side of the room, noticing them move slightly as if in confirmation. Yes, he would be very interested to make the acquaintance of one who spoke with God. For when he did, he would introduce the prophetess to *them*...

MIKE TAYLOR'S INJURY healed rapidly from Nancy's care. The evening after the Trylithians' attack, she gave his injury site another dose of healing rays—to good effect. Kaity watched her administer the aid, still awed to see her friend transformed into Apotheka. Mike's flesh knitted at a faster rate, and the wound remained remarkably sterile. In addition, his bruised knee bone had healed enough that he could walk a little, so he began helping with odd jobs around the base. Finding himself useful instead of useless, he at last seemed content. Chrysta was also sweeter and kinder toward him than she'd ever been before.

Nothing could heal the group's supply situation, however. Samantha gathered them in the Commons to report that their water would run out in two weeks. Kaity couldn't stifle a shudder. The men volunteered to double their search efforts, with Mike vowing to join them once he recovered sufficiently.

The survivors sat down for dinner, their discussion turning to the orbs. Samantha, Nancy, and Mike were eager to use them, yet Dudeman and Matt voiced uncertainties. Chrysta and Sharko seemed undecided, and Kaity confessed to feeling unsure. The tutor retired to the kitchen afterward to do dishes. She scrubbed the face of a dish that refused to give up its stubborn stain, growing increasingly frustrated as she tried using minimal water. Sharko walked into the sideways kitchen as she slammed the plastic plate down.

Why did the entire world seem turned against them? First losing everything, then running out of supplies, then being hunted by Vogul's crew...

"I hate this kitchen!" Kaity exclaimed. "I hate this stupid ship and our hopeless water search and...and I absolutely love you!"

Kaity rushed to her husband and embraced him tightly. Sharko laughed at her sudden switch in mood, returning the hug before smiling down at her.

"I think I might have a solution to our water problem," he said mysteriously.

Kaity cocked her head to one side.

"What might that be?"

Sharko merely led her out of the kitchen in answer, down the hall—or was it up?—to the Commons. Samantha still sat there, reclining at the table. Sharko requested that she bring out the bags in which the crystals rested.

"No offense to your leadership," he said kindly, "but maybe God gave us these orbs for more than self-defense."

"I'm glad you believe my vision," Samantha replied, and happily fetched the two sacks. "Everyone else—especially Dudeman—seems hesitant to even touch these gemstones. In spite of the recent attack! What is your plan?"

"When James transformed, it was into a fire form," Sharko explained. "My thought was that maybe the crystals follow common elements. If Nancy's is a healing form, and Dudeman's is a fire form, then..."

"...one could be a water form!" Samantha exclaimed. "That's brilliant! I feel a fool for not thinking of it myself."

"Sharko often has good ideas," Kaity said, clearly proud of her husband.

Samantha decided to broach the plan to the others the following morning. However, when Kaity and Sharko walked into the Commons for breakfast, Samantha met them with a rueful look.

"Matt and James left at dawn to look for water." She did a face-palm. "I guess those military men and Eagle Scouts are a bit too efficient!"

"That means we can't try the orbs together until tonight." Sharko rubbed his chin thoughtfully. "Unless we want to do it separately?"

"If Matt returns to discover there's a water Form, and his trip today was in vain..." Samantha trailed off. "'Grumpy' won't do his mood justice! I say we wait for them, but put another plan into action that's just as important. We desperately need to fortify and conceal our base!"

"Because of Vogul!" Sharko snapped his fingers, and Kaity felt a chill run up her spine.

"Matt and I discussed plans to hide it," Samantha began. "Really, it's God's mercy we're mostly buried. We could cover the broken storage bay with a tarp, and pile sand over it, and..."

Kaity found herself zoning out as the prophetess rattled on, her engineer side clearly showing. While they discussed various measures, her mind wandered to their encounter with the aliens. She recalled their first sighting, in the barrel of Vogul's gunship. The desert seemed suddenly unsafe. She couldn't help fretting for the two men out there in the open, right now, looking for a vital resource. Suppose the aliens found and killed them? They could be missing for weeks! Regardless of all they'd been through, their situation had hardly improved, and Kaity found herself questioning why God had brought them to Sahara. Her earlier outburst reflected a greater sense of misery. She prayed the orbs would truly provide answers. The galaxy seemed out to get them, and hope was running as dry as their dwindling supply of water.

DUDEMAN AND MATT RETURNED at night, exhausted. It had been a miserable day, hotter than usual and with a scorching wind. They relayed news which had become maddeningly typical: no signs of water. To their surprise, this didn't faze either Samantha or Sharko.

"Um, do you two have something up your short sleeves?" Matt inquired.

"Maybe," came Sharko's mischievous reply.

"Friends and fellow Earthlings," Samantha said loudly, "it has been Sharko's observation that our crisis could be solved with these crystals. Since we know very little about them, I propose we all try our hand at the orbs and see if more of us can transform—and into what. After all, there are *eight* of them and eight of us."

"I'm game!" Kaity cried out, and they spread the crystals across the Commons tabletop. Dudeman flatly refused to participate, slinking off to his room and muttering warnings if anyone tried forcing him.

Nancy didn't need to test out a crystal. Samantha removed the orange and clear orbs from the bags, since their forms were known. For the rest of the humans, a game of trial and error ensued. Kaity eagerly picked the blue crystal, then the green, without success. Some approached the orbs fearfully, while others, like Sharko, grabbed for them with gusto.

To Kaity's amazement, Sharko's first choice resulted in instant transformation. He took the blue crystal from his wife, and the form of the tall, brown-haired truck driver was replaced with a man in a spacesuit of sorts. Spears of flame ran down the sides. Sharko's helmet featured a dark visor in front, with yellow fire down the top and back of the headgear. Blue, yellow, and orange were the dominant colors, and a sword with a hot, bright spear of flame materialized in one hand. A gun, similar in model to Nancy's, rested in the other.

"I mean, *I* knew you were hot, Derek, but seriously!" Kaity joked. Laughter erupted from the others.

"My name is Blaze!" Sharko corrected, and then grew perplexed. "How did I know that?"

"There are many things we still don't understand," Samantha reminded. Her own hand gravitated toward a red gem. "I can't explain it, but I have a theory. Wait..."

She made a signal for everyone else to watch, then raised the red crystal high. Light overtook her form. Samantha's arm dropped, and it seemed her entire body rose a foot off the ground. The brilliance faded, their eyes recovered, and Kaity and the others beheld Samantha the Transformed. The prophetess' outfit was part armor, part spacesuit, and part dress. The predominant color—red—matched her sundress, and she wore a helmet with a gray visor. Her hands grasped two alien pistols with long, slender barrels, and she appeared even more confident than usual.

"I am Crosshair," Samantha said, in a voice filled with wonder. "I am accuracy and discernment. I feel as if I've existed before my birth date, and yet—I am also Samantha."

"Crosshair? That was the name of the person who brought this crystal!" Kaity noted. "Remember the stories on the wall?"

Gazing around at the others, it struck Kaity that these new forms were glorified versions of themselves. She could see Nancy in Apotheka's face, and yet...something more. It was as though imperfections had been lost, refined away, and left with a wholeness so beautiful it pierced her heart. Kaity yearned to join them. She longed to taste and see what this level of existence meant.

Reaching a trembling hand out for the purple orb, Kaity stretched her arm skyward and closed her eyes. A feeling of intense light burst all around her. She floated in warmth and security, as if entering a sun that did not burn, a flame that healed instead of harming. As abruptly as it came, the sensation drained away. She came out of it knowing she had on different clothes, and feeling that her body was in better shape than ever.

"My Darling, you look like a medieval princess!" Sharko, or Blaze, exclaimed. Kaity clasped hands with her husband and saw that her sleeves fell open in a bell shape. Purple gloves covered her hands, a sword hung in a scabbard from a belt, and a shield was slung across her back. Kaity danced, feeling the swish of a perfectly comfortable skirt against leggings. She felt her head, and was delighted to discover a crown studded with gems. The purple jewel glinted from its place at the crown's center. More than her appearance, however, Kaity *felt* different. She possessed more courage, and knew that her name followed accordingly. She was Valora—valor itself.

"What shall we call ourselves?" Samantha asked, her voice still full of amazement.

"Starganauts!" Kaity exclaimed, letting Sharko twirl her around. "Your cousin brought along *Jason and the Argonauts*. Since it's a story about a group that goes on a quest, I guess my mind just took it from there!"

"Starganauts. I like it!" Matt exclaimed, and the name met with unanimous approval. At least, seven of the eight agreed to the term, for James Erskin remained shut-away in his room.

One by one, everyone present found their crystal. Mike's was the white orb, which transformed him into Ninjarak. A muscular man clothed in white, he carried a long, solid, metal bo staff for a weapon. Chrysta, with the green gem, turned into a woman in a tight-fitting but modest, one-piece suit. Metallic green stripes ran down the sides of the suit as well as the helmet, and she declared herself as Vipress. A gun and a hooked, poisonous knife confirmed her name of choice.

Kaity noticed that each "form," as Samantha dubbed them, incorporated the orb into its design. Whether in a piece of armor or weaponry, every orb was inset into a form's gear to simplify keeping track of it—and make it easy to transform back.

Matt was the last of the company to transform. Doubtful of the crystals as ever, only the transformation of the entire group convinced him that the "strange alien tech" wouldn't prove harmful. He picked up the last crystal remaining: the yellow one.

"I've followed you longest, *Prima*." Matt shot Samantha a wry look. "I can't say I haven't doubted you, but who am I to be the only one refusing to try this? Heck, if it helps us find water, I'm in!"

With that thought, Matthew Sanchez shoved his hand into the air and the let the light consume him. All of the others had shut their eyes when they transformed, but Matt's remained open. They glowed more brilliantly than the sun.

"Can you see it?" he exclaimed in amazement.

"See *what*?" Samantha questioned.

"All the colors, the brilliance!"

The light around Matt faded. Standing before them, regal and proud, was a warrior clad in silver and bronze. Strange tracery adorned his garb, and in both hands he held two long, thin, pole-like swords. Live lightning crackled around them. The bolts appeared suspended in mid-strike, sparking and moving but never threatening to leap from the confines of the foils.

"It is lightning I carry," Matt said majestically, "so I shall claim it as my namesake. I am Thunderbane!" He crossed the lightning swords in front of himself.

The humans glanced around the Commons at each other, filled with wonder to see themselves as Starganauts. Sharko sensed a burden of responsibility he could not explain. Samantha felt an uncharacteristic levity of soul. Kaity, as Valora, could only clap her hands together in delight and continue letting Blaze twirl her around.

She knew this day was momentous. These transformations would change their futures forever. Though they hadn't found an aqua form, they at least possessed a defense against the hostile agents of Vogul. Kaity felt her faith rewarded, even as Valora encouraged her to thank God for this turn of events. The Lord had proven faithful. He'd given them a way to survive and thrive...in an alien desert on a distant world. Truly he'd sent Samantha's vision to aid them, and Kaity felt excited to see where these forms might take them.

<9>

Confrontation

Two powerful legs churned up a trail of dust. A figure crested the undulating dunes beneath the clear morning air, not pausing once for rest or catching his breath. Sharko, in the Form of Blaze, sped along at an inhuman pace. Racing faster than most athletes on Earth, Blaze crossed large amounts of sand with ease. It felt amazing being in Starganaut form. Running seemed exhilarating instead of tiring. Breaths came steadily, and not until the middle of the day did Sharko's legs begin to burn. Yet even their burning was a good pain, not a harsh one. Sharko hoped their glorified bodies would enable them to cover greater distances and thus find water farther out.

Chrysta went north, the others went east and west, but Sharko headed south. Mike had stayed at the base to allow his body to heal fully, while Dudeman simply refused to help. In spite of the groups' experience the previous night, he would not even go near the orbs.

Kaity and Samantha had watched Sharko, Matt, Nancy, and Chrysta depart early that morning in Form. The prophetess had instructed them to take a direction and run, and Kaity marveled to watch their superhuman speed. While her husband churned up sand, Samantha sidled over to her. The prophetess' face shone with wonder, her brown eyes following Blaze's disappearing form.

"'The Lord is the everlasting God,'" she said mightily, as Sharko's boots carried him effortlessly. "'He gives strength to the weary and increases the power of the weak...those who hope in the Lord will renew their strength. They will soar on wings like eagles; they will run and not grow weary, they will walk and not be faint.'"

"That is the best analogy I can draw for these forms." The prophetess turned toward Kaity. "The Bible speaks of us having glorified bodies one day.

Although we carry the wounds of this world into the transformation, I cannot help but wonder if these altered bodies are a shadow of that promised form."

"Whatever they are, they've given us hope in the face of despair," Kaity said quietly. "Surely these are gifts from God."

"Now we know why He brought us to Sahara. The question only remains: will these forms also help us survive against Vogul?"

Sharko Anderson wondered the same as he glided over the barren desert landscape. Although not outspoken about his faith, the truck driver from Earth had been a Christian since his parents' deaths. Losing them at 17 had plunged him into a dark depression, but a pastor took the young, saddened teen under his wing. He'd helped him through his grief, and Sharko gave his life to Christ a few months later. Part of him had converted for the chance to see his parents again, as both were believers. The other part acknowledged a deep hole in his heart. Though he had grown up a moral person, Sharko came to understand that true faith meant a relationship with Jesus, not merely keeping rules.

He reflected on all that God had done in his life since that day. The Lord had taken a selfish young man and given him compassion. He had molded him from immaturity to wisdom. He'd thrust a hesitant follower into the leadership role of his family and, Sharko reflected ironically, He still had shaping to do in *that* department.

All throughout the day, Blaze ran, keeping an eye out for signs of water. He also cast a wary glance at the horizon for alien hovercraft, yet none crossed his path. Feeling exhilarated but exhausted, he turned back toward the base as the burning sun began its slow arc toward the horizon. Water might have eluded him today. Still, Blaze felt confident that God would provide it. With the ability to look farther and longer, it would only be a matter of time...and faith.

THREE DAYS PASSED WHILE the Starganauts hunted for water. Despite the advantages of Form, the life-saving substance eluded them. Not even severe rationing halted the steady drain of their supply. A general aura of quiet panic pervaded the air, for it felt like their sinking reserves mirrored the sinking feeling in their hearts.

Sharko Anderson understood the seriousness of their situation. Worry flooded him where faith had recently been; foremost for his young bride, then for himself and the group. He could tell to what degree it impacted each of them. Chrysta seemed to share little of the groups' fears, tangled up in her own struggles. Nancy, Dudeman, and Matt appeared anxious, while he could sense Samantha's concern mirrored his own. Mike was unreadable, and as for his wife?

Kaity couldn't fully comprehend what it would mean to run out of water. Sharko knew. His bride wasn't the most aware of harsh realities. Living a sheltered life before this, Kaity did not understand loss as deeply as Sharko. She tended toward optimistic naivety, often failing to see the bigger problem looming on the horizon, if temporary frustrations were alleviated.

Sharko tried to accept this, but one evening, he found himself thoroughly sick of it. Tempers flared into a heated argument. Words began flying through the air like arrows, and Sharko Anderson spent his first night sleeping in the Commons. Out of compassion, Dudeman talked to his best friend until Sharko fell asleep. The quarrel proved short-lived, however, so Sharko awoke only one morning shaking the sand out of his ears.

Samantha, meanwhile, worked with Mike and Dudeman to secure their base. As Ninjarak, Mike had healed enough to walk great distances. He accompanied the prophetess and Dudeman to the ship graveyard Kaity had encountered, where they gathered scrap metal and any useful materials not ravaged by sand and time. The prophetess discovered several alien skeletons, marveling at the extraterrestrial cadavers. One resembled their blue-skinned pursuers, while most stretched taller, with odd torsos and long, egg-shaped heads. Even though they excited Samantha's scientific fascination, she felt slightly unnerved around them.

"There's more than one type of alien here," she commented to Ninjarak, while he and James stripped some wires. "In this galaxy of wonders and terrors, we are far from alone."

The trio headed back to base with their haul. Matt used the metal to fashion a door to the Commons. Welding pieces together with Thunderbane's foils and Blaze's torchsword, he managed to improvise a door that mostly shut the desert out. The survivors also salvaged metal posts. From the posts, they stretched out *The Deliverer's* white landing chute like a tarpaulin, covering the cave-like opening where the storage bay had separated from the shuttle. Mike drove the posts deep into the dune, Chrysta and Kaity showering sand from its crest onto the tarp to conceal it. The result yielded a base camp hidden from prying eyes, with a door in case the survivors got unexpected company.

Samantha rested easier that night. She awoke feeling some measure of peace and with her mind on her next task: the orbs. They both thrilled her and struck her with awe. Surely God's purposes involved the crystals!

The survivors kept them in a sack in the storage closet near the kitchen. The prophetess tiptoed over and gingerly lifted them out of their resting place inside an open, metal box. She spread them on the Commons table, careful to keep them atop the cloth sack so they wouldn't roll. Each orb radiated soft light—an unspeakable power contained. Where had that thought come from? Samantha longed to learn more of these orbs, yet lacked the proper facilities. If only! On Earth, they could've studied them at MIT. She revolved the green one in her sunburnt fingers.

"What secrets do you hold?" she wondered, hair falling in front of her face. "Do you activate a kind of sophisticated tech? Or does a touch of the miraculous flare within your semi-transparent depths?"

She grasped the crystal between her fingers, driven by a sudden urge to test its mettle. She slammed it against the smooth, dusty tabletop, jarring and hurting her fingers. She held it up. Nothing. The orb appeared wholly unaffected, but there was a noticeable dent on the table. Startled, Samantha rose. Perhaps the orbs were indestructible, yet what of their Forms? They knew so little about them, so she resolved to put them to the test...with her fellow survivors' cooperation.

———————✦✦———————

THE STARGANAUTS ROTATED shifts in their quest for water. Only four went out at once, meaning each person got a break every fifth day. Samantha used this to her advantage, and Apotheka became her first test subject. The prophetess grabbed a pen and notepad, asking the healer to perform various tasks and jotting down the results. Despite being so far from Earth, Samantha's experiments felt like a slice of home. They discovered that Apotheka could control the intensity of her gun's healing and killing modes, and that the medical crest in the middle of her belt activated her energy shield.

Thunderbane was fun to work with. Apart from a flurry of puns and jokes, he showed his cousin what the lightning foils could do. Flicking them on with the touch of a button, he hacked at pieces of scrap metal and even charged the foils to emit a focused pulse. Samantha theorized this would devastate electronic devices, and wished they had a spare one to investigate her hypothesis. She transformed into Crosshair to test his armor and her pistols. His heavy plates resisted damage from her searing plasma bolts. As for the pistols, Crosshair could fire one, precise shot at a time or several shots in a rapid burst. Her visor's reticule also allowed her to zoom, increasing accuracy.

Samantha moved on to Ninjarak and Vipress. Chrysta's green suit was part armor, part mesh-like metal. Her toxin gun shot a poisonous, acidic goop with a similar range and coverage as Fyromaniac's flamethrower, and her knife dripped deadly poison. Vipress tested it on a snake that wandered into the storage bay. The creature died an agonizing death in a matter of minutes and Chrysta recoiled, distressed by the snake's suffering.

"I'm not sure I like this," she said, transforming out of Form. That was the last Samantha got out of her for a while. Ninjarak proved more helpful. Aside from his bo staff, the white ninja's special ability was a stealth mode built into his suit. Activating it made his footfalls as light as a cat's, and his suit changed color to blend with the surroundings. It wasn't full camouflage, but against the dune or in a dark hallway, Samantha struggled to see him.

She wrote down Blaze's two weapons: a sword of flame and a plasma carbine. His "torchsword," as they dubbed it, had features of a welding torch mixed with a longsword. Two thin, hot flames shot out of small nozzles near the tip and crossguard of the sword. These nozzles were aimed directly at each other so that the flames made a continuous "blade" of fire in the front. Consequently, the weapon could be used as a literal torch to cut through metal plating. Blaze's carbine proved equally deadly. It shot rounds of plasma like a rifle, and came with a special sniping mode.

After recording information on Blaze, the prophetess summoned Valora. Samantha directed her to attack a rock near their base to gauge the hardiness of her sword and shield. Both ended up damaging the rock more than *being* damaged. The knight Starganaut also stumbled across a button on her gauntlet, which raised an interlinking visor of armor to cover her exposed face. While its spaceworthiness was debatable, the visor contained eyeholes and seemed airtight.

Samantha crossed Valora's name off her list and came to her last test subject. James Erskin. He'd flatly refused to transform a week ago, and couldn't be bribed to don Fyromaniac's Form. Should she even try? A pang of guilt seized her as she realized James hadn't really been on her mind. He was clearly a non-believer, yet the only thing she cared about was using him as a test subject.

Their lives were in peril, and James would be sent to Hell the moment he died. *Just like my...* Samantha cut off the thought. It pained her too much, and wouldn't it be a terrible failure on her part? So few had listened, when she had preached of Earth's coming doom. She *had* to save him, or at least, fail trying. Biting her lip, Samantha trudged in the direction of the storage bay. Studying his Starganaut Form was the least of her problems. He needed Jesus, and she alone could persuade him!

JAMES ERSKIN FELT NOTHING but unrest. As his fellow survivors searched and secured their base, he drifted further into melancholy thoughts...and further away from everyone. Perhaps it was the others' blind faith. Maybe it was their naïve industry or the generally high tensions running through the air. James couldn't put a finger on it. He merely knew that the more time passed, the more convinced he became that God hated them. Death by dehydration increased as a painful possibility.

Every night, when the others returned or rested, Matt or Sharko entered the base to give the same, fruitless report. Dudeman refrained from crashing the party and saying, "I told you so." Instead, he would lean against the tarpaulin covered with sand, watching the fall of night over their wasteland purgatory. He'd found an oddly-shaped trinket in the ship graveyard, and he'd fiddle with it while watching the sun sink into what passed for west.

Behind him loomed the dune; gray and ominous. James paid it no heed. Tonight, his mind hovered over a solitary question. Why had fate led him to take a crazy risk, enter a space shuttle, and zoom off into the stars? It made sense to spare the others from Vogul—they were all Christians—but he was solidly against it.

James Erskin believed that waves could be rough or calm, because he'd seen it. His foster parents had put their faith in the unseen, and it left them blasted to oblivion with the rest of Earth. Atheist, monk, Dalai Lama, imam—all were consumed by Vogul's unquenchable fire. What did it matter in the end? He could put his faith in a potato, for all he cared.

No. That was insulting. Faith in God couldn't be reduced to that level. After all, he'd heard some amazing stories. Christianity had too many martyrs to be so easily dismissed. Maybe that was it. Perhaps God delighted in seeing His followers die. Such devotion must appease him, as blood appeased the gods of old. That would definitely explain how he could let Earth be consumed! Dudeman had spent much of his life just assuming God didn't care, so this posed a new revelation.

God *must* be distant and cruel. He'd saved them from destruction, only to prolong their suffering and kill them in the desert. Samantha's vision was a sham, and they'd all die. If that lunatic who incinerated Earth didn't find them first.

SAMANTHA WATCHED DUDEMAN from her post by the storage bay's mouth. She'd observed him several times, walking outside and engaging in mental debates with himself. She could tell by how he fiddled with the trinket. Sometimes he threw it down. Sometimes he sulked back into *The Deliverer*. Ultimately, his problem was a spiritual one, and Samantha was going to deal with it. Dudeman avoided talks about faith like the plague, but she would change that. She took a few steps forward, yet halted.

Hesitation took over. Should she pray first? Was this God's leading, or her own? That was ridiculous. Of course God wanted her to save this unbelieving man! Samantha brushed aside the gnawing feelings of warning and strode forward. She knew exactly what she'd say. She would win Dudeman Erskin to Christ.

"You think God is uninvolved, like your biological parents."

Dudeman nearly jumped. He hadn't heard Samantha's approach, nor seen her coming across the reddened sands. Had she known his thoughts? *It's a coincidence*, Dudeman reasoned.

"Comin' to visit the enemy, man?" he questioned aloud.

"I'm hardly a man." Samantha put a hand on her hip. "And it's no coincidence. God told me to visit you out here, because of the battle that rages in your heart. How long will you fight it, James?"

"You're joking!" Dudeman snorted. "I don't have a clue what you mean."

"You feel God's tug at your heart. You can't dismiss Christianity as easily as you'd like. *I* would know."

"Ahem! *You?*" Dudeman almost coughed with laughter. "Okay, where are the cameras?"

"I'm serious! You're an unbeliever raised by Christian parents. I'm a believer, but I was raised by nonbelieving parents. A lot of our group thinks I barely mourn for them. I can assure you, I grieve deepest of all. Why? Because I *know* they went to Hell, and there was nothing I could do about it."

Dudeman felt surprised to hear such emotion in Samantha's normally-strong voice.

"I chose faith in Christ, and I lost my relationship with them." Her face dimmed with sorrow. "One was an atheist. The other was into New-Ageism. When I learned of Earth's destruction, I contacted them. I tried to tell them, warn them, plead with them! They just hung up the phone. James," Samantha's voice dropped to an earnest whisper, "don't hang up the phone on God. He is calling you to Himself. Don't you see it?"

For the entirety of her disclosure, "Dudeman" Erskin stayed silent. He merely stood for a while, digesting—Samantha hoped—her words. The sun sank out of view. As night fell over this part of Sahara, so a new day dawned in distant regions. The dunes had been steadily turning red, but now the colors flared brilliantly. The orange orb of day dropped out of sight, and everything faded to gray.

"I understand now, why you came out here," Dudeman said at last, turning slowly to face Samantha. "You feel guilty. This isn't about concern for my soul, Preacher woman. This has to do with you wanting to assuage that guilt by making a convert. Well, have fun! I'm not about to be won over by emotion or obligation!"

"You're mistaken." Samantha kept her cool despite his rudeness. "I only wish that you could know the joy, the security, the peace of being saved by God's son and knowing Heaven awaits you!"

"Explain me this, Prophetess!" His tone dropped to a snarl. "How can a God who 'loves' and 'saves' us let us die from lack of water? Where's the kindness in that? Your God sends people like your parents to Hell, and you know what? I don't give a crap about your feelings or your self-righteous bull!"

Samantha felt as if she'd been slapped in the face. Dudeman could see it on her features. He almost felt sorry, but pushed it aside. She was pestering him yet again! Why couldn't people stay out of his business? He expected a biting reply. Samantha was certainly adept at verbal sparring. Instead, her shoulders drooped in sadness.

"You know not what you refuse," the prophetess said simply. She walked away, leaving Dudeman alone on the desert hillside with nothing but the wind and his anger. *Good*! He told himself. *Maybe she'll leave this topic alone, too*! Yet beneath these words, in his heart of hearts, he felt more turmoil than relief.

ACROSS THE GALAXY, Tormac Durag rushed around in haste, pausing at various consoles in the control hall of his palace to issue commands. The Myds, the dreaded Myds, had descended on Trylithia an hour earlier! Their warships sent Lidexid into a greater chaos than its entire war with the rest of Duskrealm. In the control hall, Durag could hear—and feel—the explosion of nearby bombs. The semi-translucent, curving wooden walls shook, only bolstered by a strong, reinforcing metal frame. Igassa flowers in lanterns illuminated the space with a cheery orange glow that contrasted with Durag's dark mood.

It wasn't right. How could the sun-god Kroth do this to them? Lidexid had been the mightiest, wealthiest nation-state of Trylithia. For centuries, it had conquered its surrounding Duskrealm states, exacting tribute and building a glorious kingdom. Suddenly, leaders had arisen among the subjugated nations. Durag bitterly recalled the chain of catastrophes. His predecessor ruled too harshly, so the people of the surrounding colmits had gathered strength and declared war. Lidexid fell from a glorious nation to a tattered, war-torn country. Lives and land were lost in increasing number as the years dragged on. Now the capital itself lay besieged, but not by domestic invaders. The beleaguered Lidexan fleet could not hold back the fury of the extraterrestrial Myds.

The Myds came from a neighboring planet. More advanced than anyone else in the Gorvan System, it was their gunship which Durag had stolen. Vogul had met with the Myds six months earlier, outside the capital city of Ondoi. Myds were a secretive, xenophobic race, and would not allow any foreigners into their metropolis. Vogul had toured the impressive gunship on the grassy plain by Uudmet Sea. The first ever built, Durag had offered Modoi all the riches of his kingdom for the power of the gunship. The Myds refused the deal, so Durag moved to the next stage—theft. He knew that stealing from them was stinging a sleeping bear, to use one of Vogul's metaphors.

Now the Myds stood poised on his very doorstep. It had taken time, as Durag had covered his tracks well and waited a month before the theft. Yet the Myds managed to find the instigator. Durag would feel the bite of their retribution shortly—unless he could escape! As he issued final orders, he closed out the data consoles and wiped the systems clean of encrypted files. Hovering through the door, two bodyguards of the Skull Warrior Order fell in behind him. The Skull Warriors comprised an elite group of Trylithians with special powers. Durag possessed few after years of war, so he valued every officer.

A long hallway stretched between the fleeing Trylithians and the hangar. The space ran between glowing, white tree trunks, arching to form a frame inset with diamond-patterned panes of clear or purple glass. The company had reached the halfway point when Durag throttled down his hoverboot rockets. He dropped to the floor with metallic clank, and the Skull Warriors followed suit. Durag said nothing. He simply stared. The Skull Warriors followed their leader's gaze to the outside world.

The twilit capital of Lidexid burned. The forms of panicking Trylithians silhouetted against flames, a building of wood and glass crumbling from laser fire, a starship crashing down—each hit the tormac as though he, not Lidexid, suffered from attack. A tear trickled down his impassive-looking face. It wetted the mouth-cloth of his people, and only a hovering sound brought him back to realization. His nephew Jixa sped toward him from the direction of the hangar.

"Uncle! They are about to bombard the palace! *Come!*"

Jixa's urging snapped Durag out of a sorrowed trance. He was Tormac. Upon his shoulders lay the burden of leading a retreat. They would withdraw to the mountain stronghold of Rac Itor. Perhaps the Myds would be satisfied with their present destruction and not pursue. Tormac Durag doubted this, but even denial gave him a thread of hope to cling to.

Durag did not feel safe until his flagship took off. Seated beside his nephew on the bridge, the tormac turned to Jixa. With their escape out of the way, he could focus on a task which he trusted only his advisor and relative to carry out.

"Jixa," Durag began, "since the Myds are after us, I fear for Vogul and the gunship. What if they are detected? Stattar is too close to Modoi, and we cannot risk our enemy finding the *Draxalis* when we need it most. I have a task for you. There is a *Dezaptor* class starship in the hangar bay of this craft. Go and look for Vogul in the vastness of Stattar. I want you to find him before the Myds do."

"I shall do as you ask, Uncle," Jixa said firmly. He unbuckled himself from his seat, but paused. "May I ask what you hope to accomplish at this hour by finding the gunship?"

"There's been a change of strategy," the tormac explained, narrowing his eyes. "We will not be firing upon Dalar 2 and Vexador. Modoi, homeworld of the Myds, has become our new target!"

JAMES ERSKIN SHIELDED his eyes from the glaring sunlight. Sweat trickled down his face and back, while sand blew against the scarf he used to shield his mouth. He stopped at the crest of a dune, Matt as Thunderbane falling in beside him. The sun felt absolutely scorching. Despite sipping water from their mutual canteen, his lips were cracked. He was in an ill-temper, and a frustrated Thunderbane hardly fared better on the attitude scale.

Starganaut forms still unnerved Dudeman. He would not touch the orange orb, but he couldn't help admiring Matt's armor. Thunderbane's Form was built like a tank, with thick, overlapping plate armor, solid metal boots, and broad, two-toned pauldrons. The lightning foils hung through special sheaths on his back, their electric elements powered off.

"Curse this blasted sun!" Dudeman exclaimed, while they trudged over cracked plains. Throughout their time on Sahara, the surfer had noticed the days growing hotter. At first he doubted himself, yet he'd soon realized the correctness of his senses. They appeared to have arrived in spring, and summer threatened to engulf them. It was already hot enough. Although nobody had a thermometer, Dudeman estimated that the day's heat peaked above 100° Fahrenheit. He hoped fervently the temperature wouldn't be climbing much higher.

Heat waves shimmered upward from the sand. The horizon appeared as if it held the promise of silver pools of water—a beguiling deception. A lone cactus cast a shadow beneath the blazing noon sun, and Dudeman halted after the thousandth step. He took a swig from their canteen.

"Why do we even bother?" he asked. "This stuff will just run out. We'll die on this planet, so very far from home. What is life? What is death? Is God merely a construct?"

"Is it time to turn back again?" Thunderbane questioned, raising his eyebrows humorously. "When you wax philosophical, James, you've had a long day..."

"I mean, you all hate me anyway." The surfer didn't hear him.

"You don't exactly make yourself lovable.

"What's that supposed to mean?" James turned on him suddenly, his jaw taut.

"Whoa, chill out! I didn't mean to offend you."

"Exactly! You have a negative opinion of me, too! You *all* do!"

Dudeman prattled on, Thunderbane enduring his existential rants all the way back to their base. They reached the buried *Deliverer* at sunset. Dudeman resumed his usual position to watch the sinking sun, but it offered no pleasure. So what if the ball of gas dropped out of sight and left the world in soothing darkness? Not even the nights were cool any more. If thirst didn't kill them, the burning heat would.

Samantha was wrong. God existed purely as a figure of myth, leaving the world alone except when He came down to torment it. Why then could he not stop thinking about their conversation? Dudeman spent a restless night wrestling to find an answer. Unable to, he awoke the next morning feeling the futility of their task before he arose. At least tomorrow would be Sunday. Dislike their Christianity though he might, he appreciated a day of rest.

"You had an argument with Samantha, didn't you?" Sharko asked the question at breakfast. They were the last two left at the table, and Dudeman treasured what moments he spent with his best friend. Being a newlywed occupied Sharko's time, and he often went out looking for water alone. Dudeman couldn't keep pace with Blaze, and he barely managed when accompanying Matt.

"I don't want to talk about it, man."

James brushed the topic aside as he munched on his muffin. Without milk, cold cereal was a thing of the past, so they'd been eating dried fruit and muffins thawed from the freezer.

"Dudeman, come on!" Sharko gave his friend a pointed look.

"Why does she have to pester me, Dude?" the surfer groaned and sipped some artificial orange juice. "How I miss fresh fruit. I'd even eat broccoli at this point!"

"Don't skirt the question."

"*What* question? You don't bother me with your Christianity, man! Why does she have to go shovin' it down my throat?"

Sharko said nothing for several minutes. He scratched his chin, and Dudeman studied him. Was Sharko at a loss for words?

"You're right," he said slowly, thoughtfully. "I always gave you space. I didn't talk about my faith much, because I didn't want to offend you. But I'll tell you something, James. Maybe *I* was wrong. Maybe Samantha is right."

Dudeman looked as stunned as he felt. Sharko's first words put him at ease, but he soon disliked what he was hearing.

"We're past political correctness," Sharko said, gazing levelly at his friend. "When God strips away the comforts of this life, He often does so to remind us of what truly matters. Such is the case for me, and I've come to realize...I didn't speak about my faith enough. My brothers, relatives, and every friend I had except for you? They're gone."

Sharko's voice sounded deeply regretful, and Dudeman shifted uncomfortably.

"The greatest cruelty isn't in speaking," he continued, "but in saying *nothing* at all. I've been silent far too long. God isn't your biological dad, James. He's not your mother who abandoned you, for reasons we'll never know. He's more perfect than even your foster parents. I know those two are in Heaven, eagerly hoping to see you there. What's holding you back?"

For a moment, Sharko thought Dudeman might be swayed. The surfer's lower lip quivered, betraying an inner battle with his emotions. Finally, he glanced at Sharko, his face like that of a scared animal. Words failed him. He quickly rose, grabbed the bag of dried fruit, and marched to the door of the Commons.

Matt passed by him, seeming surprised by his brusque manner. Dudeman merely grabbed his canteen and empty water cartons and set out. His silence pained Sharko more than words ever could. The trucker realized that his reluctance to alienate a friend had led to silence regarding his faith. For the first time, he recognized the fault of his inaction. He'd been termed a "nice guy," but Sharko Anderson wanted much more. As he mulled over their conversation, an idea suddenly came to him. He might not convince Dudeman, but God wasn't finished with his tasks yet.

Inspired, he rushed off to find Samantha. First he would tell her, and then he'd head out across the dunes. The time for playing it safe was over.

SAMANTHA HARRIS SAT alone in her bedroom. No light was on, no sound could be heard, and she bowed her head as one ashamed. She'd acted on her own volition the other day, instead of obedience to God. Ever since her conversation with Dudeman, Samantha realized her mistake. James now avoided her, looking past her instead of *at* her. She'd let her ego dictate the sharing of her faith, not true compassion. *I blew it*, she thought, bowing her head to pray. Again, her strong will had hurt someone instead of helping them. Dudeman was correct. Her motivation had been converting him, to make herself look good.

Throughout life, Samantha had enjoyed challenges. Making the highest grades and attending the most prestigious university daunted many, but Samantha attacked each path with gusto. She'd become an engineer at a respected firm, landing a salary of six figures by the age of twenty-three. She'd accomplished so much, and been so governed by accomplishment, that she realized the old habits were creeping back. Making Dudeman a Christian was her continual crusade—a feather in her cap, a challenge to be conquered.

The prophetess had let pride crowd out the Holy Spirit's voice. That still, quiet stirring, warning her that the timing wasn't right. Now, James' heart seemed even more closed to the gospel than before. Yet worse than this, it raised a question Samantha tried often to push aside. *Am I leading everyone because it's best for *them**, she asked God, *or because it makes *me* feel good*? Samantha knew her tendency to be in control. She'd been at peace with her role as prophetess and leader since their escape from Earth. At least, until her vision and the words of the Lord's servant.

"There is one trial that faces you soon," the starlit man had said, "and you will have a hard time of it. Remember my advice, Daughter: let go. There is one among you who is destined to become the leader. It is his responsibility to step up, and yours, to step down."

These simple declarations tormented her psyche. After Doomsday, no one had been capable of leading but her. Tough and already prepared for the worst, Samantha alone possessed the strength and vision to lead them. She'd naturally become their leader, but what now? All she could think of to solve the water crisis was searching for a source. *How's that going for you*? Her mind asked mockingly. Suppose she was bungling the entire thing? Suppose God would raise someone else up to supplant her? That angered Samantha. She clenched her fists, but that still, small voice reminded her that telling the Lord how to use her wasn't her job. As a pot had no right telling the potter how to shape it, so she must submit to God's role in shaping her life.

"'Each one should use whatever gift he has received to serve others,'" Samantha recited, "'faithfully administering God's grace in its various forms.' You have given me the task of speaking Your truth, Lord. Just because it's the task of another to serve, or lead, doesn't mean you are displeased with me. I cannot begin to see just how these crystals will impact us. I will admit, though, leadership *and* speaking Your words are two very full-time jobs."

Samantha pondered her tiredness. Leading them was exhilarating, wonderful, and totally wearing her down! She had found herself forgetting to seek the advice of others. That stopped today. Today, she resolved to start the process of letting go, trusting that God would help another to step up and lead. At least, the woman who enjoyed being in charge would try.

A light rap on her doorframe snapped Samantha out of her musings. Sharko Anderson appeared.

"Am I interrupting? Sorry."

"No, you're fine," Samantha stated, straightening. "What's up?"

"I noticed a canyon on one of my trips out. It's too far to reach in a day's travel, but an overnight journey might be sufficient. Of all the places we've searched, it's the most likely location for water to pool. There could be another cave, too."

"Sure," Samantha said. "Why don't you take my cousin or James?"

"They're already gone," Sharko answered, "but I think my Form could hike through the night."

"Alright, but be careful," Samantha cautioned. "It's a good idea, and I'm open to any ideas at this point! We've only got three day's reserves left, Sharko. "

"I'm not surprised." The trucker exuded seriousness. "Well, I'd better be off! I feel like the Holy Spirit gave me this idea, so we shall see!"

"We shall indeed." Samantha saluted him, then turned her thoughts back to the question of leadership. A funny feeling settled in the pit of her stomach. Could God's choice possibly be...?

The timing made her suspicious, yet the timid truck driver usually avoided responsibility. Pushing the thought aside, Samantha tried to relax. They'd come to Sahara as part of God's plan. He wouldn't let them die out here in the wilderness, so she prayed Sharko's intuition would prove their salvation. They didn't have much time—or options—left.

———— ✕✕⎜⎜⎬✕ ————

SWEAT BATHED THE BODIES of the Trylithian searchers. Across the trackless wastes, Vogul's teams carried out their hunt, driven mainly by fear of their crazed leader's wrath. Most of them soldiered on miserably. Wearing kilts, metal chest plates, and boots, their entire bodies were devastated by the harsh climate. Their colmit of Lidexid, in Duskrealm, possessed a cold, dark climate. The high seldom surpassed 60 Earth degrees. Only Dalar 3's coldest night dropped down to this temperature. Harsh, hot, and blinding, the wasteland planet confounded their sensors by appearing as one huge ball of heat.

Vogul adjusted their searching schedule to compensate. The world cooled sufficiently overnight for heat signatures to stand out, so the search parties avoided this hassle—and the burning heat—by combing the planet from midnight until mid-morning. Despite this, the Trylithians suffered greatly. They would hover across the endless sands until they reached the brink of collapse, forcing Vogul to grant them a respite. Their energy shields could ward off weaponry, but nothing except spacesuits could save his soldiers from the heat. Those proved an impracticality, as the wearer would sink too far into the sand. The hovercraft teams fared a little better, yet the wind which whipped across their decks stayed hot.

To his credit, Vogul braved the desert with his men. It was no small feat for a human in his mid-forties, and he grew to hate sweating in the dark. The madman also hailed from a cooler place. Vogul Bay's coastal summers were a good twenty degrees cooler than Dalar 3's spring. At least, that was the season Vogul judged it to be. And temperatures simply kept rising.

Through days of unbearable heat, through harsh winds and over the most desolate of landscapes, they went. Yet day by day, week by week, they drew no closer to the object of their hunt. The sandstorm a month earlier had wiped out the shuttle's crash path. The wreckage of the shuttle's storage bay could offer no clue as to the direction of the crash site. Vogul grew steadily angrier, and would take to walking some distance away, only to rant with himself.

"Why will you not answer me?" he demanded, shaking his fist at the sun. This particular period of searching, he had decided to halt an hour after dawn. They waited in a circle for the dropship to pick them up, and Vogul stood apart from his men as usual.

"You showed me the path to follow!" he declared. "You spoke of my destiny. Answer me!"

Vogul whirled in every direction, as if expecting someone to reply. Snarling in anger, he bent down and beat at the ground, sending dust flying up into his own airways. Choking, Vogul spat the sand out of his mouth bitterly. He marched back to the ring of Trylithians, all murmuring to each other in low tones.

"I see how it is!" he said nastily, drawing the plasma pistol he carried from its holster. "You all hate me! I can sense it. Beyond your prejudice at my otherness lies a loathing fear! Ha! GOOD!"

Vogul pointed the pistol at one of his men. The Trylithian held his arms up in a gesture of pleading.

"Master, what have I done to displease you?" he questioned in Trylithian. Vogul, eyes glittering with malice, shoved the gun into the male's chest.

"You cursed people are incompetent!" he cried. "I should kill every one of you, but—" he paused. "I hate my own kind more. Humanity is so pathetic, so shortsighted and hypocritical! I came from a great family, but do you know what they thought I was? MAD!"

Vogul nearly snarled the word. The Trylithian gulped nervously. Out of the corner of his eye, Willum noticed one of the other Trylithians move his hand. The male reached slowly for his gun. Without a moment's hesitation, Vogul shoved his current victim back. He whirled and fired at the male. The Trylithian straightened, his hand falling short of the pistol handle, his face frozen in shock. The others, cowering, looked on with fearful eyes. Vogul merely laughed.

"At every turn, fate seeks to thwart me!" he exclaimed. "I will not be stopped, not by the desert or by a traitor in our midst! If I do not see every one of you working your hardest to find these infidels, I'll shoot you all!"

Those assembled did not speak. A stony silence fell, only broken by the reverberating roar of the landing Trylithian dropship.

"We return again at midnight!" Vogul commanded, and the Trylithians rose at once. They flooded up the landing ramp for their first break from heat the entire day. Vogul, smug and supreme, merely strode up after them. The

Trylithians needed motivation, and what better agent than fear? Vogul understood too well the power of it. He himself was held captive by a dark will that terrified him, even as it guided his steps...

SHARKO TRANSFORMED into Blaze for his trip, grabbing a backpack of supplies. He stopped by Dudeman's tiny bedroom to say goodbye. The man sat on his cot, cross-legged and reading one of Matt's books. He merely grunted in response to his friend. Ever since their awkward conversation, James kept increasingly to himself, and Blaze felt the distance between them palpably.

"I'd like for us to talk when I return," he said.

"I wouldn't," Dudeman replied, sticking his nose deeper into the book. Blaze bid him farewell and walked into the Commons, his shoulders slumped in disappointment. His wife's smile greeted him in the Commons, cheering him up. At least one person loved him enough for a send-off! Kaity walked with Blaze to the broken storage bay, where he raised his visor to kiss her goodbye. Beneath the shade of the tarpaulin, the air felt almost cool.

"Please be wary," Kaity cautioned, failing to hide the worry on her face. "Vogul's aliens are out and about, and the desert can be treacherous at night."

"You know me," Blaze replied, giving her a reassuring hug. "I'll keep an eye out, and God will protect me. I just...*feel*...that this is right."

"I love you." Kaity kissed him again, and their lips lingered. She squeezed his gloved hand, and he backed away, letting it slip slowly out of his fingers. Then, turning, Sharko set off on his extended journey. He'd grown so accustomed to leaving for a day and coming back, yet something about this particular trip caused his throat to tighten. Determined, Blaze tackled the desert at a jog. His thoughts kept him company. Dudeman, water, Vogul, hiding—all the dilemmas of their situation tumbled within his helmeted head. He weaved among the dunes, cresting a massive one late in the afternoon to gaze upon the canyon he'd observed earlier.

Descending, Blaze headed towards it. He was trekking across a plain of sand when his eyes widened in amazement. A set of tracks stretched before him, curving in from east of his position and seeming to lead toward the canyon. At first, he guessed it must be Vogul's search teams, until he recalled that hoverboots didn't make tracks. Moreover, the footprints appeared humanoid in shape. His pulse quickened. He flicked on his torchsword via a toggle in the hilt, holding it in one hand while he cradled his plasma carbine in the other. Cautiously, he followed the tracks on a downward path.

The canyon's mouth appeared in the ground ahead of him. Blaze paused, knowing he faced a clear dilemma. If the maker of the tracks proved Trylithian, he could be walking into a trap. Yet if some other alien had made them, the canyon might hold their first, lasting source of water.

Blaze made his decision and strode forward through the canyon. He glanced to the right and left, moving quietly but with determination. The walls of the arroyo showed the varicolored layers of rock beneath sand, smoothed by the wind. Here and there stood twisted, wholly strange rock formations. They seemed almost like ancient, warped statues to his Starganaut eyes. Sharko knew danger might lurk behind any one of them, but as he progressed farther without incident, he inadvertently relaxed. Near the end of the canyon, after passing the last formation, this calming of his nerves cost him.

"Stick 'em up!" a voice cried harshly, right behind him.

<10>

"We've Got Company!"

Afternoon waned to evening as Kaity Anderson worked outdoors with Chrysta. The two women scrubbed the surfaces of their solar panels, sweat dripping from their faces. The rosy evening light cast a glow over the flat surfaces. Matt had rigged the panels on the sunny side of the dune, to power their daily activities, yet dust was a constant culprit. It settled on the sparkling panels, reducing efficiency with a nasty coat of brown that only thickened over time. Due to water scarcity, the women's sole weapon against the dust was cleaning solution and paper towels. Heat radiated through the white fibers of the towels, threatening to burn Kaity's fingers.

"I'm sick of doing this!" the tutor moaned, wiping her forehead. "I swear this world is getting hotter."

Chrysta muttered her agreement, and Kaity reflected on their plight. She felt so tired of rationing and of working in the sun! Kaity missed her comfortable hammock by the sea and the wonderful commodities of town. What she wouldn't give for an iced coffee or a beach chair under an umbrella! She voiced her thoughts to Chrysta, who snorted.

"My life's been nothing easy for way longer than yours."

"What do you mean?" Kaity cocked her head to one side, intrigued. Chrysta seldom opened up like this.

"Money was always tight, but I had my family. We loved each other, and although times were tough, we stuck it out. I always felt understood by my parents and siblings. Then I married Mike. He seemed like such a nice guy...so understanding, too! Only after we married did I find out he got all his previous insights from his sister. I became a hysterical woman trying to explain my feelings to a clueless husband. And things only got worse."

Momentarily, Kaity forgot her own complaints. Chrysta seldom shared past history, so she said, "Things got worse with Earth incinerated?"

"Oh, things were bad even before that!" Chrysta's tone dripped with irony, her scrubbing intensifying. "Mike couldn't make a decision to save his life. Always hesitating and considering yet one more option! I made the majority of our income, and when he went back to school, I had to get a better job...which I hated. Yet I could've endured that, if only, oh if only...!"

Her face darkened, as though with unspeakable sorrow. Kaity waited, breathless, wondering what Chrysta would reveal next. She gave a slight shudder, and shrugged.

"I've gone without water, a car, internet, electricity," she concluded, "all because my husband couldn't take a job and go with it! At last, he goes to college! At last, he starts getting an education to pursue a career, and bam! Earth is zapped, and we're sent halfway across the universe to Lord knows where. Sometimes I feel like we have the worst luck in the world."

"Wow, I'm sorry," Kaity said, after a long pause. Her own sorrows paled in comparison.

"Does it ever end?" She stopped scrubbing. "I've been told by people 'that's just life.' They say it's a series of hardships and trials, but what about the good times? Mike and I have experienced so few. Does it ever get any better?"

"I don't know," Kaity admitted, her own arm slowing as she pondered Chrysta's words. "We're trapped in this desert, staring at dehydration and friendless in a hostile galaxy. It's hard to know what we'll encounter, but I can tell you this. Life hasn't been all roses for me. I've had my share of thorns—trials, disappointments—but I've always trusted God."

"He can get you through anything, Chrysta. I'm saying that as much to myself as you!" Chrysta grinned as Kaity continued. "We've got to remember that this life isn't all there is. One day, death will overtake us, but that won't be bad. As my favorite author Tolkien describes it, going to Heaven is like a curtain of rain rolling back to reveal silver glass. There is a greater life for us, beyond death."

"What if those ideas are simply the stuff of stories?" Chrysta asked. "I thank you for your encouragement, but how can you stay so...so optimistic?"

"Because I lived it, too." Kaity said emotionally. "There was a time when my mother went through cancer. My father's appendix burst during this, and he had to go in for emergency surgery. I was thirteen. Life is confusing enough for a girl fresh into adolescence. Twice I thought I might lose my parents—and all within the same month! But our whole church prayed for my mom and my dad. I didn't lose either of them, but I had to go through a very dark time. If it hadn't been for my church and Nancy, I'm not sure where I would be."

"Samantha keeps telling us that being here, on Sahara, is no accident. I believe her. Why else would God give us the crystals? Why else would he inspire my husband to go out looking for water? Yes, life is uncomfortable. Yes, darkness seems poised to overtake us. But we have a Hope and a Deliverer. Even if He takes us home, I will still trust in Him. He is the same God who healed my parents, and they reside in Paradise with Him. I will see them again. That is His promise, and not only to me."

Chrysta went back to cleaning her solar panel and remained quiet. Kaity couldn't be certain if her words had produced any effect, but Chrysta looked deep in thought. The women finished their task and retreated into the shelter of the base, relieved to be out of the heat. Kaity cast a last glance out across the desert as they went, biting her lip. She already missed Sharko. Despite her words to Chrysta, a part of Kaity feared him being alone in the desert with Vogul's crew on the prowl. She tried to calm her rising feelings of anxiety by shooting a quick prayer to God. Then she trudged to the kitchen to start dinner. Life's responsibilities didn't stop just because of one newlywed's worry. Did they?

WHILE SHARKO TREKKED to the canyon, Nancy Cooper raced across the dunes. Exhilaration filled her despite the afternoon heat. In the Form of Apotheka, she aided in their perpetual search. She couldn't explain it, but all her senses were attuned. She observed a lizard wandering across a flat patch of earth, and skidded to a halt. Bending down, she watched the little creature skitter in a zig-zag fashion across the grains. Its scaly back glistened, and she asked aloud, "Now where do you get your water from? Oh, I see. No answer? You must be the strong, silent type."

The lizard scurried away, and Nancy laughed at her own joke. A part of her realized the irony, though. She felt like there was no man left for her. Nancy would admit it to no one but Kaity, despite how deeply it hurt. There had been a cute coworker at the police station, a Christian and an upstanding guy. He'd just started noticing her, and then quite literally—boom! Earth went up in incineration, and she was left to ponder what could never be. Left with just enough to cling to, but not enough to justify mourning a lost opportunity. Wasn't that the story of her life?

What were her chances at love here? Even in Starganaut form, Nancy couldn't brush aside the feelings of loneliness. Matt seemed an okay guy, for someone not her type. Dudeman—Nancy didn't even try imagining herself with that temperamental non-Christian! Faith mattered in a spouse, and she didn't see much in either candidate.

Of course, there was more to her loneliness than mere singles' blues. In the destruction of Earth, she had lost her parents, three younger siblings, and relatives. Suppose her immediate family had never moved from Vogul Bay. Might they have boarded *The Deliverer* and survived? She could never know, but she missed all of them terribly. Only Kaity's presence and Mike's recovery made life bearable. Suddenly, a thought entered Nancy's brain. Whether it came through Apotheka's clearer voice, or her heavenly Father's prompting, she could not identify.

I am not alone. I am more than a conqueror through Him who works within me.

Nancy brushed the dirt off her white healer's smock, as if symbolically ridding herself of contaminating thoughts. It was true. God loved her, and He'd preserved her for a purpose. He had never left her without resources in the past. Even when her hopes of being a nurse had failed, and her bank account dropped to double digits, God saw to her needs. If marriage was her path, He would supply the right man at the right time. If singleness loomed in her future—Nancy merely hoped she wouldn't be forced to marry just to continue the human race.

"If Eve didn't have a choice, then I guess I'm in good company!" she told herself and, with a laugh, she picked up speed.

The healer didn't intend to, but she found herself nearing the plateau as she prepared to return to *The Deliverer*. Without finding even a sign of water, she felt intensely frustrated. She was so wrapped up in her thoughts that the sharp cursing of an alien voice startled her. Apotheka dropped to the ground. The level, barren plain around the tableland offered little cover. She shimmed over to a rock, raising her head slightly to view a sight that made her heart skip a beat.

Several terribly long minutes elapsed before the danger of discovery passed. Apotheka watched the figures who had caused her to duck zoom off. The moment they disappeared from view, she rose and began running. Her feet kicked up sand as she raced beneath the afternoon sun, heading westward with urgent steps.

BLAZE DROPPED HIS WEAPONS and whirled around to see a figure in dusty rags. A gun pointed directly at him, and at first, he didn't recognize its make and model. Once he did, Sharko's entire body drained of tension. He doubled over in laughter. The strange figure merely stepped forward, brandishing its weapon all the more.

"I tell you, you're my hostage!" a woman's voice called out uncertainly. "I *will* shoot you, alien scum!"

"With your big...powerful...gun?"

Sharko was so lost in fits of laughter that he couldn't speak. Whatever the person in front of him might be, she held nothing but a useless garden hose nozzle! Her confident blustering was simply comical.

"No funny business, Mate!" the woman cried, taking another step forward. Her voice sounded Australian. "I demand to know what you are and what your plans are! I saw your confederate out on the dunes earlier, clad in white and carryin' a gun!"

"Relax, 'Mate.' I'm American!" Sharko laughed. "You can put that thing down."

"Of course you're American!" the stranger accused. "All the aliens on TV are!"

"But I'm not an alien." Before the woman could aim with her weapon substitute, Blaze reached up and pressed a button on his helmet. The opaque visor of the headgear slid up, revealing his human features. "Do you really expect to harm me with a *hose nozzle*?"

"Oh my gosh, he's a changeling!" The woman shrieked and took off down the canyon. Sharko had to fight back a fit of laughter. All the way she went, the woman screamed a name at the top of her lungs.

"*NICKYYYYY!*"

A brown-haired human in his late twenties leaned over a piece of machinery. With a wrench in one hand and stained coveralls over tattered clothes, he busily worked to restart a generator before night's stars dappled the sky. The man and his machine sat in the deepening shadow of an overhanging bluff. A bunker of sand ringed the area in front of the bluff, creating a semi-circle that sheltered a row of cylindrical buildings. Beyond this, a sea of shallow dunes extended, broken only by the mouth of a canyon. The man heard his sister's voice calling from over the sand bunker. He didn't bother looking up from his task or even greeting her. Though a year younger than his frenetic sister, the young man bore a calmness that stemmed from greater maturity.

"What's got you this time, Abby?" he inquired lazily. "Run into the Hawkesbury River Monster, did we?"

"No, no, this time Nicky, it's *real*!" Abigale Dundee blurted.

"Yeah, and I'm sure Bigfoot's right behind him." Nicholas Dundee chortled, shaking his head.

"Heavens, Nicky! He followed me!" Abigale shrieked and made a mad dash for their living quarters. Nick straightened from his work, expecting to find the usual—nothing. He jumped, his face turning ashen with shock as he beheld the alien figure in front of him. Blaze raised the visor, and Nick Dundee breathed a sigh of relief.

"Crikey, Mate!" he coughed. "You gave me a go! You're human, aren't you? Wait—HUMAN!"

Nick jumped backward, tripping and landing on his rear. He was scampering off the ground before Blaze could say "hi," and sealed himself into their shelter in a matter of moments.

Sharko Anderson merely waited outside, stunned to have found fellow humans on such a desolate, remote world. He could understand their skepticism. Already, he'd surmised they must be astronauts from the Australian Space Agency's expedition. The crew and shuttle had lost contact with Earth years earlier. How had they ended up on this world so far away? Were they the only survivors? Blaze could tell he'd frightened them, but he barely cared. Right now, any humans were the most welcome sight in the galaxy.

IT TOOK A GREAT DEAL of knocking and coaxing for Blaze to draw Abigale and Nick out of their shelter. When he did, he spent several minutes simply reassuring them that he was real.

"You're not a desert mirage?" Nick asked skeptically.

"For the third time, I'm from Earth!" Blaze exclaimed. "I'm a human like you. How long have you been here?"

"Too long," Abigale spoke up, hanging her head.

"We lost count after year one," Nick added. He grew excited. "So if you're from Earth, that means the Yanks sent someone to find us? You're the rescue party at last!"

Blaze bit his lip. How could he possibly break the news about Earth to them? Instead, he decided to keep it vague.

"At present, *we're* in greater need of rescue. You've lived here several years. Obviously, you have some source of water. Can you take me to it?"

"Absolutely!" Nick exclaimed jauntily. He led the way with a smile, showing Blaze a tiny opening in the bluff's face just large enough to squeeze through. Through a dark, natural tunnel they walked, descending rapidly. The Starganaut nearly slipped on the steep slope, but Nick was used to it. He carried a torch made of native brush to illuminate the crazy path. About five minute's travel downward led them to a faint sound Sharko had almost forgotten.

Water.

Rounding a bend with pounding heart, Blaze beheld the wonderful sight of a rushing, subterranean stream! In the darkness, the droplets sprayed upward to dash against faint, rock walls. His boots squished against damp earth, and the smell of wetness wafted sweetly to his nostrils.

"It's an underground river," Nick remarked, as Blaze laughed with delight. "It flows through here pretty quick."

The Starganaut didn't think twice. He changed back into human form and dived face-first into the refreshing coolness, not even bothering to strip off his shoes. Nick watched, half-shocked at the transformation but amused by his actions. Sharko splashed around like a happy child, letting the dirt and grime of months in the desert wash away. A stream of water! An entire living, moving vein of it, buried beneath the lifeless sands!

"What in Straya was *that*?" Nick questioned, once Sharko emerged from the water. He covered his eyes as the trucker transformed back.

"It's an alien technology we found," Blaze said. Nick's questioning eyebrow only rose higher, so the trucker waved a dismissive hand. "I'll explain more later. How do you draw water from this place?"

"I set up a system to divert some of it for storage." Nick looked ready to burst his coverall buttons. "Come. I'll show you the cistern where it collects!"

"Cistern?" Blaze asked in wonderment. "You mean there's more?"

"A whole cavern full, Mate!" Nick replied, adding with a laugh, "and I'd thank you to keep out 'o that one!"

The Australian led Blaze farther into the earth, through a tunnel that spiraled downward and followed the route of the piping. Even before the trucker saw Nick's cistern, he praised God for this find. Water! The Lord of Heaven had at last answered their pleas! After Blaze observed how much was in Nick's storage cave, he couldn't wait to race back and tell the others. Yet the blackness of night replaced that of the tunnel when they emerged from it, reminding Blaze he'd be making the trip in the dark. Only this time, he wouldn't be travelling alone.

"I'm not sure about leaving the base," Abigale said hesitantly, to Blaze's proposal.

"Come on, Sis, it'll be fun!" Nick said enthusiastically, shouldering an odd-looking stick. "Best travel on this planet's at night."

"I know, it's just...my garden," Abigale protested weakly. Blaze gazed over at the tubular building, a greenhouse made from shuttle wreckage and possessing a slatted roof.

"We haven't left this place overnight in forever," Abigale continued. "It's become such a part of our lives, it...it frightens me to think of leaving."

"It's just a place," Nick soothed, smiling at his sister. "We're about to go with this fellow and meet more people! Your radishes and carrots will be fine!"

Abigale looked very reluctant, but Nick coaxed her in the end. Blaze led the way back through the now-familiar canyon. The Australians needed to walk swiftly to keep up with him in Form. They were well accustomed to the climate, however, and only Abigale paused once, to look back forlornly at the weathered compound she called home.

NANCY, MATT, AND MIKE returned to the Starganaut Base tired and at different times. Matt as Thunderbane came lumbering home first, and Chrysta all too happily greeted Ninjarak when he came through the storage bay door. Apotheka returned, breathless and with troubling news, as Kaity was bringing their dinner into the Commons. The tutor could tell instantly that something was wrong and Samantha sprang to her feet.

"What happened?" the prophetess demanded.

"Vogul's men found the plateau!" Apotheka declared, changing back into Nancy. "I saw them poking around the damaged hovercraft, and they found at least one of the bodies. It didn't seem they discovered the cave, but—"

"The net draws tighter around us," Samantha finished. Her face darkened, and Kaity felt afraid. "They'll surely have seen the wreckage from our crash. Now they've stumbled on the site where we were attacked. It's just a matter of time before they find this base."

"I wish we hadn't needed to leave that hovercraft there!" Matt said, from his seat at the dinner table. "Blasted alien controls were impossible to figure!"

"Nobody blames you, Matt," Kaity reassured. Nonetheless, the icy fingers of fear clawed at her heart. Sharko was out there. Alone. Thankfully he'd gone in the completely opposite direction as Nancy, but suppose...?

At that moment, Mike and Chrysta entered the Commons from the bedroom deck. The way they held hands and smiled warmly at each other sent a pang of longing through her heart, and Kaity suddenly couldn't breathe. She couldn't think! She couldn't stand it anymore! She slammed her tray of food onto the table and rushed from the Commons, to the surprise of everyone.

"What's eating her?" Matt questioned critically, and Nancy seemed poised to follow her friend.

"You've been through enough, Miss Cooper." Samantha stopped her. "I sense Kaity needs some time to herself, and you could use some dinner."

Apotheka couldn't argue, yet she disagreed with the prophetess. If she could state one fact confidently about her friend, it was that Kaity needed to talk things out. Time to herself often made things worse.

The tutor tore through the sideways hall, to the alcove she and Sharko shared. She slipped miserably into bed. The emptiness of the spot next to her cut into her like a knife, and she rolled onto her side, anxiety knotting her stomach. How she missed her old life! Those carefree times when her hardest decision involved tutoring clients, and her budding romance with Sharko made every day like spring.

Kaity buried her face in her pillow and sobbed. She felt like such a hypocrite. Here she'd been telling Chrysta everything was all right, and sounding so sure of her faith! Yet with Sharko gone, she just couldn't feel at peace. He was the one thing God had let her bring from Earth—her shining beacon of light in an otherwise dark existence. The groom she had walked the aisle to. Her Blaze. Just the thought of possibly losing him shattered her. Coupled with their dwindling water and the encroachment of enemies, Kaity felt crushed beneath a pile of emotional burdens she couldn't carry.

Even if He takes us home, I will still trust in Him. Her own words echoed mockingly in her mind, and she drifted into a restless slumber. Nightmares rent her sleep—images of her husband dying, Earth obliterated, Vogul leering over them, laughing as his men shot them. The orbs couldn't help them. The armor and weapons melted from them. He was coming, coming, fueled by an insatiable appetite to kill them that didn't even make sense. And behind him trailed shadows, massing like phantoms poised to strike. Kaity tossed and turned, and though she slipped out of consciousness, she could find no rest...

A GENTLE KNOCK ON THE doorway brought Kaity out of her tortured slumber. She glanced up to see Nancy, a tray of food balanced on one hand. She sniffed, smelling the aroma of muffins. Breakfast already?

"It's just after dawn," Nancy supplied, taking a bite. "I had to make sure you were okay. I checked on you last night but you'd already hit the sack. Anything you'd like to talk about?"

Without hesitating, Kaity burst into a torrent of words. Nancy simply sat on the floor beside her, nodding and offering an occasional comment.

"Well goodness, I don't know why you'd feel that way!" Nancy said sarcastically, once she finished. "It's not like we lived through an apocalypse, only to face death by dehydration. Oh wait..."

Kaity dried her tears, chuckling slightly in spite of her mood.

"What do you need?" Nancy swallowed her last bite of canned peaches.

"I guess I simply needed to vent." Kaity paused. "It's ironic, because I told Chrysta to have hope just this afternoon, and now here I am, a mess in need of a friend."

"God wouldn't have made friends if we didn't need them!" Nancy said. Her voice was encouraging, but tired. "Kaity, Sharko will be fine. I wouldn't worry until tomorrow. You know the man you married—he's more than competent to take care of himself."

"You're right. Of course!" Kaity said humorously. "He's built truck-driver tough *and* he's got a glorified body. I suppose I let the heat get to my head."

"I doubt it's the heat," Nancy reflected, stretching. "After all we've been through, I can't blame anyone for despairing. Hey, I've been meaning to ask," she added, "how are you doing with the loss of your parents? We've talked about your homesickness and current things already. I just wanted to know."

"Fine, I guess."

"You know 'fine' stands for freaked out, insecure, neurotic and empty, right?" Nancy eyed her friend humorously, then grew serious. "I guess we're all a bit 'fine,' really. I'm still coming to terms and accepting it, but it's hard to acknowledge. Everyone and everything is missing from our lives. How about you?"

"Nancy, to be honest, I'm not taking it well." Kaity's voice shook. "I keep having dreams about being back home, and then I'm jarred into reality every time I wake. It's not that life is all horrible. I'm young, married, and have a wonderful husband. And that's just it—this hurts Sharko. Part of being married is leaving your old life behind for a new one. We've had extreme circumstances, but life on Earth was so good, and life here is so *miserable*. I'm unhappy, and while Sharko talks of plans for the future, I can't even imagine a future without Earth."

"You had a good life," Nancy agreed. "Better than mine, and mine wasn't too shabby. I didn't know if my mother was a Christian, and now, I won't until Eternity. I have regrets—you at least had the comfort of Christian parents. But you're right, Kaity. You have Sharko."

"Sharko tells me he feels less significant than my parents," Kaity continued, ashamed. "I talk about them so much, he once joked that he wished he was dead so he'd at least be central in my mind."

"It sounds like you have a problem," Nancy said gently, "with letting go of the past."

"I'm aware of it. I just don't know what to do. You and Sharko are the only advisors I have now. My mom used to give the best advice."

"Have you talked to God about it?" Nancy's pointed question left Kaity feeling a bit defensive, but she knew her friend wished only to help. Before she could answer, both heard running footsteps. Chrysta burst in, a smile plastering her face.

"You'll never guess!" she exclaimed. "Sharko is back, and he's got company of the bipedal kind!"

"Like...ostriches?" Nancy questioned, confused. Kaity could only feel the greatest sense of relief in the galaxy.

"Even better!" Chrysta said happily, and she dashed out of the room. Nancy and Kaity sprang after her. They emerged into the sunlight to see the last sight they could have expected. Kaity filled with joy, racing toward the armored figure she'd feared she might not see. Blaze! Her husband was home, and he'd brought an answer to prayers in their hour of direst need.

"AUSTRALIANS, MATE!" Nick cried loudly. "We're not Brits, we're Aussies!"

Samantha Harris blushed with embarrassment at her mistake. She had asked what part of Britain Nick and Abigale hailed from, only to be met by Nick's outburst.

"Sorry," she mumbled, and the rest of the Starganauts were surprised to see their fearless leader so taken aback.

"Have no fear!" Nick clapped her on the shoulder heartily. "It's so good to see other human beings, you can call us Yanks for all I care!"

"I feel flattered," Matt said sarcastically, but he couldn't suppress a grin. Nick and his sister proceeded to go around their entire base and through it, exclaiming at every nook and innovation until even Sharko grew sick of it. Between exclamations of "crikey" and "it's a beaut," the Dundee siblings filled the Base's interior with more words in one day than the Starganauts used in a month. It was after nightfall when they ate dinner together. Nick and Abigale's eyes bulged at the sight of microwaved pizza and canned green beans.

"Well I'll be stuffed!" Nick exclaimed. The siblings tore into the processed food as if devouring a steak dinner.

"I think...I'm gonna die...from a cheese coma..." Abigale said, exhaling slowly and with her eyes half-closed. "We've eaten nothing but lizard and snake, and I can tell ya, they *definitely* don't taste like chicken!"

"Rather gummy and stringy," Nick added, making a face. "And don't tell me you blokes have toothpaste? By 'eavens! We've had to make our own nasty paste-stuff like the Aztecs, which only Abigale knew about from books."

"If you would kindly pause from talking for a moment," Samantha finally said, between clenched teeth, "Sharko and I wish to converse with you."

"I don't know if you're aware," Sharko began, "but there are aliens in the galaxy."

"Aliens? I've seen my share." Nick waved a dismissive hand. "At least, I found their cadavers. There's quite a field of crashed ships other side of my bluff, not to mention one in your stretch o' the Outback. It's my hobby, you see, tinkerin' with old wrecks. I haven't figured half the tech, but I'm close to finishing a hovercraft of sorts. Just missin' a key part."

"Which part is that?" Matt, ever the mechanic, questioned him eagerly.

"The hoverin'," Nick admitted, with a humorous grin that set them all chuckling.

"I could do with less chatter," Kaity said, at the end of their first night with the Dundees. She and Sharko walked hand-in-hand, pacing *The Deliverer*. "They do add a lot of humor to our table. You said they have their own homestead, with a garden and a cavern full of water?"

"That storage tank has plenty to last us for months," Sharko said happily, "and with less conservation! Ten minute showers, Dear! TEN MINUTES!"

He caught up his wife and twirled her around, Kaity's feet almost hitting the wall of the shuttle. She didn't care. Simply knowing they weren't alone in this wasteland made a world of difference. They had trusted God to help them find water. He'd not only provided for their physical needs, but He'd given them hope and humor at a time when they needed it most. With Nick and Abigale, the possibility of restarting the human race seemed much more reachable. The possibility of planting gardens and growing food seemed tangible, and Kaity felt strangely sad.

She brushed it away. Tonight they were happy, holding hands, forgetting about all that was lost. Tonight she'd give thanks to God and enjoy the blessings He had given. The biggest of those, drawing her into loving arms as they drifted to sleep, was her tender husband Sharko.

THE LANDING RAMP OF the Trylithian dropship fell to the sand. Willum Vogul clanked down its length in hoverboots fashioned especially for him. He wore a strip of cloth over one shoulder and a brown, leather-like hauberk. His helmet, brown as well, possessed a visor that covered his eyes but exposed his mouth. A chainmail-like mesh could be drawn up over it, yet Vogul—unlike the Trylithians—preferred to have his mouth free and clear.

The landing site lay near a plateau. This was where his men had found the old hovercraft, discarded and glistening in the early morning sun. Though the shifting sands obliterated footprints, the vessel stood empty with no sign of its crew. That provided clue enough.

Vogul stooped, taking the sand in his bare hand and letting it slip through his fingers. He hadn't felt sand like this since his last time at Vogul Bay. Earth. He'd spent so much time on Trylithia, but still it didn't feel like a true home. He could barely remember the shape of a palm tree or the scent of a lavender field. No matter how much he hated his own kind, Vogul couldn't shove aside a twinge of regret for destroying his birthplace.

It did not matter! He threw down the remainder of the sand in his palm with disgust. How much were the Earthlings like these maddening grains? Willum Vogul did not give up easily, yet it seemed an improbable feat to find these humans in the vast wasteland. Even with their search parameters narrowed, which direction should they go? And were the survivors stationary, or on the move? Vogul did not know that their shuttle had survived. All he knew was that it had crashed and left a partial trail, erased by nature and sandstorms. If only Lidexid wasn't hated by most of the Gorvan System! He might have put into a space dock to install sensors, but the risk of discovery by the Myds was too great. And it would have taken precious weeks he could ill afford.

"I wonder if the tormac knows of my absence yet?" Vogul pondered. "I'd love to see Durag's face if he ever discovered how I sent his tracker to Stattar Nebula. Hopping mad would be an understatement, once he realized where I've taken his precious *Draxalis*."

"Let us hope we do not see his face!" one of the Trylithians muttered. "Our loyalty to you means execution by Tormac Durag."

"And your cowardice to *my* face merits execution from me!" Vogul snarled. He grabbed the Trylithian by the shoulders and flung him back. The others paused, looking to their leader and expecting him to light into the male with his fists or a gun. Vogul often abused the crew. They were used to being an outlet for his rage, but this time, he stopped after taking a single stride forward. Something deep within him caused him to cringe and writhe slightly.

"What is it? Where must I go?" he demanded, of thin air. "There!" he turned to his men. "Let us examine this plateau. Perhaps they camped nearby!"

The Trylithians gave each other knowing looks. Vogul hadn't earned his reputation as a crazed man for nothing. Sometimes they caught him whispering to himself, and other times, he appeared to be cringing from an unseen fear. The madman from Earth led the way, and they searched hurriedly around the plateau. The heat of the day was rising, threatening to blind their sensors. They had but an hour left when luck led them to the cave opening.

The Trylithians turned on their lights, and Vogul held up his hands as the form of the scorpion statue startled him.

"Ugh! What is that?" he exclaimed, bad-tempered.

"Statues, master!" a Trylithian answered. "Carvings of desert creatures."

Vogul surveyed the space with interest. This was no ordinary cavern. Four statues rested on a sandy floor around a pedestal of the same stone. There were insets within the statues, all empty, and writings in several different languages along the walls.

"I know Trylithian and English," Vogul said, gesturing to the writing by Jordaccis, "but what are these?"

"Trade tongue, old Paradeesian, Myd...not sure," another soldier spoke up. "I only know three."

Vogul's face suddenly turned ashen. The human's entire demeanor changed.

"Out!" he yelled unexpectedly. "Leave me this instant! There is something I must see *alone*!"

The baffled Trylithians could only scramble to follow his orders. They dashed out of the cave, knowing better than to question the madman. Vogul approached the central pedestal slowly. Examining the stone plinth, he found the faintest of etchings carved in its surface. They were indiscernible until Vogul directly shined his light upon them.

"No, it cannot be!" he cried, pain abruptly seizing him. Clutching at his skull, Vogul writhed around, clenching his teeth and dropping the light.

"*We have heard*!" a multitude of voices suddenly proclaimed. The darkness of the cave deepened, and Vogul cowered in fear as he felt the familiar presence of that which had changed his path so many years ago.

"*We have seen*!" the voices continued. They were hollow and yet overwhelming.

"What must I do next?" Vogul begged. "You told me that keeping them from the crystals was paramount! It never occurred to me that this cave would be on the world where they crashed! I'm sorry. They have them, and I couldn't have prevented it!"

"*Pathetic! Excuses*!"

In their rage, the voices sounded even more terrifying. The blackness in front of Vogul increased, encroaching on the panicked man. Willum backed away as the shadows threatened to touch him. They had enveloped him be-fore—with painful results to both body and psyche.

"I-I'll do better!" Vogul pleaded. "I will keep them from leaving this plan-et alive! You are wise, oh Future-Seers! Everything is as you told me, and I know I am privileged to have been chosen—"

"Save your flattery for those beneath you!" the multitude snarled. *"You have but one task, one work to do. You have a month to find the Eight. Failure is not an option. You know what will be done to you for failure!"*

The darkness swallowed Vogul in deeper shadows than the cavern ever could. He clutched his skull, screwing his eyes shut, gritting his teeth togeth-er, and crying out in pain as the voices entered his head. His mind filled with images—horrible images! Agony gripped him at the familiar sight racing through his mind again, overwhelming it. Then, suddenly, they were gone. Vogul, released, fell forward on his elbows. He was panting heavily.

"I will not fail!" he vowed, picking himself up. "I welcome my destiny to be their downfall. If I must consume this entire planet, so be it—*but I will crush them!*"

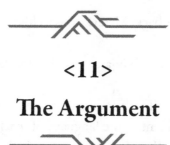

<11>

The Argument

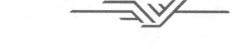

The discovery of water flooded the Starganauts with hope. Samantha spearheaded a planning session after dinner to extract the substance and cart it to their base. Nick suggested that completing his hovercraft would make the task easier, so Matt, Sharko, and Mike changed into orb Form and followed Nick to his homestead. Dudeman elected to remain back at the base, quiet and sullen as usual. It pained Blaze how little his friend wished to engage with them, but what could be done? The four men set out late in the afternoon, Nick telling them how he and Abigale ended up on the desert world.

"A lot of it we don't know, really," Nick commented. "We were part of the Australian Team sent on a Mars mission."

"I recall," Blaze put in. "Earth lost contact with you about three years ago?"

"Four," Nick corrected, and he shook his head. "Abby and I, we simply went into cryosleep with the rest of our mates. When we woke, the shuttle was crashed right into the rock beneath this overhang. Our mates were crushed, and the glass of our sleep pods had broken on impact. I can tell ya, we were sick as dingoes! Without a wakin' process, our bodies took a while to come good."

"We never did find out how we got here. The date in our shuttle's half-workin' computer told us it'd been six months since we nodded off. That contraption soon carked it, so we buried our dead and started huntin'. Water wasn't a problem due to our one stroke o' luck."

"The underground stream," Blaze supplied.

"You seem rather cheerful for someone stuck in the heat so long," Mike, in Ninjarak's white ninja garb, made the comment.

"I grew up in the Outback, Mates! I was a child of the bush. Bivouacking and an' all that."

"Is he speaking English?" Ninjarak joked. Thunderbane shot him a withering glance.

"He speaks mechanic. That's good enough for this 'Yank.'"

Nick proved quite fluent in the language of machines. While the others sported water cartons, Thunderbane carried four Trylithian hoverboots they'd salvaged from the attack of Vogul's crew.

The men reached the Australians' homestead as dawn grayed the horizon. Nick was soon showing them what appeared, to Ninjarak, as junk heaps. Blaze and Thunderbane recognized them as alien machines, similar to a few from the ship graveyard. One orderly pile of parts proved to be Nick's hovercraft, and its functionality impressed Thunderbane. Composed of obviously dissimilar materials, the Australian joked it was a Frankenstein of a vehicle. Nonetheless, he'd managed to cobble together working controls and a running engine. He simply lacked a method of flotation and propulsion.

Blaze was more interested in seeing the Dundees' homestead, while Ninjarak expressed a desire to visit the cistern. Both men split, leaving Thunderbane and Nick to the scrap piles. Matt changed out of Starganaut Form to more comfortably assist the Australian. After they disassembled the Trylithian hoverboots, Nick held up two disc-sized circles of metal they'd removed from the bottom of the gear. Matt squinted at them in the morning light.

"I don't know what the 'eck these are," Nick exclaimed, "but they appear to cause the hoverin' usin' magnets of some sort! The rockets are a separate system. This might just work! You seen one of these before?"

Nick took Matt over to a spherical part covered by a tarpaulin. Throwing the tarp back, he revealed a sturdy, octagonal box of metal and glass. A rock resembling hematite—yet translucent—hung in the middle, inside a smaller, round frame.

"What is it?" the scrap worker asked.

"Some kinda alien power source. A current flows into the octagon from the frame, an' it glows bright-red. When I hook this beaut up, the consoles come to life!"

"Are you sure this thing is safe?" Matt gazed skeptically at Nick.

"Hey, I'll take whatever power source I can get!" the Australian sniffed. "Between my sister's runny mouth and chattin' with the lizards, there's aught much else in this desert but lookin' for odd objects! Kept me sane! So did hope for Earth! What?"

A forlorn look flashed across Matt's face as he spoke the name of their home world. It hadn't occurred to him that the Australians didn't know.

"'Mate,'" he said kindly, "I...we...we didn't exactly leave Earth by choice."

The color drained from Nick's cheeks. The peppy Australian grew ashen while Matt related the events of the last several months. The gunship, the pink wave of death, fleeing through the warp tunnel, crashing...endless trekking for signs of water. He listened without comment, probably shocked into silence. At long last, after many moments where nothing sounded but the bitter wind, Nick spoke.

"Abigale's gonna be crushed."

Matt's brows rose in surprise as the man continued.

"I mean...I can't believe it, what a shock...but Abby! My sister is sensitive, Mate. I've done my best to be like her older brother, despite bein' a year younger. Abby's greatest comfort was thoughts of home. But now? No Outback. No trips to Sydney and nights downin' amber fluid with the mates. How'd you all cope?"

"Many of us believe in Christ. We look to Jesus for our strength in this hardship, and to my cousin. Samantha is a prophetess of God. She saw Earth's coming doom, and she also saw something else. A future. A life other than this, in a distant city."

"I'll have to break the news to Abby when we get back." Nick hung his head, his joviality completely gone. "I don't want any of you breathin' a word. I know how to tell Abby, and I suspect she'll be cryin' heaps."

"What about you?" Matt questioned. It was unlike the stoic salvager, but he felt a special bond with the Australian mechanic.

"I'll sluff along, same as always. It's a blow, but findin' you Starganauts has cheered me for the first time in years!"

Nick slapped Matt on the back, and the two men resumed their shared task of making the hovercraft dune-worthy.

SHARKO EXPLORED THE Dundees' establishment out of Form. Their homestead, as Nick called it, was an admirable complex for two humans alone. It rested beneath an overhanging sandstone bluff, reminding Sharko of a Native American ruin he'd once visited on Earth. Eons of blasting wind had eroded a sizeable alcove, depositing sediment farther down, which Nick formed into the crescent-shaped bunker to encircle his homestead. Although this diminished the resulting courtyard's size, Nick's junkyard of alien scraps still fit.

Three cylindrical buildings rested against the curving bunker. Partly sunk into the ground, they were fashioned out of the sideways ruins of their shuttle. Nick kept junk in one, while the middle building served as their living quarters, with a small kitchen, beds, and a firepit. The third structure resembled a greenhouse. The wall forming its roof had been cut to make slats, allowing sunlight to fall on the dirt floor teeming with plants. Sharko would later learn that Abigale's garden derived from the progeny of seeds brought on the Australians' space mission. Their task was to establish a colony on Mars, so plants theorized to grow on the Red Planet had composed part of the ship's manifest. Sharko recognized wheat, carrots, radishes and strawberries—to his surprise.

The sight made him think of the unexpectedness of God. They had been searching simply for water, never dreaming the Almighty would lead them to much more! The Australians came as a welcome boost to morale, and Sharko knew the blessing was mutual. *Thank you, Lord, for guiding me to this canyon through your Spirit*! He thought. It felt strangely wonderful, taking the initiative, and that somehow troubled the trucker.

Sharko backtracked mentally. No. He wouldn't go there! Despite feeling a greater urge to speak up at meetings, Sharko determined this wouldn't become a pattern. He'd been having ideas for solutions to their problems lately, and Kaity had encouraged him to tell Samantha. He balked at the idea. Leadership was a dark road Sharko didn't wish to travel. Not again.

His parents' plane crash was the tragedy that had propelled him into manhood. *Far too quickly*, he reflected. At seventeen, Sharko had gone from an immature, thrill-seeking teenager to a sober man providing for a family. Aside from his grandparents, there had been no one to offer guidance. The burden of leading his two younger brothers fell upon his shoulders, robbing him of years which should have been exciting.

He hated leading. He hated responsibility. He felt the weightiness of having to make decisions which could affect those he loved for years to come. He often took a long time to mull over many options before proceeding. Kaity praised his leadership of their family, but Sharko felt it was just her heart speaking. He did not see himself spearheading anything, and yet in the uncomfortable role of maturity, he had experienced his greatest growth. Through hardship, he'd become a Christian and drawn close to God.

His involvement in spearheading their latest search felt so natural; like putting on a well-fitting glove. It baffled and perplexed him. Though Dudeman didn't speak to him much, even the surfer had voiced a desire to see his best friend become more active in leading them. Sharko wondered if this could be the start of something greater, and his heart began to race. Reluctance. Fear. Doubt and anxiety crept over him, threatening to overwhelm him, so he stopped his self-guided tour of the Dundee homestead. Turning toward the tunnel opening, he transformed and descended to the cistern. Mike would be there, and Sharko figured he'd join the college student to start the task of hauling water.

Nick's stream sat in pitch darkness. Mike, in the Form of Ninjarak, reclined next to the water's edge, his boots off and his feet dangling in the rushing current. He'd felt his way through the passageway with the aid of night vision, a feature of his sleek helmet. Overcome with nostalgia for the beaches of home, Ninjarak had been sitting and enjoying the water. He nearly jumped as someone came up behind him, filling the darkness with light.

"Relax! It's just me."

Sharko, as Blaze, pointed his gun forward, illuminating the space. Ninjarak rose, and both men walked to the cistern, which Blaze estimated must be larger than most water towers. It was about half full. A hole in the roof revealed Nick's pipe outlet. A small stream trickled out, sending echoes of falling water throughout the space.

Filling up the water cartons and hauling them to the surface proved time-consuming. Nick set out a large, metal tank near the tunnel's mouth, and into this they poured roughly twenty cartons' worth. Even in glorified bodies, they dripped with sweat from the labor. Ninjarak and Blaze had just leaned against the rock wall of the alcove when Nick let out an exclamation of "Crikey! She's gorgeous!"

They looked up to see Nick proudly hefting himself onto the deck of his scrap-metal hovercraft. He pulled a lever, pressed a button, and connected a tube from the spherical power box. The entire craft floated into the air! It hovered roughly five feet above the ground, making only a whirring noise. Nick powered the vehicle off and stepped down.

"All we've gotta do is strap the rockets on the back, an' we'll have a proper craft!"

"Are you sure this can carry the water tank?" Blaze asked skeptically. Nick and Matt exchanged knowing glances.

"Mate," Nick said boldly, "by the time we're done with 'er, she'll butter your toast, scramble your eggs, and make your mornin' coffee!"

True to his word, Nick and Matt had the hovercraft ready a few hours later. All four men worked together to carry the heavy tank of water, setting it carefully on the hovercraft's deck. The ship was mostly open to the elements, with but a thin railing running between metal plates at the front and back to keep one from falling off. They strapped the tank to the hovercraft's floor and proceeded to find handholds. Nick fired the engines, and the four humans took off.

The desert raced by in a blur as they skimmed over it. Blaze was lost for words. If someone had told him a year ago he'd be riding a hovercraft on a strange planet, in alien armor, he would've laughed. Hovering was a strange sensation. The ride felt unbelievably smooth and the hovercraft stayed exactly five feet over the ground regardless of terrain. Thus, when they encountered a sand dune, the entire vehicle tilted backward, then forward. More than a little water sloshed out of the tank's open top from this, but the men enjoyed being splashed.

Dudeman would love this! Blaze thought, with a pang. His friend's distance pained him. How long would he continue to lose himself in books, barely venturing from his room? How many evenings would he depart after dinner on a long walk? James couldn't physically avoid everyone in the tiny space, so he emotionally withdrew. He hadn't shaved, and Blaze remembered his attempts to speak to his friend. Dudeman would become angry and sullen, and even Kaity couldn't pry a conversation from him.

A spiritual battle raged within him, and Blaze prayed for guidance. *Should I speak to him, Lord?* He questioned earnestly. *If yes, how? If so, when? Please give me the words and the ability to know when I must use them, or hold my tongue.*

The hovercraft sped onward, carrying Blaze along with his thoughts. In the evening light, a figure hunkered down against the crest of a dune. A gun barrel followed the hovercraft, cat-like eyes narrowing at the end of its scope. Once the hover vessel drew out of sight, the Trylithian rose to his feet and activated hoverboots. He skimmed across the sands, straight to the rendezvous point where Vogul's shuttle would pick up the search teams. Willum lounged beneath an awning, sipping ice-cold water. A group of four Trylithians stood around him, stationed for his protection as the man awaited the return of search parties.

"My master!" the Trylithian exclaimed. "I saw the enemy! The humans! They have a hovercraft, and they are heading north!"

"North? A hovercraft?" Vogul sat up.

"What is more," the Trylithian continued, "I saw water sloshing out of a tank on the ship's deck!"

"Captain!" Vogul called, to the leader of his guards. "Com the shuttle and tell them to hold off! North with water, you say?"

"Do you want us to head that way?" the Trylithian asked excitedly.

"No, wait!" Vogul held up his hand. "If what you say is true, we would do far better heading south."

The Trylithian cocked his head to one side in bafflement.

"South?"

"Because they are hauling water," Vogul continued gleefully, "that means they've found a source! The answer is simple, my comrades! We find their water and lay a trap! We've spent far too long searching for our prey. Now, we wait for our prey to come to us!"

———✠╫╲╲╁╫✠———

THE MEN RETURNED TO the Starganaut Base in time for dinner. A fourteen-hour journey by foot, the hovercraft cut the commute to Nick's homestead down to two hours. Kaity and Chrysta set plates of rice and canned chicken in front of everyone, and Samantha declared it was the grandest meal they'd eaten since the Andersons' wedding feast. Nick and Abigale insisted on doing dishes, and the mood in the Commons was joyful.

Sharko watched Dudeman closely during the entire dinner. He deliberately followed his friend back to the sleeping quarters, calling him before Dudeman could enter his room.

"James," Sharko said firmly, "you can ignore the rest of us, you can avoid me, but you can't hide from God!"

Dudeman stiffened at his remark. Turning on his heel, he glared at his friend.

"Really, dude?" he asked, his tone disbelieving. "I expected something more chill. Like, oh, you know, 'how are you, Dudeman?' 'Been okay, Dudeman?' You're just as bad as her!"

"Samantha's timing and tactics might have been misplaced, but her message rang true. It's a message you've run from all your life."

"You shut the devil up, you hear me?" Dudeman rebuffed.

"Only one Man shuts the Devil up," Sharko retorted mightily, "and He has the power to transform you in a way no crystal could. James," he softened, "whenever you encounter something you don't like, you shut it out. You've always been like that, and what has it gained you? You look miserable and haggard, and I know why you're doing this. You're afraid."

Dudeman settled down a little as Sharko's tone softened. He placed a hand against the wall, leaning his weight on it wearily. He gave an ironic chuckle.

"I guess you can still see right through me."

"I'm your friend," Sharko replied. "I do care about you physically, but spiritually, all the more."

"What has God gained you, Man?" Dudeman's tone dripped with contempt. "I see so much suffering in your life. We're both in the same boat, in this freaking wasteland!"

"It isn't what I've gained. It's what I've lost."

"I don't follow." James was utterly confused.

"In America, a young man was always told to follow his dreams. Live for yourself! Get rich, work hard—play harder! When I became a Christian, I gave up pursuing that dream. I lost my pride, my self-reliance, and my bondage to sin. I realized how empty selfish living is. I gained something *greater*. A purpose. A Savior. A hope, in life beyond this temporary and broken world. Jesus said, 'The man who loves his life will lose it, while the man who hates his life in this world will keep it for eternal life.'"

"I don't understand, Man. *Hate* is a pretty strong word."

"You don't get it because you lack the Holy Spirit," Sharko said kindly. "I don't mean that in offense. All your life, you lived under a Christian mom and dad. You fought against their boundaries and—to be fair—they weren't exactly strict. 'I can't accept a God who'd allow me to be an orphan.' I still remember you telling me that in college. You know what? I lost my parents too, James, but God got me through it. It hurt so much that some days, just getting out of bed was a struggle. But in the end, I came to see who God truly is: loving, a Father—One who gives us choices. We continually choose sin, yet He continually forgives us. To you, God is cruel, distant, and constraining. I know Him through the person of Jesus Christ: loving, close, and freeing."

"But what about history?" Dudeman spat. Sharko recognized the signs of his friend growing angrier. *What should I say, Lord?* He asked desperately.

"God ordered whole people groups killed," Dudeman continued passionately. "He had all manner of innocent people put to death! Who could follow a God like that?"

"You're right that God commanded the deaths of nations," Sharko answered, "but they were far from innocent. Many were extremely wicked and practiced every sin under the sun. God gave them repeated chances to repent. Only after their continued refusal did He judge them...and death surely comes to all of us in the end. The question, when You stand before God, is this: Will He see your wickedness, or Christ's righteousness? It isn't a matter of history, James. What your rejection of Christ comes down to is two things: fear and anger."

"You are afraid. You fear God will abandon you, just like your parents did. You are angry, because you don't want to give God control over your life. We can argue semantics 'til we're blue in the face. James Dudeman Erskin," Sharko's voice was passionate, pleading. "Jesus Christ is knocking at the door of your heart. He wants to come in and make it clean. Only then will you find true peace and an answer to the conflict within. Will you open that door?"

Dudeman breathed hard. He was still leaning against the wall, filled with emotion, his face downcast. Sharko paused to pray fervently that his friend might accept Christ. Dudeman had been fighting all of His attempts for so long. At last, Dudeman gave a shudder and surveyed his friend with the same cornered look as before.

"I just can't believe, Man!" he cried weakly. "God's always been an absentee Dad, and...and He'll never be anything else!"

With a violent motion, James slammed the door to his small bedroom, shutting out Sharko and any possibility of redemption.

———— ‡‡⧵⧵‡‡ ————

"I'M SO SORRY, SWEETHEART."

Kaity sympathized with her dejected husband after his return to the Commons. Side-by-side at the table, Derek had shared about his talk with Dudeman. Kaity gave him a sympathetic rub on the back. It slightly relieved his agitation, and once he relaxed, an idea came to him. His interview with James might have gone south, but there was still daylight left.

"Honey, come for a ride with me!" he exclaimed, extending his hand to his wife with a dramatic flourish. Seeing him brighten up, Kaity took it with a happy laugh.

The newlyweds went in Nick's hovercraft. Derek took particular delight in piloting their new hovercraft, and Kaity closed her eyes and dreamed they were back on Earth, back in his truck. He was simply taking her for a warm summer's drive. She opened them as Sharko pointed out the scenery.

They travelled so far and so fast that the landscape changed. More spots of dry brush, darker sand with tints of orange, and several plateaus—Kaity took it all in. Mesas rose like delegates presiding at a giant convention, clustered in circular fashion around desolate valleys. Their flat-topped heads fell to bluffs of varying shades of red and orange, stratified and smoothed by the wind. Everything seemed to glow in the evening air. Alien cacti raised a tangle of twisted arms toward the sinking sun as if protesting its heat, and Kaity even noticed withered green foliage on some of the brush.

"There must be more groundwater here," Sharko remarked, as he slowed to a leisurely hover, then stopped the craft. "Isn't it grand, Kaity? It reminds me of Utah and Arizona, back home!"

"It *is* lovely," the tutor had to agree. "We crash-landed in the ugliest section of desert."

"There must be water deep down!" Sharko exclaimed. An idea suddenly seized him. "Kaity, what would you say if I told you I wanted to build us a house here? That I see this as someday being our valley? We may have stumbled upon this by accident, but I'm beginning to think maybe God brought us here on purpose."

Her husband spoke the words happily, but Kaity felt inwardly crushed. Crushed, because the thought of putting down roots drove home the reality of being away from Earth. She did not want to settle here. There must be more to the galaxy than Sahara. Sharko noticed her hesitancy, and his shoulders drooped.

"I mean, we don't have to." Kaity could hear his dejection.

"My Dear, I'm sorry. I truly am," she said softly. "I just feel like Sahara isn't our home. I want to find someplace better, more habitable, more..."

"...like Earth?" Sharko ventured. Kaity couldn't make eye contact. He'd hit the nail straight on the head. Sharko placed a hand on her arm and surveyed his wife, sympathy in his hazel eyes. "Earth is gone, my Love. I know it hasn't been easy for either of us. It's hit you especially hard, but we can't keep wishing for something impossible."

"It doesn't make the yearning less," Kaity said bitterly, shading her eyes from the sun. Just their brief stop had caused her to overheat. "Where you see Utah and Arizona, I see the worst of Death Valley. Are we destined to dig wells and eat snakes the rest of our lives?"

"We can't know," Sharko admitted, "but my dearest, I once asked you to try moving on from the past. It's kept you from enjoying our married life and the blessings God has given us, even here. Have you been trying?"

Kaity bit her lip. How could she meet Sharko's gaze? Longing for her old life and family was an ache that wouldn't go away. Earth was no small thing to lose. Samantha spoke of a lofty future. Kaity couldn't see anything besides subsistence and pain looming in the murky unknown.

"Take me back," she said, choking up. "I love you, and I appreciate your sentiments, but I'm not certain I'm capable of what you ask. I *have* to hope that somewhere, out in the big, wide galaxy, there's a place like Earth."

"So I am not enough?" Sharko said at length, visibly hurt. "As my efforts to James were? Insufficient?"

"That's not what I meant!" Kaity protested, but the damage was done. Though she tried to plead with him, all Sharko could feel were barbs of pain. Husband and wife headed back to Base, silence presiding over the hovercraft. Sharko churned with emotion, stung by pangs of inadequacy. Later, Kaity cried silently as she felt the absence of familiar arms around her through the night. Backs to one another, husband and wife fell into uneasy sleep, feeling farther apart than they ever had before.

\<12\>

Pursuit

Breakfast the following morning went awkwardly. Dudeman and Abigale remained conspicuously absent, and the trouble between Kaity and Sharko was obvious to everyone. Nick had told Abigale about Earth's fate, and he informed the group of how hard she'd taken it. She was not to be disturbed until her tears subsided. Nancy attempted to avert unpleasantness by broaching the subject of Dudeman.

"I know you've been praying for him all these years," she told Sharko. His face betrayed sad bewilderment.

"I just...I felt like the Holy Spirit was guiding my words," he said. "How could they have produced so little effect?"

"Oh believe me, they had an impact!" Matt exclaimed. "I heard his fists banging into the wall this morning!"

Samantha paused from wolfing down her stale breakfast muffin to console Sharko.

"Sometimes, God uses us," she said, "and we don't see the results for years. I certainly regret doing the opposite of you: confronting James for my own ego instead of his salvation. You've planted a seed. It's up to God whether it grows. Now, about today's schedule—"

Samantha abruptly cut herself off. Her morning custom included outlining their daily plan and coordinating with the others. She was about to present her ideas, but felt God tugging at her heart to be silent. *Why, Lord?* She asked. *Because I want you to let someone else plan the day, Daughter,* came the reply. Samantha could hardly believe it! Again, she heard the familiar whisper of a Speaker who had calmed seas and formed oceans! Yet it did not amaze her so much as anger her. *Surely I am capable, Lord!* she protested.

You are capable, yes, but that is not my design for you, the Speaker corrected.

Samantha remembered her dream of distant battles and a gleaming city.
She recalled the Lord's Servant telling her she must acquiesce her leadership
to another. Though God had not revealed who that other was, Samantha had
an idea. *It would help if You confirmed who I must give this mantle to,* she said,
still annoyed. *If You show me this, I will do what I can to prepare Your leader.*

I will grant your request, though you will resent it, the Speaker answered.
He had maddeningly read her thoughts...of course! Being God's prophetess
was a high privilege, but since her boss was the all-knowing, all-powerful
Creator of everything—it came with downsides, too.

Samantha looked up to see everyone at the table staring. Her face
flushed. She'd been leaving everybody dangling with a half-finished sentence.

"You were mentioning the day's schedule, *Prima?*" Matt mercifully volunteered. Samantha regained her composure and prepared to speak, yet
paused as Sharko reached for her cup.

"Refill?" he questioned courteously. All he did was politely offer—a nonchalant gesture—but it told Samantha everything. A growing suspicion, because of his recent success, crawled into her psyche.

"Sharko," she said, forcing cordiality, "why don't you come up with a
schedule for the day?"

"*Me?*"

"You've been fronting this entire thing," Samantha pointed out. Sharko
hardly knew how to answer her. He felt scared, privileged, and too emotional
all at once.

"I—I guess I could," he stuttered, looking to Kaity for support. She merely crossed her arms and looked away. Whatever remained of his confidence
fell, trampled, to the dust. Yet he'd already said yes.

Formulating a plan took the distracted Anderson awhile, but by mid-
morning, they boarded Nick's hovercraft. The deck of the ship stretched just
large enough for five of them plus the water tank. Sharko, Samantha, Matt,
Nick, and Kaity manned the vessel, all in Starganaut form. Nancy had origi-
nally been slated as the fifth person, but she insisted Kaity go along—to her
friend's dismay. Dudeman wouldn't even answer their knocks, and Mike and
Chrysta insisted on staying because of a date. The couple left for a morn-

ing walk before the others departed, reminding Kaity with their loving looks how poorly her own marriage was going.

Mornings were the only time to traipse across the sand as the days became unbearably hot. Many of the survivors from Earth did outdoor work in Starganaut form, because the suits warded off the heat. The group that left with Sharko transformed before boarding the hovercraft. All except Nick, at least.

"Blimey!" Nick exclaimed. "You'll need to fill me in on those magic crystals, Mate! I didn't know all of ya had 'em!"

Crosshair told Nick about the orbs while he piloted their craft. The prophetess enjoyed the feel of wind whipping against her red helmet and visor. They skimmed along at a high speed, their sailing smooth except for an encounter with a steep dune. Crosshair's stomach dropped as their craft crested it, abruptly diving and speeding down the slip-face. They rushed by sand that looked like sculpted ripples, red-tinted ground, a cluster of cacti. Scenery Crosshair had never seen before slipped by, along with the whipping wind.

Nick maneuvered their craft past a canyon, throttling to a stop before an overhanging bluff with a hillock of sand in front of it. He used the last momentum of the engine to drift over the hillock, then braked the craft. The three buildings and his junk piles met Crosshair's eyes. She glanced over at the others, noticing that Valora and Blaze appeared wretched and unable to enjoy anything. Matt, as Thunderbane, looked like a kid on his favorite theme park ride.

Nick prepared to alight, then jerked back his foot.

"No, no, this is all wrong!" he exclaimed.

"What do you see?" Blaze questioned, for he appeared to sense something amiss as well.

"Tracks," Nick murmured. "Tracks and...my dingle-hopper isn't where I left it!"

"Excuse me?" Crosshair coughed.

"Dingle-hopper! It's my name for that machine over by the watcha-ma—never mind! In plain English, someone's been here!"

"Let's hope it wasn't Goldilocks," Thunderbane couldn't help commenting. His words ended with the sharp report of an alien rifle. A searing bolt of plasma smacked into the ground inches from the front of the hovercraft!

EVERYONE ABOARD THE hovercraft jumped at the unexpected shot. It came from the bluff top, and another followed soon after.

"Back up!" Valora screamed.

"I can't back 'er up, Mate!" Nick shouted, cranking a hard right. "She only goes one direction, and that's forward!"

A dozen Trylithian faces popped out. Several guns went off as Nick punched the rocket engines. The hovercraft turned so sharply it nearly capsized. Up the sand bunker it slid, and then they were racing over the dunes. Several moments passed, after which all breathed a sigh of relief. Valora glanced back and her heart sank. Three ships were darting after them!

"I see them!" Blaze yelled, and all hostilities between husband and wife ceased in the face of danger.

The Starganauts prepared for the assault. Kaity, as Valora, prayed their enemies didn't have mounted guns. Her fears were assuaged as the Trylithian hovercrafts approached without firing a shot. The closest one rapidly gained on them, until its crew hovered within range. The high whine of pistols and the crack of rifle fire caused everyone to duck except Nick. He clung to the helm doggedly, zigzagging sharply to shake their enemy.

Blaze whipped out his gun and took aim. His plasma carbine flashed in the sunlight, the flame tracery on its barrel matching the designs on his armor. Crosshair carried dual pistols, which she put to good use. The other Starganauts had no such advantage. Valora's broadsword and Thunderbane's lightning foils were melee weapons. Both Starganauts did their best to stay down as their friends and foes dueled with ranged weapons. Shooting from a moving hovercraft proved challenging, yet Crosshair scored the first kill. Her aim outmatched Blaze's, despite flourishing her pistols between trigger pulls.

A second Trylithian went down before Blaze found a good opening. A Trylithian raised himself up to fire. Blaze squeezed the trigger, scoring his first kill. Bereft of his crew, the pilot of the hovercraft throttled to a stop. The other two vessels screamed forward. Five Trylithians occupied the second hovercraft, while the third boasted a crew of four. The one with five rocketed forward, its pilot cranking the control stick sharply. The hovercraft skidded over, slamming into the side of Nick's. The Starganauts were jolted but held on. Again their enemy rammed them, but this time, one of the soldiers jumped as his craft hit theirs. He landed solidly on deck. Thunderbane met him with two crackling swords.

The male looked different than his comrades. He wore only a kilt, a chest-protector of metal, a headdress of small axe blades, and an ornate mouth-cloth. At his left side, a shrunken skull dangled from a chain strapped to his belt. The male gripped two scythes in front of him, parrying Thunderbane's mighty attack. Because of the scythes' wooden handles, the lightning swords failed to electrocute the male. Thunderbane swung an arcing blow at the Trylithian's head. A round energy shield materialized, halting his attack and taking the brunt of the force.

The Trylithian thrust both blades together in a pincer movement. The attack would've chopped an unarmored opponent in half. Instead, it sliced Thunderbane in the midriff. A weird sensation spread over him. Feeling his breastplate, he held up a few fingers. Blood dripped off of them. *I guess we aren't invincible in these after all.* The thought felt...disembodied? Matthew Sanchez had never been stabbed in battle before. He hadn't even been shot while in the army, so being knifed was a strange sensation.

The third hovership roared alongside them, loosing its own champion. A hulking Trylithian in plating jumped across, landing next to Nick. The Australian ignored him and continued his crazy maneuvers through the dunes. The champion readied his axe to strike the Australian. Valora rushed in to parry. Hardly knowing how she dared it, she successfully blocked his attack. She was frightened beyond reason. She'd never fought before, or faced the possibility of killing or being killed. But the others were occupied returning gunfire.

I'm gonna die! she thought, parrying again and feeling her arms shake. Her heart raced faster than the hovercraft. Nick propelled their vessel toward their opponent's, ramming into it. This threw Valora off balance, and she flew face-first into the railing. Her ears rang. The impact hurt, and she reached wildly for a handhold to avoid falling to the punishing sands below. Had her inner monologue been correct? Would this alien warrior finish her?

DUDEMAN PACED HIS SMALL quarters restlessly. He alternated between slapping the palms of his hands against the thin, metallic walls and sitting and fidgeting with his fingers. He knew the others had left. He guessed it must be past morning, now, but he couldn't stand to leave his quarters. A hurricane of emotions assaulted his aching heart. The sight of anyone threatened to unleash them! He must stay inside and be done with this! He couldn't imagine the actual battle going on near Nick's homestead, for a spiritual battle tore at him.

"If you truly are who You claim," James finally shouted, "then show me You're real, God! Show me a sign that You were ever involved in my life, even ONCE!"

Dudeman expected a voice, a bolt of lightning...anything. Nothing came. He started to relax, feeling vindicated. Maybe God would wimp out after all. Suddenly, his eyes flashed to a scene he couldn't place. It was so vivid that it startled him. A young woman, visibly pregnant, sat in a doctor's waiting room. He saw her only from the side, but black hair like his cascaded down her back. She fidgeted nervously, her eyes darting first to the receptionist's desk, then to a long corridor bordered by rooms with closed doors.

A woman walked out of a room. She appeared pale and gaunt, tears sliding down her face. James saw her expression, and it broke his heart. Regret, sorrow, depression—her very soul seemed wilted. She glanced up at the black-haired woman and something snapped within. Rushing forward, she crouched in front of the expectant mother, grasping her arms with an intensity that scared the other woman.

"Don't do it!" she screamed. "Don't get rid of the life inside you! Oh God, I will never forgive myself!"

Hospital staff dashed to the raving woman. Authoritative voices silenced her, dragging her off.

"Pay her no heed, Miss," a nurse said, with a sickly-sweet smile. "She's here because she's a little crazy and needs some help. The poor thing."

The nurse moved on, but the black-haired mother's fingers fidgeted faster. Her eyes shifted left and right. Her entire body began shaking, and when a nurse called her name, she could bear it no longer. Rising, she hurried toward the door. Past the voices of the calling secretaries, past the other hapless souls waiting in the office to be ushered in, she dashed out of the clinic and straight to her car. She raised a cell phone to her ear.

"John, I've changed my mind." Her voice sounded shaky, but resolute. "I want to keep our baby. I want to call him James."

James "Dudeman" Erskin recoiled physically as if in shock. He fell against his cot, landing ungracefully on his side. Breathing hard, he rose slowly and gazed at his reflection in the metal wall. It looked indistinct and blurry, like his life. Yet while the reflection remained unclear, everything seemed to come into focus in his mind. He finally saw how Sharko was right. His life, the very fact of him being here, could be traced to the sovereign will of God. Just as their survival, discovery, and protection from Vogul.

What if his mother had continued with the abortion? What if the other woman hadn't stopped, hadn't given her an extra push to run out of that clinic door and give her unborn son the future which James now experienced?

He'd been so angry for not having his biological mother. Never had it occurred to him that his very birth was the result of God's mercy! He'd felt resentful and bitter towards an absent father. What if his father had cared more about a cover-up than his life? For the first time as an adult, Dudeman started to cry. They were not the selfish tears of pity, but the watery offerings of a man at odds with God for decades, yet now humbled.

Humbled. James felt so low in comparison to the Almighty that he couldn't speak. He could not even lift his face. His pride had been completely dashed to pieces.

"Lord, I am a sinner," he said brokenly. "Save me. I put my trust in your Son and in Jesus' death on the cross. No more will I rage against you. No more will I break into tirades to escape the truth. I need You. Come fill me. Forgive me of my sins."

Again, James expected a voice, a bolt of lightning. Nothing. Yet stirring within his heart, he felt peace. It was a calmness starting small, like a tiny flame catching onto a pile of wood. But the calm, like the flame, soon spread. It settled over his entire body, bringing warmth and a feeling of wholeness James had never known. The hurricane stilled. A sensation flooded him as if something missing had been brought home; something lost was finally found. James knew it could only be the Lord. Twenty-four years later, the God who'd saved him as a baby was saving him again.

Dudeman Erskin, angry surfer from Earth, gave his heart to Christ.

NICK RAMMED THE ENEMY craft again. The Trylithian champion skidded but held his ground. Valora, slightly dazed from her encounter with the railing, sprang up just in time to avoid another blow. She defended herself, feeling utterly useless in combat. The inborn skill of her Form was the only thing that saved her. Valora's prowess made up for what Kaity's civilian lifestyle lacked.

The two foes stepped apart, and the alien stared at her. The Trylithian's fly-like, ice-cold eyes bored into Valora, sensing her fear through mere contact. He attempted to slay her with an upward swing that would've ripped into her stomach. Valora didn't have heavy armor like the others, but she remembered her shield. The device easily fit over her back, connected by magnet to a strap. With lightning-fast reflexes, she reached back, slid the handles over her arm, and deftly blocked the blow.

I just did that! Seriously? She thought. Filled with boldness, Valora brandished her sword and charged the champion. Her broadsword went right through his shield but was thwarted by his axe! The tutor barely blocked a punishing counterattack. Despite this, Valora's Form flooded her with something she hadn't known in her first Trylithian skirmish—courage. Without knowing why, she held her shield high and stared down the burly Trylithian. A replica purple jewel, akin to the orb embedded in her crown, glowed from the center of the shield. Its glow increased in intensity.

"By the power of courage, begone!" Valora screamed. A shockwave of energy shot out from the shield. The Trylithian's eyes snapped wide open. Before Valora's jaw could drop in wonder, the champion with nerves of steel turned and jumped back aboard his hovercraft. The shockwave hit the rest of the crew, who cried out in panic. The terrified pilot turned their hovership around so quickly that it spun out of control. The vessel flipped onto its side, spilling its Trylithian contents across the sand. Nick punched the engines and they continued fleeing, the capsized hovercraft fading into the distance behind them.

—————\|\|\|\|—————

WHILE VALORA FOUGHT the champion, Blaze and Crosshair struggled to fend off their other opponents. Between the two enemy vessels, six Trylithians were shooting at them. One hit Nick in the shoulder, though the Australian insisted it was a trifle. Crosshair nailed two Trylithians in one glorious volley. Blaze managed to injure a male by shooting between the rails of the enemy hovercraft, though he got hit twice in the armor for it. Thunderbane's battle was grueling. The Trylithian with the scythes proved a master warrior. Already bleeding, Matt had difficulty staying focused. His enemy struck twice in the same wound. Thunderbane cringed, backing up and doubling over in agony. The scythe-warrior moved in for the kill.

A purple knight with a shield leaped into the fray. Emboldened, Valora stabbed at the male's back. Unfortunately, he dodged out of the way, whirling on her. The alien threw his scythe into her sword, sending the blade flying from her grasp. Valora attempted to hide behind her shield, but the Trylithan wrenched it out of her hands and tossed it. The device hit the deck and skidded off the hovercraft, joining her sword on the Saharan surface.

Bereft of any defense, she was seized by the Trylithian. Though Valora struggled wildly, she felt a sharp jab in the neck. Everything appeared to grow distant. A queasy feeling knotted her stomach and the fight drained out of her. Valora slipped into unconsciousness.

The Trylithian, carrying her in his arms, made a running jump for his hovercraft. Crosshair and Blaze had picked off all but the pilot of his ship. The scythe warrior barely cleared the gap with his burden. The moment he landed, the hovercraft roared away. Thunderbane shook his lightning foils after it.

"Follow them!" Blaze commanded. Nick Dundee gritted his teeth and turned. Despite pushing the craft full-throttle, the enemy hovership was outpacing them steadily. Blaze paused, breathless with disbelief. Everything he loved and cared for was being carried off across the sands of fate. Worse, so much worse, their last parting had been fraught with turmoil and pain. No chance to say "I love you." No chance for reconciliation. Desperately, Blaze raised his carbine and fired at the pilot of the retreating ship. He would not let his wife slip into the distance!

His shots missed four times in a row. Crosshair took a cue and peppered the fleeing craft with pistol fire, wisely aiming for the larger target—its engines. One shot managed to hit home. It slowed the craft down a little, but not enough. The pilot glanced back nervously. Blaze steadied his weapon. He held his breath. It was now or never. *God of Heaven, guide my shot*! He said silently, and squeezed the trigger.

The bolt of searing plasma raced out of the barrel and struck the engine squarely. It sputtered out, and the hovership slowed enough that Nick began gaining on it. Even then, Blaze beheld a sight in the distance that made his blood run cold.

A dropship. The hovercraft was heading straight for it! Should they fail to catch up, their enemy might make it aboard with Kaity as his captive! Blaze could just make out her limp form, still held by the male. His blood boiled.

In the grasp of his foe hung his past, present, and future. In enemy arms dangled the mother of his children, the wife of his youth—the woman he'd vowed to protect and cherish with every breath. He had been wrong to equate her words with a lack of confidence in him, and what did it matter, anyway? He would win her back. He would fight to the death! He was determined to do everything in his power to protect that which he loved more than anything in the galaxy.

"The water tank!" he realized, with a shout. "We must lose it! It's slowing us down!"

"But our hauling—!" Nick began, through the pain.

"That's my WIFE!"

Nothing could dissuade the determined husband. Eagerly he tore at the straps holding the tank down. Crosshair joined in, until they unfastened enough to send the tank sailing backward off the craft. It jounced and jolted before skidding to a halt, dented and dusty but none the worse. Without its weight, the craft gained speed. Nick closed the gap, until he hovered directly behind the Trylithian vessel. The enemy warrior had laid Valora on the deck by this time and stood, waiting, scythes crossed in front of his chest-plate. Crosshair aimed at him, but Blaze pushed her pistols down.

"I'll handle him," he said simply, shouldering his carbine. Blaze moved to the back of their hovercraft and ran the length of it, catapulting himself forward in a flying leap. He landed on the deck, rolled beneath the Trylithian's flying blades, and sprang to his feet.

The warrior tried impaling him. Blaze deftly parried both scythes with his torchsword and bracer, knocking them downward. The Trylithian dodged a deadly swing and slashed Sharko's arm. The wound barely made a scratch, but it startled Blaze. He went in with torchsword pounding, forcing the warrior into a frenetic defense. His sword went right through the energy shield, forcing the male to block the hot blade left and right. He inched backward unknowingly, toward the railing of the hovercraft. Suddenly, the Trylithian held his scythes outward and crossed the blades.

Blaze felt a crushing pain seize his abdomen. It seemed like the jaws of some wild beast, but there was no such animal in sight. He could hardly move. Grimacing, he cried out in pain as the male drew the blades even closer together. The sensation in his midriff increased to unbearable intensity. Thunderbane, Nick, and Crosshair could only watch helplessly from the other craft. Were they about to lose both of the Andersons to Vogul?

THE TRYLITHIAN'S EYES bored into Blaze, willing him to give up. He released whatever hold he'd created and rushed the weakened human, but Blaze anticipated this. Even in his pain, the Starganaut swung mightily. The Trylithian's right scythe pole snapped from the blow. Grabbing his other scythe with a gloved hand, Blaze snapped it as well. The Trylithian tackled him in response—just as the pilot made a sharp turn.

Warrior and Starganaut rolled heavily into the railing. Valora too rolled across the deck, bumping into the pilot's low-set chair. *Thank you Lord*! Blaze thought briefly, with relief. The hovercraft reached the dropship but screamed past, not bothering to throttle down. With the Starganauts hot on his heels, the pilot wasn't about to risk them boarding the dropship.

The scythe-warrior, bereft of weapons, grabbed Blaze and threw him. The Starganaut flew haplessly over the railing. He twisted in midair and caught the rail with both hands, his feet skidding mere inches above the gritty ground. Sand flew against his helmet, but the visor preserved sight. Blaze felt a crushing pain again. This time, it was the warrior's boot on his hand! He grasped another part of the railing, only to have his other hand trampled.

Doggedly, Blaze held on, fighting his inclination to let go and relieve the pain. Shoving aside the injury to his hands, he focused on Kaity. Despite her Starganaut form, she lay limply on deck, looking pale and helpless. Rage boiled inside of him. Blaze pulled himself mightily over the rail. The Trylithian's boot met his helmet...with no effect! Blaze was truly enraged now. Rising, he pointed at the Trylithian with his torchsword.

"You kidnapped my wife!" he dashed forward, the heat of protective fury coursing through his veins. "You can incinerate my planet, you can blow up my base, but don't you ever, *ever* KIDNAP MY WIFE!!!!"

The Trylithian scythe-warrior blinked several times. He toppled over, a shocked expression beneath his mouth-cloth. He had been run cleanly through; the blade so searing it cauterized the gaping hole. The enemy pilot quickly threw down his pistol, and the hovercraft skidded to a halt. He groveled on the ground, expecting a shot in the head from the vengeful human. Instead, Blaze extended a hand.

"Up you get! There's a good alien," Blaze said, shocking the Trylithian pilot with his mercy. The male could only understand his body language, but that problem was soon rectified. Nick brought the Starganauts' hovercraft to a swift halt beside Blaze. All three humans gazed at him in amazement. A limp Valora hung in his arms and the Trylithian pilot walked freely beside him. Crosshair jumped out and relayed Blaze's message to the alien that he would remain unharmed.

"It isn't our way," the prophetess translated. "I don't know what treatment you've endured under Vogul, but he's an abnormal example of humankind."

Blaze and the others were forced to listen, uncomprehending, as Crosshair and the Trylithian exchanged many unintelligible words.

"Helpful chap," Crosshair said, once they were finished. "He was so grateful to avoid a torchsword through the skull that he gave me instructions on how to pilot his craft. In exchange, he asked that we leave his dropship alone. I guess that's one Trylithian we stumped with kindness. Apparently, Vogul beats lesser crewmen like him." She gazed across the dunes darkly.

"Is your wife all right there?" Nick asked, gesturing to Valora.

"I hope so," Blaze replied anxiously. "How are you holding up, Thunderbane?"

"For losing some blood in this abysmal waste...not bad!" came Matt's cheeky, weak reply. "I'm kind of thirsty, though."

"Havin' a hole in ya will do that!" Nick said cheerfully, grimacing from his own injury.

"Let's head home!" Blaze exclaimed. Nick declared he was fit enough to pilot their new hovership if Crosshair would share the instructions. Blaze readily volunteered to fly their own craft back, and gently laid Valora on the deck.

"I only pray this is not a precursor to Vogul discovering our base," Crosshair said grimly, voicing the fears of all. They retrieved Valora's sword and shield, and their water tank, from the scorching ground. This accomplished, they set out through the shimmering heat to the one sanctuary Vogul hadn't yet discovered.

JIXA OF TRYLITHIA TRAVERSED the outskirts of Stattar Nebula, frustrated and angered. Over a month of searching for Vogul yielded nothing. Because of Stattar's effect on sensors, he'd been forced to conduct a physical search for the gunship. After combing what he imagined must be every nook of the nebula, he and his small crew came up empty. The gunship was either cleverly avoiding his search, or simply wasn't there. Whatever the case, Jixa broke out of the greenish-blue nebula and into open space. The stars provided a welcome sight, and he attempted to establish a com connection with Tormac Durag.

Jixa's uncle had been holed up in Rac Itor, a mountain fortress, while Trylithia erupted into war. The Myds who'd bombed Lidexid turned from their destruction of one colmit and started bombarding others. Soon there was an all-out skirmish between several colmits and the Myd interlopers. This proved advantageous for Durag, who most Trylithians forgot in their scramble to defeat the attackers. However, as Jixa tried again and again to establish a link that ended only in static, his heart faltered. He felt that something must be terribly wrong, so he decided to proceed directly to Trylithia.

A few days' voyage brought them back to the ringed orb of home. Trylithia was divided into distinct climate regions, whose delineation was visible from space. They neared Duskrealm, and every Trylithian aboard sat aghast. Ruined cities. Forests burned to cinders. Citadels blasted apart. Crashed ships, both Myd and Trylithian, littered the apocalyptic scene. For a moment, Jixa feared all of Duskrealm was gone, but they came to a deeply-shadowed forest that seemed undisturbed. Several towns could still be seen, safe and secure for now.

He breathed a sigh of relief. Only portions of Duskrealm were ravaged by war, and they passed several patches of destruction scattered between unbroken wilderness and the usual signs of habitation. A few times, a voice came over the com demanding to know his identity. Jixa simply told them, and no one fired a shot.

The ship did not encounter a single Myd. Jixa began to relax, settling back into his seat. They crested the great, rocky ridges of the Rac Mountain Range and his heart sank. His blue face fell in sorrow. Jixa wailed in the buzz-like tongue of his people as the ship hovered before a horrible sight. Where the mighty fortress of Rac Itor used to stand, there were only craters.

Rac Itor had been perched upon two, steep slopes. The castle portion had nestled on a ridge of rock, with a bridge crossing a chasm to a spur, upon which sat the smaller but more secure keep. This was why the fortress had remained impenetrable for so long, and no Trylithian would destroy it with gunfire. The Myds were not so respectful.

Jixa's pilot brought the ship in closer. Aside from a few chunks of masonry, the entire fortress had been blasted from the mountainside. Jixa could tell, even before scans confirmed it, that no life remained in the rubble. *What if Uncle fled before this?* His mind hoped. His sharp eyes, accustomed to low light, spotted the glint of something.

Landing in the midst of the crater, Jixa alighted on the blasted rock. His long cape flowed in the wind of the chill heights. Striding forward, he bent down and removed an object from atop the ashes. It couldn't be! Jixa recoiled as if stung, dropping the half-melted crown that was all too familiar. A head-dress of axe blades, fit for a tormac. Every shred of doubt within Jixa fled from his numbed perception. His uncle was dead. Durag and his court, slain in a Myd bombardment!

Anger replaced shock. The Myds had done this...but no! Who truly bore the blame in causing this chain of tragic events? Whose persuasions had Durag heeded? Whose plan involved stealing from a people deadlier than they? One name, like a bolt of lightning, struck his enraged brain. Vogul! Before the man from Earth, all had been well with Lidexid. Vogul had suggested they steal the gunship, and now, the entirety of Duskrealm paid the price.

Jixa retrieved the fragmented crown. He vowed to his uncle that Vogul would be brought to justice. He had no more business upon this world. The Myds were an unconquerable foe, and engaging them in warfare was like stepping on the toe of a giant. Without colmit and without tormac, Jixa determined he would set out and pursue the only enemy he could touch.

He would find and kill Willum Vogul.

<13>

The Plan

The Starganauts leaped into action as soon as they reached their Base. Nick and Crosshair parked their hoverships in the storage bay, and Blaze lowered the tarp covering its opening. Mike and Chrysta rushed out to help offload the wounded. Prophetess and Australian pushed sand down over the tarp, completely hiding the otherwise-gaping hole. Crosshair retraced their tracks, wiping them out with a broom before carefully crawling back under the cover. She lowered it in such a way that from the outside, the dune looked like any other.

Inside *The Deliverer*, Apotheka tended to Nick and Thunderbane's injuries. Matt's wound was worse than he would admit. Apotheka gasped as her scanner revealed he'd lost a considerable amount of blood. Her healing gun restored him to a functional state, and Nick's arm, she healed entirely. Sadly, Apotheka could do little for Valora. Sharko had changed back to normal, and he helped the nurse strip off his wife's armor, revealing an interlocked, mesh undersuit of royal purple. Apotheka examined her, but couldn't counteract whatever serum lay behind her blackout. She had no way of taking a sample to analyze it, so she checked Valora's vitals and advised that they keep her in Form.

"Will she be all right?" Sharko asked desperately.

"I believe so," Apotheka answered, "though how long it'll be before she's with us again...I can't tell."

Sharko reached down and gently caressed his wife's cheek. He seemed lost in melancholy.

"It's ironic, how one day's tragedy can make the disagreement of yesterday appear so utterly petty."

"I guess that's part of marriage." Apotheka shrugged. "At the end of the day, you love your wife. I know Kaity will see that. I *was* next to her at the altar, y'know."

Dudeman charged in at that moment. His red-rimmed eyes formed a contrast to his face, which glowed with delight. He appeared ready to burst.

"I did it, Man!" he exclaimed. Everyone ceased what they were doing and turned to look at him, surprised. "I accepted Christ! Oh..."

Seeing Kaity and Matt put a stop to his excitement. He was instantly by Sharko's side.

"You okay, Bro?" he asked, putting a comforting arm around his shoulders. Sharko shoved it off and gave him an incredulous look.

"Get out of here!" he said impishly. "James Erskin, accept Jesus? Really?"

"Truly," Dudeman said, his glee returning, "and completely."

"That...that's amazing!" Apotheka exclaimed, and Mike and Chrysta expressed guarded enthusiasm. Even Matt put in a weak hurrah, and for a moment, their spirits lifted. Samantha could not have been more flabbergasted. Dudeman? James Erskin, the man who exploded in fits of anger, who withdrew, who had rejected salvation again and again? She felt too overwhelmed with happiness to realize her disappointment that *she* hadn't been the one to convert him. That would emerge later. For now, she took the news as a welcome boon after so much anguish and peril.

The Dundees were not present to hear the good news. The Starganauts had let Nick and Abigale use the cockpit as their room, and two sleeping bags barely fit. In this miniscule room, Nick approached Abigale. She sat crosslegged on the floor, her tears cried out, her heart lapsed into despondent acceptance.

"Not just Earth, but our homestead, too? *Gone*?"

Abigale spoke so shakily that Nick feared for her, but she smiled wanly. He took his sister's hand comfortingly, letting her see the sorrow in his own face. His lip quivered, and tears began to fall from his eyes.

"We've come through so much," Nick whispered. "I truly thought, 'at last! Finally we'll be rescued, fair dinkum!' I must've marked out two years on the wall of our module, waitin'. Knowing that everythin' which got us through it is gone..."

"What will we do, Nicky?" Abigale could barely speak, a new wave of tears assaulting her. Nick let go, rising to his feet with determination.

"We help the Starganauts, that's what!" he declared. "They're all we've got, but they're better company than cacti! Less prickly, too!" he grinned comically, and Abigale chuckled despite the circumstances. Earth might be gone, but in this feeble fragment of humanity, there remained a strong reason to persevere. That, at least, provided some relief.

STRANGE VOICES CALLED to Kaity Anderson from a distance. A monster held her in its clutches, and blue stretched everywhere. Kaity struggled violently but her body was paralyzed. She couldn't move an inch, and felt more than saw the creature leap across a great chasm. The abyss extended so far down that its depths petered into darkness. Kaity felt the jolt of the monster's landing, but suddenly, she found herself in a field on Earth. It was a green place—a solitary place. She could hear waves crashing nearby, though hedges and trees obscured her view of the ocean. She nearly tripped over an unknown object, and caught herself on it. It felt cold and hard, and she recoiled when she recognized it. A tombstone!

"Kaity!"

A familiar voice called her name. She whirled in the speaker's direction, beholding the person with amazement and joy. Her mother! All fear sank before an onslaught of relief. She rushed to her mom, to embrace her, yet could make no progress. Kaity again experienced the sensation of paralysis. She stood, frozen, only five maddening feet from her mom.

"Why, oh *why*, did you and father not join us?" she asked, tears streaming down her face. "Why did you sacrifice your lives for earthly things? For useless *stuff*?"

"We made a serious mistake, dear Daughter." Regret permeated her words. "But even our foolish choices were not outside of God's plan. This path you tread is a road you must travel with your husband. We missed our chance. Your father and I did not understand until it was too late—until the weapon had discharged and we saw death sweeping towards us."

Kaity struggled to breathe for the tears. She longed with everything inside her to feel her mother's comforting arms. She could not. Something continued holding her back, keeping them apart. Her mother gazed at her with compassion.

"You do not need me any longer," she said gently. "You are your own woman now. Your father and I are in a wonderful place—a land without pain. Jesus has wiped away our tears, although for you, there await many trials. My daughter, you have lived far too long with the past in your heart. You must cling to God, and to your husband. You must leave us behind. Mourn for us. Miss us and remember us! God made emotions so we could feel them! But do not let grief hold you back from living! Be the wife and woman God called you to be."

"I don't even know how!" Kaity lamented, wiping strands of hair out of her eyes. "Everything blew to pieces on my wedding day! I began my marriage by losing all!"

"Not everything was lost to you, my dear," her mother countered, and abruptly, Kaity heard Sharko's voice. She felt him caressing her hand tenderly, and became acutely aware of feeling very cold. It was an odd sensation after months of uncomfortable heat. Her eyes opened slowly, and she observed Sharko kneeling beside her. He held one of her hands in his. His mouth moved as he spoke tenderly.

"I love you, my Dear, and one day..." he trailed off. His mouth burst into a happy smile. He fell to his knees, grabbing Valora and hugging her to himself like a ragdoll. Kaity didn't know whether to feel stifled or insanely loved, but she was soon beaming as well.

"She's all right! She's going to be okay!" Sharko exclaimed to everyone, before turning back to her with a tear running down his cheek.

"I was SO worried. And look at you!"

"Sharko," Valora began, after a pause, "there is something I want to tell you."

The trucker politely shooed Nancy and the others away. Kaity's best friend had been approaching, but a look from Sharko made her understand.

"Yes? What is it? Anything, Darling!"

"I owe you such an apology!" Valora gestured contritely. "This fight, our argument...I've come to see that I've been selfish. I haven't been the wife you needed or deserved. I've been stuck in the past, placing more value and love on those departed than my own husband! Part of it is the novelty of our marriage. I had just left my parents to start a life with you. It isn't easy adjusting from daughter to wife, and with them dead...I'm so, *so* sorry, Honey."

Sharko gave a deep, drawn-out sigh. He took her hand, enclosing her fingers in his. Touching his forehead to hers, he stared into her sky-blue eyes.

"This morning, all I could feel was frustration and anger," he confessed. "This afternoon, all I could think of was saving you. You're more precious to me than you can ever know, Kaity. Thank you. I love you, *deeply*, and all's forgiven."

Sharko gently kissed her on the forehead. To Valora, all worry and uncertainty faded away with that token of tenderness. It was not wrong to grieve for family lost, but no longer would loss be the focus of her life. She had a husband, and although the forces of evil threatened to annihilate them, they had the orbs. Despite everything in their past, Valora truly felt a sense of hope. Vogul's minions hadn't stopped them. Nick's cistern would supply them with water, and her husband loved her very dearly. For the first time, Valora found herself looking forward to the future with anticipation.

THE TRYLITHIANS GATHERED in the courtyard of the Dundee homestead to watch an execution. Willum Vogul strode out in his armor, his gloved hand firmly around the grip of a plasma pistol. Against Nick's embankment of sand, a bound Trylithian could be seen. The male was the warrior who had foiled their ambush of the Starganauts with a premature shot. He kneeled in the sand, his face upturned to Vogul. Willum strode forward, whirling to face the onlookers once before delivering his execution. The light of dawn cast everything in a gray pallor.

"This is how I tolerate failure!" Vogul cried, and he aimed at the defenseless Trylithian's head. The Trylithians surrounding cringed as he shot the male point-blank. The warrior was dead before he hit the grainy ground.

"Yes, yes, I do this for you!" Vogul shouted maniacally as he squeezed the trigger again. "For *you*!"

Willum's words were directed at the sky. They merely strengthened the assumptions of those watching in horror that the human must be insane. The middle-aged madman ordered several males to remove the dead Trylithian. No one else moved. Most of the victim's compatriots were shaken into stunned silence, but one male, a commander, walked forward approvingly. Unlike those who feared and hated Vogul, the commander liked his barbaric methods. A model of Lidexid's brutality, he was the reason the other colmits had turned upon the violent nation. He, and enough of the other Trylithians, approved of Vogul's violence—even if they resented his mood swings.

"My master," the commander said, "what is our course of action? We have one of their watering holes...possibly a secondary base. Do we hold it, and let them die of thirst?"

"Thirst is not good enough for them!" Vogul sneered. He handed his plasma pistol to a quaking attendant. "We're now aware of the general location of their base. We use it to root them out. With our crew of 200 and our ships, they won't stand a chance."

"But my master, wouldn't it be wiser to stay indoors?" the commander questioned carefully. "It's nearing Dalar 3's summer, and it climbs to over eighty *caj* by mid-morning."

"100 Fahrenheit?" Vogul snarled, despite the fact that his body also hated the climate. "Pah! Your men are cowards. We will search the desert, by foot, by hovercraft, and by ship! I will leave forty warriors here, should those pathetic humans be foolish enough to attack. The net draws closer around them. They will be caught, and I will finally rid the galaxy of their filthy presence!"

"And after that, Master?" the commander asked. Vogul gazed toward the open, shadowy tunnel that led to Nick's cistern. His eyes seemed to be looking past it, at something invisible. The commander couldn't be certain, but for a brief second, it looked as if a shadow passed between them and the sun.

"We will be exalted as the saviors of the galaxy!" Vogul exclaimed. "We will have riches, power, and glory that cannot be imagined!"

It was a lie. Vogul knew it, but he spoke with such passion that the commander smiled beneath his mouth-cloth. There would be exaltation, true. There would be the fame and glory of saving, but not for them. Only Vogul would receive a reward. The rest of the crew, he intended to leave someplace where the vengeful Myds would capture them. Despite the fact that these people had saved him, Vogul saw them as something to be used. They served as disposable tools for his greater purpose, and their gullibility would prove their downfall.

NIGHT DESCENDED ON the shimmering desert like a hawk swooping upon its prey. Hot winds turned to warm, the burning sands cooled, and for a brief moment, the ferocity of the sun abated. Even the cacti appeared wilted beneath the cool light of the stars. On this moonless night, the only security to be found rested in the dune-covered base of the Starganauts. Yet for the eight, and the Dundees, security was the last feeling in their hearts. Gathered around both tables of the Commons, they used what precious paper and pens they still possessed to map out a plan of action. Kaity didn't know what outcome their meeting would yield, but her shoulders felt tight with anticipation.

Nick spoke first. The excitement over James' conversion abating, the prattling Australian could hold it in no longer.

"We're discovered! Foul blighters have our homestead *and* our water!"

"And they're likely eatin' my garden, too!" Abigale huffed.

"We must claim it back!" Nick exclaimed. "I won't sit on my hands while they run their grimy boots all over the place!"

"Caution, Mr. Dundee!" Samantha ran a hand through her chocolate-colored tresses. "This is bad news for us all, not just you. Vogul knows where we draw water from. I fear this will force a confrontation. Even with these crystal suits, I doubt we'd have the strength to fight his entire company. Yet I agree we can't give up on your homestead. Not with only one tank's worth of water. Anyone have thoughts on solving this problem?

"We could take their homestead back," Mike suggested, "and fortify it!"

"Forgive me, but *our* base stands a better chance," Matt spoke up. "Stealth seems our only option for survival."

"We can't let them keep us from that water," Dudeman pointed out. "After Sharko just found it..."

"What about a compromise?" Nancy asked rhetorically. The eyes of everyone turned to her. "We *must* have water, but it's possible Vogul's entire detachment isn't at the homestead. There were about a dozen Trylithians shooting at you. The gunship must have a crew bigger than that."

"Good point," Kaity agreed, proud of her friend. "Do you remember when we got swallowed up by Vogul's craft? He had a lot more Trylithians in his 'welcoming committee' than there were at Nick and Abigale's base."

"Are you suggesting we take it back?" Matt's mouth twisted disapprovingly. "As you mentioned, there were at least a hundred Trylithians in his crew complement. If we take the homestead, those hundred will fall on us like a hammer."

"I'm sorry to say, but he's right." Chrysta's words ended with a sympathetic glance toward Kaity.

"I'm *not* suggesting two bases!" Nancy interjected. "Will you please let me finish?"

"With this fruitless discussion? Sure!" Matt said sarcastically.

"Hey, you're all ignoring the fact it's *my* homestead!" Nick roared.

The meeting soon erupted into chaos. Everyone talked over everybody else. Listening was rendered impossible, and Kaity covered her ears, leaning against her husband and pleading with him.

"Sharko, please do something!"

"Me?" Sharko seemed surprised.

"You've always been good at calming tense situations. I saw you do that many times in arguments. You even calm me down! Just please do something!"

"Samantha is our leader," Sharko rebutted. "I hardly think I can offer more than a prophetess of God could."

"Our 'prophetess' is in the thick of it!" Kaity nodded in Samantha's direction, rolling her eyes. The normally-dignified prophetess stood up from the table, both hands on her hips, her tone scolding. She was alternating between arguing with her cousin and trading verbal jabs with Nick. Abigale dashed from the table, bursting into tears, and Dudeman could be heard over the din, shouting, "Hey, stop behaving so un-Christian-like, Dudes!"

"Honey, I know you don't see yourself as much of a leader," Kaity continued. "But lately, I've wondered if you shouldn't take a more active role. Whatever the case, please just shake some sense into them!"

Sharko rose from his seat, his quiet calmness a sharp contrast to the clamor in the room. Looking as reluctant as he felt, he balled his hand into a fist and set his jaw.

"Shut up!" he shouted. "Everyone, please, BE QUIET!"

A STUNNED SILENCE FELL on the arguing humans. Sharko's thundering words came out with uncharacteristic force and authority.

"Do you hear yourselves?" Sharko questioned loudly. Again, stunned silence prevailed. "If we can't agree on a simple thing like this, how in the galaxy can we expect to outwit Vogul? For months, we've experienced the unity of survival and common purpose. What happened? Why are we so divided right now—so pessimistic and ready to blame?"

"We're being driven completely by emotion," Sharko continued nobly, "instead of a balance of heart and logic. Most of all, we're not being led by prayer. In other situations, we've prayed and diligently sought the Lord's leading. We need to do this before we crumble as a team. So Vogul has our water? So Vogul has your base? God gave us this rust-bucket in a dune for our protection, and we have time! We've got enough water to last for several days. We must seek God's will first! Whatever follows, I shall trust in His guidance."

"I didn't open us with prayer." Samantha paused, a look of shame crossing her face.

"Then would you please close us with it?" Sharko asked. The prophetess recovered her cool, and led them in a prayer that calmed everyone. They split apart for the night, without further arguments. Kaity beamed to see her husband step up, yet his actions produced a far different result in Samantha.

The former engineer tossed and turned and could not fall asleep. She felt a profound sense of failure. *Why, Lord? Why did I forget when we needed to seek You most?* The prophetess could not find an answer, but something was distracting her—taking her mind off of her routine responsibilities.

It was worry. Worry, because Sharko seemed to be God's next choice for their leader. Samantha did not want to relinquish her leadership. Yet by her very stubbornness, she'd revealed why God had chosen him. *I'm slipping*! She thought, with self-accusation. *I know what I must do, but I want the opposite. I...I resent him for bringing James to Christ. What is wrong with me*?

"You are unwilling to let go of control," a familiar Speaker said. Samantha shook her fist at the darkness.

"Control? Then what do you call that entire year I trusted You?" she snapped. "I gave up my career, my savings, my credibility, to preach from street corners and get branded the town lunatic!"

"It is true that You let me lead you on Earth," the Speaker affirmed, "but after Earth, you have slipped back into your natural tendencies. For my servants, I desire a leader who seeks to avoid control rather than gain it. I will grow Sharko in ways he cannot imagine, and You do not wish to impede this, Daughter. You can choose to, but it will not come without a price."

"You find worth in your position," the Speaker continued, softly. "You find value in being the head of things, liked and admired as a leader. But that is not my plan for you. Daughter, if you only fully trusted my words! If you only believed in your heart that I sincerely love and value you! Not for what you accomplish, but for the simple fact that I made you and you are my child!"

Again, as she so often did, Samantha felt stricken by humility. God needed to be obvious to get through her thick skull, and tonight was no exception. However, she also sensed God's overwhelming love, and this encouraged her. Despite enjoying leadership, it was exhausting. Samantha laughed ironically as she reflected on her present tiredness and drooping eyelids. She rolled onto her stomach. Resolving to give God the wheel, she at last found the peace which had long eluded her, and drifted off to sleep.

MORNING DAWNED, HOT and blinding. The ground started radiating heat waves almost immediately. From a distance, the desert sand appeared to end and a pool of silver water begin, yet this was a mirage of the desert. It reminded Chrysta and Mike Taylor of their own illusion—their shared secret.

Hand-in-hand they walked, enjoying the fresh if not grainy air. A brisk wind kicked up, and Mike wondered if another sandstorm would blow through. It seemed a reflection of their marriage. Rough, hard, and unpredictable. Starting out, they'd had little money, multiple jobs, and college tuition. Those would have been bearable with a better relationship, but Chrysta and Mike had struggled with issues that made living together difficult. On top of this, and hardest of all, they kept a painful secret from the others. Chrysta had nearly told Kaity about it, but Mike wished to hide it. As he'd concealed the seriousness of his wound from Chrysta, so they concealed this truth from the Starganauts.

It was for the best. Knowledge would only upset the others and depress their hopes on this world. Husband and wife whispered to each other, though nothing but the wind and cacti could overhear. The oncoming storm would wipe out their trail of footprints, yet they stayed alert for signs of Trylithians. Hand-in-hand they traversed the ever-shifting dunes, which cast long shadows where secrets basked.

In the Commons, Samantha continued the previous night's meeting without them. Everyone appeared calmer from a good night's sleep, and even Nick and Abigale looked less agitated. Kaity and Sharko took their usual seats, and Samantha gestured toward the trucker.

"Mr. Anderson, as you all know, had the good sense to call for a break last night. Since he's continually demonstrated clear-headed thinking, we agreed that he would lead this assembly. He also has a plan, which I believe you may approve."

Kaity smiled, appreciative of Samantha's praise toward Sharko. She squeezed her husband's hand under the table, telling him without words how proud she felt.

"Thank you," Sharko said to Samantha, before turning to the others. "I want to start by saying that I consider all of you my brothers and sisters. I hope I didn't hurt any feelings last night, but my intention was for our benefit."

"We hear you, man!" Dudeman exclaimed, speaking for the group.

"I had an idea last night that could only have come from God." Sharko fidgeted, somewhat nervous. "I think it's pretty clear that we're divided. Some wish to assault the enemy and reclaim Nick and Abigale's home. Others think it's wisest to stay put and out of sight. My thought is: What if we can accomplish both?"

"Both, Mate?" Nick seemed thoroughly interested.

"And how do you propose that?" Matt raised a skeptical eyebrow.

"Just listen closely," Sharko began, and the others leaned forward in rapt attention as he carefully outlined his plan...

———————— ✝✝⟋⟋⟍⟍⟋⟍ ————————

WILLUM VOGUL RECEIVED news of an approaching sandstorm only two hours into the day's search. He'd been skimming along in a hovership looking for footprints, trash...anything to give them a trail to their enemies. Vogul indulged in his usual fit of rage before consenting to pull out. He could not argue with an approaching wall of sand, so he left the garrison of 40 at the Dundee homestead with orders to search the property for information. To the 40 Trylithians, this was nothing new. It would be their third search of the Australians' effects, but Vogul was obsessed and they were dutiful.

The Trylithians started by rummaging through Nick's outdoor junk piles. They posted a lookout on the crest of the sand bunker, to watch for the storm and the Starganauts. The male's eyes soon bugged from a sight in the distance. His headdress flew back as he turned to report a high wall of sand rushing toward them. The Trylithians took cover. For over an hour, the sandstorm blew through Nick's junkyard, carrying off smaller scraps and reshaping the dune bunker. Once the storm passed, the Trylithians funneled out of the buildings to resume their posts.

Outside of the Trylithians' sight range, the Starganauts prepared to move in. They'd departed for the homestead as soon as the sandstorm died down enough for visibility, their intention to strike when the enemy least expected. Nick's sand bunker shielded them a bit from detection, but they needed to move along the bluff to approach the homestead covertly. The alternatives were a flat plain of sand with no coverage, or the obvious canyon, and Sharko's scheme depended on surprise.

Kaity, in Valora's form, paused before the coming battle. Her heart beat wildly. She'd faced the Trylithians in recent combat, but this felt different. Now that they were the attackers, she feared facing the aliens. What if she was shot? Could she bring herself to kill someone? What if Sharko couldn't save her this time? What if they failed, and God's plans for them came to nothing?

It was foolish, thinking the Lord's will could be thwarted. Valora's logical side told her this. Yet she knew that sometimes, God called his followers to make sacrifices. Sometimes, His will came at the ultimate earthly cost. *Even so,* she thought bravely, *if my life ends here, it will simply begin in Heaven. This, *this* is the hope we have, no matter how dark or frightening the trial. If anything, Father, my greatest regret in battle is sending unbelievers into a painful Eternity.*

As if sensing her confliction, Blaze squeezed his wife's gloved hand. He walked to the front of the group of ranged combatants. Those with melee weapons, like Valora, would follow behind those with ranged. Samantha, Chrysta, Nancy, and Sharko carried guns as Crosshair, Vipress, Apotheka, and Blaze. In contrast, Dudeman, Matt, Kaity, and Mike's forms of Fyromaniac, Thunderbane, Valora, and Ninjarak possessed close-ranged armaments.

The heat of the desert felt oppressive, even to her enhanced body. Valora awaited the signal from her husband, who moved ahead of them all. The Starganauts pressed their bodies against the layered sandstone of the bluff, moving so close to it that the Trylithians couldn't see them from the homestead. Blaze crept up Nick's embankment and peeked around the corner of the rock alcove. About ten Trylithians patrolled the courtyard beneath the bluff's shadow, tense and alert.

He quickly drew back. Casting one final glance at his wife, Blaze prayed for success and that Kaity might be spared, whatever the outcome. He raised his arm toward the heavens and let it drop. Crosshair, Vipress, and Apotheka raced forward, carrying the assault. Blaze followed closely, giving the melee fighters their signal. Fyromaniac took a position in front of Valora, counting audibly to four.

"We go in there and hit them heavy, Man," he said, his voice intense. "Kaity, you stay behind me. It's gonna get rough, and Sharko will kill me if I let anything happen to you. Besides," he added, with a grin, igniting the flame on his gun, "you wouldn't want to miss the toasted Trylithians!"

Fyromaniac's humor relieved some of their tension. The newly-saved surfer motioned with his weapon, and they charged into the fray.

<14>

Blaze of Glory

The courtyard flooded with weapons' fire. Hot plasma bolts streaked through the air, striking sand and stone. Crosshair led the attack, and the shooters had the easier task. Catching their foe completely off guard, the three women let loose with a hail of fire. They took down four Trylithians within the first seconds, before the aliens could even activate energy shields. Crosshair was impressive in form, simultaneously running while making the enemy duck with the accuracy of her projectiles. Vipress' toxin gun spewed bolts of poisonous goop that immobilized one Trylithian through his shield. Apotheka's gun was set to kill, and she laid down suppressive fire.

Blaze picked off two snipers from the bluff top before the melee fighters entered the fray. Trylithians flooded out of the homestead's three buildings. Fyromaniac's flamethrower forced them to quickly dive for cover. Despite staying out of Form so long, the surfer showed remarkable skill. He single-handedly cut a swath through the emerging enemies, while Valora cut down any who tried to approach him from behind. She hesitated with her first kill, feeling strange to take even an alien's life. Yet her blow stopped a scythe from embedding in Fyromaniac's back, and she pushed through it after that. It was kill or be killed—no time for emotions.

Ninjarak and Thunderbane formed a deadly duo of death. The ninja Starganaut delivered punishing blows with his white bo staff, while Thunderbane finished off opponents with a swipe of his deadly lightning foils. Thunderbane's electric swords had to hit an enemy's shield several times to disable it, but the bo staff sailed right through, crunching bones.

The Trylithians were in utter chaos. Most of them had been indoors, so more than a dozen were cut down before the commander of the garrison ordered his troops back. He didn't wait for the last few stragglers, but sealed the thick metallic door to the Dundees' living space. Two males didn't make it inside. Seeing they were shut out, the pair whirled and charged their Starganaut opponents. Both met swift ends.

The battle ended almost as soon as it began. None of the Starganauts had been critically wounded, though Apotheka and Ninjarak sported minor wounds. Thirty one Trylithian warriors lay dead on the ground. The remaining nine had holed up in the cylindrical housing unit of Nick's compound. The same door that Blaze could not open earlier now stood in their way, and the Trylithians were doubtless contacting Vogul about the attack.

Fyromaniac reached for a square-shaped charge. A string of six explosives hung from his belt, and he placed one right next to the door. Taking a Trylithian communication device, he fiddled with it until he was certain he'd activated it.

"Hey there, my blue-skinned friends!" he exclaimed, in a cheerful voice. "Just a friendly call to let you know I rigged an explosive on your doorframe. Try calling Vogul, and you're done. Try coming out, and I blow you up. My friends and I would like you to stay where you are. We don't want to kill you, but...I rather like a good fireworks show! That's kaboom, for you Trylithian-speakers!"

A series of angry, guttural words came from the other end. Fyromaniac winced and flicked the device off, turning to his friends.

"I guess they got the message," he said sheepishly. Valora could only assume that he'd gotten a string of alien expletives. Blaze walked atop the sand bunker and flashed a piece of metal in the sunlight, making certain to face away from the bluff. Within minutes, a humming sound approached. Nick Dundee piloted their hovercraft over the sand bunker, resting it in the courtyard and carefully avoiding the dead as he hopped out.

"Crikey!" he exclaimed. "Do I need to ask how the fight went?"

"Quick, let's load the water!" Blaze urged. The Starganauts began the arduous task of filling the tank on the hovercraft, and only Fyromaniac didn't help. Instead, he guarded the trapped Trylithians, taking a moment every hour to remind them of the explosive. He hoped they wouldn't realize he had no way of actually monitoring their attempts to contact Vogul. Then again, bluffing was James' strong suit.

The Starganauts worked fast. They managed to haul six loads of water before sunset reddened the sky. They were just filling their tank a seventh time when Fyromaniac rushed up to them.

"I went to give my usual com," he said, "and the Trylithian just laughed at me. I think he's informed Vogul, and we're about to have company!"

The words hardly left his mouth before Blaze heard the sound of a distant engine. He strained his eyes against the horizon, and fear seized him. High in the sky but rapidly approaching were four alien starships!

BLAZE CALLED FRANTICALLY for the others to run. Ninjarak, Apotheka, and Nick were in the middle of carting water containers, with Thunderbane up on the hovercraft deck, busily dumping them into the tank. It felt like barely a minute—mere moments—before the ships descended upon them. Green-and-yellow crafts, shaped like tadpoles, screamed toward them. Dart-like bullets cut into the sand with machinegun bursts, and the Starganauts around the hovercraft scrambled for cover.

Apotheka threw herself beneath the vessel. Thunderbane dodged behind the water tank, but Nick, hapless Nick, froze to the spot. A double line of dart fire ripped through the ground toward him. He looked paralyzed, and then a figure clad in orange, red, and yellow threw himself over the Australian. The desert seemed to hold its breath. The dread sound of metal ripping into metal amplified in Blaze's ears. The ships passed, and Fyromaniac rolled limply off the top of the man he'd saved.

Blaze's blood ran cold. He saw Valora emerging out of the water tunnel and shouted at her to stay put. Fully aware the ships could come back at any moment, he dashed across the open courtyard and frantically examined the surfer.

"James!" Blaze cried. His best friend lay unconscious, blood seeping from beneath his armor.

The trucker was numbly aware of Apotheka and Thunderbane shoving him aside and grabbing Fyromaniac. Nick, more shocked than hurt, leaped to his feet. Blaze felt the Australian grab him by the arm, leading him quickly to the shelter of the tunnel. At a distance, the Trylithian ships turned around.

They skimmed low for a second run, the pounding of their cannon fire ending in an explosion which confirmed they had destroyed the hovercraft.

Inside the cave, Apotheka looked desperately for a way to strip off Fyromaniac's armor. Dudeman himself had failed the first time he transformed, which felt so long ago. However, Apotheka found a button on his belt. She discovered that by clicking and holding it down, the armor casing unlatched. Thunderbane helped her tear it off and turn Fyromaniac on his stomach. The black shirt underneath his armor was badly torn by wounds from the darts. Punctures peppered his back, like stab wounds from a dozen large needles. Apotheka quickly switched her gun to its healing setting, but her tensed muscles and uneasy motions betrayed her anxiety.

Ninjarak held up Fyromaniac's armor suit. About a dozen foot-long projectiles stuck into it, each like cones of metal—thin and ending in a needle-sharp point.

"He threw himself over me," Nick could only say, in amazement. "He took these nasty things *for* me."

"And saved your life," Thunderbane said sarcastically. "One of these would've killed you easily, 'Mate!'"

"Now isn't the time to be rude," Blaze rebuked, and all fell silent. Crosshair, Valora, Vipress, and Ninjarak had been underground during the attack, so the trucker quickly explained the situation.

"There's a simple solution," Crosshair said, once he finished. "We wait them out until night conceals us."

Blaze wrung his hands at the suggestion. Had the prophetess forgotten that Vogul possessed more forces?

"We can't," he countered. "Those ships are just the first wave. It's Vogul we're talking about here. He's been trying, obsessively, to hunt us down. He's spent months and valuable resources. He knows we're pinned, so he'll send in ground troops, hovercrafts...we *have* to leave."

"And go where? Right into enemy fire?" Vipress exclaimed. Despite her physically enhanced form, as Vipress, Chrysta's personality had been altered the least of them.

"We can't stay here," Apotheka put in logically. "Dudeman may die. I need stitches and bandages! This gun is great, but I can't figure out half the settings!"

"How on Earth would we escape?" Ninjarak questioned. *That* stumped Blaze as well. Fortunately, Valora snapped her fingers together.

"The hostages!" she cried. "We exchange their lives for ours!"

"It's worth a try," Apotheka conceded, and Blaze agreed. Crosshair used the Trylithian communicator to contact the captives, still imprisoned in Nick's house module. Their commander merely sneered, issuing a chilling reply.

"Vogul is willing that we die to destroy you!" Crosshair translated.

Static sounded on the other end, telling everyone the male had flicked off his com. Suddenly, the earth around them shook. A low rumble drifted in from the cave opening, dirt fell from the ceiling...and Blaze knew. The Trylithians in the bunker had killed themselves. Either by detonating Fyromaniac's charge or an explosive of their own, they had just blown themselves out of the equation.

THE TRYLITHIANS' SUICIDES left the Starganauts at an utter loss. Crosshair felt sick to her stomach, and not only from fear. With the option of hostages gone, their choices dwindled to two extremes: staying or running. Staying meant the risk of reinforcements pinning them in, and Nick informed Crosshair and Blaze that no tunnels branched off from theirs. The passageway dead-ended at his cistern. It had merely one exit, which now led into the deadly fire of their enemies. However, flight appealed even less. In the face of starships, Crosshair calculated they'd be cut down before cresting Nick's sand bunker. The homestead's open courtyard offered almost no protection.

"Well this is peachy," Thunderbane muttered pessimistically. "We can either die now or die later! I knew I was being an idiot when I volunteered to build you a spacecraft, *Prima*!" He faced Samantha in the dim illumination provided by the lights affixed to their guns. "Where has all our faith led us? Into a deathtrap, of course! It seems we aren't out of one situation before we're in another. Out of the frying pan and into the literal fire!"

"Matt, be quiet!" Crosshair chided. "The Lord didn't vaporize Earth. He's the one who delivered us from it, and He'll continue to rescue us, because death is not our fate. At least...not yet."

"What if you live, but we die?" Valora questioned, with a shudder. Crosshair placed a comforting hand on her shoulder. Even after all their perils, Kaity remained largely unchanged. If only she would let go of the past, and embrace the courage God intended to cultivate in her! Crosshair smiled in a way that made Samantha show through.

"'Do not let your hearts be troubled,'" she spoke majestically, "and do not be discouraged. 'God cannot be mocked. A man reaps what he sows,' and men like Willum Vogul sow *much* evil. A time is coming soon when darkness will have its heyday, but dawn will break over his sins."

"Which should we choose, though?" Nick broke in. "It's good talkin' about God an' all that, but what about now? Dudeman took the bullets meant for me! I'll be mad as a cut snake if we don't get him back to Base!"

Crosshair said nothing. The others waited for what felt like an hour, though it was truthfully but a few minutes. The prophetess had closed her eyes and furrowed her brow, which Thunderbane recognized as her thinking expression. Finally, she sighed and hung her shoulders.

"I don't know," she admitted painfully. "I've been praying and weighing all the pros and cons, and I haven't the slightest clue."

"I say we go out in a flash of glory."

Blaze walked into the light projected from Vipress' gun, crossing his torchsword over his breastplate.

"I don't think that's a good idea, Sharko," Crosshair advised, yet Valora held up a hand.

"I'd like to hear my husband's idea."

"We have four powerful guns between us," Blaze began, "so we've got a weapon to cover each ship. The longer we stay, the more likely Vogul's ground troops will arrive. The challenge is breaking free from this place. Once we hit the courtyard, we split up. Ninjarak and Thunderbane, being melee fighters, will carry James. The rest of us will run in different directions and try taking out a ship before meeting back at our base."

Blaze further outlined that Valora should be given one of Crosshair's pistols, and Nick would make a run straight for the base to shorten his journey. As the only non-Starganaut of the group, the Australian agreed to it.

"Me and Thunder should be the last out," Ninjarak suggested. "That'll give you the opportunity to draw fire, and it should make carting Fyro easier."

None of the Starganauts objected to the plan. Crosshair had to admit that it beat being trapped and dying liked caged animals. She carefully picked her way through the dark, to the tunnel entrance. The desert shadows were elongating as daylight faded into dusk. In the near distance, the four alien ships circled like birds of prey. Crosshair drew back. Although initially unsure of Blaze's plan, a thought formed in her mind of how to improve it.

"I like your pan," she said, "but I might have a better strategy to deal with these aggressors. If Vogul is anything like I suppose, he wants some fun with us before he kills us. We may be able to use that."

"What are you proposing?" Blaze questioned. Crosshair smiled slyly and outlined her amendment. At the end of her proposal, Vipress jumped up and down in glee. Valora felt nervous, yet Apotheka voiced a cautious optimism. Even Thunderbane seemed impressed, and Blaze nodded in approval.

"We'll do it your way," he said, "but follow my lead! If this works, we'll be able to walk out with weapons in hand and no starships pursuing us!"

Blaze took the com again, sending a message out on all frequencies. Now they simply needed to wait for a response, and pray Vogul fell for their deception.

———— ✣ ————

"THE STARGANAUTS ARE surrendering!"

"*What*? You're not serious!"

Vogul's face twisted in utter disbelief as the Trylithian next to him repeated the news.

"They're surrendering to the ships you sent ahead," he persisted, and handed Vogul his earpiece. The madman listened in amazement as Sharko's voice requested safe passage into the open, where he and his friends would lay down their arms. Finally! His long search would be over! Their demise would secure his future and maybe, just maybe, the nightmarish will that set him on this path would flee! The Voices would be gone again, leaving him to enjoy his position of power in peace. Trembling with excitement, Vogul answered the Starganauts via the ship's com.

He settled back in the copilot's chair and watched the darkening desert go by. The loaded dropship which carried him headed toward the Dundee homestead. Vogul had departed from his gunship on this craft after receiving a call for help. He'd sent four starships ahead to assess the situation and engage any hostiles. His troops followed in several dropships—eighty men, altogether. After so many of his men perished in the hovership attack, Vogul didn't wish to take any chances. He also knew these humans had found the crystals. Reports of advanced armor suits and weaponry confirmed this, simply adding to his urgency.

At the Dundees' base, the Starganauts carefully walked out of the tunnel with their weapons in the air. The starships hovered in place, about twenty yards above the ground and spread out to form a semi-circle around the alcove and dune bunker. They pointed their cannons right at the humans. Blaze led the way, acting nonchalant. Valora's veins coursed with fear, but her panic served to convince the watching pilots that this was a victory. She carried one of Samantha's pistols in her hand.

While she walked, she thought of the prophetess' risky but clever plan.

"We fake Vogul out," Crosshair had said, smiling slyly. "Sharko, we have a way to communicate with the Trylithians. Offer to surrender. We can walk out with our weapons in hand as if we're going to lay them down. Then, we shoot at the ships. We'd get a much better shot with them standing still than as moving targets."

Valora hoped that Crosshair was right. She tried to brush aside her fears and focus. The plan was being enacted now! Nick Dundee purposely tripped, giving them their pre-planned signal.

Before the ships could react, all five of the Starganauts with guns took aim and fired. Blaze charged up a shot. It hit a ship squarely in the windshield, taking out the pilot. Vipress focused her acidic projectiles on an alien's hull, burning a hole through the bottom of it. Crosshair and Apotheka peppered another fighter with fire, and Valora nervously shot a volley at her mark.

They fired continuously. Vipress' target exploded in midair. Blaze's mark slowly lost air and crashed. Apotheka and Crosshair's target turned tail and fled, while Valora's swooped toward them. It was met by a spray of flames. Ninjarak, sporting Fyromaniac's gun, filled the air with an inferno. The ship, blinded, crashed right into the alcove behind them. The Starganauts rushed forward to escape the shrapnel. Nick sprang to his feet. As Ninjarak manned the flamethrower, Nick helped Thunderbane carry Fyromaniac's limp body. Everything seemed to be going better than anticipated, and Valora felt worry draining out of her limbs.

They ran for ten minutes without pursuit. Across the cooling sands, over the wild and barren bleakness, they dashed toward freedom. They would make it. Valora could feel it in her bones. Surely God went with them! This would mark the turn of the tide—another day in which they'd evade Vogul!

Blaze, at the front of the fleeing party, skidded to a halt. Dropships were rapidly approaching, encircling them in the crimson light. They plummeted down, landing ramps bursting open and Trylithians pouring out. Before they could avoid it, the Starganauts found themselves clustered in a circle, surrounded by blue-skinned foes. Alien guns stared them down from every direction. They were trapped! It was over! In the span of only an evening, they had fallen from their greatest victory into crushing defeat!

"I'm afraid there's no way out of this one, my Love," Blaze said to Valora ruefully, before the entrance of a single man silenced everyone.

Vogul, Willum Vogul, came arrogantly down a landing ramp. None of them had seen his face since their first encounter. Four months of dauntless searching had added more lines to the troubled, gaunt visage now stretched taut in victory. A smile of morbid satisfaction twisted his lips, and his eyes blazed like coals. Valora could only clutch her husband and cower in fear. Even Crosshair appeared shaken.

"I have dreamed about this moment!" Vogul exclaimed, rubbing his hands together gleefully. "I've fantasized about it longer than you can know! I considered, 'what would be the most appropriate end for the humans who've continually eluded my grasp?' and I decided, 'why not keep them in suspense?' Hold on!" Vogul paused, glancing around as if panicked. "Where are the other two?"

"What other two?" Blaze feigned. Valora almost blurted out her surprise at their absence, but bit her tongue. Hope leaped within her chest, for Nick, Matt, and Dudeman were missing.

"I know there are eight of you!" Vogul shrieked, striding around like an irate prison warden. "I was told! There are eight insets for crystals in that cave! Where are the others?"

"They spontaneously combusted from your bombast!" Crosshair said cheekily. Vogul snarled and spat at her.

"Fan out and find them!" he ordered, to a unit of six soldiers. "Tell me the moment you spot them!"

The Trylithians left the circle, and others stepped forward to fill the gap. While Vogul turned away, Crosshair flicked up her visor, emboldened.

"¡*Corre, Primo*!" she shouted, at the top of her lungs. "¡*No mires atrás*! *Y recuerda, hay un...barco...intacto*!"

"Shut up!" Vogul snarled, and he slapped her brutally. Crosshair winced from the impact, but ignored the pain. "Whoever you're babbling to, my men will find and extinguish!"

"For your information, that was Spanish!" she shot back. "And good luck finding a translator!"

Her feisty comeback enraged Vogul, yet he calmed himself, his mouth morphing into a triumphant expression.

"No matter!" he exclaimed. "It is pointless for any of you to run or deliver garbled messages. It always was. You're going on a journey, to a place I've spent four months preparing for you! We're going on a ride together...to the *Draxalis*!"

THE STARGANAUTS WERE fleeing through the desert. Nick and Thunderbane kept falling behind, due to the added burden of carrying Fyromaniac. Nick suffered the worst, since Thunderbane's glorified body amplified his strength and endurance. Nick finally tripped and fell. He lost his grip on Fyromaniac, and only Thunderbane kept the injured Starganaut from tumbling with the Australian.

Nick got up with his clothing and hair full of sand. Thunderbane called to his compatriots. Whether the wind carried away his voice, or they simply didn't hear, the other Starganauts continued on, heedless. They retreated into the distance as Nick took hold of Fyromaniac.

"We gotta catch up!" he urged. "I'll be right as rain."

"Wait!" Thunderbane pointed toward their companions. Two dropships fell from the sky, and the duo watched in horror as Trylithians encircled their six teammates. Thunderbane bade Nick to set Fyromaniac down. The Australian could sense his urge to help the others. The Dundee did as he requested, and Thunderbane crept forward, shielding himself from detection using the dunes. He could hear a voice—Vogul's—yet couldn't understand the words. Nick trailed him. The moment he caught up, the Australian grabbed his armored arm.

"You can't go and aid them, Mate!" Nick exclaimed. "Look at all those aliens pourin' out of ships! You've as much chance as a gecko with a dingo! An' what about our mate here?"

Thunderbane hesitated, unwilling to leave their companions. Yet his soldier's sense recognized the truth in Nick's assertions. The two crouched to make themselves less visible to the enemy, but Vogul and his men were focused on the six Starganuats in their trap.

"We need to shoot through!" Nick persisted. "Leave quickly, to you Yanks! Vogul may not know someone's missin', but I'd rather not find out!"

Thunderbane bit his lip beneath the gray, opaque visor. How could he ever make a rational decision? The pressure of time running out, countered by the impossibility of a rescue, forced his mind into a fog. Suddenly, Samantha's voice cut through the evening air. Thunderbane's brain translated: *run, Cousin! Don't look back! And remember, there's an intact ship!*

"What was that?" Nick demanded, while the sound of a slap rang out.

"Our cue to leave!" Thunderbane exclaimed. He was thankful for his cousin's words, though her statement about a ship left him confused. "Do you think you can make it back to Base? We can't go back to your homestead!"

"No idea." Nick shrugged.

The roar of engines sounded. Thunderbane turned to see Vogul's ships taking off, their compatriots held within as prisoners. He felt like cursing.

Two groups of Trylithians remained on the cool sands, conferring together. Thunderbane didn't need to understand their language to realize they were search parties. Nick suddenly knocked on his pauldron.

"Hey Mate, we'll never make it to *The Deliverer* with these blokes on the lookout. We've gotta find a faster mode of transport than our feet, an' I may have the answer!"

"What in the galaxy are you proposing?"

Nick bade the Starganaut to pick up Fyromaniac. The two men lifted their limp burden, the Australian mechanic explaining as they walked.

"I know you wanna avoid my homestead, but Vogul's men aren't there right now. And what modes of propulsion are lyin' about, their owners *very* dead?"

Realization crossed Thunderbane's face like the inevitable dawn.

"It's crazy enough it might work," he said, and Nick led the way, groaning under the strain of the unconscious Fyromaniac.

THE AUSTRALIANS' HOMESTEAD proved ominously dark, yet deserted. They set Fyromaniac down and began pulling off pairs of Trylithian hoverboots. Dragging everything into Abigale's garden module, they risked using Thunderbane's foil for light. Minutes dragged by, feeling like hours. Nick fiddled with a boot, easily switching the hover mechanism on via a wireless toggle. The rocket portion took longer to figure, with Nick at last concluding the wearer pressed down with their toes to fire it.

Thunderbane acted as a test subject. Since Trylithian toes were shorter than human, Nick cautioned the Starganaut to press down lightly. Both men winced as Thunderbane fired up a pair of boots, taking off like a shot and smacking into the metal wall with a loud clang. Several accidents later, he managed to circle the module without a mishap.

Nick, fortunately, proved a quicker study. A few painful falls accelerated the bruised Australian's desire to learn. Thunderbane almost found himself laughing, and probably would've indulged in mirth, under better circumstances. The Starganaut hovered shakily outside, avoiding a painful encounter with the doorway as he throttled his way to the top of Nick's dune bunker to assess their situation. His heart sank. Lights in the distance! The Trylithians were coming, and they hadn't figured out how to carry Fyromaniac! He furrowed his brows, trying to puzzle out a solution. *Come on, Matt! Think! You're in glorified form. Of course!*

Thunderbane zoomed back into the space, whacking against the doorframe in his haste. He grabbed Fyromaniac unceremoniously and threw the man over his shoulders like a sack of seed. *At least we stripped his armor,* he thought, grateful for the reduced weight. *And it will come back to him the next time he transforms, anyway.*

"You crazy rat bag! Watcha doin'?" Nick cried.

"The only thing that will get all of us home!" Thunderbane replied.

Fyromaniac remained unconscious as Australian and Starganaut headed for the Base. They zoomed through the nearby canyon, praying the Trylithians wouldn't detect them. Nick almost hit the canyon wall multiple times, and Thunderbane nearly dropped Fyromaniac.

Somehow, miraculously, they made it. Flying over the nighttime sand, they at last drew to within sight of their sanctuary. Thunderbane recognized the distinctive dune, even in the dark. He placed Fyromaniac on the floor as soon as the duo retreated under the storage bay's tarp, muscles aching. Nick collapsed, breathless, body dripping with sweat. Keeping his legs steady had drained an incredible amount of the Australian's strength.

"Will you be okay?" Thunderbane asked, chest heaving.

"I'll come good tomorrow." Nick gave a careless wave of his hand, and Thunderbane alone had enough stamina left to take off the boots, blot out a few yards of their hover tracks, and replace the tarp. He mounded some sand to close off the gap they'd entered through, and hoped it would be enough. His whirling mind wondered what to do.

Thunderbane removed the crystal from his breastplate and transformed back into his regular self. Cradling his forehead, Matt sat on the dusty ground and felt helpless. True, he'd been a soldier. True, he'd seen action and felt the adrenaline rush of battle. This was different. He'd been under a commanding officer. He had always excelled at going with the flow and following orders. The calm attitude he projected was normally how he felt. Now, worry and panic overtook his usually laid-back demeanor.

What would happen to them? They were four, only four: himself; an exhausted mechanic; a wounded man; a hysterical botanist. His actions would determine whether they lived or died. He alone bore responsibility for what remained of the Starganauts. Yet his heart quaked with fear, for the deeper question lingered before him: could a follower become a leader?

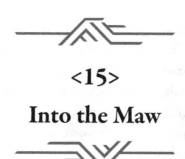

<15>

Into the Maw

Kaity Anderson rocketed skyward to an uncertain fate. The desert disappeared from view as she ascended, up into the outer atmosphere where the air spread thin enough that stars burst forth in glory. A backdrop of dark blue set with glistening diamonds, its beauty escaped Kaity's notice during the harrowing flight. The alien dropship rattled as they crossed the burning thermosphere. Flames obscured her view through the cockpit window, and everything felt like a mockery of their escape from Earth.

They ascended to their deaths. Like foxes cornered by a hound, they cowered in abject fear. On the surface, Vogul had forced the six Starganauts out of crystal form. The armor suits were nearly impervious to weapons' fire, but Vogul had opened Crosshair's visor again and pointed a gun barrel at her forehead. Though no scientific expert, Kaity understood that even a glorified body couldn't survive at point-blank. Vogul took the crystals and handed them to a Trylithian who appeared—like the scythe warrior from the hovercraft—to be part of his special forces. Kaity overheard him designate the alien as "Skull Warrior." Whether that comprised the male's actual name or a group one, she didn't know.

Skull Warrior had departed on another vessel, their chance of recovering the orbs slipping away with him. It didn't ultimately make any difference. The humans sat on the dropship floor, handcuffed in curious alien restraints which tightened when one fought them. Mike discovered this the hard way.

While Chrysta huddled against her cringing husband, Kaity sat with Sharko's arm around her. She could feel how tense he was. He had hated flying ever since a plane crash killed his parents, but the destination was also a cause for fear. Normally, Kaity would have cowered like Chrysta during a journey to execution. She found herself, strangely, trying to be brave. She made an analysis of her surroundings to see if there might be any hope of escape. Nancy noticed her glances around the cabin, and did likewise. Her best friend tended to be more observant and less emotional under fire. Kaity greatly admired this trait. It was part of what made Nancy such a gifted medic—if only the former secretary would see it.

"Stop looking around, my dear. It won't do you any good!"

Vogul gleefully watched them from the cockpit, clearly enjoying the ability to witness every moment of their suffering. *What could make another human being so cruel?* Kaity wondered. *Especially to his own people? How could a man find it within himself to kill everyone on Earth with no regard?*

"I see you're worried sick about something!" Vogul snarled, throwing his verbal darts at Samantha. "Or *someone*. I know Matt Sanchez is your cousin. I know a great many things...things you won't ever discover, in your steadily shortening lifespans."

The prophetess did not meet his gaze. Grim and pale since their capture, Samantha now raised her head slowly, scorn replacing her serious demeanor.

"I see a burning ship," she said scathingly. "I see a falling emperor and a fading future. Those belong to you, I think."

"Bah!" Vogul seethed with contempt. "You're better than petty attempts to prophesy out of thin air! We're both aware that your journey ends on my vessel."

"What of *your* journey?" Samantha's question came with a pointed stare. Vogul looked away. "Does not the guilt of the blood of Earth haunt your waking steps? Wrack your mind with nightmares? You killed *billions* of people...and even that was not enough! No, you had to follow us here, bent on ridding the Universe of every single Earthling. *Why?* If you're going to kill us anyway, at least tell me the reason."

"I will, Prophetess," Vogul answered cryptically, "but not today. I'll be kind enough to inform you that your deaths will not happen immediately. I have *big* plans for you before the end."

Willum Vogul smiled sadistically. His words were more misery than comfort, and Kaity's heart sank as a great, black object blocked out the stars. How ironic fate could be! She had recently let go of the past to embrace the future. Now, that future would be tragically cut short.

Kaity snapped back to the present. The gunship loomed ever closer: a spider drawing them into its web. The first time, they'd been swallowed into the *Draxalis'* massive barrel. This time, they were enveloped by a hangar the same brown hue as the gunship's interior. They appeared to go through a shield, and their dropship landed with a dismal clank in a hangar clad in metal. They had arrived. They had left the soil of their temporary home, to die within the hardened ribs of a gunship far from Earth.

THE TRYLITHIAN SEARCH party tracked the fleeing humans for several hours. Darkness proved their enemy but the Starganauts' ally. The humans stayed ahead of handheld sensor range, so the Trylithians used searchlights to illuminate the double trail of hover troughs leading through the sands. It was slower going than their quarry, and the aliens reached a sea of massive dunes by midnight. The humans' hover-trail suddenly petered out, near the slipface of a nondescript hill of sand.

The six Trylithians readied weapons and gathered at the crest of the mound. No sign of their human prey could be found, yet coming up empty was not an option. Vogul expected success, for failure merited execution. The Trylithians shuddered as they remembered their comrades who had been shot to death. They separated to search thoroughly, leaving the warrior with the best night vision as a lookout atop the dune. The Trylithians were about to despair when one of them gave an exclamation, shining his light on a strange, reflective surface.

Beneath the hoverboots of the enemy, Matt Sanchez listened and waited. As he heard them cry out and talk animatedly, a sickening realization sank in. They must have found the solar panels! Nobody had thought to cover them up!

Matt's pulse quickened as the tarp overhead shook slightly, an alien skimming over it. He hoped fervently he'd done a good job covering their trail. Suddenly, he remembered the skylight! When their ship crashed sideways, one porthole window remained open to the sky, sand funneling through it until a sinkhole formed. Nick had rigged a fake rock of sorts that could be rolled over it. Matt rushed to the Commons and looked up through the skylight to see the blackness of night. His stomach clenched with fear. The sky-light was open! What if the Trylithians discovered it?

Nick's snores drifted to him, and he observed Fyromaniac stretched out on the floor nearby, his chest rising and falling. The fire Starganaut had awakened after their arrival, in much pain but able to bear it. He managed to fall asleep after Abigale tended to him with what resources they had. With Nancy among the captives, necessity had forced the Australian woman to be Fyromaniac's nurse. She now paced the Commons nervously, pausing when she noticed Matt looking at the ceiling. Her gaze moved upward.

"Crikey! We forgot the skylight!" she cried softly.

"Don't you think I know?" Matt let out a long sigh. "*¡Dios ayudanos*! Let us pray they simply don't see it."

Sand suddenly fell from the ceiling, as if in answer to his musing. Abigale quaked with fear.

"We *must* do something!" she cried, in a low voice. "They already have the others. To die down here, separated from them—it's too much to bear! We never should've done this! We knew it was hopeless...!" she burst into hysterics. Matt grasped her around the shoulders and shook her.

"Listen to me, Miss Dundee! *Listen*! We're not dying down here. Not by a long shot. I've got a revolver, and it's dark out there. I'm going to do something absolutely crazy, and I need your help!"

Abigale seemed to come to her senses. She wiped away her tears and set her jaw.

"You're right!" she declared. "God bless the Yanks! You're stubborn as a bull, but by golly, you've got heaps of courage!"

The Trylithian search party assembled atop the dune. Murmuring in their buzz-like language, they agreed that the humans must be close. Yet where?

"Perhaps they are underground," the leader said. "Our sensors can't penetrate the soil very far."

"Do you hear that?" another Trylithian said, and the aliens glanced around. "It is very faint."

"I hear it, too!" The leader held up his four-fingered hand. "The sound of sand falling...and something being scraped."

The aliens glanced in every direction but one. A few yards from them and a bit down the slope, a figure emerged slightly from a hole in the ground, bathed in shadow. Wearing dark clothes and holding a black revolver, he took aim at the one holding a com device.

BANG! The sharp report of a gun snapped the taut silence of the night. The aliens' leader slumped, his device falling to the sand. The Trylithians swung their lights around in confusion. Matt fired again, taking out another alien who was reaching for a second com device. The ex-soldier breathed a sigh of relief. The Trylithians didn't appear to possess shields, for his revolver rounds hit them unimpeded. He didn't wait for the Trylithians to pinpoint his position, but slid hastily down the ladder, jumping off before he reached the portion which Abigale tightly held.

Matt prayed he'd taken out the only aliens with com devices. Suddenly, the silhouette of a Trylithian blocked out the starlight of the exposed hole! Abigale thrust the ladder up, catching the alien in the hoverboots and knocking him back and out of sight. The male righted himself and attempted a shot, but the shaft of the skylight blocked it. It smacked into the sand just above the opening, and Abigale quickly lowered the ladder.

The Dundee breathed a sigh of relief, but Matt held up a cautioning hand. Though the skylight seemed impervious, a grenade might be tossed in, and it was only a matter of moments before the tarp would be discovered. Heart pounding, blood pulsing, Matthew Sanchez moved swiftly to the hover bay. He could see the tarp shaking from activity above, and hear hoverboots. Any minute, any second, they might enter.

He placed his finger on the trigger and deliberately slowed his breathing. How much ammunition did he have left? There were only seven rounds, and he vowed to save one for Vogul. Matt did not imagine he'd ever see Samantha again, but he was determined that everyone here would survive. To do that, he risked staying out of Starganaut form. The clink and glint of Thunderbane's heavy armor would alert the enemy. Stealth was his greatest weapon, now. Stealth, and his soldier's senses.

Body tensed and alert, Matt slipped out from the protective cover of the tarp and aimed to kill.

THE INTERIOR OF THE *Draxalis* was fascinating and foreboding. The gunship's hallways stretched high but somewhat narrow, their walls paneled in brown, metal plates ribbed by pipes and circuitry. It felt oddly cold, but the Trylithians seemed right at home in the environment. Vogul alone donned a coat, and he led the party down a long, main corridor. They descended a level in an elevator, Vogul and his guard of twenty escorting them to a room in which sat four posts. They were evenly spaced at the corners of a low platform, and the Trylithians herded the Starganauts into this area. Vogul pressed a button on a wall console near the door, activating the prison's "bars."

Kaity had never seen anything like them. Rods of blue energy shot out, spanning the gaps between the posts to form a square enclosure around them. Mike made the mistake of treading too close to the bars, and jerked his hand back suddenly. The flesh was seared where he had touched a bar, and he gritted his teeth in pain.

"Serves you right!" Vogul snarled, leering at them through the cage. "Why couldn't you just be a good little group of humans and surrender? No! I had to traipse around a burning desert for months looking for you!" he shook his fist at them. "Now who has the upper hand?"

"Save your gloating!" Samantha stepped forward to face him, fearless. "You're like a cat with a mouse. You can't just kill us. You're obsessed with having your fun before wiping out every last one of us. Why?"

Vogul gazed at Samantha strangely. The Harris couldn't tell why he did this, but it made her uncomfortable. Vogul took a few self-important paces back. He seemed about to speak, but a Trylithian burst in. Kaity recognized Skull Warrior.

"Sir, we have lost contact with the surface team!" he declared. Vogul turned on his heel and marched out, leaving the Starganauts in silence. Kaity didn't know whether the Trylithian's words boded well. She merely hoped they were an answer to her prayers that Matt and the others would safely escape.

Sharko and Mike assessed the alien cell for any possible weaknesses. They gingerly examined the posts, trying—unsuccessfully—to budge one. Samantha merely sat on the metal floor, her legs drawn up under her chin. Kaity, noticing the prophetess' inaction, plopped down beside her.

"It's useless," Samantha said sadly. "We can't break out of this one."

"Samantha, what's wrong?" Kaity asked. "You're usually in charge or doing something about the situation. You seem overly worried."

"I am. Vogul...he's...*attracted* to me." The words came haltingly. Kaity's eyes widened.

"Samantha, that's horrible!"

"Perhaps," Samantha rejoined, "but it could work to our advantage. Vogul is a monster, but he's an intellectual one. He may try to charm me, to win me over. Even men like Willum desire someone to share life with. Man's craving for companionship traces back to the Garden, after all. We may find an advantage in this."

"An advantage?"

"I might be able to accomplish something," Samantha explained, "by being the only one he takes out of prison. He enjoys our verbal spars. No matter what darts I throw at him, I've begun to realize he likes it. While I'm out of here, I might be able to disable this cell, a critical system—even kill Vogul himself."

"I'd think that would be first on your agenda," Kaity commented dryly.

"Killing in battle is one thing." Samantha shook her head. "Killing a man simply when the opportunity strikes? I don't know. I think...only in self-defense could I do it. Killing Vogul may be on your minds, but there's another option I'd like to try."

"What is that?" Kaity questioned.

"Saving him."

ON THE BRIDGE OF THE *Draxalis*, Vogul foamed with fury. No! The fates must be bent against him! How could two Starganauts elude his men? Hadn't his men reported hitting one? At least one of them must be injured. Vogul glanced around. The bridge appeared oddly deserted.

"You promised glory," he murmured between clenched teeth, "but all I've reaped is suffering! Toil!" He glanced around again, but there were no shadows—no Voices answered. "Fine! Be quiet. If you're so all-knowing and wise, why have I been thwarted at every step?"

Vogul suddenly felt a chill running down his spine. Seized by the creeping feeling of someone behind him, he swiveled in his seat. His eyes nearly popped out of their sockets. He saw a figure of shadow, with only mouth and eyes visible against the blackness. The mouth twisted in a smile that glowed, while the eyes burned with flame. The smile of the shadow radiated with gloating—and Vogul knew he was going to die.

"Master? Master, awaken!"

Vogul straightened in his captain's chair. It had all been a nightmare! He blinked, but no one loomed behind him. The Skull Warrior's scornful face met him instead.

"Are you sound?" the alien questioned, tilting his head to the side.

"Perfectly!" Vogul snapped, grabbing the report from his officer's hands. "Is this the approximate location where we lost contact?"

"Yes," the warrior said. "I can send a team down immediately."

"No!" Vogul held up a hand. "I'm done going down to them. We have a gunship. I say we give our Starganaut guests an encore performance...with their brethren in the front row!"

"You wish to bombard Dalar 3 from orbit with the defense lasers?"

"No, I want to blast this entire planet!" Vogul exclaimed. The Skull Warrior's eyes widened in shock.

"You would discharge the entire gunship, simply for two humans?"

"Isn't it the perfect revenge?" Vogul sneered, his eyes glistening with madness. "They watch the world burn all over again, but this time, they're losing the last of their friends and family!"

"My Master, it is a ridiculous! I—" the Skull Warrior stopped himself. The look on Vogul's face told him that arguing was useless.

"The search is over!" Vogul snarled, rising. "I simply have one unfinished thread."

Vogul summoned two guards and entered the elevator from the bridge to the 2nd deck. He passed a few underlings as he walked. Altogether, the *Draxalis* boasted seven decks. Though meant to be manned by a larger complement, Tormac Durag had only spared 200 men to crew the stolen Myd craft. Vogul approached the prison room, his heartbeat quickening. He cared nothing for most of the Starganauts, but one in their midst intrigued him. If he could but sway her, persuade her to embrace life, and *him*...Vogul smiled in anticipation.

SAMANTHA HARRIS WAS ushered along a passageway by Vogul, flanked by two stoic Trylithians. Despite the cold fear rising inside of her, she attempted to breathe slowly and pay attention. The prophetess took in many things at a single glance. A pictorial layout of the ship on one wall, fuel lines running along the tops of the hallways, and few guards on patrol. If only she could locate the crystals! They were powerless without them, forcing her to acknowledge their dependence on eight, golf-ball sized orbs they knew little about.

Down a hall they trekked, up an elevator, and through an automatic sliding door. Samantha emerged onto the *Draxalis'* bridge—a long, low, rectangular room ringed by floor-to-ceilings windows. Consoles and panels lay scattered throughout, but she had little time to study them. Vogul pushed her onward, toward a staircase near the front of the gunship, descending into the bridge floor. It led to a door which slid open at Vogul's voice command.

The madman pushed her beyond it, into a posh if eclectic room. Alien fashions collided, from the bizarre and colorful to the bare and utilitarian. A lone window revealed the ship's barrel, terrifying in its length and inspiring in its construction. Two red chairs of alien fabric adjoined the window wall, facing each other. Vogul invited Samantha to sit down, yet he remained standing and dismissed his guards. An open doorway behind her told Samantha that another space abutted this one—perhaps Vogul's bedroom or a torture chamber. *Which could be one and the same thing*, she thought, with a shiver.

"What is the meaning of this?" she demanded, outwardly calm despite her heart racing.

"You are the leader," Vogul stated. "I'd like to get to know the woman who has long held me at bay."

"'At bay' is an interesting choice of words for a *murderer*."

"The death of an individual is a tragedy," Vogul retorted. "The death of millions is a number."

"Most of them hadn't even heard your name, and you killed them!"

"Exactly!" Vogul's body tensed with anger. "I was the first human on an alien world! I was the first to travel to another galaxy! My name should've been recognized across the Earth! Statues should've been raised, monuments built, history books rewritten to feature *my* name!" Vogul's eyes gleamed with livid superiority.

"The day I was ridiculed on live TV, I learned that most Earth people are ignorant fools! Small, petty people with even smaller minds, prattling about their puny lives while wholly unable to fathom the scope—the enormity!—of the galaxy around them! I simply exterminated the vermin who could never understand distant planets and true accomplishments! My discoveries were never good enough for them! *I* wasn't good enough! People ridicule most what they don't comprehend."

Samantha felt her blood boiling. She wanted to rise from the chair and strangle him. Yet she calmed her whirling emotions. Her objective went beyond present feelings, regardless of how strong. She also realized about Vogul what few did: it wasn't apathy or superiority that truly fueled him. She knew this insight came from the Holy Spirit.

"This is all about your father," she said suddenly, quietly. Vogul's smugness vanished, his expression turning on a dime.

"W-what are you talking about?" he returned innocently. "The old codger died in the blast!"

"No, don't you distract me!" Samantha closed her eyes, her confidence building as the Lord revealed things to her; much as He had the day she met James. "I see a little boy trying hard to pour milk into his cereal bowl. You spilled just a little, but that was enough. Down came your father's disapproval—his harsh words. Years later, you built an impressive science project. You got second place. Again, his harsh words—this time, his beating hands. You know the greatest tragedy of all? You have an amazing mind, but you bent it towards evil. You were a victim of parental violence, yet you've become the worst victimizer of them all. Did you see him, Vogul, before you destroyed Earth? Did you make a special trip just to visit your father?"

Willum's mask had been slipping as Samantha spoke. Now, he threw himself into a tirade of words, his mouth almost foaming from fury.

"I asked him to join me in the gunship. I offered him a chance to live! He laughed at me! *Laughed*! Just like all the other pathetic little cockroaches crawling over the sphere we called Earth! My last words to him? 'I hope you feel every minute of incineration!'"

"You wanted him to suffer," Samantha responded, keeping her tone even. "You wanted him to pay for all the pain he caused. All the pain everyone on Earth has caused you!"

"Yes! YES!" Vogul cried out, his anger subsiding. "You know, you're the first person who really understands me." He moved closer.

"I am a prophetess," Samantha answered, shrinking back in her chair. "God grants me insights beyond human wisdom."

"But you are also intelligent!" Vogul added, seeming to forget the chasms between them. "You were an engineer! Your mind is bent to scientific things."

"How do you know that?" Samantha suddenly felt cold.

"God is not the only giver of insights." Vogul's reply came eerily, and the room seemed to grow darker. Samantha sensed another presence with them, though her eyes beheld no one. A feeling of dread settled over her, and she shuddered. No! Something was horribly wrong. More lay behind Vogul than just his emotions, and Samantha didn't wish to find out.

"I want to go back to the others!" she insisted. "Please take me back!"

Vogul rubbed his chin thoughtfully. The room definitely felt colder, and Samantha nearly felt like she would scream.

"I think I will return you," Vogul replied—to her amazement, "for now. I've a decision to make, and I need time. Return to the rest of your worthless people, but know this. We will speak again!"

WHILE SAMANTHA CONVERSED with Vogul, the five captives huddled together in the alien cell. Their worst fears had been realized. Four months they'd outlasted Vogul. Against the burning sun, the parching desert, and search teams with advanced weaponry, they had endured. To finally fall into enemy hands was beyond disheartening. Sharko and Nancy had said little during their entire imprisonment, and even chatty Chrysta seemed dumbstruck. Kaity felt what many of them did. Despair. Entrapment. Fear in the face of death. She turned to Sharko with a pitiful expression, taking his hand and massaging it.

"I suppose your dreams of our valley won't turn out," she said regretfully. "It's ironic, my Love. So many months, I dwelled on what *was* lost. Now, I mourn for what *will* be lost. I think of the milestones I wanted with you: a proper honeymoon, children, our tenth anniversary, twentieth...sixtieth. It took me six months and a journey across the galaxy to realize what was right in front of me. Now that I wish to grow old with you, I can't!"

Tears slid down Kaity's cheeks as she spoke. Sharko merely stood and slammed his fists into one of the prison poles. He paced passionately, turning to address them all as he shook his fists.

"No!" he cried. "We cannot give in to hopelessness! Look what God has done through us! What did Samantha say? He has a plan and a purpose for our lives, and I can't—I refuse!—to believe He spared us just for this. Remember her dream of a city?"

"Forgive me, Sharko," Chrysta said bitterly, "but Vogul may be torturing or violating our prophetess right now! You think a God who lets that happen won't allow us to perish?"

"We don't know if he is," Sharko countered. "Listen to me! Look at yourselves! We have one real defeat, and we're all drooping faces and sorry spirits! God is with us. There's got to be a way of escape, and we will find it!"

"What do you suggest we do?" Nancy asked, logical as always.

"Why don't we pray for Samantha?" Sharko questioned. "Why don't we ask God to spare her from harm, and bring her back? To have Vogul extend us more time?"

"I doubt that'll happen!" Mike snorted.

"Nonetheless, doesn't Jesus say; 'ask, and you'll receive?'" Sharko persisted. "Nothing is impossible with faith in Christ."

"He's right!" Kaity exclaimed defiantly. "Let's all join hands."

It was several minutes later when Samantha returned, a bit unnerved but unharmed. As she shared how Vogul unexpectedly let her go, all eyes turned to Sharko. Kaity hugged her husband tightly, and Samantha glanced around the group with a confused smile.

"Um, did something happen while I was away?"

Kaity filled her in on their prayer session, and the prophetess nodded approvingly toward Sharko. *You were right, Lord—as usual*! She thought.

Aloud she said, "Well done! I have a bit of intelligence to share, too. I noticed an illuminated map of the gunship in one of the halls. While there wasn't a neon sign that said 'crystals' anywhere, I did spot an unusual chamber next to the engine room."

"How did you know what it was?" Kaity questioned. Then she recalled how Samantha had read alien writings in the orb cave. "Oh. Right."

"This chamber was plasma storage, I think," Samantha continued. "We may not be able to find the crystals, but plasma can be volatile if it gets out of containment." She winked.

"You mean blow up the gunship?" Mike caught on.

"You're crazy!" Nancy said disparagingly. "No offense, but *we'll* go down with it!"

"Possibly not," Samantha rejoined. "I saw a hangar bay on the same floor. It's a long shot, but we might be able to figure the controls. Or take a hostage to pilot."

"So you're suggesting we fly out, before it goes boom?" Matt was very interested. "That could work."

"What about the crystals?" Kaity asked, and all fell silent. Samantha placed a motherly hand on the former tutor. Although she didn't consider Kaity a close friend, she viewed her as a dear soul, and liked her very much.

"Kaity," she said, "perhaps the orbs aren't in our future. It was fun while it lasted, but God gave us that alien tech to survive Sahara. If it must go down with the ship, I'm sure it's His will."

"Are you?" Nancy's pragmatic voice cut in. "If we manage to break free—which is our first problem—I have an idea for how to find them. Guards."

"Guards?" Matt repeated. Samantha snapped her fingers.

"Look for the door with a sentry! Of course! What a dunce I've been. I'll wager Skull Warrior is babysitting the orbs, probably on another deck. Maybe I'll ask Vogul for a tour." Samantha shrugged at the others' incredulous stares. "What? Vogul has a thing for me. As disgusting as that is, I may be able to use it to even further advantage."

"Just make sure *he* doesn't take the advantage!" Chrysta pointed out. Samantha pretended to brush her comment off. Yet she too felt the icy chill of fear, and it wasn't Vogul alone who frightened her.

WILLUM VOGUL PASSED a restless night. He battled against the dark will that drove him, twisting and clawing the air in his sleep at times, as if fighting invisible adversaries. Vogul, agent of destiny, knew he must kill all of the Starganauts. Vogul, man of Earth, desired a wife from his own kind. What better revenge than to force the prophetess who'd proudly opposed him into marriage? Trylithian women held no appeal, and he doubted they were compatible, anyway.

Vogul was in deep, emotional upheaval, and not only from confliction. Samantha's words churned up a sea of rage, pain, and fear that Willum had swept under the rug much of his forty-seven years. She seemed to understand him, yet her empathy brought fresh agony. How could the engineer from Earth do this to him?

It is not the woman! The Voices hissed, from the darkness. *It is the I AM!*

Vogul felt himself jerk physically, as if snapped to a different plane. He stumbled through what was once a city square, now blasted. People surrounded him in various states of panic, but they stood frozen—frozen in time. Children, adults, the elderly, even pets, crowded the square. Their skin looked like obsidian and their eyes were ashes.

Blood trickled down Vogul's pants, dripping from his hands as well. He recoiled in shock, and suddenly, he was falling towards a great, red ocean. The surface parted, swallowing him. Black, wispy hands of shadow reached for him. At first, Vogul thought he would be saved. But the hands grasped at his clothes, pulling him, dragging him down into the depths of the ocean of blood that was his—all his doing! He heard the Voices mockingly crying, *"What is the death of one man? Billions are but numbers!"*

Vogul snapped awake in terror, his mouth tasting of ashes. Shaking, he walked to the bathroom of his quarters and began scrubbing his hands fervently in the sink. He stopped himself. No blood could be seen dripping or staining him. It had been a nightmare...all a nightmare. His com light blinked. Vogul got up wearily and flicked it on.

"Yes?"

"Sir, our ship is approaching from Dalar 3!"

The familiar voice of his Skull Warrior captain sounded excited.

"When we hailed it, one of our men answered. He said he was the only survivor from the search team."

"Meet him and begin debriefing," Vogul commanded, stifling a yawn. "I'll be there shortly."

He flicked off the com and changed mechanically from night clothes to his customary garment. It was Trylithian in fashion with modifications to look like a t-shirt and pants. Despite his hatred for Earth, Vogul could never entirely get away from it. He put on his desert hauberk, fastened his shield belt around his waist, straightened his shirt sleeves, and ran his fingers through his hair. Upon the messy blond tangle, he placed his brown helm, pausing momentarily to look in the mirror. Still no crimson stains. Only the face of a seasoned warrior stared back at him. Feeling relieved, Willum marched out and headed for the elevator. He had a loose end to tie up.

THE SKULL WARRIOR AND several Trylithians stood at attention in the hangar bay. They waited for their *Dezaptor*-class fighter to land. The larger starship had been left behind for the six-member tracking party, and the landing ramp came down with a clank. The surviving Trylithian descended slowly, stiffly. The Skull Warrior saluted him in Trylithian fashion, cocking his head to one side.

"Are you injured, warrior?" he questioned.

"Not at all!" an American voice cried from inside the dropship.

"Stick 'em up!" an Australian one chimed in. "This is a rescue!"

The Skull Warrior staggered back as a bullet entered his exposed side. Thunderbane leaped from the hold, shocking two Trylithians as he sliced into them. The remaining warrior made a mad dash for the com. Nick aimed Matt's revolver and shot him between the shoulder blades. The male fell against the wall, reaching upward to an alarm button that would spell discovery. His hand was mere inches away when another revolver bullet hit him. He gasped, his fingers slowly sliding down the metal, paneled wall. Nick whirled to cover the Trylithian survivor.

"I do as you ask," the male said haltingly. "I get you inside and I contact *Draxalis*. What more you want?"

"For you to count little koalas in your sleep," Nick replied. "To go 'bye-bye,' as you Yanks say!"

He moved over to the male and hit the back of his head with the revolver. Nick and Thunderbane moved the unconscious Trylithian into the dropship to hide him—Matt giving the Australian a rueful look.

"You know, you used the last of my two bullets," he remarked. "One was meant for Vogul."

Nick ignored him. He thrust the empty gun through his belt and picked up the alien's weapon, relieving the Skull Warrior of his com device as well.

"Could come in handy," he commented, and Thunderbane nodded with approval.

The Starganaut led the way. His lightning swords popped and crackled as he leaned around the corner of the open doorway. The hallway appeared clear. Yellowish lights illuminated it dimly, and they could hear the steady rumble of the ship's engines. Thunderbane and Nick crept along the tall corridor, every sense alert. The Starganaut soon turned off his lightning foils to aid in their stealth. Nick didn't notice. His eyes traced the length of the corridor. While the *Draxalis* was mostly barrel, seven living decks comprised the aft portion of the gunship. They were simply laid out, with perfectly straight hallways extending along both sides of the gunship for a good distance. These were broken up by doorways and the occasional, unfinished alcove. At the midpoint, front, and rear of the living decks stretched connecting passages, allowing for foot traffic to cross from the port to starboard sides.

Thunderbane and Nick neared this middle hallway, and Nick glanced back to see a Trylithian rounding the corner of the rearmost passageway. He yanked Thunderbane into the middle hallway. Chancing another glance, he observed a company of four Trylithians advancing. He gulped and drew back. Vogul was leading them!

Nick carefully told Thunderbane about his discovery, and both men rushed to the starboard side of the gunship. They could only guess that

Vogul's destination must be the hangar bay. All Hades was poised to break loose. The Starganaut shook his head.

"We *must* find the others!" he exclaimed. Peering around the corner, Thunderbane observed a hallway that was deserted but for a single sentry, farther down. He reached for an explosive hanging from his belt. Nick had thought to bring along a few from Fyromaniac's gear, yet as the Starganaut clutched their only grenade, the Australian objected.

"I should prob'bly take out this one," he said. "Never know when we might need that, Mate."

Thunderbane replaced the grenade grudgingly, Nick creeping forward to sneak up on the male. He dared not risk a shot. The noise might alert the crew, and he wasn't confident in his aim at this distance. Nick noticed that a long section of the wall was missing its paneling, creating alcoves and patches of pipes and wiring that jutted out. It was the perfect cover for an approach!

The Australian shimmied along the exposed wall, ducking behind a pipe or panel whenever the guard's head turned his way. The fact that a guard stood on duty was a relief. It had to mean the others were alive and trapped, here, behind this alien. Nick made his way painstakingly. Years of practice hunting indigenous animals had honed his stealth skills. There were few greater motivators than a full belly, and he imagined the Trylithian as a steak on legs. *Maybe I shouldn't*, Nick told himself, as he involuntarily licked his lips.

The Australian slipped to within three yards of the sentry. The opening in the wall ended here, forcing him to attack at the loss of his surprise. Muscles tensing, Nick waited until the Trylithian looked away. He half-slid, half-ran at the alien. The guard heard him and whirled around. Nick pointed what he believed to be the gun barrel at the alien.

"Care to be a steak—I mean mate!—and open the door?" he questioned, shaking his head to clear it.

The door slid back. Nick forced their 'friend' into the room beyond, and Thunderbane followed. The door closed behind them, and the two humans stared in disappointment.

"You've got to be kidding me!" Thunderbane moaned. A cage sat in the center of the room, barely three feet tall. Inside rested the sack of crystals! They had succeeded in finding the orbs, but not their friends!

"Does this mean they're all dead?" Nick gasped. "Are we all that's left, Mate?"

"Of course you are!" the Trylithian hostage sneered, in stilted English. "And Vojul kill you also!"

An alarm suddenly sounded. It grated their tense ears, and Nick moved his captive in front of Thunderbane.

"What you do, pale-flesh?" the Trylithian spat. "Slay me?"

"We're going to abide by the Geneva Convention," Thunderbane said, with a smirk. His fist shot out and hit the confused Trylithian in the forehead. The male slumped to the floor, unconscious.

"Never gets old!" Thunderbane exclaimed contentedly, before sawing at the cage bars with his electrified swords. He managed to cut through a few, and pried them completely apart with his bare hands until he could reach in and retrieve the crystal bag.

"That superhuman Form is simply ace!" Nick said admiringly.

"Come on!" Thunderbane ordered, rushing to the door. "We've got to see if our friends are alive, and then we find Vogul! Whatever their fates, I'm determined to make certain of two things, Nick. The Trylithians will never leave with the orbs, and Vogul will never live to enjoy his victory!"

<16>

Samantha's Choice

Willum Vogul strode angrily down the corridor of his gunship. Trylithian warriors poured out of their barracks to join him, as it had been their evening hours. Most climbed out of bunks and into their limited armor suits, consisting of a metal chest-plate, wrist- and shin-guards, boots, a shieldbelt, and a headdress. Vogul dispatched additional men to the lower deck, praying the two sentries outside the Starganauts' prison had held their ground. So far, his efforts to contact them yielded static.

Before this, Thunderbane and Nick found the same schematic of the ship that Samantha had seen. It was impossible to determine their friends' location, but Matt had a theory. The level of power being used in a room on the second deck seemed greater than the others, and it looked about the size of a dormitory. Throwing caution to the wind, the two raced for the elevator. They stepped in front of the double doors just in time for them to slide back, revealing three Trylithians. Thunderbane leaped at them with his lightning swords, and they rode downward with the still-sizzling bodies.

"Are you sure this is deck two?" Nick asked. "These alien symbols are all gibberish!"

"I saw this symbol next to the second lowest floor," Thunderbane persisted, and they burst out of the elevator together. Two Trylithians guarding a door saw them and fired. The humans jumped back into the elevator, and the Starganaut bent down suddenly. He put on a belt from a dead warrior, and tossed another to Nick.

"Try this on for size!" he exclaimed. "I believe I saw our friends push...*this*...button!"

A shield snapped on around him, vanishing within seconds from sight. Thunderbane put on a burst of speed and dashed toward his opponents. Plasma bolts smacked into his shield, only to be absorbed! He executed a roll on the ground, sprang upright, and let loose with such a flurry of attacks that the first guard's shield broke. He lopped his foe's head cleanly off, and Nick advanced with alien weapon drawn.

The remaining Trylithian threw down his plasma pistol and drew an axe. Thunderbane faced him, and the two circled each other, alert, tense—watching for any opening. The male's shield hummed, and he rushed the Starganaut. Thunderbane slashed the male's shield five times before it buckled, yet received a bruising blow to the torso in return. The Trylithian warrior suddenly swung his axe in a powerful, arcing motion. Thunderbane parried his attempt and did a cross chop. The Trylithian moved to block, but his axe handle snapped under the force. He drew a dagger. Too late! Thunderbane ran the Trylithian through and he collapsed, his body convulsing from the shock, joining his brethren among the mounting dead.

Nick dashed to the door console. He tried desperately to unlock it—without success. Thunderbane grabbed the door and attempted to bodily move it, but it wouldn't budge. Disgusted, he bade Nick stand back. Thunderbane placed one of Fyromaniac's smaller explosives on the door console. There was a loud explosion. A smoking hole appeared were the console had been, and the door slid open. The six Starganauts, their energy cage, and the bleak interior were revealed.

KAITY COULDN'T BELIEVE her eyes as their rescuers entered. Matt and Nick! They were okay and, even more amazingly, they'd come to free them! The Creator had not abandoned them to death. Vogul's time of gloating was over. They would escape, and outlast him, and she prayed that this day would spell his doom.

Sharko rose and greeted Thunderbane and Nick heartily.

"You two are the best!" he exclaimed, adding quickly. "Is Dudeman...?"

"Stable, for now," Thunderbane answered, "though I believe Miss Cooper's services are long overdue."

"Praise Jesus!" Samantha declared, beaming. "I knew I could count on you, *Primo*!"

"Nick here might've helped, too," her cousin said modestly, but Samantha knew he liked the praise.

"It's great you have the crystals!" Kaity affirmed. "How will we get free, though?"

"I have an idea," Thunderbane answered. "Remember how I can release an electrical pulse with these, Cousin? You may want to stand back!"

The six Starganauts huddled together in the far corner of the small space. Nick closed his eyes, and Thunderbane dipped his swords into two separate energy bars. Sparks flew, and blue electricity surged from the bars to his foil blades and back. The energy beams began to destabilize. The lightning of his swords jumped into the beam. The sound of electricity popping and crackling grew to almost overwhelming intensity. Suddenly, something went wrong. The blue energy of the bars shot down Thunderbane's swords. The bars had completely destabilized, but the energy was now flowing into Thunderbane. The convulsing Starganaut gritted his teeth and held his ground.

"GO!" he cried, and his comrades needed no second urging. Nick tried madly to find a shutoff switch while the six rushed out of their cage. The Dundee gave Samantha the bag of crystals, and she handed an orb to each of the humans—Sharko's blue, Kaity's purple, Nancy's clear, Mike's white, and Chrysta's green. Kaity breathed a sigh of relief as she felt the familiar, wonderful feeling of lightness, and became Valora once more.

Bolts of electricity leaped from the posts of the prison. A surge of power shot down Thunderbane's foils, followed by an electric explosion. The Starganaut flew back, armor sizzling, slamming into the wall with a metallic crunch. The others had all transformed and were free—just in time! The energy bars snapped back into place. The entire prison cage shot out a few tendrils of blue lightning and gave a final popping noise. Valora and Apotheka rushed to Thunderbane, but his pride was hurt more than his body.

"I wouldn't be much of a lightning guy if I couldn't withstand a little electrocution," he said humorously. He wheezed as the women helped him up. "I'll be all right."

"It's good to have these pistols back!" Crosshair happily flourished her matching guns.

"Where to now?" Valora inquired.

"We have a Trylithian ship in a hangar a few decks up," Thunderbane answered, but Crosshair and Blaze shook their heads.

"We discussed a plan while we were in here," Blaze put in. "We mean to destroy the gunship. Vogul will only blast Sahara if we return to the surface, and who knows what other evils he'll use this ship for? This ends, *now*! How many explosives did you bring?"

"Half of Fyro's," Thunderbane replied. "I've got two timed charges and a grenade left. I fail to see how we can destroy an entire ship."

"It's not the firepower," Crosshair interjected, "but the placement. We know Vogul's beam is highly volatile stuff—plasma, most likely. If we can find the storage tanks..."

"We can blow through them and unleash the plasma!" Blaze finished.

"Follow me!" Crosshair ordered. "We need to get back to that schematic!"

"Um, guys, we've got trouble!" Vipress cried. She was standing by the doorway with Nick. Crosshair poked her head out and, to her horror, saw several squads of Trylithians thundering towards them. A few carried scythes and axes, while most had guns, and she dodged back as plasma bolts smacked into the plating right next to her!

PANIC SEIZED HER HEART. The bolts continued to pepper the doorway, and Crosshair turned to her colleagues. The prophetess felt shaken. About thirty Trylithians were closing in, with countless more charging down the hallway. She could not even see Willum Vogul at the back, but proximity hardly mattered. They were trapped!

Blaze walked up behind her.

"Move back," he said authoritatively, turning to face the room of uncertain faces. Many were shielded by visors or framed by alien helms, but all shared fear and worry. As searing bullets struck the wall outside, as the sound of tramping boots drew nearer, he drew his rifle and torchsword, raising the latter.

"Today may be our final hour!" he exclaimed loudly. "Today we may go out in a blaze of glory, but we shall not go silently into that good night! We fight! We race into the maw of death and danger, knowing God is with us! Though darkness may overtake us, dawn comes upon its wings! Who's with me?"

Valora felt a rush of pride at her husband's brave words. Her heart swelled with admiration, respect, confidence. She brandished her sword as Valora, and the Starganauts raised a shout as one. Their battle cry surprised the Trylithians, who could hear it as they reached the doorway. Even Vogul heard, and a tendril of fear wrapped around his blackened heart.

"For Earth!" Blaze cried, dashing into the maelstrom of gunfire.

The hallway erupted in chaos. They charged out of the room and right into the thick of Trylithian bodies. Scythes and axes came out. Those behind their blue-skinned allies were unable to shoot, for Trylithian was so intermingled with human. The Starganauts' armor protected them from the initial volley, and then it was close combat.

Thunderbane made a dramatic entrance, swinging his electric foils in a fearsome flurry of lightning. Valora came behind Blaze, slashing right through enemies' shielding with her broadsword. Crosshair let loose with a point-blank volley, and she directed the shooters farther down the corridor. Here, at a slight distance, they carefully picked off some of the melee fighters. Ninjarak burst into the fray with his bo staff whirling, knocking opponents off their feet. He finished them with a crushing blow to the skull. Vipress sprayed acidic poison, scalding her enemies and eating right through their armor. Trylithians seemed to be everywhere, and Valora was so focused that she didn't even notice a scythe-warrior draw blood until she felt wetness on her sword arm.

"How dare you harm my wife!" Blaze yelled, and the scythe-warrior received a flaming sword in the face. It was impossible to tell how they were faring. For every Trylithian they killed, more came to replace them. They fought for their very lives, but they also fought with an amazing sense of unity. Ninjarak would knock a foe back, and Thunderbane would finish him. Crosshair, Vipress, Nick, and Apotheka would surgically pick warriors off, and Blaze stayed ever vigilant in holding their frontline. The truck driver from Earth had changed drastically. Hesitant to lead or voice an opinion, he was shouting orders and encouragement from their head, dauntlessly cutting a swath through onrushing enemies.

The flaming torchsword seared its way through several Trylithians. Blaze confronted a particularly skilled warrior, with a skull dangling from his belt and a sabre in his hand. The warrior feinted an attack from the right, but suddenly stabbed to the left. He caught Blaze in the stomach, though the armor stopped his sword. Blaze executed a counterattack, but the Trylithian dodged it. He unleashed a rapid succession of blows with his sabre, putting Blaze on the defensive. The Starganaut stepped back, and for a moment, they stood perhaps seven feet apart. That was all the Trylithian needed. He held both arms out suddenly and, just as quickly, slapped them together in a pincer motion.

Blaze remembered, too late, what the champion of the hovercraft had done. The familiar, biting pain knifed through his midsection. He still couldn't grasp how the mere motion of alien arms could physically harm him, but it staggered the Starganaut leader. Before he knew it, the Trylithian came in low. He thrust his sabre upward, through the small gap of Blaze's armor between belt and breastplate. The blade punched sickeningly through.

VALORA SAW THE TRYLITHIAN stab her husband, and felt the world slow down. Her heart pounded more loudly than the clanging of metal. A lump clogged her throat. She wanted to scream, but nothing came out. Watching in horror, she beheld her valiant husband double over in agony and sink to the floor.

The enemy took full advantage. The warrior prepared his sabre for a final, powerful thrust. Valora was too far away to stop him. She heard a shout, and suddenly, two plasma bullets ripped into the male. The Trylithian fell, and she glanced back to see Crosshair, her pistols still extended and smoking. Ninjarak and Thunderbane charged forward to protect their leader. Valora gave a cry and joined them. Fury coursed through her body, and she swung her sword with the might of anger. Slicing a foe, she extended her blade and twirled around, slashing several males at once. Tears streamed down her face. She imagined the worst, but there was little time to think or feel in the press of battle.

Apotheka picked her way over the bodies of the dead to examine Blaze. The Starganaut's pained grimace revealed the depths of his pain, and she removed the breastplate quickly. An artery had been cut by the Trylithian's blade. Although in a glorified body, Blaze was bleeding substantially. Apotheka switched her gun to its healing setting, a ray of blue enveloping the wound. She hoped desperately that her gun could knit his damaged flesh enough for him to stand.

Meanwhile, the team continued fighting. Trylithians fell like wheat before a harvester, and as one alien toppled over dead, Crosshair beheld the face of the enemy. Willum Vogul paced at the rear of the Trylithians, and she realized he must be unleashing his entire crew at them. As the melee fighters continued to drop, weapons' fire from the gunmen began reaching the Starganauts. Thunderbane was peppered with shots but his thick plating held. Ninjarak received minor burns from plasma bolts, and Crosshair had to duck as enemy fire sped her way.

The key to everything was Vogul, yet...not in a way the others would understand. Crosshair could see fear and surprise in the evil man's countenance. He was watching the Starganauts lay waste to perhaps 60 of his men. He seemed ready to bolt—ready to reveal the self-centered scoundrel he was—and she must follow. Despite the fact that he had murdered billions, Vogul was still just a man. Every human shared two things in common: mortality, and the need for a Savior.

Although her heart went against it, Crosshair knew she must confront him. The battle was physical, yes, but a greater one raged spiritually inside this twisted soul. The abused child inside of Vogul needed to hear the truth. Regardless of what happened, Vogul would be executed for his crimes—but he deserved a chance at repentance. Like anybody else. Samantha could sense God's full leading in this. It was all that kept her from aiming for his head and squeezing both triggers.

"Nick!" Crosshair turned to the Australian, firing around the blasted doorway at the Trylithians. "I need you to relay a message to my cousin."

"All ears, Mate!"

"The plasma storage tanks are on deck 5, just before the engine room. Matt will know where to place the charges. 'Taxu desrec' will give him five minutes to run! Please tell him not to look for me."

"*You* wait five minutes!" Nick protested, but the two were briefly interrupted by shots whizzing by. Nick took down the alien shooting at them, and resumed. "Where are you headin', and why can't he follow?"

"God walks us through the hard trails of life," Crosshair explained hastily. "We all have our paths, and every path has its end. My path may be heading in that direction, and I would thank you not to get in my way. Any of you."

"Now listen here!" Nick exclaimed. "That's bull dust, and—"

"This isn't a debate." Crosshair swallowed hard. "Your mission is to destroy this ship and get off. Mine...is far more complicated than you can ever understand."

With that, Crosshair looked up, and saw Vogul slowly beginning to draw back. His Trylithian force couldn't be more than twenty warriors, now, and Crosshair gave Nick the infamous look that told him better than to protest.

"It is time!" she announced, withdrawing down the corridor. She had a hunch as to where Vogul was fleeing. Moving stealthily, she made her way to the hallway which connected to the other side of the gunship. Halfway, she found an elevator door. Crosshair rode it up to the highest deck, and emerged onto the *Draxalis'* expansive bridge.

At first, she didn't see Vogul. Though familiar from her previous visit, she was finally able to take the space in. The gunship's bridge contained one long, low room, ringed by floor-to-ceiling windows and with consoles spread out in an orderly fashion. Above these consoles hung flat screens—the only obstruction to a spectacular view. Crosshair was dazzled by the brilliance of the stars. Burning in the midst of the massive black vacuum, they almost made her forget her reason for coming. But a figure lurked ahead of her, half-bent and mostly obscured from her view by a hanging screen. His fingers pressed buttons left and right, and as the elevator door made a clinking sound behind her, she realized he was throwing the ship into lockdown.

She was trapped!

THE BATTLE WITH THE Trylithians wound down. Apotheka had moved Blaze to the room of their former prison, to be out of the battle zone, and she'd been able to heal him almost fully. Vogul's melee fighters were all but fallen, leaving Thunderbane, Valora, and Ninjarak to wreak havoc on the ranged Trylithian warriors. Vipress and Nick supported them, and Apotheka moved freely about, tending to her companions' minor injuries almost as fast as they arose. Her form's strong shield protected her from stray shots, until the battle was won and the corridor fell silent. The Trylithians had fought to the last man, refusing to surrender. If nothing else could be said for them, they made stubborn, brave foes.

Their dead, blue bodies choked up the corridor. Valora felt slightly sick. Fury over her husband's wound had long subsided, and she stepped over the dead, almost slipping on green, alien blood. Fighting in the desert had been one thing, but having so many corpses confined to one area—she felt ill. Was battle truly their calling from the Creator? The horror of killing, and the terror of fighting, sent shivers through her.

"She did WHAT?"

Valora's musings were interrupted by the outcry. Thunderbane was shaking Nick. The Australian shoved the Starganaut away and appeared insulted.

"Mate, I'm tellin' you, I couldn't stop her," Nick said defensively. "You know how your cousin is!"

"So knock her out!" Thunderbane exclaimed, grinding his teeth in frustration. "You do realize she could DIE?"

"Look, we've put the Trylithians to cream! The eight of us slaughtered big mobs of 'em. Sam wanted us to place charges and scatter, an' that's what I figured we'll do."

Thunderbane calmed slightly and gave a long, drawn-out sigh of resignation.

"I think it might be best to split into teams," Blaze interjected. "One team can be tasked with finding the closest ship to the storage room. Another could plant the charges and set a timer."

"And I want a third to search for my cousin!" Thunderbane insisted.

"I agree," Blaze affirmed. "Though I highly respect Samantha, we're not going to let her be a martyr. We'll find her, if we can. If we run out of time, we'll return to the ship," he added, to assuage his wife's look of concern.

All of those present agreed to the plan. They decided that Nick, Valora, and Vipress would seek out the best hangar to escape from. Thunderbane chose Apotheka to look for Crosshair with him, since his cousin might be injured. That left Blaze and Ninjarak to find the storage bay and place the charges. Thus resolved, the Starganauts set out for their respective destinations.

Valora's team had the easiest task. Aside from the encounter with an occasional Trylithian crewman, they met no resistance. They simply rode to Deck 5 with the demolition team. Nick couldn't remember the location of the hangar, so they tried every door along the hallway until they found it. The *Dezaptor* starfighter stood ready to depart, looking large enough to transport all eight of them. The landing ramp was still down, so they stepped inside the alien vessel.

Valora immediately noticed metal ribbing, long windows, and a bulbous cockpit. The ship's cabin looked smaller than she had imagined, but large enough. Aside from the cockpit and a pilot's chair, simple cushions lined the floor, and alien circuitry ran everywhere. Nick sat down in the pilot's chair and slapped his palms together.

"This is gonna be fun without our hostage!" he said sarcastically. "Gee, I just love those strange symbols and this odd doovalacky of piloting apparatus! An' here I failed my high school Japanese."

Deciphering symbols was the last thing on Blaze and Ninjarak's minds. Once they reached the plasma storage chamber, Blaze used his torchsword to cut through a section of the tall, locked metal door. With Ninjarak's bo staff as a lever, they dislodged the section and it fell loudly into the room. Inside, two massive tanks confronted them. The material that comprised them, however, was a complete surprise.

"Umm...those are shields, aren't they?" Ninjarak asked. The two men exchanged worried glances. They had imagined the storage tanks to be solid, box-shaped containers made of a material that could contain plasma. Little had they imagined that the storage tanks would be solid, metal frames with see-through shielding for "walls."

"What on Sahara are we going to do?" Ninjarak questioned, throwing up his hands in frustration.

<17>

Shadows

Crosshair walked toward Vogul boldly. Her pistols rested in their holsters, for her intention was to talk. Willum heard the prophetess approach. He peered out from behind the console screen, a gloating expression crossing his face.

"I hoped we'd meet once more, before the end!" he exclaimed. "You just can't resist me, can you?"

Crosshair's face contorted in a look of disgust.

"My coming has nothing to do with attraction," she spat. "You're a depraved man, Vogul, but you're also deeply lost. You think you yearn for connection with another human being, but I know the shape of the hole in your heart. It can only be filled by one thing."

"Don't patronize me!" Vogul gritted his teeth. "Awfully stupid of you, Miss Harris, wandering off by yourself. What did you really hope to accomplish? I know your plans! This gunship cannot be destroyed."

Crosshair was momentarily taken aback. How *could* he know? For one with so much knowledge of her and future events, it baffled her how could he struggle to find them in the vast desert. Was he being informed by some being that could transcend time? Had he found an artifact that revealed the future? Whatever the case, the source of his knowledge was impressive but not limitless. *Only the Lord is all-knowing*, she reminded herself, taking comfort in that fact.

"Every giant has a weakness," she countered. "For some, it only takes a shepherd boy and a stone."

"You're no shepherd boy!" Vogul hissed disparagingly. "The days of Earth are over! Your God can't help you here. I'm about to kill your entire group! Myd ships are crewed by robots, you see." His tone took on a crazed quality. "As such, they have a failsafe in case enemies invade. Every large ship can vent toxins into the air system, and that's what I'm giving to your friends! They're all going to suffocate, leaving you alone...with *me*!"

Vogul attempted a smile, but it came out looking ghastly.

"Think of it, Samantha! The last man and woman from Earth! We are the next Adam and Eve! You continue to resist, but you know you want me. You understand me, as I understand you!"

As he spoke, his tone softened. He moved closer, like a shark circling its prey.

"You and I aren't too dissimilar. You were a woman of renown on Earth—an engineer. You and I share a high intellect. Those *others* you travel with...they're not like us. We were both ostracized by our people: I, for my discovery of an alien world, and you, for leaving a successful career to preach about Earth's end."

Crosshair paused. Should she play along, or state her intentions? The longer they talked, the more it delayed Vogul's release of the toxin.

"I can't argue with you there," Crosshair said, to Vogul's pleased surprise. The madman relaxed. Could it be? Despite their bitter introduction, this girl from Earth appeared to be warming up to him!

"Your companions will die," Vogul said, feigning sadness. "They are not fit, but you! With a mind as open as yours, who knows where destiny might take you? *Us?*"

"It is true," Crosshair stated. "I've never felt quite like the others."

"Which is why I'm making you the offer of a millennium!" Vogul exclaimed. He was now so close that his body trembled. "Samantha, why should we continue being enemies? Despite all that I have accomplished, I feel alone. You too must feel it—the loneliness of greatness? Why not stay here with me? You're a beautiful woman, and I am a successful man. I know you have high standards. Just say the word, and I will marry you and forget about your friends' iniquities. I wield power in a galaxy where humans, well..."

Crosshair pretended to think for several moments. At length, she smiled coyly, leaned forward, and took his hand. Vogul lit up. It had been so very long since any woman noticed him. His own mother had never given him affection—not even a hug. The Starganaut smiled.

"I cannot accept your offer," she said, "without first putting forth one of my own. You are an intelligent man, yet you killed so many people. But God is a merciful creator. It is not too late for you to accept His Son's forgiveness for the terrible sin of destroying Earth and its people. Surely conscience must claw at you? Surely regret must seize at your heart, even more than loneliness. Will you repent? Will you confess your sins, and pay for your crimes?"

Vogul shoved her hand aside, his mouth curling into a snarl. He appeared as vicious as an animal, and struck her. To this, Crosshair merely jumped up, drawing her pistols. Vogul too whipped out an alien pistol, and the two faced one another, waiting to see who might make the first move.

"I'm not sorry for what I did!" Vogul roared. "I haven't a drop of regret for silencing those inferior beings you call people! They rejected me. They deserved what they got, and if you remain blind...I thought you, *you alone*, were open to reason!"

"Your reason is madness!" Crosshair cried defiantly. "Your mercy is murder! Your words are poison. I'd rather marry a pile of dung!"

Vogul's face contorted in fury.

"Then I *will* kill you!" he screamed, and lunged at her. Crosshair fired her pistols. She was so close, but to her shock, a shield materialized. It absorbed her shots seconds before Vogul jumped on her. She had underestimated his strength. Despite her glorified Form, he grabbed her wrists and pushed her to the floor. There they grappled, until he grabbed the crystal at the center of her choker and ripped it out. His action filled her with an odd sensation.

The light of transformation blinded her. The moment she could see, a fist crashed into her face brutally. She was Samantha Harris once more, and Vogul hauled her bodily to her feet. He slammed her against one of the bridge's few pillars, holding her throat between his hands. Samantha clawed at him with her fingernails and kicked hard. Vogul simply ignored her and began to squeeze.

"You idiot! You don't understand how I went against *their* wishes! How much I sacrificed trying to save you! You knew your answer before we spoke. You came here simply to die!"

"Not to die!" Samantha choked out. "To convert you! And if not that, then...to buy my friends...time...to stop you!"

Lack of oxygen began to take a toll. Vogul squeezed with every ounce of strength in him, his face bright red with exertion and anger. Samantha's life was draining out of her. Her orb tossed aside, her Starganaut strength gone, she looked upward as if toward Heaven and waited for the Lord to take her home.

BLAZE AND NINJARAK were in a crisis. Sharko, as a truck driver, was at a complete loss when it came to destroying the generators. Ninjarak had minored in computer science in college, but even his knowledge proved useless for interfacing with the alien system. Neither could read a word on the console, anyway.

"Drat that stubborn woman!" Ninjarak exclaimed, and Blaze knew he meant Samantha. "Figures we'd lose our engineer when she's needed most!"

"Being able to read this would definitely help," Blaze agreed. The massive storage tanks were cylindrical in shape, squat, and broad. They both appeared full, the purplish plasma inside looking almost beautiful through its encasement of shielding. A kiosk with a panel and flatscreen stood between the generators, doubtless controlling some aspect of them. The bases of the tanks rose a good six feet, prompting Blaze to surmise that the shields' generators must be built within.

"Well, we can't take out the generators," he said. "We could try blowing the frame, but we'd risk setting off the plasma instantly."

"What about these tubes?" Ninjarak questioned, pointing down to some thick, flat pipes that ran through the floor and connected to the generators' foundations.

"I'm not about to randomly blow up conduits," Blaze rebutted. "For all we know, these might be supplying fresh plasma to the tanks. Would you walk around and see if you can find anything else? I think I'm starting to understand something on this dratted console!"

Ninjarak skirted one of the large tanks. On the opposite side from Blaze, he found another panel. This one was set into the base, and displayed a bar of blue, green, and red color, along with alien lettering and symbols. Ninjarak gave a yell, and Blaze jogged over to him.

"I haven't a clue what the heck this is," he admitted, "but you instructed me to—"

"I know," Blaze interrupted, motioning him aside. He gazed intently at the panel, flexing his fingers. "I believe this word, ulac, means 'control.' This bar...see how it has a marker which fluctuates ever so slightly? I wonder..."

He pressed a button on the screen, and the marker rose toward the red zone. He continued pressing it, until a warning light flashed. Blaze grinned with satisfaction. Ninjarak stared at him, uncomprehending.

"Mike my friend," Blaze said with a grin, "I believe I've found where to place the charges."

"Here?"

"These, I believe, are the temperature controls to the generators. We plant explosives here and take the whole system out. The generators will over-heat, and, well...you're the science major."

"They explode!" Ninjarak exclaimed, and he rubbed his hands together eagerly.

"Samantha instructed us to give ourselves 'taxu desrec,'" Blaze continued, "five minutes. Let's hope all goes as intended. If not, we should at least be aboard that escape ship."

The two Starganauts each took one of Fyromaniac's charges. Hardly daring to hope they were correct, they placed the explosives and set them for five minutes in unison. Blaze and Ninjarak dashed to the doorway, squeezing through the hole in the metal door. It was done! Beyond belief, they had defeated Vogul's crew, and now they would destroy the gunship that had decimated Earth. The *Draxalis* would not last to harm another world.

"WARNING! WARNING! TEMPERATURE control failure in plasma storage!"

An alien, artificial voice announced the alert over the ship's com system in Trylithian. Vogul cursed and dropped Samantha like a bag of rocks. The prophetess crumpled to the ground and lay still. For a half moment, Vogul looked down at her limp form. He shook his head.

"So dies Samantha Harris, Prophetess of God," he said darkly, as he moved to a console on the bridge. "No matter! I shall throw up a shield around the room! These Starganauts won't stop me yet!"

"*Fool! They have already!*" a multitude cried, from the shadows. Vogul turned to see a cloud of darkness spreading across the room. Shadowy shapes moved about inside of it, barely distinguishable in the blackness. Vogul felt himself shaking, but he tried to remain calm.

"*It is too late for a shield!*" The Voices hissed. "*You have failed us yet again! You were warned!*"

"No! No, I haven't!" Vogul countered. "My wish to keep the Prophetess alive was an indulgence. I acknowledge that, and beg your pardon now! But there are things that can be done! I can blow up this entire ship!"

Willum Vogul was so preoccupied that he didn't notice Samantha regain consciousness. The Prophetess raised her head weakly, starting with fright at the terrifying sight before her. She watched the exchange, greatly troubled in spirit. Was she...were the shadows...demons?

"*Imbecile!*" The Voices shouted, infuriated. "*We gave you everything, and you have never served us! You are weak and pathetic! You deserved the ostracizing of your world!*"

"Shut up!" Vogul snarled. "Just...*shut up*! Look, there's the girl! She stirs! Can't you do something about her? Can't you see I brought her here for you to slaughter?"

The mass of shadows slithered toward her, and Samantha screwed her eyes shut and clasped her hands together. Darkness and coldness beyond bearing surrounded her. She felt a slimy, icy substance envelop her, and her body grew faint yet again.

'*The Light shines in the darkness, but the darkness has not understood it,*' she prayed. *Lord, protect me from this evil!* Her body froze in abject terror. It felt like she lay there an hour, yet within moments, the shadows retracted. They re-amassed with an angered screech.

"*We cannot lay a claw upon her!*" the Voices screamed. "*She is protected by the I AM! You have no conception of what has begun!*"

"Why are you able to affect me, if not her?" Vogul's voice quavered.

"*It was a mistake,*" the Voices continued. "*You are a mistake, and your usefulness has run out!*"

All light seemed to leave the room. The stars glittered more brilliantly in the darkness, and Vogul began to back up slowly, toward the glass at the very front of the bridge.

"Please, don't kill me!" he begged.

"*You will receive the mercy you granted to Earth*!" The Voices roared. Vogul cowered in fear, and Samantha watched in horror as tendrils of shadow flicked out suddenly, touching the human and causing him to shiver. Vogul turned and bolted, but he was without direction. He smacked into the glass plate, and had only moments to whirl around before the darkness swallowed him. His mind pulsated with pain, and the most unearthly cry Samantha had ever heard erupted from his mouth.

Her heart pounded, even as her brain remained fuzzy. Samantha crawled numbly across the metal floor. Her crystal lay not far from where she'd fallen, and she reached for it madly. Vogul screamed in agony, and then something dreadful happened. The great throng of shadows launched into him. Though Samantha couldn't see anything for the darkness that covered him, she heard the ghastly sounds of the Voices tearing him apart, intermingled with Vogul's dying screams.

The force of their attack was so great that the glass pane behind him cracked and shattered. Nothing could be seen of Vogul as he was wrenched violently into space. Only a great mass of shadows, and a slight trail of red, marked the passing of the madman who had destroyed Earth. Willum Vogul was gone forevermore.

SAMANTHA TRANSFORMED into Crosshair. She was barely in her suit when she felt herself being sucked out into space. The room was suddenly freezing, and all gravity left. Crosshair slid back along the floor, flying up into the air. She grabbed for the metal post, catching on with both hands and clinging desperately.

Despite her glorified body, the damage to her regular one had weakened Samantha greatly. Her Starganaut armor protected her from exposure to space, but her helmet visor was still open. She felt a frigid rush of air smack her face. An unimaginable force pulled at her and, for one terrifying instant, she thought the Voices had seized her again. She couldn't let go to close her helmet, but lack of oxygen and exposure threatened to finish her.

I was right, she thought, holding on between oblivion and eternity. *I figured this would be the end of me, and it is. Stupid, stubborn Samantha! At least I was stubborn for You, Lord. Into Your hands I give up my spirit, willingly, happily, knowing I have served You well. In the end, that is all that matters.*

Crosshair suddenly dropped to the floor. A containment shield had automatically kicked in, covering the hole in the glass plate. The room's gravity and oxygen were restored. It was still bitterly cold, and Crosshair could hardly move.

"Warning! Warning! Generator heat critical! Plasma ignition in four desrec!"

The announcement roused Samantha slightly, and she saw a sudden explosion. The elevator door blasted open, her cousin and Apotheka emerging through the smoke. They rushed over, and she dimly heard Thunderbane give an exclamation.

"*Prima*! Are you okay? Where's Vogul?"

"Torn apart by the forces that drove him," she said weakly, and the two Starganauts gingerly picked her up. They wouldn't understand the literalness of her answer until later.

"We've got to get out of here!" Apotheka reminded. "You're going to be fine, Samantha. There's not much my gun can do with asphyxiation, but you'll recover."

"Thank goodness for Fyro's grenade!" Thunderbane added, and the two moved toward the elevator.

The rest of their trip seemed a blur to Samantha. She vaguely recalled being ushered down a hallway, and then they entered an alien ship, and she was plopped down near Valora. Nick sat in the pilot's chair. As soon as the hatch clanged shut, he started the starship. There was a slight sputter, but the engines awoke with a roar. Nick steered through the hangar's containment shield and out into space, just as the first explosion burst through Vogul's gunship. The outer hull ruptured along several other places, traveling down the length of the gun barrel in a sight that, to the Starganauts, was beautiful to behold.

"All this toil, suffering...this long nightmare," Valora said softly, leaning on Blaze's shoulder and watching the fireworks. "It seems like a dream to see it finally ending."

"We aren't outta this one yet, Mates!" Nick called. "That blast knocked the engines of the gunship offline! It's gonna fall into a decayin' orbit, along with heaps of the debris!"

The *Draxalis* ruptured from another explosion, and chunks of the ship started flying toward them as if to emphasize his point. Nick kicked on the fighter's boosters and began dodging shrapnel. Missiles of brown and gray metal zoomed by, beating them to the thermosphere of the planet. And behind them, like a great rod of doom, the gunship was falling into the atmosphere of Sahara.

NICK STRUGGLED TO AVOID the pieces of flying shrapnel. Their ship burst through the thermosphere with flaming chunks of gunship all around, and the seven Starganauts held on grimly as their fate was determined by the steady hand of the Australian. With the massive size of the gunship, there seemed an endless barrage of debris. Their ship wasn't the most maneuverable, and Nick went into a roll to avoid a cluster of chunks the size of beach balls. He uttered a garbled oath as the craft jolted from an impact to the engines. Still they rocketed through the upper atmosphere, and Kaity, as Valora, tensed with fear. The sound of air whistling by reached them all.

"We're going to crash...*again*!" Vipress shrieked. Crosshair was still too groggy to be of help, but Blaze jumped to his feet. He braced himself near the cockpit, just behind Nick, as another piece hit them.

"What's the situation?" he asked with authority. The Australian pressed buttons madly, attempting to slow their descent.

"I dunno if these ships carry air brakes or somethin'," he replied, "but we're gonna crash, Mate!"

"Can this thing land?" Blaze suggested. "If we're going to crash, we can at least minimize the damage."

"Lift me up! I *must* see the controls!"

Crosshair's voice was weak but persistent.

"I can read Trylithian!" she nearly shouted, and Valora and Ninjarak helped her up. With Crosshair urging haste all the way, she reached the pilot's console as the desert floor drew nearer.

"There! That button!" she cried, leaning forward and pressing it herself. There was the sound of something being retracted, followed by a metal clank. At the same moment, Blaze pointed to a long, flat stretch of desert to the right of their current trajectory.

"Land here!" he exclaimed. Nick reactively jerked their ship over, and the Trylithian craft screamed toward the sand.

"Nose up!" Crosshair commanded. At the same time, she held down the button. The ship was rapidly falling. It nearly hit the sand, but suddenly launched upward. Crosshair had activated a set of landing thrusters. Again, the ship fell towards earth, and again, she activated them at a calculated moment. They were slowing down a little. Reaching the best-looking stretch of desert, Nick gritted his teeth and went in for a landing.

"Get ready for a bumpy ride!" he yelled. "We'll either make it, or we're dingo stew!"

"Brace yourselves!" Blaze called, and Crosshair wisely slid into the copilot's chair. The ship smacked into the ground so hard that the craft bounced and cleared air. Valora dug her gauntleted fingers into her seat cushion and winced. Their vessel landed with a slight crunch, jolting the entire group of cringing Starganauts before bouncing again. The ship appeared to land on some sort of skis, and started skidding quickly across the grainy terrain.

Sand flew into the windshield, but Nick managed to see just enough to slide around the occasional rock. All of them hung on grimly. All remembered the shuttle crash, and felt deep pits of fear in their stomachs. It seemed the world couldn't stop rushing by. As if to add to their dilemma, they slid into a field of ancient, crashed ships. Dodging rocks and metal wreckage, they continued on, slowing with every yard...but not enough! The ground ahead seemed to disappear, and no one needed to suggest they were skidding right toward a cliff. Nick had already guessed they were, anyway.

"You're not gonna believe this," he piped up, "but this cliff ahead is the bluff overhanging my homestead!"

"Great! We're going to crash at your place...literally!" Thunderbane said with sarcasm. "How comforting is that?"

"Oh, shut up, *Primo*!" Crosshair exclaimed, and she jammed her fingers into the console. The landing thrusters activated, flipping their ship. The Trylithian craft did a 360-degree turn in the air, along with Valora's stomach. It smashed into the sand and continued sliding, albeit more slowly. The ship came to a scraping halt merely ten yards from the bluff's edge. Nick breathed a sigh of relief. It was an amazing crash-landing. The outside of the ship had been badly scraped, but the hull remained largely intact.

Blaze urged everyone out immediately.

"We've still got shrapnel incoming!" he shouted, and even Nick scrambled to do his bidding. The eight humans bolted from the crashed craft. Valora, gazing up, could see shrapnel descending like a meteor shower. They ran straight, interested in distance more than destination. At last, they reached the scarp of a sand dune a fair ways off.

They stood on it and watched the impact of the debris. Chunks of flaming shrapnel, ranging from the size of a snowball to the size of a mailbox, slammed into the sand where their ship lay. Debris hit the planet all around them too, but they seemed to be out of any missile's trajectory. Nick wore a mixed expression. He seemed crestfallen from losing the alien ship and seeing shrapnel hit his homestead. However, he also reminded Valora of a kid in a candy store.

"It's bad for my home," he said, "but look at all those spare parts! Alien tech that's new and grand! I could spend years workin' on—!"

He stopped abruptly as a gigantic piece of the *Draxalis* hit the earth just over the bluff. His mouth twisted into a glowering frown.

"That *was* your homestead, wasn't it?" Valora asked gently. Nick couldn't speak. He nodded slowly, and then the shockwave of the impact reached them. They were all standing on a sandy slope, and Crosshair, weakened, staggered and fell right onto her bottom. For a moment, a horrified look crossed her face. She'd fallen in a highly ungraceful manner. Everyone glanced at the Prophetess, so grave, so dignified—except for this moment.

Crosshair burst into laughter. One by one, laughter infected the group of weary but victorious humans. Even Nick started shaking with mirth, giggling at himself for his comment about spare parts.

"We did it!" Crosshair exclaimed. Thunderbane helped her up, and the Prophetess, looking much better from her ordeal, bade them all to hold hands and bow heads. They prayed, right there, right in that field of falling wreckage and arid waste. Crosshair thanked God for keeping them all alive. She thanked Him for sparing them, strengthening them, and bringing them back safely. She concluded by praying for their future and for Fyromaniac, whose present condition none of them could know. At last, with a hearty amen from all, she turned to them with a smile—so rare, for her.

"Well, we know which way our base is from here!" she said. "We'll never have to fear Vogul again. We survived!"

"And we are free!" Valora agreed. The Earthlings raised a shout of victory which carried on the desert wind.

<18>

Homecoming

Two happy reunions ensued at the Starganaut Base. Abigale squealed as she ran into her brother's arms, exclaiming repeatedly how proud she felt of Nick. Sharko and Dudeman's reunion was far less melodramatic, though still moving. The injured surfer was lying inside of the Commons, on a clean sleeping bag, when the seven Starganauts entered. Apotheka had immediately started healing his wounds with her gun. Once Dudeman felt well enough to sit up slightly, Apotheka turned her healing gun on Blaze's stab wound. The injury had mostly healed from her earlier treatment, but now Apotheka finished the job, enabling Blaze to kneel painlessly by Dudeman. He removed the crystal, gazing with great relief upon his longtime friend.

"I think I'll be okay, Man," James said reassuringly. "Hurt like heck, but the pain's better now. You have no idea how hard it was, lying here while those two were up there. Wished I could've joined them!" he settled farther down onto his pillows, and grimaced. Sharko merely shook his head.

"I'm just glad you're okay," he said, a tear coming to his eye. "I thought...we didn't know..."

"Hey, I understand," Dudeman remarked. "I did a lot of praying here. About all I could do, with this pain. I'm just glad Vogul's gone and we can finally settle into this place. I mean, no beaches or anything, but hey! At least we don't have bloodthirsty Trylithians after us!"

"Still the same old James." Sharko grinned. Dudeman risked leaning forward, and though he grunted, he caught Sharko's arm with a hand.

"Not the same, Man," he countered, and pointed to his heart. "Better than ever."

Sharko digested his friend's words long into the rest of the day. He and Kaity decided to walk out and sit atop the dune over their base. It was sunset. The shadows lengthened as the heat of the day lessened, with everything bathed in a crimson glow. Kaity always liked sunset the best. It was the rare time of day when the desert landscape actually held some beauty, and it brought with it the promise of night's coolness. She kissed her husband, and they held hands as they sat side-by-side. She thought back over their long sojourn here, while Sharko's thoughts remained on their deliverance from a madman.

"I still can't believe Thunderbane took out *six* Trylithians with a revolver!" Kaity exclaimed.

"It was clever of him and Nick to repair that crashed ship," Sharko added. Kaity knew he referenced the ship he'd shot down during their assault of the Dundee Homestead. Its crash had been the softest of all, and doubtless the one on Samantha's mind when she bade Matt and Nick to utilize an intact vessel. Nick had proudly shared the story of working overtime to find scrap and repair it in one night. Matt and Abigale had pitched in, and forcing their Trylithian captive to fly it had been a feat.

Matt and Nick's heroics had led to their victory against Vogul. Kaity looked back over their entire time together and could see God's hand working to shield and guide them. Their escape from Earth, their journey through the vortex, their fortunate crash site—truly there was a Creator watching out for them. Kaity had known Him since the age of twelve, and now Dudeman was part of their spiritual family.

"It will be interesting to see how James is, now that he's got the Holy Spirit," Sharko said thoughtfully, gazing off across the sand.

"I certainly won't miss the expletives," Kaity teased. She grew serious. "My Dear, what will become of us now?"

"I suppose we'll put roots down here. Wherever *here* is. Hopefully the Trylithians will be too afraid to bother us. Who knows? Maybe someday we'll be their friends."

"Or their gravest enemy," Kaity said wryly. "Who can tell what the future holds?"

Sharko shrugged, then rose and took her by the hands. Helping her onto her feet, he added, "One thing I do know, my Love, is how much I'll enjoy spending that future with you."

"Vogul is gone. Can you believe it?" Kaity asked. Sharko squeezed her hands and gazed tenderly into her eyes.

"The future is bright. Our path is cleared, and now, we begin the rest of our lives."

"I can't help thinking about all we've lost," Kaity started, with a sniff. Sharko gently wiped the hair from her cheek, and caressed it.

"We've lost more than most in this far-flung galaxy, but God has also granted us blessings we could never have imagined."

"Truly." Kaity's joy returned. "We are alive, my Dear. And today is a time to celebrate what we hardly dared hope for: victory against Willum Vogul!"

WHILE THE ANDERSONS basked in the glow of sunset, Samantha Harris sat shrouded in shadows. She'd withdrawn early to her room, and was melancholy despite the happiness of the others. A gentle knock on the door brought her back to reality. Sharko had suggested a celebration that night, and Samantha knew she must attend. Yet there were questions—mysteries unanswered—that remained to torment her mind.

"What's wrong?" Matt asked, sauntering into the room. Samantha had drawn her knees up under her chin. She sat on her cot, facing the wall. He knew what that posture meant.

"Was witnessing Vogul's death really so bad?" he asked. "Y'know, half of us thought you were crazy going off to try turning him."

"Shadows. Voices," Samantha said darkly, and shuddered. "Matt, I saw it all. Remember the broken window?"

"Yeah, that seemed weird."

"You may think me crazy, but I saw *something*." Samantha's lips quivered. "When I told you how Vogul died, I meant it literally. There were...shadows...voices...a demonic darkness that descended on the bridge. It attacked me, and I think God protected me, yet I couldn't breathe. I wasn't fully cognizant, but it was real! I *felt* the evil in that place, and it surrounded him, Matt. Vogul died because he failed a vile master. The shadows tore him to pieces. I heard it—his screams were like nothing I've ever..."

Samantha trailed off, unable to speak further. Her face looked ashen, and she turned toward her cousin.

"What if Vogul isn't the end?" she questioned. "What if a greater enemy awaits us, out there, lurking in the blackness of space?"

Matt pondered his cousin's words for several moments.

"If there is one, I think we're more than ready for him." He smiled comfortingly, and his cousin relaxed. "Are you going to tell the others about this?"

"Eventually," Samantha confessed. "With everything that's occurred these past few days, I felt it best to let them recover first."

Matt nodded, adding, "Remember, *Prima*, this doesn't mean we're in danger. That force might only be attracted to great evil. Vogul was really wicked. We're righteous compared to him."

"Are we?"

The lingering look Samantha gave him unsettled Matt. She shook herself. "I'm sorry. I should be celebrating the present instead of musing about what could be. I must recall my vision of a grand and glorious city. I don't know if it was a metaphor, or a picture of our futures, but it somehow gives me hope. This desert won't be our final resting place."

She grasped her cousin's hand briefly and squeezed it. Matt wondered at her statement, but shrugged and walked back into the Commons. He saw Nancy tidying up the space in preparation for their victory party. Mike entertained Dudeman at the table with a story, while Chrysta prepared a special dinner. How good it was to be home, and safe! Vogul had hounded them since they'd left Earth. Now, they could at last enjoy a peaceful and secure existence.

LIFE RETURNED TO NORMALITY for the survivors. They were back to scrubbing solar panels, sweeping excess dust out of the Commons, and taking five-minute showers. Occasionally, they would all savor the rare microwaved food. Matt and Sharko started supplementing their diet with native wildlife, and Kaity soon agreed with Abigale that the alien armadillo was both gummy and stringy. Yet her heart hoped for more than this.

What was this bland tranquility? Kaity would have laughed at herself, mere weeks ago. She had longed for life to feel "normal"—now, she almost despised it. The dull monotony was only broken by Sharko's excited monologues concerning their valley. He spent hours drawing up plans for a house that would be partially sunk into the ground. The way he carried on animatedly was very endearing, if not a tad long-winded. Nick, too, attempted to experiment with some crashed ships in the field near his homestead. His dream was to make one space-worthy.

It surprised Kaity when Mike and Chrysta called for an assembly in the Commons at lunchtime. All the tutor knew was that they hoped to share some news, though what it might be remained the subject of speculation. At last, noon came. Almost seven months to the day since their flight from Earth, they gathered around the dusty, white tables, Nick and Abigale joining them. Mike led the meeting, his fingers moving ceaselessly, his eyes roving around the room uncomfortably. Whatever news they had could not be positive.

"Chrysta and I wanted to begin by saying we're sorry," Mike said awkwardly. "We've concealed something from you which we probably shouldn't have. With the threat of Vogul, we kidded ourselves into thinking this was fine. Now that he's out of the way, we feel bad, because our secret impacts everyone."

Chrysta took a firm hold of her husband's hand and leaned forward.

"Mike and I, you see, are unable to have children."

Chrysta could barely keep her voice together, but the news dropped into the room like an exploding bomb. Kaity stared in surprise. Even Samantha's mouth fell open in astonishment, making her feel better about being fooled. Everyone was stunned to some degree.

"It's a painful secret we've borne since our wedding," Mike continued brokenly. "Chrysta was having...issues...after we got married. We went to the doctor, and that's when she was diagnosed with infertility. On top of all the other things we faced in life...we were so ashamed...so confused...!"

"My one dream in life was to be a mother," Chrysta interjected, through tears. "I wouldn't even talk about it to Mike, but it caused strife our entire marriage. I am the reason none of you knew. Partially, we didn't want to drain the hope out of the group. Really, it was my shame at feeling half a woman.

My bitter disappointment, when so many other things in life had been let-downs."

There was silence among the Starganauts for a while. Kaity didn't feel so much hurt as very compassionate toward Chrysta. The seamstress's snappish behavior suddenly made sense, and she wished she'd offered Chrysta more pity than blunt truths.

"I'm so sorry," Kaity said.

"What a terrible burden," Nancy added.

"This...does change things," Samantha spoke, at last. "With you unable to bear children, that only leaves the rest of us. Matt and I are cousins, and Nick and Abigale are siblings, so we can guess who we're all going to be marrying."

"I just became the most eligible bachelor on Sahara!" Dudeman quipped, but his humor fell flat. "Sorry."

"This is serious, James!" Sharko reproved. "We're talking about building a new human race here. With Vogul dead, that's become our top priority."

"Can you forgive us, for concealing this truth?" Mike questioned. He was beyond contrite.

"Of course we can!" Sharko said graciously. "It's not like you can help it, and we all understand why you hid it."

"You are forgiven for the lie," Samantha affirmed, "but no forgiveness is necessary for your reasons."

Chrysta breathed a sigh of relief, and managed a half-smile.

"Well, I'm glad that's over!" she exclaimed, and Mike squeezed her hand. "It's funny how burdensome a secret can become, yet how quickly the truth lifts its weight."

"So it is to accept Christ," Samantha commented. "We're weighed down heavily by our sins, yet in an instant, Jesus lifts them from our shoulders. We are free from their bondage, and it is a wonderful feeling indeed."

The Starganauts disbanded from their meeting with much murmuring. Kaity and Sharko stayed at the table with Mike and Chrysta to discuss the situation further. Nancy walked back to her quarters, and everyone else stood around talking except for Dudeman. The surfer had taken up his old habit of leaning against the sand dune, but now, he did so to spend time with the Lord. He was gone less than three minutes before he came racing back, out of breath.

"You're not going to believe this, but some alien ships are approaching! And they're *not* Trylithian!"

———— ✕✕✏✏ ————

THE COMMONS BECAME a flurry of activity. Crystals were passed around, weapons checked, and Starganauts gathered once more.

"Did they seem hostile?" Samantha asked, before she transformed into Crosshair.

"I...I don't know," Dudeman replied. "Given our experiences, what do you think?"

"One or two of us should go out to meet them," Sharko, as Blaze, answered. "Crosshair, you and I are the logical choice. I won't risk anyone else. Thunderbane, ditch the foils and grab your Trylithian repeater. All shooters, I want you to station yourselves just outside of the Base entrance. That includes you, Nick."

"Oh, jolly!" the Australian complained, but he nonetheless grabbed the pistol he'd taken from Vogul's crewman.

It was barely afternoon. The scorching sun hung overhead, the day was bleak and blinding, and the sky looked its usual dusty blue. Three alien spaceships had freshly landed on the ground not more than fifteen yards from their Base. Blaze realized, with chagrin, that these newcomers had likely found them because their tarp was up. Several of Nick's scrap projects were also positioned around the dune. Believing the worst to be over, they hadn't been careful about hiding themselves. He hoped they wouldn't pay for it.

Crosshair and Blaze strode boldly forward, their clothes flapping in the brisk, hot wind. They held their weapons at the ready, but did not brandish them. A landing ramp descended from the foremost craft. A figure wearing a long, colorful cloak came striding down, followed by three persons who appeared to be guards. These carried weapons, while their leader merely had a pistol hanging from a holster at his hip.

The four were surprisingly humanoid in stature and shape. All wore helmets and were fully covered. Their garb consisted of armor plating over shirts and pants, predominately white and tan, with black trimming and blue accents. They marched out in a soldierly fashion, their faces obscured by dark, blue visors. No one could tell whether their intentions were friendly—or otherwise. The leader walked forward unafraid, gesturing at them animatedly.

"Ajuu r'eda teploff riadeem," he said hopefully, pointing up at the sky. "Guuzkat Vexadori? Ee'oah tluk gevorti?"

Crosshair took a step forward.

"I think I understand him," she said, in amazement. She proceeded to return his alien inquiries in perfect, if not awkwardly accented, language. The alien grew excited from her response. He nearly jumped up and down, and Crosshair turned to Blaze. She put up her visor and smiled broadly.

"Derek, you're going to need a chair! These aliens are called Vexadorians. They came from another world to meet us. *Us*! Because we took out a gunship that threatened to annihilate them!"

"Vogul?" Blaze looked astonished, but his amazement was about to deepen. At Crosshair's removal of her visor, the alien leader gave a startled cry. He moved forward, and Blaze eyed him warily. The prophetess merely faced her new friend and watched him slide his own visor upward with the click of a button on his helmet. Her smile faded into shock. Beneath the mask of green was revealed a smooth-skinned, tan face. Two blue eyes peeked at her beneath brown hair, and only the alien's surprise outmatched her own.

"He's..." Crosshair began.

"...Human!" Blaze finished. From somewhere behind them, an Australian voice cried out in disbelief.

"Crikey, NOT AGAIN!"

THE "ALIEN" HUMANS stood before the Earthlings, as equally surprised as the Starganauts at finding their own kind. The four Vexadorians chattered wildly in their tongue. Crosshair joined in mirthfully while Valora and the others trickled over from their posts. It was a strange thing, making contact with humans from another planet. To Valora, it felt like meeting relatives from overseas for the first time at a family reunion. Apotheka and Thunderbane were stunned. Abigale was laughing at Nick's remark, and Vipress and Ninjarak smiled happily.

Blaze took a while to recover from his shock but, once realization dawned on him, he shook the lead human's hand heartily. The Vexadorian stared at him in puzzlement, yet smiled after Crosshair explained. He returned the handshake with an over-zealous attempt of his own, which would have wrenched Blaze's arm off, in human form.

"They've thanked us for stopping Vogul," Crosshair relayed. "They asked if we needed anything, and their leader offered to give us a tour of their world."

"A...*what*?" Blaze's jaw dropped. Valora could hardly comprehend it all. To tour an alien world...full of humans? She couldn't have dreamed up an offer so wild! Yet here it was, standing before them in the form of four humans from another planet. She wondered if they had cities and civilizations on their world. The Vexadorians before them seemed polite enough.

"Is there a translation for 'heck yes?'" Fyromaniac chimed in. Crosshair chuckled and said a few words in Vexadorian. The leader laughed with amusement, and extended a hand toward them all.

"That means 'come,'" Crosshair interpolated. "He's inviting us onto his craft right now—if we desire to depart so soon."

The Starganauts gazed at each other. Blaze wondered if this could be a possible trap, but Valora's heart harbored no shadowy suspicions. Vexador was one of the places mentioned in the crystal cave. More than this, she felt that these aliens could be trusted. They had come in a friendly, open manner, and appeared even more excited at the meeting than the survivors.

"Why not?" Apotheka spoke up. The secretary from Earth walked forward, pausing to glance back at the others. "We've come this far. We can always fly back and get our luggage. I don't know about you, but I'm ready for a change of scenery!"

"I can't argue with that," Blaze said at last, and the Starganauts and Australians followed the Vexadorians into their ship.

THE TRIP TO THE OTHER humans' homeworld of Vexador took only a few hours. Their ship was extremely comfortable and very advanced, but the Earthlings barely took note. They passed through a vortex of swirling, green tunnel. Valora watched the patterns pass by, endless in their variations and mystery. Crosshair spent the most time speaking to their new friends, and once asked if they'd heard of a shadowy being that spoke in a multitude of voices.

"Perhaps in a Gravite legend," one of the men replied. His reference was lost on her. She didn't know whether to feel relieved or more anxious, but Valora brought her out of her fears.

"Look at all this beauty and wonder!" the knight Starganaut exclaimed, tracing the patterns of the vortex on a window with her finger. "If this is but a taste of what these Vexadorians have to offer, I can't wait!"

She had hardly spoken when the blackness of space appeared ahead. They shot out of the vortex as if from a train tunnel, slowing rapidly before a great, whitish orb. Valora was surprised to see sand! She wondered if all the worlds in this galaxy were desert planets, but it hardly mattered. Unlike Sahara, this world boasted a city and a river, visible from space. Blaze estimated that the metropolis spread many times larger than New York City, and the Vexadorians clarified that about 20 million souls populated it.

"Are they all human?" Chrysta asked hopefully. The Vexadorian leader smiled mysteriously.

"You shall see," Crosshair translated, and the seamstress was disappointed by his reply.

Nonetheless, they continued their descent. They passed over a towering range of mountains crusted with white snowcaps and followed the course of a river which became clearer and clearer as they approached it. The line of green along its bank became a band of foliage, then individual trees stretching along a shoreline. They came to the vast city visible from outer space, and Valora gasped as enormous skyscrapers passed below. Lanes of traffic, both on the ground and in the air, moved beneath them like lines of ants. There were the tiny figures of people too, though their appearances were indistinguishable from this height.

The Vexadorian craft landed atop a skyscraper. The leader appeared pleased by their amazed looks, and he led the way down the ramp. A cool, evening breeze greeted them from the north. It was early sunset—Valora's favorite time—and she pointed this fact out to Blaze. There were several other ships parked on the rooftop, but no other people in sight.

The Vexadorians headed the procession of ten dusty Earthlings to an elevator shaft. The lift looked just large enough to accommodate them all. For the first few floors, they were surrounded by solid walls. Suddenly, their elevator reached a level where one corner was all glass. Crosshair gasped in amazement.

"The city from my vision!" she exclaimed, and everyone was drawn to the windows.

The alien metropolis stretched before them, bathed in the comforting glow of a rose-hued sunset. The faces of the towering skyscrapers flashed crimson, their enormity creating valleys of shadow where the sun could not reach. From here, the lights of streetlamps and hovercars flickered, illuminating aisles of lawn and trees bordered by moving sidewalks crowded with pedestrians.

Valora had to catch her breath as the elevator descended downward, steadily downward, taking them closer and closer to a sea of humanity which none of them could have imagined. They were people—human beings! She was close enough now to see them clearly, and tears started streaming down her face. Tears of relief, of burdens lifted, of gratitude for answered prayers, flowed freely. Yet she also laughed out loud for pure joy. Crosshair was right. God had spared them for a purpose greater than they could have believed, and now, that purpose seemed poised to unfold.

"Humans!" she cried aloud, beaming. "Millions and millions of *humans*!"

Blaze, Crosshair, and the rest of them were caught up in the laughter of disbelief. The elevator reached ground level and they stepped out after their Vexadorian rescuers. Valora clung to Blaze's arm and knew that everything would be all right. Sahara no longer needed to be their shelter. They would return to that world to gather their possessions, and come to live on this one. She sensed Blaze shared her sentiments without even needing to ask. They would learn the language of fellow humans on a distant planet, and they had an entire city and way of life to discover.

Vexador. Whatever its meaning, whatever its place in the galaxy, this gleaming metropolis stood high above the desert sands—civilized, teeming, promising. It was the city of Samantha's hopeful vision, and to Kaity, its one meaning would eventually and forever become "home."

A BLUE-AND-GREEN TRYLITHIAN craft descended upon the desert sands of Dalar 3. The ruin of Vogul's gunship lay strewn across the dunes, stretching across such a vast area that it could be seen from space. Jixa, nephew of Durag, walked down the landing ramp with a dull clank of titanium boots. The blasting heat was the first thing that hit him, and he squinted to shield his sensitive eyes from the glare and blowing sands. Surveying the sprawling wreckage of the downed gunship, he knew there could be no survivors. There was also little chance of salvaging it to create a new weapon for his colmit—although he doubted he had enough colmit left to defend.

Jixa activated the hover function of his boots and carefully picked his way over the rubble. Behind him, his crew began the lengthy search for evidence of what had transpired. Even hovering, Jixa could smash into some of the more tilted chunks of hull if he wasn't careful, but he wished to scope out the entire field. One person alone interested him, for if anyone had survived via an escape pod, it would be *him*.

The Trylithian made it to the top of a dune. He was hovering down its slip-face when the sands suddenly gave way. He fell over twenty feet, smacking into the ground so hard that he bruised a leg and broke one of his hoverboots. He was too hurt and winded to realize that he'd dropped off a sheer cliff, or that his hoverboots had lessened the fall.

Jixa gave a cry of enraged pain. It was lost in the gaping, shadowy maw before him—swallowed up before echoing back out. Blinking, Jixa staggered into the coolness of the shaded recess. To his great surprise, he found himself in a primitive hangar. A dusty sand glider sat in one corner, along with a pile of scrap metal.

Could this be it? The Human Base? Jixa had heard reports of eight humans from Earth who were rumored to have destroyed Vogul, but he wanted the facts for himself. He swore bitterly. He could hardly think for the pain, but the young Trylithian held onto various pieces of machinery and metal to keep from hurting himself. He cursed the humans who had hollowed out this place which had nearly been his death.

The Starganauts! That was what they called them! Jixa could not grasp then how crucial a role they would play in his own life, but he swore a single, overarching vow. Whatever the future brought, he would make them pay. He would seize their source of power. For, as long as they existed, Trylithia could not rise to dominance. As long as they lived, they were the only survivors he could blame for the loss of an empire and the death of his beloved uncle.

Jixa Durag would destroy these eight humans from Earth.

The End of Starganauts Book One
The adventure continues in
Starganauts: Vengeance of Sorrow...

<Join the Gorvan Club>

Gain access to a free e-book, The Sorcerer's Realm! This epic, Christian sci-fi adventure is perfect for fans of Star Wars and Star Trek. In addition to the free e-book, you will be the first to read snippets from my works-in-progress. Join here: http://eepurl.com/gc30Pb.

About the Author

My name is C.E. Stone and I live in sunny California with my chronically-ill, cowboy husband. When not tutoring a host of students, I'm usually writing my next book or plotting a galactic takeover. ☺ I created Starganauts at the age of 10, expanding its universe and stories in the form of mock "TV shows" I acted out with Legos.

After writing fantasy stories for several years, I started telling my best friend about my Sci-Fi universe. For 2 hours. At the end of it, she was so amazed that she insisted I write these stories down...and I haven't stopped since. It's been a fun and unexpected journey, and I hope to follow in the footsteps of my favorite authors, Tolkien and Lewis...albeit with a Sci-Fi twist.

Read more at https://www.starganauts.net/.

CPSIA information can be obtained
at www.ICGtesting.com
Printed in the USA
BVHW031718120621
609348BV00006BA/945